Crushed by Love

Nina Verona

This is a work of fiction. Any resemblance to peoples living or dead, including names, characters, businesses, places, events and incidents is purely coincidental and a product of the author's imagination.

Print ISBN: 978-1-950093-46-5

Cover Designed By Natasha Snow Designs

Editing By Dani Galliaro

To the ones who feel not enough.
Or too much.

Let this book be your reminder that you're not too much and you're not too little.

You're exactly just right.

RUIN ME.

WRECK ME.

FUCKING OWN ME.

BUT PLEASE DON'T BREAK ME.

Playlist

Summertime Sadness - Lana Del Rey

I Feel Like I'm Drowning - Two Feet

If I Weren't Me - Katherine Li

Nothing's Gonna Hurt You Baby - Cigarettes After Sex

Foolish Games - Jewel

Kissing You - Des'ree

Crush - Cigarettes After Sex

Streets - Doja Cat

Cherry - Lana Del Rey

August - Taylor Swift

Poison & Wine - The Civil Wars

Logical - Olivia Rodrigo

Sad Movies - Still Corners

Falling in Love - Cigarettes After Sex

Work Song - Hozier

New Years Day - Taylor Swift

Crushed by Love is recommended

for adult readers only.

.

Please be mindful of your triggers

before proceeding.

This book contains content including but not limited to depictions of sexually explicit encounters, bullying, sexual harassment, childhood trauma, generalized anxiety disorder, alcohol abuse, drug abuse, adult drowning, bodily injury, loss of limb, and even death.

Part One

"My only love sprung from my only hate, Too early seen unknown, and known too late! Prodigious birth of love is it to me, that I must love a loathed enemy."

William Shakespeare's Romeo and Juliet

One

I feel him before I see him. Some people are special that way. They're born with extra gravity pulling in the rest of us mere mortals. Regular people don't have a choice in the matter, same as we can't choose the laws of physics. And this man? This man is all gravity.

His bronzed form slices through the crystalline water, arms rotating in powerful arcs, muscles taut and flexing with each stroke. If he notices me ogling him from the pool deck above, he doesn't acknowledge it.

But I can't look away.

"You aren't to speak to the twins unless spoken to first." Mrs. King's silky voice frays my thoughts as she motions to the man in the water. "And they won't bother you. They're very familiar with how to behave around the staff."

Her words ring in my head and all I can think is, *There are two of them?*

I follow my new boss across the pool deck to the guest house, my cheeks warming from far more than the summer sun. She's probably used to people fawning over her twin sons, but that doesn't make getting caught with my mouth hanging open any less embarrassing. I force myself to focus on her instructions and not whatever that man just did to twist me into knots.

Mrs. King is very thorough, going over every nook and cranny of the guest house, just as she did with the main house, detailing exactly what she expects of me. Basic cleaning, laundry, and dusting daily. Deep cleaning and fresh sheets twice a week. Windows as needed in between the professional window cleaners. Try not to be seen, never be heard, and stay out of the way. If there's a visible mess anywhere, I'm already failing. And if I do anything to embarrass her, I'm gone.

When she leads me back to the main house ten minutes later, the pool is empty without even a ripple on the surface. I'm a little disappointed.

"Under no circumstances are you to get involved with Ethan or Cooper. If something happens, if they make an advance towards you, anything at all, you're to tell me straight away."

I blink at her, stunned that she'd think I'd stand a chance with someone who looked like that Greek god in the pool. "Am I making myself clear? You have my number."

"Yes, ma'am," I mumble. Again, my cheeks are flaming, and again, I'm beyond embarrassed.

And a little annoyed.

And a lot caught off guard.

She studies me for a long moment, her eyes roaming up and down my body, and I wonder what she thinks of my unruly ginger hair, or the too many freckles spilled across my pale skin, or the way my second-hand clothing is a tad too big and a lot too old. She pins me with her judgmental gaze and I get my answer--she doesn't think much of me at all. Her stare is calculating. It's as if she's able to see little thought bubbles forming inside of my head questioning: Was that one Ethan or Cooper?

Are they identical twins? How old are they? Obviously older than me.

I force the curiosity away.

Mrs. King smiles ruefully, like she's the prize-winner at my expense. She's first and I'm last. A nervous itch crawls up my spine. "You're to start immediately," she says. "I will be back in a few weeks to check on things."

"You're leaving?"

"Yes, I've got obligations in Manhattan. My husband and I will come and go throughout the summer, but the boys are staying put." She purses her lips. "It's their last full summer here and I'm sure they'll keep you busy."

I gape at her. "Keep me busy?"

Her eyes flash with something unreadable. "With cleaning up after them, doing their laundry, whatever they need. Now, get to work."

She struts away, and I return to the sizable broom closet next to the even larger kitchen pantry for cleaning supplies.

Nothing in the job description said anything about living alone with two twenty-something-year-old men. I wasn't expecting to be staying here without my new employer actually on-site. That, and I totally got caught checking out her son. Who could blame me though? But more to the point--why did she seem annoyed to catch me doing it?

Ugh, rich people are so confusing, but I'm not here to figure out how rich people operate. I'm here to clean up after them and get paid, so I'd better stop my wayward thoughts right here and now before the anxiety slithers in.

With that declaration in mind, I gather the all-natural cleaning supplies into my caddy and pull my hair up into a messy bun. I set out to tackle the first of many bathrooms, a massive grin on my face because I still can't believe I landed this job. How many people get to say they're the live-in housekeeper for one of Nantucket's nicest beach estates? And while cleaning isn't glamorous, I'm also barely out of high school. Graduation was mere days ago. I got this gig so fast despite not having much work experience. Two weeks after submitting my application, and a week after the online interviews that I took at my local library, here I am––in over my head and crossing my fingers that I don't screw up.

My electric nerves settle to a low buzz the rest of the day. I'm used to the anxious feelings lurking in my chest. As much as I hate anxiety, I've coped with it since childhood and have learned to function around it.

The house seems deserted, which helps. Even if I'm alone, I'm careful to orbit around where I think people could be. I steer clear of the dining room at dinner time and save the bedrooms for tomorrow. I'm not good with people and never have been, so I'll deal with them on my second day here.

Finishing my duties that evening, I head downstairs to unpack my suitcase into my new dresser. The room is basic, but I don't mind. I'm used to basic. I didn't bring much because I don't have much. It doesn't take long to get everything put away, tucking my clothing into neat little squares, one on top of the other. I quickly shower and change into jean shorts and a long-sleeved t-shirt that's seen better days, but that doesn't matter right now. What matters is that I made it here, that I followed through on something positive, albeit terrifying, and I'm immensely proud of myself.

You. Can. Do This. I tell myself between long slow breaths, then slip my phone and house key into my pocket and head back upstairs.

The Kings have a private chef who will leave meals labeled for me. I tiptoe into the kitchen after she's finished for the evening to retrieve my personal chicken and pasta salad, imagining myself as quiet as a passing shadow. What did Mrs. King say? *Try not to be seen, never be heard, and stay out of the way.*

The meal is delicious, and I savor each bite as I hover over the counter. It's truly phenomenal, and not just because it's the first thing I've eaten since this morning. I barely had enough money to get myself from western Massachusetts all the way out to this island, taking a redeye bus across the state last night to catch the ferry this morning. A gas station donut was good enough to get me through the journey. My stomach isn't ready to be done when I finish the last of the container, but I'm not sure I'm allowed to go rummaging through the pantry or fridge. I clean up and head outside to the detached garage instead.

If you could even call it a garage.

The building is larger than half the houses back home in Pittsfield. Then again, this house is bigger than anything I've ever seen in person. The average person wouldn't imagine a massive estate when told to picture a beach house. Sure, they might picture something nice, but the Kings' place is next level. The sprawling mansion is a modern vision of whitewashed concrete, dark woods, clean lines, and expansive windows. It sits high on a bluff overlooking a secluded beach--complete with three stories, a walkout basement, twelve bedrooms, sixteen bathrooms, two kitchens, three family rooms, a game room, a theater room, two dining rooms, a gym, an office, a wine cellar, and who knows what else I'm forgetting from my tour.

Oh, that's right, a guest house.

The garage stands separate from the main house and has ample space for the four luxury vehicles parked inside. I've never driven a car and wouldn't know the first thing about any of these. I steer clear as I make my way to the back where Mrs. King told me I could pick out a bicycle to use for the summer. And thank God for that because my phone is just a dinky flip phone and definitely not anything that can do more than talk or text. I can't afford to call a standard cab company every time I want to leave the house, and this place is too far to walk to town with my limited free time. So, biking it is.

Bikes and me—we've never had the best relationship, mostly because they symbolize the kind of childhood I missed out on. It was only a couple of years ago that I even touched a bike. My last foster parents insisted I learn when they found out. They took the time to teach me, and if they hadn't moved across the country for a work transfer a few months later, I would've happily stayed with them until graduation. Sure, they cried about it, said they wished they could get the paperwork together in time to adopt me so I could come along, but ultimately, they left me behind.

It's not like I was surprised, or even angry. I wasn't—I'd numbed myself long before they could hurt me. What did anger me was my case worker placing me in a group home to finish out my last two years of high school. Those places are the worst, and the one I landed in was so overcrowded and depressing that it nearly sucked the life out of me. I'd have done just about anything to get out of there, including taking this job. But at least I got to move away right after graduation and bid farewell to the system.

The pastel bikes are lined up in a tidy row, reminding me of shiny Easter eggs. I select a pretty blue cruiser with a white basket attached to the handlebars. It's adorable in a way that makes me hesitate. What happens if I mess it up? I could crash it or scratch it or pop a tire, and I don't know if I'd have enough money to replace it. How expensive is a nice bike like this?

But I need transportation, so I wheel it out to the driveway and hold my breath, suddenly nervous to climb on. Is it possible to forget how to ride a bike? I guess I'm about to find out.

The rubber handlebars bite into my palms as I push off the stone driveway. The inertia is quick, but my muscle memory is

quicker. I squeal, delighted I didn't forget how to do this, and pedal out to the main road with spirits lifted.

This isn't so bad.

The grassy fields surrounding the Kings' estate are a vibrant spring green, swaying with the ocean breeze. The sunset paints the sky neon, streaks of fuschia and blood orange reflecting off the endless sea. It's the kind of stunning I thought only existed in the movies and it wraps me up in fresh scents of salt and sea. No movie could compare.

I ride two miles down the hill and another out to the boardwalk, glad I paid attention to the area when I arrived this morning. I don't have any spending money yet, so I'm not going into any of the shops or restaurants, but I'm eager to explore what will be my new home for the next three months. I've never truly been at home anywhere. Maybe this time will be different.

Once I reach my destination, I park the bike and lock it, walk down to the beach, and plop down in the sand to watch the waves roll in. The ocean is much bigger than I imagined. I knew it was big from videos and pictures, but seeing it in person really puts it into perspective. It makes me feel small but not in an insignificant way—in a calming way. The bright sunset fades into night, but I don't want to leave. I breathe in the salty air, dig my hands into the warm sand, and close my eyes, letting the sound of crashing waves wash over me.

This is the most free I've felt in ages, and I sit like that until the light fades away and I can count the stars. Or attempt to anyway. I've never seen so many stars before. Back home light pollution blocks most of them out. I almost wish I could stay out here all night and see what they look like hours from now, but I'm sure I can sneak out in the middle of the night sometime at the beach house and stargaze from there.

It's going to be a perfect summer. This is my fresh start into adulthood and I don't even care that I have to work long hours.

I'm used to working full-time in the summers and juggling after-school jobs. With this one I'll have some money in the bank when I go to college in August. I've worked in an ice cream parlor and a movie theater, so it's not like housekeeping is my first stint into employment. I'll keep that giant house sparkling and make the most of my free time when I'm not catching up on sleep.

Catching up on sleep is exactly what I should be doing right now.

My eyelids flutter, the exhaustion of the long day setting in. The air is growing chilly, and I still have to bike a couple of miles back to the house. I trudge back up the beach, pausing to study a group of young people several yards over. A glowing bonfire crackles, illuminating about twenty people. It's hard to tell from here, but I think they're older than me, probably in their twenties. They look like they've done this a thousand times before, meeting here in the summers to huddle together and drink and laugh and talk.

And kiss.

A couple that could be the poster child for PDA demands my attention. They're kissing with no concern for their surroundings, lying intertwined in the sand only a few feet away from their group. The woman's leg hooks around the man's torso, shorts riding up to barely cover her ass. The man grips her with his large hands. She rolls her hips and I'm struck with the thought that they might have sex on this public beach. Their forms flicker in and out of view with the firelight, little flashes of something I shouldn't be watching.

But I can't stop.

The sight of them, of his hands on her like that, of her body arching against his, stirs something within me. What would it be like to be touched by a man? To be wanted like that? How would it feel to have his hands on my body?

I wouldn't know. Maybe I should, but besides a few kisses, I've never let myself get close to anyone.

The woman breaks away with a giggle, rolling back to comb her hand through her tangle of blonde hair. The firelight reveals the man's face. I inhale quickly and step back, heart thundering. He didn't see me before and he doesn't now, but I can't unsee him just like I can't reverse gravity.

He's the gorgeous man from the pool.

Two

I'm certain it's him. Even though I haven't studied the intricacies of his face, that spark of recognition splinters through me. It's an internal knowing, an admission that he does something to me. He makes me want more than I've wanted before, to be someone I've never been, to test the laws of gravity.

As if hearing my thoughts, his eyes snap in my direction. My chest burns and I sink further into the darkness. He can't see me, can he? There's no way, it's too dark out here. But his gaze stays pinned to where I stand and I begin to doubt myself. Could he be watching me watching him? With looks like those, he's probably used to all eyes being on him, but right now, he's staring at me. I swallow hard but I don't turn away, not now that his face is trained in this direction, and not a moment later when the woman kisses the tanned column of his neck.

"You don't have to watch the fun from back here," a gravelly voice chuckles, and I nearly jump out of my skin.

A man approaches from behind, car keys in one hand and a case of beer in the other. His brown hair is long enough to hang around his chin, with just enough curl that I have the sudden urge to sink my fingers into it. His midnight eyes travel over me with mild interest, the hint of a smirk playing at his Cupid lips. A blush spreads all the way down to the tips of my toes. Is being a ten on the hotness scale some kind of requirement to summer on Nantucket or what?

"You're welcome to join us," he says, tone criminally dark.

Is he inviting me to the bonfire? Or is he calling me out for watching the couple and inviting me to do the same thing with him? I don't know, but I don't say a word. Not because I don't want to say anything, but because I physically can't. My throat is empty and my mouth is as dry as the sand between my toes. Did I trade my voice to a sea witch in exchange for a place here and just forget about it? Because I seriously cannot utter one word.

But maybe that's because I'm inexperienced in every way. He's out of my league. I'm not wealthy. Not beautiful. Not outgoing. Too young. Too mortified. And definitely too chicken shit to take this handsome stranger up on his offer.

"Or maybe you like to watch," he continues with another low chuckle. "I'm not into voyeurism personally, but suit yourself."

And then he's gone, invitation revoked, walking away from me and toward the bonfire as if I were nothing but a shadow.

Story of my life.

Hands. Teeth. Tongues. Skin. My eyes fly open and I suck in a heady breath. My entire body is vibrating. A prickle of shame overtakes me when I realize that I was dreaming of sex. The kind with zero inhibitions, like I was made for it and actually knew what I was doing. Part of me wants to sink back into sleep and continue where I left off, to slip my fingers between my legs, but instead I sit up and blink at the bedside clock.

It's 4:45 a.m. I'm awake an hour earlier than needed. I've planned to do a thirty-minute run every morning since running is the only thing that clears my mind. Normally I'd go for an hour but I don't want to wear myself out too much before working. Then I'm going to shower and get dressed, have a quick breakfast, and start work by 7. It's the only way I'm going to finish work in time to have any kind of social life in the evenings—once I make some friends, of course.

I rub my face, already feeling the frustration tugging at my eyelids. Frustration because I'm still so tired, and frustration because I want things that I haven't allowed myself to want before.

I've never come close to having sex, which didn't bother me up until now. In high school, the other girls were either racing to lose their v-cards or holding onto them as if they were precious gifts, but I was hiding mine. I didn't want to lose it because I didn't want anyone to get close to me like that. It didn't matter how attractive a guy was, or how sweet, I refused to entertain the thought of anyone being able to hurt me. As far as I'm concerned, loneliness is better than abandonment. And sex? Sex is intimate. It's letting someone in both figuratively and literally, opening yourself to heartache on the deepest level, and I'm not ready for that.

So where did that dream just come from?

And who was the man in the starring role?

He didn't have a face, but his hands were possessive and his lips like crushed velvet. His movements were demanding as his body dominated mine, taking and giving in an addictive cycle. He knew exactly what he was doing. And somehow, despite my lack of actual real-world sexual experience, so did I. If I were a betting woman, I'd put a million dollars on my sex dream starring the man from the swimming pool yesterday. But maybe it was the handsome stranger who'd spoken to me on the beach.

I plop back onto the pillows and groan, clutching the sheets between my needy fingers. My breathing is still fast and my limbs are heavy with lust but I refuse to indulge in this anymore. It's ridiculous. This isn't me. I've never allowed myself to lust over complete strangers like I did yesterday, like I'm doing right now. Their images are currently a slideshow in my mind despite my pathetic attempts to extract them.

It's a bizarre distraction and nothing but trouble.

I need to stay focused on the job. I'm already out of sorts here and I'm still baffled as to why I was hired when there must've been better candidates. But I'm determined to prove myself and make the most of it, if only for the sake of having a wad of cash and the ability to pay for a better phone and other necessities when I go to college in August.

I need to forget all about the beach bonfire and the bruising longing I felt as I watched the couple. In fact, I need to forget all about men in general. I can date when I get to college. Better yet, I'll date after I graduate and have a few years to build my career first. That's probably unrealistic, probably the musings of a shy and anxious girl, but it's also the only way I know how to protect myself.

Right now, I need to work, so I get up early and begin my duties an hour ahead of schedule, pushing everything else from my mind.

That plan unravels not much later when I'm mopping the kitchen floor and a young woman prances in, her long stick-insect legs bare under an oversized men's t-shirt and her shiny black hair a mess of sleepy curls down her back. She clearly didn't have to dream of sex last night. She got to do the real thing. Looking past me, her eyes zero in on the state-of-the-art espresso machine that could very well belong in a Starbucks.

"Would you like something to eat?" Camilla, the chef, strides in from the pantry to address this barely-dressed woman, cans of ingredients stacked in both of her sun-spotted hands.

"I don't usually eat breakfast." The young woman yawns and motions to the espresso machine. "But I'll take a cappuccino and you should already know Cooper's order."

"Of course," Camilla replies, setting to work. She's Italian and I can't wait to see what she's able to create in the kitchen. Based on the food she cooked last night, and the fact that such wealthy people have hired her, my expectations are high.

The young woman turns on me, her scrutinizing gaze roaming from the mop in my hand, to my simple outfit of jeans and white t-shirt, to my makeup-free face. "You. Be helpful and bring our drinks up to Coop's room."

Did she just tell me to be helpful while I'm literally mopping?

My jaw tightens and I blink at her, instantly disliking her for treating me like I'm her personal assistant. Do I look like Cinderella? I'm hoping this isn't what I signed up for, but Mrs. King did say I was to take care of whatever the twins needed, and this girl is clearly sleeping with one of them. I guess today I'm their housekeeper *and* their coffee delivery service. Not a big deal if I don't make it into one, except now I have to officially meet them and that makes me want to crawl into a hole.

The woman is staring at me like she expects me to say something. "What's your name?" Her eyes narrow, scanning me like I'm the competition, which is ridiculous considering she looks like she just strutted off a 2000's Victoria's Secret runway. "You're not the old hag they had cleaning last year. Too bad, she was good."

Old hag? I have no words for that.

"My. Name. Is. Arden." I grip the handle of the mop tighter.

"Arden." She turns the name over in her mouth like it tastes sour and cheap. "I'm Bree." Her eyes narrow. "Don't forget it." She spins on her heels and disappears up the stairs.

Mind reeling, I turn to Camilla. "Is she here a lot?"

"She was last summer," she sighs. "She's one of Cooper's regular girls."

"He has multiple girlfriends?"

She shakes her head and the wrinkles around her eyes and mouth deepen. "They're not girlfriends. They're female friends who stay over. Cooper's never had a real girlfriend here as far as I know. I've been their Nantucket chef for fourteen years now. I've known him since he was a child."

"So you only work for them during the summers?"

She nods, offering a small smile. "I live on the island year-round. I've been here for forty-two years. Raised three children here. They're all grown up and living on the mainland now."

Wow, so she's a local, and if I had to guess I'd say she's in her sixties, which means she really knows her stuff. She's going to be useful when I have questions, but of course, I don't want to bother the woman too much. She seems busy as hell.

I wrinkle my nose. "I still don't know which one is Cooper and which one is Ethan."

I remember what rooms are occupied from my tour yesterday, but I haven't been formally introduced to anyone here besides Camilla and Mrs. King herself. And I'm pretty sure Mrs. King has already left for Manhattan. And who knows when I'll finally get to meet Mr. King. I don't know much about the man, except that he runs a billion-dollar media empire and probably doesn't have a lot of time to vacation in Nantucket. He seems like the kind of person who buys luxury real estate as an investment--not to actually enjoy it for any length of time.

Either way, I still haven't figured out if the man from the

pool and the bonfire was Ethan or Cooper. Considering the girl that man was kissing last night was blonde and not a brunette, I'm going to guess he was Ethan, but who knows? This is a whole other world than the one I'm used to, and making out with one woman on the beach and bringing another home to sleep with could be a regular thing around here. Just like having "regular girls" is a thing for Cooper King.

"They're fraternal twins," she says, "but they look a lot alike. You'll figure it out quickly, though it helps to remember that Cooper has the brown eyes and Ethan has the blue."

"Where to?" I set down the mop and rub my palms against my shorts.

"Upstairs, third door on the left," Camilla instructs, finishing off the drinks and sealing the lids on tight before handing them over. They heat my palms and smell mouth-watering. Definitely better than the cheap stuff I'm used to. I salivate, tempted to taste one, but I won't, nor will I ask her to make me one. But I did watch her carefully and think I might be able to pull off a decent coffee for myself tomorrow morning. I prefer iced. Does that mean I just make a regular coffee and pour it over ice? I have so much to learn.

She returns to her meal prep and I need to hurry and get this over with so I can finish the floors and get out of her hair. Cleaning isn't easy work, but no doubt cooking gourmet meals is harder. I wouldn't know the first thing about it, would probably burn the whole house down before managing anything half as decent as what she can produce.

Ignoring the tension in my chest, I climb the floating stairs and gently knock on the door. Nobody answers so I knock harder and the coffee sloshes around in the cups. I go still, wincing as I wait for it to settle. Spilling it wouldn't be a great way to introduce myself. I stand in the hallway and gaze at the crisp white walls with the occasional piece of expensive-looking artwork, then down at sleek hardwood floors. I love the upscale modern design, but it's probably going to be a pain in the ass to keep this house clean. Every speck of dust, every smudge, every grain of sand trudged in from the beach—all will be glaringly visible in here.

I wait for the door to open, but nothing.

"I got your coffee," I call out.

And then I have the thought that Bree and Cooper are having morning sex in there and I should just leave the coffees in the hallway for them to retrieve when they're done.

The door flies open and I step back, taking in the man from the pool. He's a force, looming over me. And he's shirtless, that dark brown hair perfectly tousled from sleep. His boxer shorts sit low on his sinful hips and I instantly blush. And not just from the low boxers--it's the obvious morning wood he's sporting under those boxers that has my attention.

Dear God.

And his sleepy blue eyes? They're heavy on me. Taking me in. Traveling me up and down like they're not quite sure what they're looking at. Emotions flash behind those pretty eyes, shock and then sadness, anger and then forced indifference. It all happens so fast that I nearly miss it and have no idea what to make of it.

Is he angry that I spoke to him? His mom said I wasn't supposed to speak to them unless spoken to first. *Shit.* Day one and I already screwed up.

"Who are you?" he asks dryly.

My cheeks flood with heat and I could kick myself. *Why, oh why, do I have to blush so deeply?* I swear, it's the curse of the redhead.

"I'm Arden. The new housekeeper," I offer brightly and hold out the coffees, careful to keep my gaze up and not on his distracting nether regions. "I can't remember whose is whose. Sorry about that."

"You woke me up."

"Uh--" I mean, technically I'm just the delivery girl. Bree woke him up. "I'm the housekeeper. I didn't know you were sleeping, I apologize."

"So you're living here then?" His lips thin, those bedroom eyes lingering on my hair for far too long. Being a redhead, I'm used to it, but that doesn't mean I like it.

"Yes," I say tentatively because somehow I feel like he wants me to say no.

"I didn't order any coffee." He slams the door in my face and I stumble back, a little stunned. He just acted as if I offended him. Excuse me, but is someone kindly bringing him coffee to his bedroom a crime? It's not even rude. It's nice.

The door on the other side of the hallway swings open, followed by a breathy laugh.

Three

"There you are," Bree whines, standing in the frame and somehow looking even more like an editorial model than she did downstairs. "Took you long enough."

I don't even know what to say to that. I obviously knocked on the wrong door, waking up the wrong twin. So the rude man from the pool is Ethan. And Cooper is? The man from the beach steps into the doorway, his dark eyes widening with playful recognition.

He stands next to Bree, dropping a kiss against her temple before addressing me with a dark chuckle. "So you're the new maid, huh?" He murmurs his words against Bree's skin while still staring at me, his hand coming to rest on her stomach, and I don't know what to make of the lusty expression on his face. Is it for me or for her? Both of us?

"Housekeeper is the correct term, actually."

"Yeah," Bree adds. "She's the *housekeeper*." She says it like it's a derogatory word.

He chuckles but I can't tell if he actually finds any of this humorous. "I guess it's only fitting that Malory and Conrad would hire someone like you to live here during the last full summer Ethan and I get to spend on the island. They're so predictable."

And I also don't know what to make of anything he just said except that Malory and Conrad are his parents and it seems like such a rich person thing to do to call your parents by their first names like that. Then again, what would I know about money or parents?

"You think me being here is predictable?" I force out the question despite the stress. All I want to do is to apologize for knocking on the wrong door and bolt out of here.

Cooper raises an eyebrow, and I can't help but think he's just as attractive as his twin brother even though they're not identical. But they're most definitely brothers, and I don't know how I'm going to get through this summer without being beet-red at all times, either from the sun or from these guys.

"You looking the way you do? Yeah, I sure do," he draws out his answer that doesn't really answer much of anything. What I should have asked is why he thinks it's predictable that I'm here. His inquisitive eyes search mine, as if waiting for me to say something more. Was he giving my looks a compliment or a criticism? Or maybe it's my young age that he's talking about?

"Thanks, Ardie." Bree snatches the coffee cups from my hands.

"It's Arden--"

For the second time in less than a minute, a door slams in my face.

Welcome to Nantucket.

I head back downstairs and return to mopping. Mind reeling at what I just experienced, I'm unable to keep my mouth shut. "Are the twins always so..." I don't finish the question because I don't want to overstep my bounds here, but seriously, *what the hell was that?*

Camilla frowns down at her cutting board. She's slicing an onion into tiny cubes like a pro. The woman is barely even teary-eyed because she's slicing so damn fast. "They're good boys when they want to be." Her Italian accent is still thick enough that I'm sure she grew up there despite her decades of living in Nantucket as an adult. I wonder what her story is? "But I'm warning you now," she continues, "when the brothers want to be bad, there's no stopping them."

"Bond villains, huh?" I tease.

Her eyes snap to mine. "I'm being serious. Don't push their buttons."

It just about kills me not to snort at that asinine comment.

"Since when do bad boys spend their summers on Nantucket?" As far as I'm concerned, they're not bad boys, they're just ungrateful douchebags with too much access to daddy's money.

Honestly, I'd laugh about this whole thing if I wasn't so pissed off by my interaction with the twins upstairs. There's no good explanation for slamming their doors in my face--even if Bree was the one to do it for Cooper. I can't very well tell them off without jeopardizing my job, so I channel my frustration into the mop instead.

Mopping is good.

Mopping is rhythmic and easy and predictable and doesn't treat you like shit.

"Just be careful," Camilla adds right before I leave the kitchen. The chopping of her knife stops and I find her eyes are on me again--older eyes, experienced eyes, protective eyes that won't turn on their employer but will warn a young woman. "The twins are no good for a sweet girl like you. Especially not Ethan."

And then she's back to chopping. Why single out Ethan

when Cooper is the one who apparently has a revolving door of women?

"Thank you." I mean it, too. I'm not used to having people look out for me, so when they do, I always appreciate it. I also take it with a grain of salt and a heaping dose of trust issues, but that might just be a me problem.

"I can tell you're a good girl. It must be one of the reasons why you were hired."

The answers to why I was hired are still pending, but I'll take the compliment anyway.

I nod. "Thanks."

She nods back, and that's that. The conversation is over.

I'm moving on with my day, but I can't stop thinking about her words of warning. They were similar to Mrs. King's warning yesterday, but it's not like I'm going to go jump on one of these guys. And it's not like they're desperate for female companionship considering what I learned about their willing rotation of women.

These men are untouchable, but I'm here to be a professional, to get my bank account ready for college, to have a nice place to live. I shouldn't worry about what Camilla said, shouldn't even think about it.

But I do.

Hours later I take my lunch break to the edge of the property. My target is the old white-washed wood veranda that sits perched on the bluff overlooking the ocean. There's a stunning beach down below but the stairs to get there are so long and steep that I'm not going to attempt them today. The wooden planks of the bench creak under me as I sit down, the wind ruffling my ponytail. I could get used to this place.

This is my chance at a fresh start.

A new me.

I finish up my meal and close my eyes for a few minutes,

letting the distant crashing of waves overtake my senses until a shadow passes over me and I'm forced to pop my eyes back open. The King brothers stand over me with arms folded and grim expressions on their similar faces. They're both shirtless with swim trunks low on their hips, their chiseled bodies on full display. They each boast perfectly rippled abdomens and well-proportioned frames. They do not make men like this where I come from.

"Can I help you?" I ask carefully. And then I remember that I'm not supposed to speak to them first. Geez, I hope I don't get reprimanded for this. It has become glaringly obvious that I'm out of my element with this family.

Ethan glares down at me and Cooper speaks up first. "That depends on what you're offering. Are you here to clean up after us or are you here to fuck us?" His tone is relaxed despite the harsh words. "Because we're not interested in tag-teaming."

I blanch and jump up, grabbing the remains of my meal and snapping the lid onto the lunchbox. "You think that's what I'm offering? That's not why I'm here."

Screw the whole not speaking to them thing—I'm no doormat.

"Isn't it?" Ethan says, deadpanned. "Look at you."

"What do my looks have to do with anything?" I'm not sure if this is supposed to be some kind of fucked up compliment or what. I know I'm cute, could even be considered pretty, but I'm no drop-dead beauty queen. "Don't talk to me like this again or else I'll tell Mrs. King."

"Are you going to tattle on us?" Cooper raises an eyebrow but his smile quirks in a playful manner and I have no idea what to make of it.

"Maybe I will. This is sexual harassment."

They're on either side of me in an instant, both staring

down as I stand rooted to the spot between them. I fight the urge to take a step back because they're not backing down.

Well, I'm not either.

"Listen, I'm a professional," I try. "I got hired to clean up after you this summer and that's the only thing you'll be getting from me."

Cooper shifts back, a bored expression passing over his face like an afternoon shadow, but Ethan doubles down, inching so close that our noses are mere inches apart. White hot heat radiates between us. A fake smile thins at the corners of my lips and when they part, his eyes drop to my mouth. For just a second, I think he's going to kiss me. And for just a second, I think I might let him. What the hell is wrong with me? I can't be a willing participant in his twisted games.

"Back off," I growl instead.

He snatches the end of my ponytail between his fingers and tugs. "Are you here to snitch on us then? Is that it? You're our father's little lackey? His eyes and ears?"

"You really think I was hired for anything other than cleaning?" I motion to the three of us standing together like this.

"Answer the question."

"No, I'm not here to babysit you. You two are grown-ass men and you're older than me."

"How old are you then, Ardie?" Cooper asks.

I bristle at the name. "It's Arden, and I'm eighteen."

At that, Ethan takes a full step back and they exchange yet another unreadable look but it's evident that my young age has rattled them. Good, I hope it bothers them that they're being inappropriate towards a girl who's barely legal.

"Mrs. King made it very clear that I am not to get involved with either of you." I can't seem to stop talking at this point. "She also made it clear that you know how to behave around the staff, which is obviously a lie."

A grin greets Cooper's lips. "We've never had a staff member look like you before, let alone one that's living with us."

"Alone," Ethan adds.

"Camilla's here too," I squeak.

He shakes his head. "Camilla doesn't live here." He assesses me like I have the answers written all over my face, then he turns to his brother. "He's up to something."

Cooper tilts his head, pondering, before shaking it. "It's not like dad to be so cruel. I think this is *her* doing."

So cruel? A little stab at my heart lets me know I've got to get out of here. "Are we done here?" I interrupt their cryptic conversation. "I've got to get back to work."

Two sets of devastating eyes cut to mine. Ethan's are blue as the tumultuous sea and Cooper's are so dark they shadow all emotion. Both I could get lost in---*I'm in big trouble.*

"Our father's reputation precedes us," Ethan says. "Don't pretend you don't know who he is. Everyone knows the billionaire media mogul Conrad King, same as everyone knows the King family is akin to American royalty."

Ice runs through my veins, zapping any heat that was there before.

"American royalty? More like royal dicks."

Cooper smirks. "That too."

I have to fight to roll my eyes. "Well, guess what? I'm not everyone. And I don't know much about your father, same as I don't know much about you two, or your family. And most importantly? You don't know shit about me."

Ethan grins like the devil himself. "Don't worry, *Ardie*. That will change soon enough."

Four

Over the next week, the twins manage to leave me alone, which is great, considering I feel like they declared war on me, but also not great, because I'm restlessly waiting for an attack.

It's morning and Bree is here again, and like the other two times she's spent the night with Cooper, she pads down to the kitchen to order her coffee.

I just so happen to be taking a break, sitting at the bar and chatting with Camilla as she slices fancy cheeses for a charcuterie board, the condensation from my drink cooling my hands. It's an iced caramel latte that I've perfected since Camilla took pity on me and showed me how to use the espresso machine.

Bree slides into the barstool next to mine as Camilla gets started on her drink order. "What about breakfast?" Bree asks Camilla, gazing around the kitchen with appraising eyes.

Hmm . . . I remember Bree saying she doesn't usually eat breakfast and now she's asking for it like it should be expected. This annoys me, but Camilla takes it all in stride, her feathers not the least bit ruffled.

"Cooper and Ethan rarely want breakfast so I don't have anything planned for today, but I can make you something if you'd like. How about an omelet?"

I sit up taller and can't help but smile as I watch the older woman. Apart from her day off, Camilla has made me breakfast every morning since I've arrived. Maybe feeding me breakfast is in her contract or maybe she actually cares about me. I'm starting to think it's the latter.

"Egg whites only, extra spinach, red onion, tomatoes, and goat cheese if you have it," Bree replies. Then she turns to me, her face propped up on her hand. "So, Ardie, what are you up to today?"

"It's Arden." I set down my drink and offer a careful smile. "Just doing my job."

She nods like she gets it. "You're a hard worker. I like that."

"Thanks." My guard is up, I don't trust her, but I don't think she's out to get me either.

"Have you made any friends on the island yet? There's a lot of really cool locals here and people who come to work for the summer too."

"Nobody yet. Are you a local?"

She wiggles her eyebrows, leaning in close. "God, no, but they are fun."

I'm not sure what to do with that. "I wouldn't know. I can't go out to the clubs or bars or anything. I'm only eighteen."

She pouts. "Aw, you're just a baby, you poor thing. You know what though, there is a club that does eighteen and older nights. It's fun, we used to go all the time before we got older. If you want to go, I'll give you the name and directions. Lots of locals and service people go there too, not just the summer-people, so you'll fit right in."

Maybe it wouldn't be such a bad thing to check it out. "Tell me more."

Sighing deeply, I step out of the shower and study my naked body in the foggy mirror. It's fine. It's nothing so perfect as the bodies I've seen out on the beach, but it's not too bad either. Truth be told, I've never really given a lot of thought to my figure in a sexual way before, not even when I went through puberty.

Looking at it now, I cup my breasts and wonder what someone else would think of the B-cups, then turn to study my side profile with its small pooch instead of flat abs, and the little bum that is definitely not the BBL so many guys are attracted to these days. The status of my hair is still up for debate. I've never been able to decide if the unique color makes me good-different or bad-different. Sometimes being different isn't a good thing. Sometimes different gets you teased mercilessly and makes you stand out when you'd rather be invisible.

I turn to the other side and adjust into a sexier position, twisting my torso and sticking out my chest and ass. Surely there's a great guy out there that would want this? A hunger forms low in my belly, but I ignore the sudden urge and laugh at myself. I'm being ridiculous again. This isn't me; this is just nerves. I get dressed for the evening, ignoring this newfound pull to explore my sexuality, especially while under this roof.

Tomorrow is my day off, so I plan to stay out late tonight and get the lay of the land. Maybe I'll even make a friend of two. There's got to be others in the service industry here that are also looking for people to hang out with. Even though I'm used to my own company, I don't want to spend the entire summer on my own.

Back home I was on the outskirts of several social circles, which is exactly how I like it. I can get invited to things when I want to go out, but I don't ever feel obligated to be somewhere

I don't want to be, nor do I get pulled into unnecessary drama. It's the kind of social life I'd like to keep going here and plan to adopt when I'm in college.

Wanting to look cute, I slip into tight black shorts and a loose silvery halter top. I don't have a lot of going-out clothing, so I hope this outfit will be good enough, and at least I can handle my bike with shorts on.

Feeling a little brave and a lot reckless, I leave my bra at home.

A half hour later and I already regret that choice, because my nipples are poking an outline through the fabric of my shirt for everyone to see, something I've never allowed since hitting puberty. I locked up my bike a few blocks away so I wouldn't look like a total dork rolling up to the club on a bicycle. And then I waited in the line with everyone else to get in. The cool evening air is not being kind to the girls under my slinky top and I've gotten more than a few side-eyes from it. People either love this look or they hate it. I think I might hate it.

When it's my turn to get up to the bouncer, he asks for my identification.

I hand it over and after glancing at it, he lets out a barking laugh. "What the fuck is this? Get out of here, kid." He hands me back my ID and then reaches past me to the next person.

My stomach sours but I hold my ground. "Don't you guys have an eighteen and older night tonight?"

He turns back to me. "Never have, never will. Come back in three years."

Several people laugh, a camera flashes, and I step out of the way, feeling as if I'm sinking into the concrete. A wave of hot anxiety flushes over my skin and I start to sweat. I've never been so embarrassed.

Fucking Bree.

But that's not even the worst of it, because when I turn

back to the gawking onlookers, one face stands out among the rest.

One face that has daggers sharpening his gaze—Ethan King.

He rushes forward and grabs my arm, his fingers biting into my bicep as he marches me away from the group of onlookers. I catch Bree and Cooper among them, Bree grinning like an evil bitch and Cooper grimacing.

I'm not sure where Ethan thinks we're going, but I choose not to fight him off. Not yet anyway. One, because he's knocked me out of my anxiety, and two, because I'm still wanting to be a little reckless tonight and I'm curious to see what he's going to do. And I'm also curious to see how I'll react to him. There's something about this man that makes me feel like a different person. Not better. Not worse. Just different. And right now, I really want to be anyone but myself.

"You can't stop me from having a good time tonight." I toss out nonchalantly.

At that, he whips me around, standing in my personal bubble with his hands on my upper arms. His touch feels electric to my nerves and my heart goes haywire at the feel of him. He towers over me and I stare up, my chin lifted. He's not backing down and neither am I.

"Why are you dressed like this?" he demands.

The audacity of his question throws me off. "Umm because I wanted to."

His jaw tenses. "You mean you wanted people to notice you."

I don't even know how to answer that, so I don't. I stand my ground and narrow my eyes. Who cares if I want to look good on a night out? Everyone is dressed up, not just me.

"Are you trying to look like a slut?" he continues.

Anger burns through me. Of every word he could've used,

why did it have to be that one? "You think it's okay to call women sluts?" I throw back.

"If you don't want to be called a slut then don't dress like one." His eyes track down my body even though we're standing so close. My skin pebbles under his gaze but I hold my ground. I won't let him rattle me. "I can see the outline of your nipples through your top, Ardie."

"And that bothers you?" I scoff.

"Unfortunately."

I can feel my cheeks burning but I won't let him see the insecurities he's just surfaced. It's not like I'm walking around topless, they're just poking through the fabric a little bit, but I feel stupid for thinking I could pull a look like this off. It takes confidence, something I wish I had in spades like so many other girls do. But you know what? Screw him and his misogyny. "Everyone has nipples, this outfit choice doesn't mean I'm a slut, and as far as I can tell, I look no different than most of the women in line to go in there."

"But you aren't like most of the women here."

I scoff. "What is that supposed to mean? Is that some kind of compliment or an insult?"

"It *means* you're barely eighteen," he hisses. "You're practically a fucking child."

"Why do you care about my age so much?" It's like there's something more going on he's not willing to admit. "Because newsflash, in case you can't tell, I'm *not* a child."

"And yet you've still got three more years before you can step foot in that club."

My face prickles and shame washes over me. I usually pride myself on being street savvy but sometimes I can be a gullible idiot. Right now is one of those times. "Bree told me this club has eighteen and older nights on Thursdays."

I don't mean to bring Bree into this but her name slips off

my tongue anyway. But why should I protect her? She obviously lied to me on purpose, wanting to embarrass me. I think she even filmed the whole thing, considering I saw her phone held up while she laughed.

"Bree?" His mouth thins into a line. "Cooper's Bree?"

"No, the French Brie. Yes, Cooper's Bree."

His eyebrow twitches but he doesn't laugh.

"Never mind." I look away. My eyes are burning and the last person I want to see me cry is Ethan. God, how could I have been so stupid? I want to wring Bree's neck for lying to me, but I know I won't. She's one of Cooper's girls and therefore untouchable. Besides, I'm not a fighter. I'm a loner. There's a big difference.

"What did she say?" Ethan demands.

I almost blurt it out but hold back. This isn't a good idea. The last thing I need is to have drama with Bree. I already have enough of it with the twins. The last week of laying low has given me a sense of confidence, one that I desperately needed. Probably a false sense, but still, I don't want it to all come crumbling down because of a bitchy girl who doesn't even know me.

"What did she say?" he repeats forcefully, then he takes my face between his fingers and forces me to look at him. In the dark, I can barely make out his features except for two navy pools peering into me, seeing far more of me than I'm ready for.

"She said the locals and service people come here for eighteen and older nights," my voice is shaky, "and I thought maybe I could meet some people to hang out with."

I feel like a loser with capital L, which means Bree won. Great.

"There's nobody for you in there. That place is the most expensive nightclub in town."

My mouth pops open with a little "oh" and I want nothing more than to crawl into a hole.

"There's nobody around here for you to hang out with anyway. You're too young."

"Am I supposed to believe nobody on this island is my age?" I roll my eyes.

"Believe what you want. I don't care."

"Really? Seems like you care a little too much."

He doesn't drop his hands like I expected. "Look, there's a divide on this island between the vacationers and the locals and the staff, and somewhere in the middle is you. You're not old enough to go to the bars, you work alone, as far as I can tell you don't have a phone, and you definitely don't have a car. Do you need me to go on?"

"I have a phone." Just a very crappy flip phone currently in my back pocket, but still, it's not nothing.

"You know what I mean. You don't have a smartphone. Do you even have social media?"

I do but it's not like I can keep up with it. I don't have internet access unless I trek it to a library and I haven't found the time yet. "Are you trying to be cruel?" I spit out. "Because Bree's already got that covered."

His eyes harden. They're no longer deep pools of blue; they're hard frozen ice. Impenetrable. I swallow hard, wetting my lips. My entire body was cold two seconds ago, but now it's burning hot. I can feel the warmth coming from him, adding to my heat. His cologne smells like rich-boy heaven and he's standing too close. He still hasn't let go of my face.

Shame on me for trusting Bree, but shame on her for pretending to extend an olive branch that was actually poison ivy.

"I should've trusted my gut when it came to that girl," I sigh.

"Funny that you thought you could believe a word out of

Bree's mouth," his sinful lips quirks into a mocking smirk, "when she clearly doesn't like you."

I grab his wrists and push him back. "I had no reason not to. Why would she lie about this? It's ridiculous."

He laughs and I'm suddenly a wounded animal desperate to lash out. *What a dick.* I don't have to stand here and take this from him. I step away, ready to take off.

"Besides the obvious?"

"She thinks it's funny? Ha. Ha. I'm laughing real hard over here." God, I want to punch that girl, but having a stable job is more important than revenge.

"Don't play dumb."

"I'm not playing anything."

His stare is like a dagger. "She's *jealous* of you, Ardie. She's worried you're going to steal Cooper away."

Oh, here we go again. "I'm not interested in Cooper."

His gaze flicks to my lips and back to my eyes. "Are you sure about that?"

"Very."

I turn and march back toward the bike rack a few blocks over, but of course he follows. My stupid tears are two seconds from falling and I can't hold them back anymore. Salty wetness streaks down my cheeks but I don't let that stop me. Walking past darkened storefronts, I'm soon back at the rack and unlocking the bike. I probably should've worn a helmet tonight but I didn't because I didn't want to ruin my hair. I can see now that wasn't the smartest decision, but neither was trusting Bree. In fact, this whole summer feels like one bad decision. Maybe I should call it quits early and go back to the group home. God, what a bleak thought. I'd vowed never to return there.

The second I climb onto the bike, Ethan's rough hands haul me right back off.

"Let me go!" I knew he was following me, but I didn't want

to give him the satisfaction of acknowledgement. Thank God I'm away from the club and that line of people with their camera phones and judgment.

"Riding a bike out here at night? You're more stupid than I thought."

"Not all of us have Daddy's car to drive around," I snap back. His tricked-out Land Rover is around here somewhere, I'm sure.

"One, that chip on your shoulder isn't doing you any favors. And two, even if you did have a car, you don't have a driver's license. I'll give you a ride home."

My face goes hot all over again because that fact about myself means he really has been checking up on me.

Ethan knows.

He knows about the foster homes and the poverty and the dead drug addict mother and the unknown father who never even made it onto the birth certificate, let alone into my life. Which also means he knows that by society's standards, I'm well beneath him. Him, and everyone in his social circles. Him and his family. Him and his stupid fuckboy brother.

And I hate them for it. And I also hate myself for even thinking this way, for even caring what someone like Ethan King thinks of me. Because logically, I understand that my upbringing isn't my fault. I was born into terrible circumstances, and they were born with silver spoons in their mouths. It doesn't actually mean my worth as a human is less than theirs. And it doesn't mean I won't make something of myself in the future, or that they won't screw up their pedigree lives. But try telling that to a girl who has been let down and abandoned by every single person? It's one thing to understand a concept logically, but it's another thing entirely to actually believe it deep down.

Without a bike, I don't have a way to get home, and I'm not

in the mood for walking, so I wipe away my tears and follow Ethan to his black Land Rover. He pops the hatch, tossing the bike inside, then slams it shut with a loud thud.

"Please don't cry," he grumbles. "I can't deal with it."

I don't even dignify that with a response.

"You are forbidden from going out on that bike at night again. Do you hear me?"

I walk around to the side of the SUV and he follows. I didn't ask for this fatherly protective attitude. Nor do I need him. I can take care of myself. And I'm definitely riding that bike *and crying* whenever I damn well please.

"Yes, Dad," I toss over my shoulder.

Big mistake.

One second we're facing off and the next he's pushing me up against the side of the car and stepping between my legs. Eyes locked, he whispers low. "I already know all about your daddy issues. But guess what, Ardie?"

Ugh, that terrible name again. But I can't think of that right now. All I can think of is him. Of our close proximity, and the way I'm burning up again, burning with humiliation, but also burning with something I don't want to name. He's so close, so attractive, and so *all-consuming*. I can't help but want him even closer, to be keenly aware of every inch where our bodies touch.

I don't know what to say, so all I squeak out is a measly, "What?"

His face softens, those blue eyes almost silver now. He looks like he's going to reply with something important, something close to a confession. But instead, he reaches behind me, and opens the door, which draws me even closer to him. He's hard all over and I gasp.

Leaning down, he whispers in my ear. "Get in the car."

"Tell me what you were going to say," I insist breathily.

He was saying something about daddy issues and I need to

know what it was. I stay rooted to the spot, secretly loving the way it feels to be pressed up against him like this. Okay, maybe not so secret. He must be able to see it on my flushed face and hear it in my husky voice. He must feel it between us, the same way I can.

"I don't want you either." He steps away and I go cold.

Ouch.

That. Was. Fucking. Low.

As he rounds the car for the driver's seat, I climb into the back and force the threat of tears to turn to anger instead. Anger for being rejected, but also anger because of course he doesn't want me. Same as my daddy probably never wanted me as a daughter.

And why do I care so much?!

Why do I feel like I'm in the middle of the desert whenever I'm around this man and he's the only water source available? Why does someone who is a complete jerk to me feel like he could be my oasis? God, I really do have issues, he's obviously the mirage and not the oasis. I should be ashamed of myself, but strangely, I'm not. Because I'm pretty sure he's lying, that he really does want me too, and for the first time since arriving here, I don't feel so powerless.

Five

Someone pounds on my door, and normally that would wake me up considering it's the middle of the night, but I've already been awake for hours. The twins are throwing a raucous party, complete with the low thumping bass of rap music and the occasional obnoxious squeal. I've been trying to read to distract myself but can't think through the noise. Next time I'm in town, I'm buying earplugs.

The pounding continues.

"Oh, hell no," I mutter. I'm off duty and I'm not answering.

"Ardie," Cooper's voice calls out, "your services are needed out here."

"I'm sleeping!"

"No, you're not." He knocks on the door again. It's past 2 a.m. now and the party still sounds like it's raging on, so I guess he's right about my lack of sleep. "Come on, Ardie."

It's now been a full three weeks of them calling me Ardie instead of Arden. Yeah, I've stopped correcting them. I know when I'm fighting a losing battle.

"Well, if I was sleeping, I'm not anymore thanks to you people," I yell.

"You mean your employers?"

It's not like he's the one paying for my salary but I wrench open the door to a very disheveled Cooper. In all honesty, that shaggy hair always makes him look a little disheveled, but tonight it's apparent that someone has been running their hands through it. Probably a woman. Bree is here more nights than the other girls, but Cooper's had a parade of women sleeping with him in the time I've been here. The guy is the walking definition of a fuckboy. But when it comes to Bree, I haven't said a single word about what happened at that club a few weeks ago. I can tell she hates it, so at least in this one thing, I've won.

"What do you need me to do?" I don't like being out of my element like this, woken up in the middle of the night. I prefer routine and predictability—sleeping seven hours a night, waking up early for a run, and following my plan for the day. Rinse and repeat.

He stares at me for a second, his eyes roaming over my pajama shorts set. I'm obviously not wearing a bra under the top but I've got my arms folded over my chest, and he smirks at that. At least he's not calling me a slut for being sans bra like Ethan did. "We need you to clean up a mess."

"I'll do it in the morning," I say, closing the door.

He catches it and pushes it back open, stepping in closer, his hooded eyes locked on me. "If you wait until morning for this one, you're going to regret it."

"And why's that?" I cock my head.

"Because it's vomit," he deadpans.

"Oh, for Christ's sake, are you a child?"

He laughs as if this is all just fun and games. "It's not my vomit. Now come on."

"No, I'll do it in the morning."

"If you want, but it'll be a lot harder to clean up if you wait for it to get all crusty."

The visual image of that makes me rethink my life choices. "And you really can't go clean this up by yourself?"

He pouts. "Please, Ardie? I'll just make an even bigger mess."

I narrow my eyes. "Are you familiar with the term *weaponized incompetence*?"

I can tell he wants to laugh and I don't know if I want to laugh with him or punch him. Maybe both. "I am, but is it my fault I never learned how to clean properly? Blame my parents."

"At twenty-four, yes, it is your fault, you big baby."

He shrugs and I want to hate him for this but I don't. I may be pissed off, but I don't hate him. I can't, the guy has a certain swagger that's too easy to love. "What will it be, Ardie?"

"You're a monster," I deadpan and he snorts, giving me his signature panty-dropping grin.

I drag myself to the closet and grab an oversized hoodie to throw on over my sleep set and follow him upstairs. We zigzag through hordes of mostly drunk people and I get more than a handful of stares. They're all preppy casual wealthy twenty-somethings and I look like I'm naked under my ratty hoodie. Some of these people just seem curious, some are most definitely checking me out, but most of them are judging me.

We take the second set of stairs and go all the way up to his bedroom.

He doesn't say anything and I glare at his back, following him inside to the mess of splattered vomit on his rug. The rancid smell is a punch to the gut. I hurry back out into the hallway away from the stench and Cooper follows. My frustration has bubbled up and any sense of professionalism is fast disappearing.

"Let me guess, you hooked up with a drunk girl and she threw up on your floor? You really shouldn't sleep with women when they're so drunk they can't even hold the contents of their stomach."

Maybe I said too much, maybe that was mean, but I'm exhausted and this is bullshit and I'm back to hating the guy. I know I'm supposed to keep my mouth shut and clean on autopilot, but Mrs. King isn't here to reprimand me.

Cooper, however, is.

His face goes pale and his eyes blaze. I don't think I've ever seen Cooper mad before, I thought he was the easy-going brother. The funny one. The one who lets things roll off his back because he's too disengaged to care. Guess I don't really know him at all. "I don't sleep with women who are too drunk." His tone is tight with anger. "I would *never* do that."

I should shut up, I really should, but I can't help myself. "Then why, of all places, was it in your bedroom that a woman threw up a bunch of liquor? I know what you get up to in there. Considering you've got a woman over every night, we *all* do."

His eyes narrow and I know I've hit a nerve. This is about to be the part where he threatens my job, maybe even fires me, but that doesn't happen. Instead, he smiles slowly, stalking in close. Dusty brown hair hangs around his face as he presses his forehead to mine. I'm frozen to the spot. This is the last thing I expected.

"You're so fucking cute when you call me out like that," he says, "but Ardie, I know what consent means. Ask anyone I sleep with and they'll tell you they want it. Not only that, but I always make sure they come back for more."

"O–okay," I breathe. "Sorry."

"Now let me call you on your shit," he continues, voice husky-soft like velvet. *Oh, boy.* If this move is how he seduces women, I get it now. "You're being pretty resistant to doing your job. Do you need to be punished for insubordination?"

My pulse thunders and I let out a slow breath. Somehow, I think I might like his form of punishment and that scares the utter shit out of me. I shake my head no.

"Hmm, too bad." He brushes past me, shoulder-checking me on his way out.

Back to being an asshole.

The anger rushes right back and I want to chase after him, but I don't. At least I got under his skin. I'm tired of keeping my mouth shut around here. Their mom hasn't set foot in the beach house in three weeks and I still haven't met Mr. King. It's just me and these entitled idiots when Camilla isn't around. If I'm going to be cleaning up vomit, I should at least be able to speak my mind about it.

I hurry back downstairs to the cleaning closet and get what I need, ignoring the guests who have moved on from taking an interest in the housekeeper. They're all probably used to staff waiting on them hand and foot. I'm just another everyday luxury to them, not an actual person who needs sleep and respect.

I set to work and twenty minutes later the rug is as good as new. Stupid as it is, I stand there for a full minute, admiring my work. I've gotten pretty decent at cleaning. And also, thank goodness for baking soda because that stuff is the kryptonite to vomit.

On my way out the door, I catch sight of Cooper's phone sitting on the dresser and a pair of noise-canceling headphones laying next to them. I already know the phone will be locked so there's no point in trying to look through it, but the headphones will help me sleep tonight even if I can't play music through them. I try them on, adjusting them down to my smaller head-size and switching on the noise canceling feature.

Sure enough, what comes out sounds like glorious white noise and drowns out most of the obnoxious party sounds.

I turn them off and stuff them into the hoodie pocket. I'll return them tomorrow. It's the least Cooper can do for making me clean up vomit in the middle of the night.

Ding! A text message pops up on his phone's lock screen. Do I touch it? No. But do I look at the text message? Absolutely. It's from his father, and when I scan the message and register what I'm actually reading, my body goes cold.

Dad: It's obvious that I got her for Ethan. I know all about your playboy tendencies and I usually look the other way but I won't in this case. She's not yours.

I stare at the text, wondering what it all means, a sinking feeling in my gut that Conrad King might be talking about me. But no, that doesn't make sense. I'm not something someone can just *get* for somebody else. I'm being big-headed about this--my knee-jerk assumption must be wrong. This text could be about anyone. There's a parade of women coming through the house, it's probably one of them. Or maybe someone from their life back in Manhattan. An escort of sorts? Somebody else . . .

I pick up the phone and click on the text anyway.

The lock screen pops up and I can't read any further into the conversation. There's no way to know what Cooper texted his father to prompt such an unsettling reply. Shit, I suddenly wish I knew more about tech than I do right now.

Ding! Another text pops up on the screen, also from Mr. King.

Dad: I mean it, Coop. Stay away from Arden. This is important.

I stare at my name for a long moment.

"What the hell?" My stomach is twisting into an unbreakable knot and I suddenly feel even more sick than when I did while cleaning up the vomit, because this text hits me center in the chest. This is a violation.

With a shaky hand, I set the phone back down exactly where I found it and dart from the room. My mind is spinning, the party's chatter, thumping music, and sharp scent of alcohol dulling. None of that matters. I make my way back downstairs.

Mr. King brought me here for Ethan? What does that even mean?

My first thought is sex, and the initial shock of the text messages is quickly replaced with anger. I'm not a sex worker. I'm an eighteen-year-old housekeeper. This is wrong.

But ... Ethan can get any girl he wants.

And if bringing me here is some kind of present for their son, then why did Mrs. King demand I stay away from him? Did she just say that to make Ethan the desirable forbidden fruit dangling in my face all summer long? She doesn't seem like the type, but I don't know her. There's got to be more going on here, but it doesn't matter because I don't want them in any capacity. Are they attractive? Yes. Have I been tempted? Undeniably. But no amount of attractiveness and temptation can make up for the fact that they're entitled assholes.

I'm hurrying down the stairs to the basement, my mind so preoccupied that I trip over my own feet.

Six

Losing my balance, I face-plant over the last four steps, ending up sprawled out on the floor. Drowning in shame, I hiss quietly to myself as the pain eats at my knees and elbows. I turn back to glare at the stairs only to find a beautiful Bree bounding down them. She's a dream woman in a tiny black bikini with a matching sheer cover-up. A delighted expression is painted on her sultry face. I really shouldn't let her make me feel insecure but she's everything I'm not.

"I know it's a party, but you really shouldn't drink on the job," she says with a mocking laugh.

On the inside, she's rotten—I'd rather be me than be rotten. And maybe it's the shock of the text messages, the frustration of being awake right now, or just that I'm fed up with her, but I am all of two seconds away from losing it on her.

I can't.

If I lose it, she wins.

So I scramble to my feet and walk away. Of course, she's not going to let me go so easily. Quick to catch up, she waves her iPhone in my face. "Can I get your okay on something before I post it?" She plays a video and ice-cold embarrassment freezes me to the spot. There I am on her phone getting shut down by the bouncer at the club. It's a quick video, punctuated by background laughter.

"You want to post that?" I say woodenly. "Go right ahead. I don't care."

I *do* care, but she can't know that.

She scoffs. "It's a *joke*, Ardie. Where's your sense of humor? Besides, I'm not posting *you* on my socials, you're a nobody. But I still had to make sure you saw it. I couldn't let something so funny go to waste. Isn't it hilarious?"

Her question is a test. Am I going to play along with her bullying or am I going to stand up for myself? If I give her what she wants, she won't stop. And if I don't give her what she wants, she also won't stop.

"I don't think it's funny." I turn to face her head on, steeling myself for a possible fight. "I know all about girls like you, Bree. I've dealt with this pity shit my entire life, and you know what?"

She stiffens and her voice drops an octave. "What?"

"You can't hurt me. I grew up fighting for myself and I'm not stopping for you. But I have real problems, and sorry but you're just not one of them."

She raises a perfectly groomed eyebrow, her face bright with challenge. "You think I want to fight you? Well, I could, I am trained in three martial arts. My father made sure of it." Her eyes travel me up and down. "And you're a twig. I could break you in two."

She thinks I want to physically *fight* her? Goes to show how little she knows of the real fights in this world, the ones that aren't done with fists.

I shrug nonchalantly. "I didn't grow up with a father. I grew up in foster care and I learned that there's a hell of a lot more to fighting than martial arts." I hate that all this mean-girl shit is so cliché, but in the real world, there are mean girls, many who are far worse than Bree. She's not my first and she won't be my last. She needs to know where I stand. "But it doesn't matter," I continue, "because I'm *not* going to fight you, Bree. I'm not interested in your drama."

The word drama seems to send her over the edge. I've struck a chord.

"Aw, you scared?" There's a vengeance growing within her, something rooted much deeper than anything to do with me. I'm just the current punching bag, someone to take out her frustrations on. But this isn't about me, this is about her.

"Actually, no. I'm not afraid of you. I don't need to hurt you because insecure people like you are already doing it to yourself on a daily basis."

Her mouth pops open in shock. "What is that supposed to mean?"

"It means you're picking on me because you're upset that Cooper won't date you for real. You're hurt by his actions, but you don't have the courage to be honest with him about it, so you're picking on me instead. You see me as someone who is unable to defend herself, an easy target. But here's the thing, I'm not playing your game. Hit me and I'll hit back if I have to defend myself, but you won't hurt me where it counts." I make sure to emphasize my last line. "Because I don't care what you think about me."

Her face reddens—she's a predator who's been caught. And what do wild animals do when caught? They lash out.

"I'm not surprised you don't have a father," she sneers, shifting closer, voice trembling. "He probably took one look at you as a crack baby and bailed."

My heart falls. People have said a lot of mean things to me over the years and I would like to let this roll off my back, but it sticks. And it hurts. But I can't let her see how sharp her words truly are to me or she'll keep going, so I don't let myself react.

Doesn't matter. She grins, triumphant.

"That's enough," a furious voice hisses.

Ethan.

We turn to find the man glaring down at us, rage darkening his features.

"Hi, Ethan." Bree has the audacity to bat her eyelashes but he's unfazed.

"Cooper, come and rein in your bitch," he booms, drawing the attention of everyone in the basement. He doesn't take his eyes off us.

No surprise, Cooper is nowhere to be found.

"Are you calling me a bitch?" Bree tries to play it off as a joke but Ethan's not laughing.

"I am. I heard what you said. That was fucking low, even for you."

I blink at Ethan. The man who has been nothing but cold towards me is now *defending* me? Is this his protective bullshit again?

"She started it," Bree tries.

"Excuse me?" I laugh.

"I doubt that." Ethan's voice drips with venom.

Bree acts shocked and innocent, making me hate her more than I already do. I'm done. I'm done being treated like her doormat, like my presence in this home warrants her walking all over me. "You targeted me, not the other way around. Stop lying."

She doesn't even look my way. "Ethan, are you really going to choose her side over mine? She's the one who looks—"

"Shut up," Ethan roars and Bree's mouth closes tight. It's not like her. Something's up.

"I'm the one who looks . . . what?" I try. "Say it."

But nobody says anything, except for Ethan yelling for Cooper again, who remains missing. Bree and I both know there's nothing she can add, that I didn't actually do anything to her but tell the truth about her insecurities.

"Where the fuck is my brother?" Ethan asks, turning toward the onlookers who have mostly stopped the party to gawk at our exchange.

"He's probably busy hooking up with someone," I laugh bitterly. My statement is true, but it also has the potential to hurt Bree, which is exactly why I turn to her and add, "Does being nothing more than a booty call bother you?"

It's petty. I know better, but I can't help it.

"We're in an open relationship. It's noncommittal." Her face is glacial, but she abruptly storms out the back door to the pool area.

Ethan takes that as his cue to drag me away from the sea of gawkers and into the hallway where my bedroom is located. He throws open my door, and pushes me inside, following right behind.

I really wish he hadn't.

Because even though the darkness makes it difficult to see the details, I still catch sight of the two naked bodies kneeling on my bed.

I yelp and turn away, my face prickling.

"Cooper, are you fucking kidding me?" Ethan's voice is sharp enough to cut. He also turns to face the door.

"Get out. We're almost done," Cooper replies hastily, as if we're the ones violating his privacy and not the other way around.

"This is my bedroom!" My face is in my hands, muffling the sound of my yelling.

"My house," Cooper replies. My stomach churns at the sound of him fucking some girl in my bed. It fills the room alongside her whimpered pleasure. Do they really have no shame?

"Get out of my room or I'll tell your father," I try.

I don't know why I thought that would work but it doesn't, because a few seconds later they let out sounds of simultaneous orgasms. My eyes are closed but I hear everything, and I have to get out of here. My stomach liquefies and I sprint into my bathroom, slamming the door and locking it behind me.

"I did not consent to that," I yell out. "Fuck you, Cooper!"

"Give me ten minutes and you can," he yells back.

"You better take that bedspread to the washing machine and get me a new clean blanket or I swear to God I really will tell Daddy King."

Cooper chuckles.

"Don't ever say Daddy King again," Ethan's voice grumbles from somewhere within my bedroom.

"Not unless you're talking about me," Cooper adds with a laugh.

His girl laughs too, calling out a quick apology, and then they all leave.

I stay locked in the bathroom, swallowing down my anxiety. The aftermath of all that adrenaline coursing through my veins has given me the shakes. I splash some water on my face and rinse the rugburns at my elbows and knees, wincing through the whole process. Great, I'm going to have to clean up after this party tomorrow while in pain.

For the first time since graduation, I'm struck by just how alone I am in the world. There's nobody being paid to look after me anymore. Not that they always did back in foster care, but absolutely nobody cares about me here. If I don't have my own back, nobody else will, that's for fucking sure. It's a lonely realization. A bitter truth.

Just breathe, you'll be okay, I tell myself over and over until I start to believe it. I have to because if I don't, my emotions will control my thoughts and then I'll really be in trouble.

"I left a clean blanket and sheets on your bed," Cooper says through the bathroom door and I jump. I wasn't actually expecting him to come back. "I'm sorry, Arden. I was angry at you and shouldn't have used your bedroom for sex. I invaded your privacy."

He's apologizing?

I don't offer him a reply. His apology is too surprising, especially with the use of my real name, and I don't know if it's genuine. Did Ethan put him up to it? Either way, I'm still angry and feeling violated, so I'm not forgiving him. The fucker woke me to clean up vomit and when I gave him grief for it, he took his hookup to my bedroom. There are places all over this house he could've done that, but he chose *my* bed.

"For what it's worth, I didn't actually mean for you to see that," he adds, and he actually does sound sorry.

Do I believe that? I don't know. I can take a lot of shit, but I can't take this.

I fling open the bathroom door, glaring up at him. His hair is a mess and his cheeks are flushed pink. He smells of sweat and cologne and I hate him. He looks way too relaxed given the situation. I point my finger, hitting him right in the chest. "If you didn't mean for me to see it, then why did you do it in my bedroom?"

He doesn't have an answer to that.

"That was fucked up," I go on. "Did you do it because I called you out on your issues upstairs?" No answer except to look away like a coward. "I may be younger than you but I'm obviously more mature. You're here in Nantucket to put your dick in any girl who will let you. I'm here to work, *to survive*."

"It's our last summer before signing our lives away," he argues, as if that makes it all okay. "You wouldn't understand."

No, I certainly wouldn't.

"Wow, poor baby. Guess what? I'm not here to play around. I don't have that luxury. If I don't collect a paycheck, I'll end up homeless." He opens his mouth to say something, but I don't let him. My words are rolling off my tongue now. A runaway train. "But even as much as I need the money, I shouldn't have to put up with you violating my privacy, not to mention with your little girlfriend Bree attacking me."

"She attacked you?"

"She's been after me since I got here. She may not have hit me, but she treats me like fucking garbage. You saw what happened at that club. Do you know she orchestrated the whole thing just to shit on me?"

His eyes darken. "I'll take care of Bree."

I scoff. "Oh really? I thought you guys hated me, so how do I know you weren't the one to tell her to mess with me in the first place?"

He shakes his head. "We wouldn't do that. Besides, Bree is pretty harmless. What damage can she really do? She doesn't even know you. Don't let her get under your skin."

His defense of her puts me in a rage. "You think calling me a crack baby is harmless? Saying that's why I don't have a dad? Or maybe you think it's okay for her to challenge me to a fight? Or how about filming me during an embarrassing moment to use against me later?" My voice cracks. "Take your pick, Cooper."

His face pales and he reaches out, as if he has a right to comfort me.

I step back. "Don't touch me."

"She did all that?" He has the audacity to sound surprised. Like, does he really not know the kind of women he's been sleeping with?

I nod and look away, tears burning my eyes.

With clenched fists, he storms from the room. I shouldn't

follow him. I know that. I know all about "shoulds." I should stay right here. I should lock my door. And I should use the headphones I buried in my hoodie pocket to help me sleep. But "shoulds" are for less curious girls than me right now, because what I do is follow Cooper out of the room.

"Bree!" his voice booms angrily as he rips into the living room. I don't think I've ever heard the guy yell. I can't tell if he's truly mad at her or if he's just embarrassed by his immature actions and is now taking it out on the easiest target.

"Where's Bree?" he demands of the beer pong players.

They exchange glances, a few of them smirking. "She's in the hot tub."

Cooper goes for the back door. The house is on an incline, so the basement walks out to the backyard pool area. Sure enough Bree is in the large adjoining hot tub. She's straddling the lap of some guy and the two are making out. Her bikini top is undone and floating nearby, and the guy's got his hands all over her breasts.

Are these people always so horny or is this Bree's attempt at getting back at Cooper for hooking up with someone else at his party? Probably a bit of both.

"Bree!" he yells and she peers over her make out partner's shoulder to land a scathing look at Cooper.

"What do you want?" she coos. "I'm a little busy here."

"Get the fuck off my property," he states, his tone cold and final.

It's a side I haven't seen of him, and for the first time since I arrived, an inkling of hope swells within me. Fuckboy tendencies aside, *maybe* he's not all bad.

Maybe.

She blinks up at him. "Wh–what?"

"Get out," he repeats, harsher this time.

She stands, covering her breasts with one arm. The water

glistens down her body as she grabs her bathing suit top and hops out of the tub, striding over to Cooper. Her face is hard, and she never once looks at me even though I'm obviously standing right next to him. "Is this because of your little maid? She's a nobody. Don't choose her side over mine."

Cooper's voice is the sharp end of a blade. "You've made her uncomfortable."

"So what? She makes me uncomfortable."

"She has nowhere else to go and you do, so you need to leave. Now."

Bree has the audacity to appear offended, which would be funny under different circumstances. "Are you kidding?"

When he doesn't budge, her lips thin indignantly. "Fine, whatever. This party is almost over anyway." She turns her back to us and hastily slips on her top and sheer cover-up, then points to the hot tub guy. "You, what's your name again?"

He has since climbed out and wrapped a towel around his waist. "Darnel." He's staring at her body like she's a cherry cheesecake and she's looking at him like he's her meal ticket out of here. Good, let them have each other.

"Do you want to take me home, Darnel?"

He nods with a smug grin.

She grabs his hand and shoots one last scathing look at Cooper before taking off with her new boytoy. Cooper doesn't appear to care. And why should he? He's not exclusive with her or any of the other girls he sleeps with. If Bree leaves, he'll just find someone else to take her spot in the roster.

My mind swirls with questions, but more than that, I just want to sleep and forget this night entirely. "This doesn't make us even," I shoot at Cooper.

"Never said it did." And then he saunters back to his party like none of what just happened is a big deal.

SEVEN

Bright and early the next morning, I hobble upstairs despite wanting to stay in bed. At least my rug burn isn't as bad as it was, but I'm definitely going to need caffeine and ibuprofen to get through all the cleaning that needs to happen after last night.

I saunter into the dining room and am hit with a savory smell. I stop dead in my tracks.

Eggs. Bacon. Coffee.

Today marks three weeks and one day since I arrived here and not once have I seen the twins eat breakfast, and after last night, they should be passed out cold somewhere. But despite the house being in total disarray, a bountiful meal is spread out on the dining room table. On one end sits Mrs. King, and on the other end is a handsome gentleman who must be Mr. King.

"Uh--hi," I mutter. "Good morning."

Mrs. King gazes up from her phone and Mr. King peers over his newspaper. I'm struck by the age difference. She looks at least twenty years younger than him, though they're both beautiful people. I once heard the phrase, "you're not ugly, you're just poor," and these two very well could be proof of that. They can afford whatever they want, including the world's best plastic surgeons, skincare, vitamins, and nutrition.

The shape of Mr. King's face is more square like Ethan's, but his eyes are dark chocolate like Cooper's. His hair is a shade somewhere between Cooper's dusty brown and Ethan's deep brunette, just streaked with highlights of gray to give away his age. He's the picture of a powerful man, the kind I can imagine has a closet filled with tailored suits. He's the type of powerful that rules over boardrooms, always in control and always on top.

Today he's in crisp golf attire and his wife is dressed to match in a white tennis skirt and top. Her breakfast sits steaming on her plate, seemingly untouched, and my stomach growls.

"It's nice to finally meet you," Mr. King says. He gives me a quick once-over and it's almost like he's checking me out. I have no idea what he thinks of my appearance. My cheeks prickle because I'm wearing basic cotton shorts and an old high school t-shirt, my mane of red curls knotted haphazardly on top of my head.

I look like I just rolled out of bed, and in fact, that's exactly what I just did.

"Good morning, Arden," Mrs. King addresses me coolly, her mouth pinched and eyes sharp with disapproval. "You'll see to this mess immediately, I assume? Or do we need to reevaluate your position here? If you can't handle this, you can either resign or we can hire a second housekeeper and split the salary difference."

Fuck. Her initial instructions cut me like a knife, revealing my mistakes. *If there's a visual mess, you're already failing.*

"Malory, that's enough." Mr. King's eyes blaze in his wife's direction. I'm confused by his immediate defense of me but I'm not going to protest.

"I can do it," I promise. "I'll get to work right away."

It's silly to be embarrassed because this mess isn't my fault. I did my job yesterday and went to bed with the house in pristine condition. The guys threw a huge party and that's not on me, but it feels like it is.

It feels like I somehow should've cleaned up already even though that would've been completely unreasonable. Not to mention, I didn't know Mr. and Mrs. King would be arriving this morning. Every once in a while, she'll call or text to speak with me about how things are going, but our conversations are brief. She never mentioned her plans.

"The twins had a wild party last night," I blurt, my cheeks flaming even hotter for doing it.

I'm probably covered in bubblegum pink splotches right about now, looking like I had a run-in with poison-ivy. The couple bristles at my words and I could kick myself. I should've kept my mouth shut and my head down. They don't want to hear my excuses and they certainly don't want me blaming their precious grown-up little boys.

"And did you participate in the party?" Mr. King asks.

He's studying me like I'm a fascinating puzzle to figure out. I don't like it. I want to ask him what he meant when he texted Cooper last night. Does he think he can buy me?

"No, I'm not here for parties," I say instead.

My eyes dart to Mrs. King and she gives a satisfied smile.

Mr. King frowns, the lines around his eyes deepening, and then he's back to his newspaper and coffee. I've been dismissed.

I hurry away, leaning back against the wall when I round the corner to catch a breath. My bare feet stick to the floor and I groan, trying not to wince as my lungs expand. I should go back downstairs and dress in something more professional. And get some damn shoes on!

I feel so stupid and inexperienced. So young. I already have an unwanted stigma from my upbringing and now they're going to think I'm an incompetent housekeeper. I don't know the first thing about removing the wine stains I saw on the carpet downstairs on my way up here, let alone this sticky gunk that's currently below my feet on the hardwood floor.

Peeling my foot from the mess, my mind swirls with ideas for how I can do a good job today. This is going to take more than baking soda and elbow grease. This is a professional job, something that might be beyond my experience.

"They threw that party because they knew we were coming back this morning," Mrs. King's voice filters from the dining room and I hold my breath. I can't help but listen to the conversation even though I know it isn't meant for me. "They made this disgusting mess for us to walk into just to spite us."

"Obviously," Mr. King replies, but he sounds unfazed. "Though it's quite stupid. It's their house too and not like we're the ones who have to clean it up."

Yeah, that would be me.

"It's one thing to throw parties but they should know better to do it when we're coming into town. Where's the respect?"

"Malory. . ."

"You're just going to let them get away with it?"

He sighs and the room goes quiet for a long moment. "It's the deal I made with them," he finally croons. There's a charm to his inflection that reminds me of Cooper. "They get free reign of the place for the summer before joining King Media in the fall. Once that happens, you know as well as I do that their lives are going to change. This is their last chance to be young. What do you want me to do about that? Take it away?"

"I want you to parent your children."

"They're not children. They're grown men."

"Really? Because last I checked, grown men don't waste their summers drinking and sleeping around and throwing parties."

I couldn't agree more.

They go silent again. Should I walk away? Would they hear me if I did? I don't move because it's like I can't, like I'm rooted to the spot now, like I'll never move again.

"You're right," he replies, "but I'm trying to make it up to them after everything they went through during the years that were supposed to be the best of their lives, especially after what Sybil did to Ethan."

Who the hell is Sybil and what did she do to Ethan?

"Clearly," Mrs. King drawls. "Arden is barely eighteen though. Leave that poor girl out of it. She doesn't need to get involved with Ethan and his demons."

My body goes cold.

Mrs. King may not seem to like me, but she's looking out for me. Looking out for me when it comes to Ethan? Why? Camilla also warned me to stay away from him.

"Arden's got a roof over her head and a good job. I provided that. Don't act like she's being victimized here. Nobody's forcing anything. Let's just . . . stay out the kids' way and see what happens, hmm?"

It sounds like he does want me to hook up with Ethan, but why? There's no logical explanation that I can think of, especially not when there are socialite girls Ethan could date. So why root for a nobody?

I swallow, hardening my resolve. We're almost through June and I leave in August. Am I going to sleep with Ethan King? Absolutely not. But I am going to figure out this mystery before I leave the island. At least it will give me something more interesting to do with my time besides cleaning up other people's messes.

My vision blurs, needling pinpricks unthreading my world. It's been a long day and I was past the point of exhaustion hours ago. I inhale deeply and drop my head down onto my arms, leaning against the cool kitchen counter. Soon. Soon I'll be sleeping. But right now, I'm helping Camilla clean up after the five-course dinner she served the family. She saved a portion for me, but I hardly ate a bite, let alone tasted it—all I want is to go to sleep and forget about this shitty day.

But even if I could lay down right now, I know I wouldn't be able to sleep, because underneath all that exhaustion is anxiety. It lives coiled inside of me like a snake and it's been sleeping for most of the summer—but now it's rearing its ugly head, fangs dripping with venom. If it strikes, the anxiety will take over, making a terrible situation so much worse.

Because I messed up today.

I messed up big time and now it's time to face the consequences.

"What's wrong?" Camilla pats me on the shoulder.

I look into her concerned eyes and crumble. "I think I might get fired."

Her eyes flare. "Why would you say that?"

I can't bring myself to explain so of course that's when Mrs. King walks in. "Arden, we'd like to speak with you in the office please."

She walks away, expecting me to follow, and I do. Time to face the music.

Eight

My nerves are threatening to overtake me as I follow Mrs. King into the office. *Breathe, just breathe*, I instruct, but the serpent is awake and coiling around my windpipe. Mrs. King folds her arms over her chest and stands next to her husband, seated at his desk. His eyes are on his computer screen for a full minute despite our presence. It's as if I'm not actually worth his time and I shift awkwardly between my feet, waiting. Finally, Mrs. King clears her throat and Mr. King looks up.

"Arden, how are you enjoying your time here?"

I don't know how to answer that, so I decide to go with the truth. "I think maybe I should put in my two weeks' notice."

Mrs. King smirks but Mr. King seems unfazed. "And why would you do that?"

I gather my courage. "I don't think this job is a good fit for me."

"Hmm." He ponders that, a line forming between his brows. "You may be right. My wife informed me of two concerning things."

He opens his drawer and places Cooper's headphones on the desk. "What were these doing in your bedroom?"

It hits me like a battle axe. Mrs. King went snooping through my bedroom and I was foolish enough to give her something to find. "I was just borrowing these from Cooper to help me sleep through the party noise last night. I promise, I was going to give them right back."

He sighs heavily. "Did you ask him?"

I shake my head.

"This could be considered stealing. These are expensive headphones."

"I'm so sorry." What else is there to say? He's right. I wasn't thinking clearly last night. I was too angry and tired. I never should've taken them without asking Cooper. What a dumb mistake to make.

"Thank you for your honesty," he replies, putting the headphones back in the drawer. "I believe you. However, the principle of this incident is concerning. Do you regularly borrow things that don't belong to you?"

I shake my head vigorously. "No, never. I didn't think Cooper would care."

"He wouldn't but be sure to ask next time."

Mrs. King is glowering at us and there's no need to guess at what she's thinking. She wants me gone and doesn't like that Mr. King is being lenient on me. "And the second issue?" she snaps at her husband.

He eyes her sidelong and I can tell he's getting annoyed with her. He turns back to me. "You've damaged the Brazilian rosewood flooring in the east hallway. Are you aware of that?"

I can feel the blood draining from my face. "Yes, I'm so sorry. I was going to tell you after dinner. I didn't realize my mistake until an hour ago."

"Care to explain?" He's calm and collected, which throws

me off. His demeanor is so unexpected because everyone else around here is a hothead.

"There was a sticky substance on the floor after the party and I tried to clean it with the natural products Mrs. King prefers but it wasn't working." I swallow hard, avoiding her laser glare. "So I used a different product on it, the stronger one I use for the bathroom tiles." The image of what I did to those beautiful floors flashes through my mind and my stomach turns over. "I took some of the varnish off."

"Yes, you did," Mrs. King snaps. "Even if you weren't going to quit, you'd still be fired for your complete lack of judgment. Do you have any idea how much those floors cost?"

I shake my head, absolutely mortified.

"Malory, you're getting too emotional about this. Please leave us. I'd like to discuss the matter of Arden's employment privately."

"But—"

"Malory." One word and she shutters her features and strides from the room like an ice queen.

"Five hundred dollars a square foot," he says and I blink at him. "The cost of that flooring is five hundred a square foot."

My mouth pops open.

"And I expect you to pay for the repairs."

I blink rapidly. "I–I can't. I don't have that kind of money." My mind races through the square footage. I don't know how many will need to be replaced. Ten? Twenty? More?

"You will have that kind of money by the end of the summer. You can pay us back before you leave."

My entire body goes cold and I lose all sense of decorum. "Do you realize what kind of hostile work environment you've created here? Do you know that I've been bullied by one of Cooper's girlfriends? That in the middle of the night last night he forced me to get up and clean vomit from his rug while he took a different girlfriend down to my bedroom and had sex with her there?" The words blurt from my mouth without much thought to the consequences. "Do you know that Ethan treats me like scum, like I'm nothing? And yet he acts like he has the right to control me."

"Are you done with your tantrum yet?" Mr. King asks.

"No!" I'm just getting fired up. "While I was cleaning up that vomit last night, I saw your text about me being here for Ethan. I don't know who you think you are, but I'm not a plaything for your son."

I feel like I'm sinking into the carpet, but I hold my knees tight and my body tall. This man could squash me like a bug if he wanted. He has all the resources in the world and I have none, but I do have my pride and I'm done letting him take that away.

He pushes back from his desk and stands, sauntering around the desk to meet me. He's so much taller than I am, taller even than both of his sons, and it takes everything in me not to get intimidated. Okay, who am I kidding? Of course, I'm intimidated. Everything about this family screams intimidation, especially the patriarch.

"Alright, let's play this out." His voice is business-like. Calm. Calculated. *Cutthroat.* "Let's say you quit this job and leave Nantucket in two weeks, because you do have to give us two weeks' notice, that's in your contract. Well, that still leaves you how many weeks until you're due to check in for school?"

I swallow hard because I know my voice is about to wobble. "Six."

He thinks about that for a long moment. "And where will you go for six weeks?"

No clue.

And that's the sad truth. I won't have anywhere to go unless I'm willing to go back to the state home, but I will have three full paychecks' worth of money saved up from this job. That will have to be enough to get something figured out. In an ideal world I would head to Boston early and find short-term lodging and employment. I tell Mr. King as much and he laughs in my face.

"The world is cruel. You of all people should know that your plan is doomed to fail."

"I'm resourceful. I'll figure it out."

He tilts his head. "You'll end up back in that state home you were living in. Is that really better than staying here?"

He's right. It's not better. Memories of the last two years flash through my mind: crowded bedrooms and complete lack of privacy, constantly having my things stolen, getting into fights with the rough girls or watching the sweeter ones get bullied, getting yelled at by the overworked adults, and sometimes even going to bed hungry. But all those things I can deal with. What I can't deal with is returning to the worthlessness I felt day in and day out. By the end, my anxiety was flaring its ugly head every time I even walked through the front door.

I never want to feel that way again.

"It's not worse," I admit.

"And what about the bill for the hardwood flooring?" he presses. "You can't pay us back if you don't have a job." His threatening question is like two hands squeezing around my neck. I know I'm breathing but it feels like I'm not. It feels like I'm suffocating, all the air in the room gone. "Do you expect us to bail out your mistake because we're wealthy?"

I give a shaky nod and he laughs again.

"Sorry, Ms. Davis, but I'm a businessman and I didn't get wealthy by letting people take advantage of my family."

What. The. Fuck?

"But--but--it was an accident and it was with a product you provided in your home."

He shrugs. “You’re welcome to hire an attorney but I don’t think that would be the best use of your already limited funds. Why don’t you take a seat and we can negotiate how you’re going to pay for your mistake?”

I can’t move. I can’t think. All I can do is stand here.

“You’re an adult now, Ms. Davis. No more relying on other people to take care of you.”

Tears flood my vision. When has anyone truly taken care of me? And now this, one mistake and I’m out thousands of dollars.

“You’re looking at ten grand in repair costs, maybe more. I pay fair market wages, but live-in housekeeping for an inexperienced woman such as yourself is hardly a lucrative endeavor. You can’t leave now and expect to pay us back for the damage you’ve caused in a timely manner. It would be so much easier to stay here and work it off.”

This. This moment is exactly why I’m going to college to pursue whatever can make me the most money. Somewhere in the back of my mind, I think there must be a way to get the damage fixed for less than what he’s expecting. But if there is, and that’s a big if, I wouldn’t know.

“Sounds to me like you can’t afford to quit this job.”

He’s right and he knows it.

And I’m too angry and upset to discuss this any further. “Fine. You win. I’m staying. I’ll pay for the repairs, just take it out of my checks.”

He nods. “I knew you’d see reason. And Arden, do me a favor, huh?”

I stare at him, not able to say a fucking word.

“Don’t talk to my wife about this. Quite frankly, it’s none of her business.”

None of her business? I nod numbly because there’s nothing else to do anymore. I’m an open chasm of vulnerability, all my insecurities picked apart by this intimidating man in a single conversation. I can't stay in his presence a second longer, so I turn on my heels and race from the room.

I'm still exhausted to the bone, but I can't imagine sleeping right now. I don't want to be in this house for another second. I hurry downstairs and grab my book, then stride out onto the back lawn.

The summer scene before me is so wonderful in juxtaposition to my mood that I could cry. It's a gorgeous late June evening in Nantucket, the sky an endless blue that will soon turn to a vibrant sunset. And the temperature? It's absolute perfection. It even smells amazing out here, like ocean salt and fresh cut grass and the hydrangeas that bloom everywhere on this picturesque island. Everything about this place should be a dream come true, but I hate it here. They've made me hate it.

"Where are you going?" Ethan's voice snaps me from my thoughts and my eyes dart to find him in the pool, arms folded over the edge as he peers up at me. I'm close enough to see the water droplets clinging to his eyelashes, noting the way they skim along his full lips. Another thing that is entirely unfair-- he's way too attractive, what with swimming laps every day on top of his already model-pretty face. I've peeked at his lithe body slicing through the water more than once but right now I really don't need him asking me questions.

I throw my hands up, shooting him the death-glare I should've given his asshole father. "None of your business, Ethan."

And then I stomp past the pool deck and out toward the gazebo overlooking the ocean. I just need to get away for a while so I can gather my thoughts. Even though Mr. King is right and I have to suck it up to pay off my mistake, I'd still like some time away from that house so I can get properly angry. Maybe scream into the wind or something.

Ten thousand dollars?

Ten grand is more than half of what I'll make this summer after taxes. I'll pay off whatever I have to and then the rest will go with me to college in August. At least I won't have to pay for my lodging at school thanks to my scholarship, but the idea that fixing the varnish on some lousy wood will cost me thousands of dollars is bullshit. Is this what it means to be an adult?

I enter the gazebo like I have a vendetta against it, plopping myself down with my book in my lap. Ethan sits down next to me as if he has a right to my company.

"What do you want?" I snap.

"I want to know if you're okay." He sounds just as defensive as I do, which is annoying and only makes my hackles rise. I don't care that he's got a gorgeous body that's half naked right now or that he smells good even with the chlorine overpowering everything or that a few water droplets are still sticking to his eyelashes and lips. None of that matters because he's the spawn of Satan. Conrad King showed me exactly where his sons get their asshole tendencies.

"I'm fine," I bite out. "Please leave me alone."

His eyes narrow on the book. "And what's so interesting about that book that you can't talk to me for two seconds?"

I flip it over and stare down at the cover. It's a smutty fantasy romance on the inside but on the outside it just looks like any other fantasy book. One of my bookish friends back home raved about it but it had a long waiting list at the library, so when I found the whole series at the used bookstore for only a couple dollars a book, I grabbed the set. "Trust me, this book is infinitely more interesting than anything you'd like to say to me."

He raises an eyebrow. "That might be true."

No, it's not. I'm bluffing, but I'm also pissed off.

"Right. So go back to the pool and leave me alone."

"Bree's not coming around here anymore. I made sure of that. If I see her, I'll throw her out myself, and same goes for anyone else who tries to mess with you." He stands and begins back down the path toward the house. "You're welcome," he calls over his shoulder.

"So you and Cooper are the only ones who are allowed to mess with me, is that it?" I call back.

He stops and turns around, a handsome smirk on his face. "Not Cooper either. Just me."

Oh boy.

That makes me stand too. "Why am I here?" I demand, walking right up to him and craning my neck to glare into his eyes. "Because I know there's something else, that your dad has ulterior motives, but nobody will tell me what's going on."

"What makes you think there's anything going on?" His eyes scour me, as if looking for something, as if hopeful. For just a moment I think that maybe there's something else here, something between us, but maybe I'm imagining things because his gaze immediately shutters.

"Your father told Cooper to leave me alone because he got me for you, as if I'm a material possession and not a person." The next part might end badly for me, but I have to ask. "Are you involved in some kind of trafficking operation?"

With that, his expression opens up, revealing something else entirely. Not something vulnerable. Not something sweet or sexy. Something entirely hateful. Vile. Rage-filled. "Is that what you think of us?"

"I don't know what I'm supposed to think!"

"Don't worry, Arden," he growls. "That's not what this is."

"Then what is it?"

"It's nothing." He emphasizes each word before turning for the house, his back tense as he walks away from me.

I imagine he's going to lay into his father, and for a second, I imagine following him in there to eavesdrop on their conversation, or maybe just so I can tell Mr. King off again. But I do neither. Instead, I head back to the gazebo and attempt to get lost in the book. Of course, I can't concentrate and end up reading the same page over and over again, not because the story is boring, but because there was one thing Ethan was wrong about today. This book isn't more interesting than what's going on in my life right now. That's fiction. This isn't.

Billionaire Conrad King wants me here for Ethan and nobody will tell me why.

Nine

On my next day off, I decide it's high time that I trek down to the King's beach. With the holiday coming up, all four of them are at the house this week and I need a break. Scarfing down my breakfast, I change into my most modest swimsuit and head out. This beach is pretty private because the only land access is through the wealthy properties lining the bluff. The stairs are steep as hell and made from the same wind-worn wood as the gazebo, so coming back up them is going to be a bitch, but that's a problem for future me.

It's early so the beach is an empty stretch of tan against the endless blue. Reaching the bottom of the stairs, I tug off my sandals and step onto the smooth sand.

A girl could get used to this.

I need to come down here more often, go running or lay out of something. The peace will be well worth the challenging stairs.

I pick a spot and lay down my towel, stretching myself out on it like a sunbathing cat. I've never been much of a tanner--

definitely more of a sunscreen at all times type of girl with my pale complexion, but I'd still like to go to college with a little bronze color. My sunscreen can sit in my bag for a little while longer. Once I feel that first bite of sun on my skin I will apply it, but right now I just want to relax and be a little reckless.

I roll my eyes at myself. Am I really so boring that I consider the possibility of a sunburn to be reckless? *Nice one, Arden*.

I gaze out at the ocean, then up and down the empty beach. I'm blissfully alone out here this morning and an actual reckless idea pops up in my brain, something the women in my books would do and something I normally wouldn't. Before I can talk myself out of it, I stand and strip naked, then sprint down into the surf. The morning water hits me in icy waves, a brutal wake up call.

I've been in Nantucket for weeks now, but this is my first time going in the ocean in my entire life. Simply setting foot here would've been ambitious, but I'm doing it in my birthday suit. That's what makes it reckless, what makes it feel more alive. And that's all I want right now, to feel so fucking *alive* that all my worries drift away.

Spreading out my arms to face the endless horizon, a bubble of laughter escapes me. This is fun. I keep laughing, taking another step and then another. I like the ocean. It isn't so scary after all.

A wave smacks me in the face and drags me under.

That humbles me real quick.

I'm spinning. Saltwater assaults my nose and mouth. My limbs flail out around me as grainy sand scrapes against my bare skin.

It's okay. Stay calm. You're fine.

It takes a few crashing waves before I can gain enough stability to stand up, but just as I do an even bigger wave pummels me, sending me right back under the surf.

The terror is instantaneous.

I thought I knew how to swim.

Turns out being able to dog paddle with one hand while holding your nose with the other is not the same thing as swimming. My skill level is nothing to take on this crushing ocean. The waves didn't look that bad when I came out here, they weren't even that big. But with each one, I'm pulled farther and farther away from the shore. Soon I lose the grip of sand under my feet. And still, I'm pushed out and under, out and under, out and under . . . I come up sputtering each time. More water in my mouth. Salt burning my eyes. Fear pounding my chest.

More waves––endless ocean.

I'm going to drown out here.

No. This will not be how I go. I refuse to let this take me. Kicking my legs harder than ever, I push the panic aside and refocus. All I have to do is float on top of the waves and swim with them back to shore. How hard can it really be?

The answer: very hard.

Before long I'm even farther out because the waves going to shore are nothing compared to the strong current pulling me to sea. I don't know enough about the ocean to understand what is happening, but I do know enough to realize that I've made a huge mistake. I completely underestimated the level that my recklessness could take me. This isn't the Nantucket Sound, this is the East side of the island. The Atlantic Ocean may appear friendly, but it's a gargantuan monster and it's going to eat me alive.

I begin to scream for help, but I'm alone out here.

There's nobody.

My limbs are getting too tired to keep fighting and the water is too much. No matter how hard I try to stay above the swells, I can't seem to do it. And forget about swimming in the direction of the shore, I don't have what it takes. I'm going to drown and my body will become shark food. Or maybe it will wash up somewhere, naked and bloated and barely recognizable.

And it's all my fault, all because I wanted to be reckless.

My vision pinpricks, black nothingness edging in. I close my eyes and keep fighting. I keep screaming. Keep moving. But with every passing second, I'm losing the fight. My death is simultaneously taking forever and not taking any time at all. These are the longest and shortest minutes of my life--and they're about to be my last.

Something slams into the back of the head. I try to scream but I'm too tired and waterlogged to get a breath out, let alone a functioning scream. This must be what drowning feels like. It's death's final blow, hitting me upside the head and I can't even scream about it.

And then I'm underwater again. I'm sinking. Fighting. *Ending.*

I open my eyes despite the burning salt. I need to see this as it happens, need to know it's real, to accept the truth. To let go.

I should be panicking but I'm not.

The world is beautiful down here too. Beautiful and violent and terrible. I can't see the ocean's bottom, there's nothing but darkness below me. It's reaching up to consume me, dark shadows that offer nothing but death. Above me, the surface is rising away in a parting goodbye. It sparkles, bright and cheery, as if to mock me.

And then someone is there, a body swimming toward me.

Strong arms wrap around my middle. Legs kick. Feet hit against mine.

I'm being pulled back up.

We break through the surface and all I can see is Ethan. Ethan is holding me. Ethan is saving me. Ethan is dragging me onto a surfboard. The plastic edge bites into my hip and then my ribs, irritating enough to bruise. So it wasn't death that hit me upside the head, it was Ethan's board.

I'm alive. I'm alive and coughing up water and crying.

"Are you okay?" he's asking me, his voice sounding far away to my waterlogged ears.

I nod but it's not true and I can't stop crying. I'm not okay. After that, how can I ever be okay? I'll dream of that darkness. It will come for me in nightmares. Surely the monster won't give up on me so easily. I've been claimed.

Ethan is cussing and then he's laying down next to me on the board, practically crushing me with his body. My breast scrapes against the plastic and I want to cry even more but how can I? I'm already crying. Waves splash over us again and again, more water spraying up into my face as he paddles us to shore. The crying turns to coughing and it's all I can do to keep from passing out.

"Just hang on, baby," he's saying, sounding angry. At me? At the ocean?

Probably me.

Maybe both.

Did he just call me baby?

It feels like ages before we're back to shore. There's so much water and then there's none and he's dragging me from the surf. I'm suddenly very much aware of how naked I am as I stumble along beside him, one of his arms wrapped around my waist. I should be embarrassed at my nudity, and I'm sure those feelings will consume me soon, but right now I'm just grateful to be alive. I gulp in air between coughing fits.

Cooper runs across the beach, sand spraying up behind him, my towel flapping in his hands. He wraps me up in the warm fabric and lays me gently on the beach. They kneel over me and I still cough.

"What the hell happened?" Cooper demands.

"I was surfing and found her out there half-drowned." Ethan's tone is as dark as the bottom of that ocean.

They turn to me, expecting an answer, but I can hardly form coherent thoughts right now, let alone string together words. My entire body shakes and I still can't get enough air. Every time I breathe, I cough.

Because my body thinks I'm still under that water, believes I'm still drowning.

The panic has finally come for me.

"She's hyperventilating," Cooper says but he sounds far away. "I wonder how much water she swallowed. Maybe she should see a doctor."

"Probably a lot. I had to swim down at least six feet to get her."

"No doctors," I manage.

Cooper pats my back and Ethan stares at me like he's staring at a ghost.

"Why the hell not?" Ethan demands.

Isn't it obvious? "I can't afford a doctor."

"To hell you can't." He sounds angry now, like it's completely unreasonable and stupid that I'd refuse medical care because of the cost. And it's not like he's completely off base because there are government programs that will pay for my medical expenses, but I can't wrap my mind around trying to figure those out right now. Besides, I'm okay. I'm breathing. I made it. I'm alive. Isn't that what I wanted? To feel alive?

Well, I fucking succeeded.

With that thought, I lean forward and vomit salt water.

Ten

The Fourth of July is my favorite holiday for many reasons, but the main one is that I love firework shows. Crowds normally bother me, but crowds watching fireworks are the exception. I don't mind all the people or the loud booms because I get to marvel at the display. Even the scent of gunpowder in the air makes me nostalgic.

All that, and I get to belong.

Growing up in foster care meant that I wasn't always included in holidays, but most people in Massachusetts go out and enjoy the big shows that the cities put on. The whole community is involved and nearly everyone I lived with would take me to watch fireworks. Even the employees at the group home made a trip out of it. It was free. It was fun. It was festive. And sitting under the fireworks, surrounded by darkness and dazzling lights and strangers made me feel like I was a part of something.

I love it, and I'm determined that tonight won't be different.

Because while I haven't been very welcome on Nantucket,

the fireworks show tonight is for everybody. I finish up my work and get ready for what will be a great night.

Standing in front of the bathroom mirror, I take in my patriotic reflection. I look normal, just like a happy and healthy girl ready for a night of celebration. Not like someone who nearly drowned four days ago. Most importantly, I look like someone who belongs, like every other American girl on this day.

After saving my life, the twins took me to the doctor for a check-up and insisted on paying for it. The doctor checked for something called secondary drowning, which is when water gets into your lungs and you end up aspirating on it later. Fortunately, I was fine and able to return back to the house to rest. The next day I got back to work like nothing happened . . . but something did happen. And every time I think about it, about how I went skinny dipping in broad daylight, nearly drowned, and was saved by Ethan dragging my naked ass to shore, I cringe.

I still don't know if he meant to call me baby. Does he even know he said that?

With a heavy sigh, I tuck a curl behind my ear and assess my distressed jean shorts, red tank top, white sandals, and light makeup. It's not perfect, but it's good enough for tonight. I look festive--that's what matters, right?

I don't know what the Kings are up to tonight and I don't really care. I'm off work for the holiday and I'm going to enjoy it without worrying about my employers.

That is until I step into the hallway and hear the music coming from out on the patio.

Another party.

Not the kind of obnoxious party from last week but the kind thrown by middle-aged wealthy people with middle-aged wealthy friends. I know better than to go out there and get wrangled into some kind of cleanup job on my day off. Besides, aren't "the help" supposed to be invisible at times like these? I slip up the stairs and through the side door to retrieve my bike from the garage. Cars are being lined up on the driveway by a hired valet and I chuckle to myself because heaven forbid rich people park their own cars.

I haven't been on my bike in a week and I smile when I climb aboard, hands flexing on the familiar handlebars.

It's going to be a good night.

It's going to be a good night.

It's going to be a good night.

That's my mantra today. I've been repeating it all day, probably because deep down I'm nervous that it won't be. I'm not someone who gets her hopes up very often, but when it comes to the Fourth of July, I can't help but want it to be great.

Even if I don't fit in.

Even if I have zero friends here.

Even if I'm too young to hang out because everyone goes to the bars that I can't get into and I haven't found anyone my own age yet. And even if Bree is probably out there somewhere plotting revenge for getting kicked out of the Kings' lives.

I swallow hard and push those thoughts from my mind, then take off down the drive. All of three seconds later, a car honks and Ethan's Land Rover drives up next to me.

"What are you doing?" Cooper demands as he rolls down the passenger window.

"What does it look like?" I shoot back, stopping on my bike to face them.

"I thought we talked about this," Ethan growls. His face is in shadow from the driver's seat but I can easily picture him when he's pissed off. "You're not to ride that bike around at night. It's not safe."

"It's the Fourth of July. I'm going to the fireworks show." I say it like it's obvious, because isn't it? I'm not going to stay back at the house and miss out on my favorite holiday just because I have to ride a bike to get down to the public beach.

"My parents have their own fireworks show already paid for and set to go off from our beach, you can stay back for that one."

My mouth drops open. "They do? But how? Personal fireworks are illegal in Massachusetts."

"Not illegal with a permit."

Oh . . . maybe I should've assumed something like that was happening, what with the party going on and all. But do I really want to stay back at the house? I'm all dressed up and I want to get out of here, not stay. Besides, I have no interest in crashing Conrad and Malory King's party, nor do I want to run into any of their adult friends. What do Ethan and Cooper expect me to do? Hide out in the bushes to watch the fireworks? No, not interested. I'm going down to the public show to fight the shitty crowds like a normal person.

"No thanks." I take off on the bike again, pulling in front of them so they can wait for me to get out of the driveway.

Ethan honks again. "Don't be stubborn."

I wave back at him. He's not going to stop me from going to the show I want to go to. Besides, it'll probably be the better one. Am I really supposed to believe that the King's private show is going to outdo the one put on by the island of Nantucket?

Well, maybe . . .

I loop around and go back to Cooper's passenger window. He's smiling at me like I'm the funniest person he knows. I glare like he's the most evil, even though he's really not. "You're going down to the public show too, aren't you?"

"Yeah, you got us there. Get in. You're coming with us."

Ethan exhales a gravelly breath, making it very apparent

that he doesn't want me getting in with them, let alone going down to the public show at all. A flash of anger lights my temper. "No, I'm fine to get myself there," I snap, taking off yet again. I pedal hard, but of course they catch up in all of two seconds.

"Just get in the damn car," Ethan demands.

"No." One word. Should be as simple as that, but nothing is ever simple with these two.

"I'm starting to think you have a death wish," Ethan yells. It's not often I've heard him yell before and it makes me listen. "First you go swimming in the ocean when you clearly don't know how to swim, and then you get on a bike in the dark on the busiest night of the summer. Do you know how many drunk drivers are going to be on the roads tonight? Do you want to end up as roadkill?"

Okay, maybe he has a point.

With a dark glare, I concede, leaving the bike at the end of the driveway to pick up later tonight and climbing into the backseat. A thought strikes me that this won't be the last time I climb into Ethan's backseat and I have to shake my head to push the thought away, because no fucking way am I going back to lusting after these idiots.

Twenty minutes later and they have no trouble finding parking because they have no problem paying a local an obscene amount of money to use their driveway. When we climb out of the car, I plan to head in my own direction because I don't want to spend the evening with these guys.

"Meet us back here after the show." Ethan catches on. "I'll take you home."

And then I'm sure he'll go to some after party. But whatever, I'll need a ride. "Sounds good," I agree.

But Cooper slings his arm around my shoulder and a stupid zing of electricity races through my body. "Nope. Ardie's with us tonight," he announces to his brother, then gives me a playful wink.

Ethan shoots him a dark look. "You're not sleeping with *Arden*."

He puts emphasis on my real name and I don't know what to do with that.

"Excuse me." I push Cooper's arm off me. "I'm not interested in sleeping with anyone tonight, nor do I need your pity. I can handle myself."

"Aw, why you gotta be like that?" Cooper teases. "But seriously, you should come with us. I won't hit on you, I promise. I'll even introduce you to our friends."

"No, you won't." Ethan is full of attitude about this and I have no idea where it's coming from. Honestly, it's not as if I want to crash their fun, but what's the big deal if I meet their friends? I've met a few of Coop's girls, haven't I? And I was seen at the party. I'm no surprise to anyone at this point. Not that I care.

I study them, noting that their casual clothing probably costs a fortune, that Cooper's longer tousled hair and Ethan's shorter dark crop both fit perfectly with their personalities. But it's the way their eyes are both so intense that gets to me the most. Even if one set is brown and the other blue, they're both able to rope me in without even trying.

Ethan is gorgeous in an obvious heart-stopping way and Cooper has that devil-may-care personality that makes his rugged good looks even better. They're definitely brothers, but they're also so different. Subtly in appearance but night and day in personality. Doesn't matter, I can't forget that they're two sides to the same coin. If push comes to shove, they're going to look out for each other and not for me.

"I don't know. If your friends are anything like Bree, I think I'm good on my own tonight."

"He means our male friends," Ethan deadpans. "He wants to hook you up with one of them. It's Cooper's way. He wants to have sex, but he also wants everybody else to be having sex."

Cooper grins. "Sex is my love language."

I scoff and elbow him, but he doesn't budge. "And that's why you want to introduce me to your guy friends?"

"I gotta make it up to you for what happened last week. Might as well have a good time the rest of the summer, right? You're off work every night, go enjoy yourself."

"Your friends are douchebags," Ethan interjects. "They're not good enough for Arden."

Warmth blooms in my chest and Cooper rolls his eyes. "*Our* friends are not all douchebags and you know it." He elbows me softly. "Ethan just wants you for himself."

Ethan grimaces and walks faster, disappearing into the crowds of people heading toward the beach and leaving us behind. Cooper and I walk together in the same direction, while my mind swirls. *He called me baby.*

"What's his problem?" I finally ask.

Cooper sighs. "It's complicated."

"You really think he wants me for himself?"

Cooper's face is unreadable but then a sly grin takes over. "Damn, you want him."

"No, I don't."

"It's alright, everyone does."

"He's a jerk. I don't want him."

"Whatever you say."

"I do say."

"Alright, well in that case, I was just teasing Ethan before. He's messed up and doesn't want anyone right now. It's a long story."

"I've got time."

He laughs. "I'm sure you do, but it's not mine to tell."

I nod. Fair enough. The mystery that is Ethan King lives another day.

"But if you want to fuck," Cooper continues. "I'm down. Or I can hook you up with one of my friends. The offer still stands."

Ethan was right, Cooper's friends really do sound like douchebags. Also, so does Cooper, but I bite my tongue because Cooper is also being friendly and I need a friend. Is he gorgeous and does the idea of sex with him intrigue me? Absolutely. But I also know the kind of guy he is when it comes to girls, and I'm not interested in something like that. At least, that's what I keep telling myself . . . ugh, why do I care so much?

"There are other ways to have fun, you know. It doesn't all have to be about sex."

Cooper just laughs. "You sound like a virgin."

"I am a virgin," I fire back.

He turns on me with wide eyes, his mouth thinning into a line. "Oh, sorry. Yes, of course. Shit. Sorry. Forget I said any of that. You definitely don't want to hook up with any of my friends then."

"Because they don't like virgins?"

His face softens. "No, because they don't like relationships."

"And that's why I'm a virgin? Because I want a relationship?"

He holds up his hands in surrender. "Don't you?"

I'm glaring, and he's frozen, which just makes me bust up laughing. "I don't know, relationships kind of scare me, but it's okay. The truth is, I don't want to have sex for the first time until I'm ready, and I think that's going to take someone special."

"Someone special like a boyfriend?"

I smile. "Yeah, probably, so I guess you're right."

"See? I thought so, and that's fine. It's smart of you to be careful with your virginity. But Arden, can I give you a piece of advice?"

Do I want to take advice from Cooper King? Absolutely not. But am I curious enough to let him continue whatever asinine thing is about to come out of his pretty mouth? Yes.

"And what's that?"

"Relationships aren't all they're cracked up to be."

Eleven

Maybe everyone gets nervous when meeting new people, but my reaction seems to be on another level. It's a personal flaw that I'd like to change. It's not that I care all that much what they'll think of me, it's that I care what I'll think of them. I have this problem of getting my hopes up with people who turn out to be disappointments. I've had friends but never a best friend. I've kissed boys but I've never had a boyfriend. I've lived with families but I've never known what it's like to belong to one. I don't even know what it's like to go to the same school long enough to memorize the fight song.

My life has turned me into an island unto myself, but I don't want to be a damn island, I want to belong to other people the same way I want them to belong to me. And that's what's so hard about meeting new people, why I get so nervous, why my hands sweat, and my words get all sticky on my tongue, and my stomach twists into knots.

My last school counselor called it social anxiety, but I think it might be more than that.

I want to change this about myself, I really do, but the thing about change is it's easier said than done. And as I walk alongside Cooper to meet up with his friends, those nerves hit me like a tidal wave. It's a physical thing that I can't just will away no matter how hard I try.

"You okay?" Cooper senses my unease.

I'm surprised he even noticed but that's probably because I'm being too obvious. I nod and force a smile. "What's there to be nervous about?"

He rakes a hand through his hair and nods. He looks older at this moment, more thoughtful and experienced. "Listen, I'm sorry about what I did to you. I know I've apologized, but I was an asshole that night."

Having sex in my bed while I clean up vomit for him and then get verbally attacked by one of his other hookups is the definition of asshole-behavior, but at least he's being nice to me now. And I can sense that at his core he's a good guy. He's nicer than Ethan, that's for damn sure. I hope I'm not deluding myself by thinking I can trust him, but I decide to lighten the mood anyway.

"Cooper King––apologize? I never thought I'd see the day." I raise my eyebrows at him when he has the gall to look offended.

"Yup, I'm an asshole."

I sigh. "You can act like an asshole, but you're not an asshole. There's a difference."

"Well, in that case, let me make it up to you."

Their friend group is gathered among the sea of people who are sitting on the beach, and Cooper plops down on the only empty spot on the blankets. He just so happens to be sitting a foot away from where Ethan is busy flirting with some girl. It's not the same girl I saw him making out with at the bonfire my first day here, and I kind of want to kick myself for noticing one way or the other. But I can't help it. It's that orbit thing again--Ethan is the center of everybody else.

I'm standing here awkwardly while the rest are sitting down and ignoring me, but at least Cooper reaches out for me. "Come on." He pats the tiny space between him and his brother. "We don't bite."

"I know I'm small, but I'm not that small, Cooper."

Someone snorts cruelly, reminding me exactly why I wanted to watch the show by myself.

"You'll fit," Ethan says. I didn't even realize he was listening.

But he's right, I probably can fit if I'm willing to give up my personal bubble. I remember that lonely island thing and step through the tangle of bodies to squeeze in between the brothers. I try to make myself as small as possible but it doesn't work, I'm still wedged between them, their bodies pressing uncomfortably against me on either side.

"Arden, this is everybody. Everybody, this is Arden."

About half the group chimes in with hellos and the other half continues to ignore me, which is fine because the last thing I want to do is make small talk. Some of them are probably friends with Bree and hate me.

Someone passes out cans of beer from a cooler and I go for a water instead. Cooper begins chatting up the girl on his right and Ethan is still flirting with the girl on his left and I'm sitting here like a third wheel. Or is it fifth wheel?

"You okay there?" the guy sitting in front of me turns around, looking me up and down like I'm a salty snack and he's hungry. Normally I find this behavior annoying, but tonight it feels validating. I put a lot of effort into my appearance and it feels good that he's noticed, whoever he is. He smiles and deep boyish dimples appear on his cheeks. It multiplies his hotness factor by ten.

"Yeah," I croak, instantly flustered. I hold up the water bottle. "It's hot out here."

Did I really just say that?

"Do you want a beer instead?"

I shake my head. "I'm only eighteen so no public intoxication for me."

"Smart girl. I'm Perry Hargrove. I'm glad to finally meet you," he says with a flirty smile, and I smile right back. It's nice to flirt. It's been so long since anyone paid attention to me like this and even longer since I let myself play.

"Hi Perry, I'm Arden," I say coyly.

"Oh, I know who you are. Everybody knows about the Kings' new girl."

"Why is that?" Interest spikes and now I truly am interested to know why "everyone" would know who I am, because I certainly don't know anybody else here besides the Kings and I feel like a nobody.

He nods towards Ethan, voice going whisper-low. "He made damn sure we all knew who you are and that you're off limits."

I eye Ethan's back with skepticism then look back at Perry, my voice dropping to a whisper. "Why would he even care who I spend time with?"

It's not like we're dating. We're not even friends, I'm not his little sister, and he's been clear that he doesn't like me. But maybe that's why. He doesn't like me, and he doesn't want me mixing with his world. Infecting it.

"He's looking out for you, that's all."

Do I really believe that?

"Don't worry." Perry pats me on the knee and adjusts himself to be fully turned around to talk to me. We're knee to knee now, and I can't help but notice how attractive he is. Smooth tawny skin, black short curly hair, thick eyelashes fanning deep soulful eyes, and full kissable lips framed by those amazing dimples. This is the kind of guy that girls flock to, and despite several stunning girls in this group of at least forty people, Perry has his attention completely on me. "Anyway, I'm not worried about Ethan," he goes on. "He's my friend, but he's not my dating coach."

"And what about me being off-limits?" I tease.

"That's up to you." His eyes linger on my mouth. "You can date whoever you want."

"Date?" The nerves are back. I barely know the guy and he's already talking about dates? Would I date him? Should I date him? Maybe I'm getting ahead of myself, it's not like he's asked me out, nor do I know anything about him.

"Yes, I would like to take you out on a date if that's okay."

And there it is.

Of course, that's the moment that both King brothers twist toward us. Cooper's grin is wide and he pats me on the knee. "Perry is a good guy, Arden. You wouldn't have to worry about a date with him."

I don't know why, but something about his eagerness to set me up with his friend makes my heart twist. Just a little bit. I shouldn't care that Cooper wants to pawn me off on other men instead of wanting me for himself or his brother. It's a stupid thing to think—barely a blip and I ignore it.

I study Perry, trying to make up my mind.

But Ethan? Ethan reacts just how I thought he would.

"No fucking way." His tone is harsh. Final.

"Why not?" Perry asks, a single eyebrow raising in challenge.

The conversation has an undertone that signals something more is going on here, something beneath the surface that I'm not catching. I probably never will because I don't have years of history with these guys like they do with each other.

"Yeah, Ethan, why not?" I add.

From my understanding, most of the people in this group have been meeting for their Nantucket summers for nearly two decades. Several of them are turned toward us now, watching the exchange like they're about to break out the popcorn.

The darkness and distraction of fireworks can't come soon enough.

Ethan keeps his eyes on Perry when he answers. "For one, she didn't say yes."

"I'd love to go out on a date with you," I quip in Perry's direction.

Cooper erupts into laughter, Ethan sneers, and Perry grins like he was just handed a trophy for having the biggest dick. Maybe I shouldn't have agreed to a date, it was probably a foolish thing to do, but it was worth it. The look on Ethan's face isn't one of disgust or annoyance, and it isn't even one of protectiveness--it's envy.

Maybe he's protective because he wants me.

But maybe that's just what I want to believe. Either way, his dark expression is quickly replaced by indifference.

"Fine," Ethan says to his friend. "If you want to slum it, be my guest."

My mouth pops open, stomach dropping. "Excuse me?"

"Not cool," Perry glares.

I'm so embarrassed I could sink into the grass and die. *Just bury me right here, please*. Right when I think Ethan might not be a total asshole, he has to say something like that.

I don't have to sit here.

Who says I have to deal with this?

I shift my weight to stand up, but Cooper pulls me back down. "Don't listen to my evil twin."

"Yeah, if anyone's slumming it, it's you. You're way out of my league," Perry adds, squeezing my knee again and smiling wide, dimples popping again.

I shake them off. "I'm fine." I point toward the park bathroom farther up the beach. "I just need to go to the restroom and I'll be right back."

I hurry away before anyone can stop me, before my anger has a chance to turn into tears and the humiliation swallows me whole. This beach only has one public restroom that's not a honey bucket and even though the line is about a mile long, I have no problem killing time by standing in it. I don't want to go back down there just yet. When I finally make it to my stall, I stay inside longer than I should.

I just need to get my bearings and I'll be fine. Slowly, I count backwards from ten and make myself breathe.

Women are talking all around me, many of the younger ones checking hair and makeup in the mirrors. Someone says Ethan King's name and my hackles rise.

"Personally, I don't see it," she says. I recognize her voice as the girl Ethan was flirting with earlier. I never got her name.

"Are you kidding me? It's obvious," another girl replies.

"No," the first one snaps. "Ethan isn't interested in a new girlfriend, especially not someone of low status. You heard him. He told Perry he was slumming it with her."

The second girl chuckles. "He was teasing *Perry*, not the girl, and you know it. They're always talking like that to each other."

They are? I freeze, wondering if this could be true.

"Whatever. The fact remains that ever since things with Sybil ended so catastrophically, he's not wanted to date anyone."

"Poor Ethan."

I roll my eyes and wait for them to leave, then exit the stall, trying to unpack everything they just said. Ethan is heartbroken over a woman named Sybil and now he doesn't want a girlfriend? It sounds like maybe she left him, but I'm not sure.

There's a story there. And that's all fine, but what does that have to do with me? Because it was my name on their gossiping tongues.

As I wash my hands and make my way back to the group, I contemplate finding my own spot to watch the fireworks alone. That should be my preference, and I tell myself it is, but deep down I know it's a lie. I want to watch the show with the guys, God help me. The King twins have a magnetic pull on me. I can't seem to resist either of them. So instead of finding a spot for a single person, I wind my way through the crowd and allow myself to be once again wedged between the two most attractive boys I've ever laid eyes on.

"She's back," Perry announces sweetly. He just might be the third most attractive boy I've ever seen and I really don't know how to handle all the attention. The guys back home never looked like models nor did they *look at me*.

Not like this. Not like they want me.

A minute later the show starts and I can finally relax. The bright dazzling bursts of fireworks shake all my thoughts away as the crowd "oohs" and "ahh" over the show. The city is shooting them from a barge out in the ocean, but we're close enough where we're sitting that we're practically right underneath them. After a few minutes of craning our necks, everyone lays back, limbs tangling together in a heap. I imagine this friend group has been in this exact position together for years now. I'm the new one, the one who doesn't fit into the puzzle, but sitting up would make that even more obvious, so I lay back too.

"I got you," Cooper hums, tucking me into the crook of his arm so I can lay my head on his shoulder. Electricity buzzes through me at the touch. I shouldn't read into it. Even if he is trying to make a pass at me, I'm not interested in hooking up with a guy who's got a different girl in his bed every night.

Besides, I'm still annoyed with him for hooking up with someone in my bed. But he knows that he messed up, which is exactly why he's doing what he's doing tonight. I'm letting him because I want a friend.

I settle in and relax my breathing. My heart begins to slow to a normal pace. The fireworks are loud and all-consuming, so it's easy to get lost in them again.

My left hand is to my side and my right is tucked up between myself and Cooper, so when someone grabs my left hand, I know for a fact it isn't him. My body goes still and I peek at Ethan. He's not even watching fireworks, nor is he looking back at me––the man is making out with the girl on his other side.

But his hand? His hand is holding mine.

Twelve

He must be mistaken, must think it's the other girl's hand that he's holding. Not mine. I try to pull away and he tightens his grip. What the hell? I try to yank it away this time, and he lifts his face from his partner. She's laying underneath him now, the fireworks long forgotten. I widen my eyes when he meets my gaze. His are lit up by the fireworks, filled with lust and malice and challenge. I pull my hand away again but he doesn't let me go. Instead, he threads his fingers with mine, squeezes, and goes right back to kissing his date.

We're holding hands while he makes out with someone else? Who does that? His thumb starts moving up and down my fingers, as if to acknowledge that this is all on purpose, and my insides explode with their own version of fireworks.

Cooper doesn't notice. Perry doesn't either. The woman on her back certainly doesn't. But Ethan's hand in mine is all I can feel. We're all lying in a heap, watching the show, and I try to do the same, try to take it in and enjoy it, try to get lost in the fireworks again, but I can't.

I can't. I can't. I can't.

My body is aflame, and Ethan is my arsonist.

Is this because Cooper is holding me and he has to compete? Maybe it's a twisted game to keep me under his spell. I don't understand anything about Ethan except for the way he makes me feel. And even when the show ends with a brilliant finale, when everyone cheers and Ethan finally releases my hand, I'm still burning. The man has struck a match to a pool of gasoline. He's started something that I can't put out no matter how hard I try. It doesn't matter that Cooper is holding me, or that Perry asked me out. None of that is relevant anymore because there's no denying the truth. I want Ethan.

The next week flies by without incident. After the fireworks all seems forgotten. The hand-holding with Ethan while he made out with another girl isn't acknowledged. Perry doesn't follow up about our date, and it's like I never cuddled with Cooper. The entire night feels like it was a dream. In fact, any possibility of friendship with the brothers also seems to have disappeared. They're back to ignoring me and I have a sinking suspicion as to why.

Because Malory and Conrad King left the day after the holiday.

Were the boys only being nice to me because Conrad King told them they had to? I thought they were extending an olive branch, but I no longer think that's what it was at all. It was a performative act for their father. For whatever reason, Conrad King wants me here and wants me to be something with Ethan. That's not going to happen, and now that Conrad is gone, I'm back to being invisible.

But that's fine. Really, it is. I don't need them. They don't need me. I don't belong in their world, and they don't belong in mine. Sometimes that's just the way it is, and I accepted that long ago. I know better than to get my hopes up or to assume the best in people. And it's not that I always assume the worst, but people make it easy. They're flawed and they make mistakes and as much as I want to belong to them, sometimes I wonder if it's worth it.

I'm finishing up a long day of cleaning and trying to decide if I want to go anywhere tonight. I haven't done much besides working and reading for the last week and I'm itching for a little excitement. The rich kids are a bust, but maybe I don't have to be a loner just because I don't fit in with them. I could try to make friends with other people on the island. I still have a month left, am I really going to leave with no new connections?

"What are you doing tonight?" Ethan's voice startles me from my thoughts and I turn to find him standing in the doorway of the cleaning closet. My eyes travel to his bare chest and the low-slung swim shorts hugging his hips. He's got perfect abs that taper down into a V and I can't help but look even though I force a step back.

"What do you want?" I croak out.

"Get your bathing suit on. I'm going to teach you how to swim."

I stare at him, speechless.

"Unless you'd rather go swimming in the nude again. I wouldn't complain. I'd even join you, but you have to promise to keep your hands to yourself." He pins me with a smirk.

My mouth pops open but I still don't know what to say.

"Not that I would call what you did a few weeks ago swimming, which is exactly why I'm going to teach you."

"Why?" I finally mutter.

He leans in closer, towering over me. Sometimes I forget how tall he is and then he does this. "Maybe I don't want an accidental drowning weighing on me. Maybe I can't stop thinking about you out there being tossed about the waves like you were. Maybe I just like to teach people how to swim. I don't care, take your pick."

"Oh--okay."

"I'll meet you at the pool in ten minutes."

He saunters away and I decide not to fight him on this despite the nervous anticipation. I can't help but wonder if this means what I want it to mean. Is he offering me swimming lessons or is he offering something else? Because I already know I want something else with him, but I also know I shouldn't get ahead of myself. It's more than likely that he'll disappoint me again.

Still, I haven't been able to stop thinking of how it felt to have his hand holding mine. He made a move but doing it while kissing another woman was confusing. It was an invitation to a twisted game. But I can't help it, I'm intrigued, and I want to play.

Which is exactly why I put on my tiny black bikini instead of my more sensible purple one-piece. I haven't worn it yet and I hope it makes him squirm.

I slip out of the back door and find Ethan waiting for me. He's already in the water.

"Are we doing this or what?" Cooper calls out, appearing from the side of the house and jogging over to the pool. He's also got his swimsuit on and also looks just as amazing as his brother, but I can't say I'm happy to see him because his presence answers my question.

This is *just* a swimming lesson.

Not a game.

Not more.

Cooper winks as he approaches, his dark gaze lingering on my breasts for a moment too long. "Damn, I knew you were hot, but you should wear that more often."

I roll my eyes.

"No, I mean it." He shakes his hair from his eyes, his teeth flashing like a predator. "If I paid you extra, would you clean in that thing?"

"Shut up!" I laugh and he takes my hand.

"Come on, let's turn you into a mermaid."

Swimming looks easy but it's not. The second I put my face in the water, panic sweeps through me and I come up sputtering. "I don't need to learn how to swim," I insist between coughs. "I'll just avoid deep water."

"For the rest of your life?" Ethan deadpans. "No. Try again."

"No? You're not the boss of me. If I don't want to do this, I don't have to."

The three of us are standing in the shallow end of the pool and I feel as if they're ganging up on me here. They look so determined that I do this and do it right. And for what? I don't have to go near deep water again and I'll be fine.

"Do you want to drown?" Cooper questions. "Because what if you can't avoid deep water your whole life? You didn't plan to get swept out to sea, but it happened."

Oh, well, there is that.

I groan and try again, repeating their instructions in my mind. *Blow out of your nose, but only do it gently so you don't empty your lungs too fast. Turn your head from side to side to catch a gulp of air as you stroke your arms and kick your legs to move forward.* Should be easy. But the water is quick to fill my nostrils and I'm not fast enough with my arms and my legs are already burning. This is a pool, I'm in the shallow end, and I'm terrible. I'd be hopeless in an actual ocean.

I come up with a groan.

"Go deeper," Ethan commands. "I'm right here with you."

I could memorize those words. Dear God. He's way too hot for me.

Taking another breath, I try again. This time, I make my way to the edge of the deep end and hold on to the tiled edge for dear life. "Really, it's fine. I just won't go in the ocean ever again. Once was enough."

But even as I say it, my heart gives a little pang.

"That was your first time?" Cooper swims up to us. They're on either side of me now and I'm reminded of fireworks. Heat floods my center.

"There's a first for everything." I shrug. "And a last."

"That wasn't your last time," Ethan states.

Whatever. He doesn't know me. I'm fine not going in the ocean again. "Most people on this planet will never see the ocean. I got to swim in it once and that's fine for me. It nearly killed me, so I'm okay with a one-time experience."

"She's okay with the one time," Cooper repeats to his brother. Then he looks at me, his eyes lingering on my lips for a beat too long. I let out a little breath and he shakes his head. "In that case, I'm going to head inside."

He lifts himself from the pool and I can't help but admire the way his muscles flex with the movement. The slick water drips down his tanned skin as he goes for his towel. He's a beautiful man and it's no surprise he has so many women willing to drop their panties for him without a relationship.

This is getting . . . confusing.

"Stop it," Ethan growls, shaking me from my ogling.

I turn on him and narrow my eyes in challenge. "Stop what?"

With only the two of us in here now, the air feels electrified, as if a storm were coming. But there's no storm, only blue skies. Blue skies and blue eyes.

"Stop flirting with Cooper. He won't be able to say no to you."

"Excuse you? I'm not flirting with him on purpose. He's just a big flirt with everyone. You know he acts like this with every girl."

"Are you telling me you wouldn't fuck him if he offered?"

My cheeks flush, images of Cooper's body flashing through my mind. "No. That's not why I'm here."

But am I telling the truth?

Doesn't matter. I'm not here for Cooper and I'm not here for Ethan either. But then the image of Ethan's body rocking into mine pops into my brain and I nearly gasp. I could probably say no to Cooper, but I couldn't say no to Ethan. If he tried to sleep with me, it would be like running into that ocean all over again. Wild and dangerous and tempting. I would do it but I might not survive it.

"Don't fuck any of our friends either, especially not Perry," Ethan continues.

I laugh at that one. "Are you kidding me? I had one conversation with Perry and you think I'm going to spread my legs?"

"Some girls do."

"Women are welcome to do what they want, but guess what? I'm not interested in fucking anyone. And I don't plan on fucking Perry, let alone going on that date."

That date that he never followed up on anyway. It's fine though, I don't need to get mixed up in all that.

Ethan swims closer, pressing me against the side of the pool. His body is caging me in and I love the way his skin feels against mine.

"Do you like sex?" he questions. I lose my grip on the pool's edge. I start to sink and grab onto the first thing I can get a hold of. His arms.

His eyes flash and biceps flex under my fingers. He moves in even closer. We're pressed together now, neither of us speaking. Nobody moves. And that's when I feel it––his erection is hard against my stomach. Something primal comes over me. He's almost pressed right where I want him to be, only two strips of fabric separating us.

I want to cry out with need. I want to spread my legs even more. I want to move against him, to let him in. My breath comes in heavy. Our mouths are inches apart. It wouldn't take much. One little movement and I could taste him. From the intoxicating feel of his hardness on my sex, I think he'd let me. He runs his nose along my cheek, his breath hot on my skin, and I nearly combust.

"Answer the question, Arden," he demands in a gravelly voice.

Cooper already knows I'm a virgin, so I just assumed that the brothers talk enough that Ethan would know it now too. Apparently not.

"Who doesn't like sex?" I breathe. I'm very aware that I'm trying to evade his question.

"Plenty of people don't like sex but that's not what I asked you. I want to know if *you* like sex . . . because if you don't, it's probably because you haven't done it with the right person."

His hand is on me then. One holding us up on the tile and the other trails down my side and scoops me up by the ass. It's only natural that I wrap my legs around his middle, that I press myself against his erection, that we both groan. *Oh lord, is this really happening?* I don't feel like myself, I feel like someone else entirely.

"I wouldn't know," I swallow hard and answer his question honestly. "I've never had sex."

He freezes, eyes studying me as they turn from liquid heat to pure ice. And then he carefully unhooks my legs and releases me.

"I apologize. Sometimes I forget how young you are."

"I'm not that—"

"Let's get back to the swimming lesson."

Thirteen

What the hell? I want to demand that he explain what just happened between us. I also want to demand he get back here and let me wrap my legs around him again. To touch me again. Ignite me again. But he does none of those things. Instead he looks me in the eye when he delivers the blow. "I'm not the guy you're looking for, and neither is Cooper."

"Okay…"

"You're not having sex this summer, Arden."

"I never said—"

"I know, but I just have to make myself clear."

"Umm—"

"There will be plenty of time for that when you get to college. Find someone worthy of your body."

"And that's not you?" It comes out incredulous.

"No," he bites out. And while I get what he's saying, that he's trying to be a good guy or some shit like that, it still sucks. Doesn't matter that I'm used to being rejected. The wound opens fresh every single time.

For days I can't get the interaction with Ethan out of my head . . . or off my body. It's like his hands have imprinted on my skin. I'm no longer in a pool but I'm still treading water, lost in that moment when he was going to kiss me. I'm sure he wanted me as much as I wanted him. But that was three days ago and he hasn't said a word to me since. He hasn't even looked in my direction. It's like I no longer exist.

I'm lost and confused and feeling more than a little stupid. And I'm also angry. Angry because why did he have to be like that? Why even put me in that position?

When I told Cooper I was a virgin he didn't think it was a bad thing, not even flinching. But Ethan? Ethan physically removed me from his body and then from his presence. I'm not sure which hurts worse.

It doesn't matter. I have work to do and I don't need to be thinking about this. He's not good for me. He's right that I'm young. I'm only eighteen and have so much life still ahead of me. College, and everything that comes with it. Ethan has already finished graduate school and is ready to move into a totally different stage of life—a career he was groomed for since infancy. A billionaire father to make proud.

So I do what I've been trying to talk myself into since I almost drowned. I finish my work and head down to the beach by myself. I'm not stupid enough to get in the water again, but I haven't been back since I nearly lost my life and I need to face that beach again.

It's a new day. I'm a different person. It's going to be fine.

I take the steps slowly, my beach bag slung over my shoulder and stuffed with a blanket to lay on and a fresh, albeit gently used, book from my collection. I've been reading so much this summer that I'm nearly through them all and have plans to visit the closest bookstore on my next day off. I would go to the library but I'm not sure how that works for non-residents, and I don't need yet another reminder that I don't fit in here.

Unlike last time, the beach isn't deserted this evening, but it's not crowded either. Only a handful of homes have access to this stretch of paradise. That's the perk of being a one-percenter. Or in my case, working for them. They can take something like a public beach and make it hard to access for everyone else, skirting the laws and essentially making it private.

I make myself comfortable and get to reading. The sun will set soon so I can't actually be out here too long, but it's nice to enjoy the crashing of the surf and the salty breeze sweeping over my body. After a little while, everyone clears out until the only other people down here are a young couple. They're playing in the water together, laughing and kissing as the guy throws the girl into the waves and she comes up squealing, then diving for him in turn. They remind me of Noah and Allie from the movie *The Notebook* and the romantic in me hopes they make it. I imagine that one day they'll be holding onto each other in a nursing home, reminiscing about a life well-lived and crying over their love.

I want that kind of love someday. Maybe it's just a story glorified by Hollywood but I believe that kind of love is possible. It might even be possible for a girl like me.

I hear someone coming up behind me and turn to find Cooper. "There you go with that voyeurism thing again," he remarks, dropping onto the blanket beside me and nodding toward the cute couple.

I roll my eyes playfully and he laughs. When I first met him I got the impression that he wasn't the type to laugh a lot, but I was wrong. He laughs more than anyone else I've met this summer. It's refreshing and completely different from his broody brother. Ethan seems to only laugh in that sarcastic scoffing way. Ethan rarely gives anyone a real smile, but when he does, it's like the sun coming after weeks of rain.

I watch the couple for a minute, noticing the way they seem to be in sync with their movements and oblivious to me and Coop watching them. It sends a pang of longing right through my heart. I shouldn't want that, but I do. I can't help it. "They're cute," I say simply and then I frown. "How come they have no trouble in the water but I was carried out to sea?"

"Because you went out at high tide," he explains. "The waves are a lot bigger at certain times of day. You're lucky Ethan was even out there. We don't normally surf this spot when the tide's that high. It's dangerous. Then again, Ethan hasn't cared about putting himself in danger ever since . . ."

His voice trails off.

"Ever since Sybil?" I try.

His eyes harden and he tuts. "You know about her?"

I shrug. "All I know is that she was his girlfriend and they broke up."

He shakes his head slowly, hair hanging around his chin as he stares off into the distance. It's like he is seeing memories play out right in front of him. He looks so sad. "It was more than that. We all grew up together and they dated all through college. They were even engaged for a few months."

"And what happened?" I'm almost scared to ask.

"That's not my story to tell."

"You've said that before."

He nods. "And it's still the truth. This is a conversation for Ethan, not me."

I suck in a breath and hold it. I guess that's fair, it's not my business, but that doesn't mean that I still want to know what happened. Not only because I find Ethan fascinating, but also because those girls were talking about it in the bathroom and my name was thrown into the conversation. They acted as if I had something to do with it, but that literally makes no sense. I didn't even know the Kings until this summer.

I need answers and I can't wait for Ethan.

"Maybe you can tell me why your dad thinks he brought me here to hook up with your brother?" I try, braver than I've been in a while. There's a fine line between courage and recklessness and I've been toeing that line ever since I set foot on Nantucket.

Cooper turns on me. "How do you know about that?"

No way in hell I'm telling him about snooping on his phone. "Nope, it's my turn to ask a question, and considering this is about me, I deserve the truth."

He leans back onto his elbows, gazing hard at the water for ages before finally answering me. "Let's just say Conrad is a big part of the reason Sybil and Ethan didn't work out."

"And what does that have to do with me?"

He swallows hard and my gaze traces the way his Adam's apple bobs against the column of tanned skin. He really is too attractive for his own good. "As misguided as it is, he brought you here as a consolation prize for Ethan. You're supposed to get her out of his system."

My insides go hollow. "Oh my God." If my question was the seed of this conversation, my anger is the resulting bloom. But this isn't pretty or soft. This is thorny and dangerous.

"Don't worry, Ethan doesn't think the same way Conrad King does." Cooper's tone turns bitter. "He doesn't think of you like that, even though . . ." Another silence. "Anyway, he's not going to use you." He looks at me sidelong. "And I won't either."

I grimace. "Your family is fucked up."

"You're telling me."

I always thought it was better to have a messed up family than no family at all, but they're starting to make me rethink that position. But at least in the King family, they have guarantees that most people don't. Need a job? Money? Medical care? How about a girl to live in your house, clean up after you, and maybe even spread her legs? Conrad King has you covered.

"Come on," Cooper says. "Enough of this. Let's go swimming."

He jumps up and grabs my hand, but I don't move. "Are you crazy? I'm not going back in there."

"You'll be fine."

"One lousy swim lesson does not make any of this fine. I'll drown."

"I won't let that happen."

I roll my eyes. "How can you be so sure?"

"The tide is low and the waves are small. Haven't you ever wanted to swim in the ocean at sunset?"

He has a point. The sky has turned to bright pink and is reflecting off the water in a dazzling light. It's gorgeous and inviting. The couple has moved much further down the beach and nobody else is nearby. It would be an experience I haven't had before.

"I don't have my swimsuit."

"Are you wearing underwear?"

"Why do I think you've asked that question to multiple girls?" I tease. I'm wearing a pair of boy short undies and a sports bra. The bottom has more coverage than my bikini bottoms, but the top has no padding and will definitely show my nipples once they get cold. But hey, he's seen it all before.

"Where's your sense of adventure, Arden?"

I let out a huff and stand, shimmying out of my top layer of clothes and laughing when he whistles. Then he takes my hand, and together we run toward where the painted sky spills into the sea.

I freeze up when the water hits my middle and I don't want to take another step. I imagine that if I do, the sand will drop away and I'll be pulled under. Flashes of nearly drowning assault my mind. Cooper is still holding my hand and I swear if he tries to make me get in any deeper, I'm going to knee him in the balls.

"Relax." He inches closer. "Listen to the waves. How do they sound?"

I swallow hard and take them in. *Crash. Swish. Crash. Swish.*

"Terrifying."

"Most people find them relaxing."

"I'm not most people."

"Yeah, I've realized that." His words catch me off guard and I turn to him, searching his face, hoping for a compliment but expecting an insult.

What I find sends my stomach swooping. It was definitely a compliment--the man is looking at me as if I'm the only sunset out here tonight. I don't know if anyone's looked at me like that before.

"Do you trust me?" he asks.

"Of course not." I don't trust anyone.

He grins, squeezing my hand. "I won't let you drown. How about I stay a step ahead of you? Make sure it's safe?"

"That seems like an okay plan."

He steps in front of me so he's walking backwards while he's facing me. He takes my other hand so that he's got both of mine in his now. But he's got more than my hands in his. He's got my life and maybe even a piece of my heart. Does he realize that? Does he feel what I'm feeling right now? Confused and excited and hopeful and terrified. *And did I say confused?*

Tugging, he leads me into deeper water.

"The waves are worse when you're close to shore like that. We'll go out a little bit and they'll be better."

"If you say so." The water is colder tonight than it looks and my skin is already covered in gooseflesh. I make the mistake of looking down at myself, finding nipples that are hard pebbles from the cold. "Oh geez," I murmur and Cooper smirks.

"Go faster, Coop." I demand and he takes a large step back, pulling me with him.

"Not that fast," I squeal.

"Look at me. Right here."

I meet his eyes and focus on them instead. The deep brown is hooded by long lashes. Long strands of his tawny hair hang across his forehead and he tosses his head back. When he does, I get an even better look at his eyes. My insides turn molten--because I can read exactly what's behind those irises.

Lust.

He likes what he's looking at--he wants me.

It makes me entirely uneasy and wholly excited at the same time, a torrent of battling emotions.

This is so confusing. There's no denying it now. I'm attracted to both of these brothers. I want them both. What is wrong with me?

"Don't go too deep," I whisper as we take another step out, this time the waves are high enough to cover my breasts.

"I'll go as deep as you'll let me," he rasps, and my cheeks flush at the sexual innuendo. But it's not a joke, he means every word. What am I supposed to do? Forget supposed to . . . what do I *want* to do?

"This is good." My voice is husky. The water is at my neck-line and his pecs. The waves are still frightening, but he's right that they aren't as bad as during high tide. And I have him to anchor me.

"What's going on in that pretty head of yours?" he asks.

"Just that I thought I understood this place but I don't." *Thought I understood you but I don't.*

His eyes search mine. "And what do you want to know?"

"Everything. I want to know everything."

"Everything?" His tone darkens and he wraps me in his arms, our bodies pressing together.

"Yes, everything," I whisper boldly, yearning to be that girl who throws caution to the wind, like Allie was in *The Notebook*.

"To do that you're going to have to let go for once."

"I don't know how."

"You do, but don't worry, I'll show you how. Are you willing to let go with me, Arden?"

No hesitation, I nod once. That's all it takes for our lips to crash together.

FOURTEEN

Kissing Cooper King in the ocean is by far the hottest thing I've ever done. He knows what he's doing, his mouth moving against mine in an expert give-and-take. I wrap my legs around his torso and his fingers dig into my ass. My mind drifts away with the surf, passion taking over as we explore each other's mouths. My hands are wrapped around his head, fingers threading into his hair, digging into his scalp the same way he's digging his own fingers into me.

I am a different person, a new Arden. I like her. And I really like him.

He pulls back for a second, searching my eyes. "This is okay?"

I can't believe I'm doing this with Cooper of all people, but I wiggle in closer. "More than okay." And then I'm kissing him again.

There are wet kisses, and then there are ocean-wet kisses. The water splashes up all around our bodies, covering us time and again with spray as we kiss and kiss and kiss.

But it's not enough for me, and I'm sure it's not enough for him either.

I break away. "Promise you're not using me?"

"Promise." His voice cracks earnestly.

Somehow, I believe him, and maybe that's naive but I don't care.

"Take me to your bedroom?" I mean it as a question, but it comes out as a plea. I'm begging for this, but I think he is too.

His eyes darken and he kisses me again, murmuring his approval against my mouth. Then we break apart and run back to the beach. I don't think I've ever packed my bag as quickly as I do now.

He stops me at the bottom of the stairs to kiss me again and I almost ask him to strip me right here but we're in public, and while there's nobody close by, I know they're out there. I'm ready to have sex, but in a bed and in private.

We hurry up the brutal stairs and then on into the house. I'm nervous, the anticipation icing my veins, but I'm not going to stop this. I thought I wanted to love someone before I had sex with them, but I've revoked that opinion. It's not that I want to get it over with, it's that my body is clearly ready and I don't want to make a big fuss out of it anymore.

Ethan wouldn't have turned me down if I wasn't a virgin. Things would've gone further in that pool. And I'm suddenly certain that things are going to be the same when I get to college, more rejection from guys who don't want a virgin. It's ridiculous and unfair but I don't claim to understand the inner workings of the male psyche.

I may not trust Cooper to save me from the ocean, but I trust him with my body. He knows what to do. He'll make sure it feels good, that I enjoy every minute of what we're about to do.

We make it all the way upstairs without anyone seeing us.

Camilla is gone for the night and I haven't seen Ethan much since he started avoiding me. Cooper swings open his door and we stumble inside the room. He pushes me back up against the door to close it and we're kissing like we're a wildfire and need each other to keep burning.

His hands are everywhere and so are mine, what little clothing we're wearing quickly stripped away. He's already seen me naked but this is so much different. That was an accident. This is a choice.

I'm down to just my panties when he takes my breast into his warm mouth, his tongue circling my nipple. Pleasure zings and I gasp on the sensation.

"You like that?" He pulls away and palms his erection. I let myself look, taking in his impressive length. I'm a virgin but I'm not totally clueless when it comes to this stuff. Still, I've never seen a naked man, not like this. It makes me nervous again.

But I nod anyway. Because I do like it. I like all of it.

He takes my hand, wrapping it around his cock. Our bodies are still freezing from the water but he's all heat down there. Thick and warm and ready. So I kiss him again, stroking him as we make out. He groans in my mouth and bucks against my hand. His tip is wet and I'm practically soaking.

I feel powerful—I never knew it would make me feel this powerful.

We fall into the bed and he retrieves protection from his nightstand. And then he kisses his way down my body, taking special care with each breast as I arch into him. He's moving lower, open mouth on my stomach, fingers hooking around my panties. Butterflies explode through my stomach. We're really doing this.

The door flies open.

"What the fuck!" Ethan fumes. Yells. Stomps toward us.

I cover my breasts and gasp as Ethan rips his brother off me.

"What are you doing?" he growls into Cooper's flushed face.

"What does it look like?" Cooper is naked and aroused, and right now he sounds as equally angry as his brother. But there's something else underlining his tone. Something like regret.

I freeze.

"You agreed not to fuck her!" Ethan roars and pushes his brother back against the wall. He doesn't even seem bothered that Cooper is bare-ass naked, that I'm only in my underwear.

Actually, scratch that––he's beyond *bothered*. He's livid.

"Get out, Ethan!" I yell and the man turns on me with bitterness in his eyes.

"This conversation is none of your business. *You* get out."

I sit up, anger springing. "Are you kidding me? How is this not my business? It's none of *your* business."

But Ethan doesn't care. He's the ultimate cock-block. He storms over to Cooper's dresser, practically breaking the drawer that he pulls open, and grabs a random pair of gym shorts. He tosses them at Cooper so hard they're like a whip when they hit him. "Get dressed," he demands.

This is the part where Cooper will tell his brother off.

He's going to kick him out.

He'll lock the door.

Ethan can stand outside that damn door and listen to us for all I care. I'll be sure to scream Cooper's name extra loud. But Cooper doesn't do any of those things. Slipping into the shorts, he simply walks out the door. Ethan's the one he cares about here, not me.

I'm dumbstruck.

Disbelieving.

No fucking way.

Ethan moves to follow, but stops and turns to me on his way out. His index finger is pointed and his eyes are two razored slits. "I told you not to mess with my brother or our friends."

"It's not up to you."

I'm shocked right now. How is this even happening? Did Cooper really walk out that door?

"When it comes to this," he circles his finger at me, as if I'm the "this" he's referring to. "It *is* up to me."

"No, it's not--"

His voice goes softer, his hand fisting at his forehead. "Yes, Arden, please trust me on this. I'm trying to protect you."

My mind swirls. "No, you're trying to control me."

"In this case, they're the same thing."

Except he won't explain it to me. Nobody will. "Fuck you," I growl.

He shakes his head regretfully. "I warned you, Arden. You won't get a second chance." And then he slams the door and I'm left sitting on the bed, my heart shattered and my pride decimated. I'm ashamed. I'm ashamed and I shouldn't be but I can't help it. It eats away at me like a piranha. The blood is already in the water. I'm already a goner.

I slip back into my wet clothing and hurry out the door. I can hear Cooper and Ethan talking in Ethan's room just across the hallway. Their voices are low but heated. I don't stick around to attempt to listen in. I've been thoroughly humiliated and I'm done. It's not only that Ethan showed up and demanded we not have sex, it's that Cooper went along with it. He just left me here. He didn't tell me to wait for him, he didn't even mutter an apology.

How does Ethan have so much power here?

Tears gather in my eyes as I race downstairs, strip off my clothes, and jump into the shower. The hot water feels nice, but it isn't enough to wash away my frustration.

Frustration with the King Brothers . . . and sexual frustration. I've never been big on self-pleasure but right now I can't help it. I slide my hand down and begin to move my fingers. A jolt of pleasure rockets through my body, awakening me. I close my eyes and imagine I'm with Cooper, that Ethan never interrupted us. He's worshiping my body. He's helping me feel good. I continue this way until I reach my climax, gasping into the water.

Then I drop my hand, defeated. Because while it felt nice, it wasn't what I wanted. Sure, I know my first time will hurt and I don't expect it to be perfect, but I'm also certain that Cooper would've made sure I had an amazing orgasm, something better than what I can do to myself.

But there's nothing I can do about it now, so I dry myself off, slip into my pajamas, and head upstairs for a quick dinner. I would skip it, but I can't get rid of the gnawing hunger without food. I'm quiet as I heat up the chicken marsala Camilla left for me. When I eat it, I can hardly taste it, my mind busy wondering what's going on with the twins.

Ethan thinks he owns me.

It doesn't matter what I have to say about it or even what Coop has to say, Ethan has sided with his father on this one. I am here for him and not for Cooper and that's just the way it is. But it still doesn't make sense.

And it's complete bullshit.

Ethan rejected me. Cooper wanted me.

The end.

With a little too much vigor, I clean up my plate and march upstairs. I'm going to chew them out, to demand an apology.

But they're not here.

Their bedrooms are empty. The whole house is quiet. And Ethan's Range Rover? It doesn't take long to figure out it's missing from the garage.

They left together.

Ethan wasn't the only one who rejected me. And as stupid as it makes me feel, I can't help but cry myself to sleep. Of course, I sleep like shit. And of course, the next morning when Cooper brings a random girl down for morning coffee, I feel even worse.

Cooper doesn't look at me.

Oh, but Ethan does. His eyes are constantly on me. Hot. Punishing.

And sometimes regretful.

Whatever I do, I won't let them see me cry, so I make myself appear calm and collected and completely unaffected. I thank Camilla for breakfast, clean up after myself, and get back to work.

It doesn't matter. The King brothers have shown their true colors. Cooper is a fuckboy and Ethan is a sadistic control freak and I don't need them. They're nothing to me. Absolutely *nothing.*

But if they're nothing, then why am I so hurt?

Fifteen

"Are you guys really icing me out?" I find them three days later walking back up from the beach, surfboards under their arms and water beaded on their bodies. It's ridiculous to be jealous of water but I am. I kind of hate myself for it but I hate Cooper even more, because he doesn't even look at me.

I stomp right up to him. "Are you serious? More silent treatment?"

He continues walking, brushing past me like I didn't just ask him a question. White-hot anger prickles over my entire body.

"It's one thing to humiliate me, to almost fuck me and then bring a different girl home instead. I can deal with all that, it's whatever. But for you to go on and ignore me as if nothing happened and I'm not even here? As if you didn't have me naked in your bed? That's fucking wrong, Cooper. I thought we were friends."

He flinches, letting out a low confession. "I promised I wasn't using you but that was a lie. So I ended it. Just let it go,

Arden." He says this as he's walking away from me. The man doesn't even slow. I watch him go, so seemingly unbothered. It's like I'm not even here, like I don't matter at all.

He was using me?

Well, fuck him.

Ethan, unfortunately, hasn't left. He's standing in the path, scrutinizing me. This is his fault too. He's got some kind of hold over his brother and has decided to use it to keep Cooper away from me. Cooper may be the spineless idiot going along with it, but Ethan's the mastermind.

"Why?" I ask simply.

His bicep flexes as he tightens his grip on his board. "You know why."

I've been holding my arms crossed over my chest in protection, but I drop them, completely at a loss. I don't understand any of this and I just want answers, and to feel better, to be included, to be liked. Maybe one day I could be loved.

But I'll take answers instead.

Answers that let me put things into neat little rows in an attempt to get some meaning out of everything that's been happening.

"No. I really don't know why because you won't fucking tell me shit." I suppress a cringe at the way I sound. So desperate. So angry. Hurt and needy.

He carefully sets down his board and stalks in so close that I have to crane my neck up. "I told you not to hook up with any of our friends and I specifically told you not to get with Cooper. You did it anyway, so now you have to live with the consequences."

And by that, he means back to invisibility.

I press my hands against his chest, pushing him back, but he just uses that as an opportunity to grab onto my wrists and hold my palms to his pecs. His skin is cold and prickly from the ocean, but it still sends a flood of warmth through me.

"You don't get to have control over this," I challenge. "It's my decision. Mine and his."

Ethan shakes his head. "You don't understand our relationship. How would you? You don't even have a sibling, let alone a twin."

"That's low." Way to twist the knife.

He leans in close, enunciating each word. "He only wants you because you're mine."

Outraged, I try to pull back, but he's not letting me. My hands are splayed out and he's breathing hard. I'm breathing harder.

"I'm. Not. Yours."

"But you are," he says simply. "And everybody knows it."

Am I really hearing this? "You don't just get to lay claim to me like that. I'm my own person."

He scoffs. "I didn't claim you. This is bigger than both of us."

"Explain it to me then."

"No."

"But I'm yours?" I dig my fingers into his chest.

His face is like a steel mask. "Correct."

"And you don't actually want me?"

"Also correct."

Something comes over me. Something primal and brimming with feminine rage. I want to test him. I want to bring him to his knees until he begs my forgiveness for the pain he's caused me. If I could make him cry, I would.

And so instead of pulling away, I surprise both of us and lean in close. I press my body against his, my hands still flat-palmed on his chest, my stomach sliding against his swim trunks, my breasts resting under his bare pecs.

"If I'm yours, prove it."

He thinks about it. I know he does. His eyes flick to my lips but he doesn't move. I don't move either. This is a game of chicken that neither one of us is willing to lose.

But his heart--I can feel it beating under my fingertips.

Faster.

Harder.

And it feels like I've won.

"Listen very carefully," I say, wetting my lips. "There are two people standing here, and in order to be yours, I would have to choose to belong to you."

I shimmy against him, feeling him harden beneath me. Normally I would jump back but not today. "I may be young, and I may work for your family, but I'm still a woman with my own opinions and wants and *needs*." My voice goes hoarse on the word "needs" and an erotic image of sex with Ethan flashes through my mind. *Shit.* It's quickly replaced with Cooper. *Good.* Then Ethan again. *Double shit.*

"I haven't chosen you back," I continue. "But I might be persuaded under the right circumstances."

I don't mean it. Really, I just want him to kiss me so I can reject him like he rejected me, to hurt him. He needs to know what I'm capable of, that I'm not some toy to be thrown around in the sandbox, to be discarded.

But he doesn't kiss me.

Instead, he pries my hands away from his body and steps back. "I have no intention of being with you. I don't want you, Arden. You were never the one I wanted. But you are mine regardless, which means that nobody else can have you."

He picks up his board, trudging back toward the house. I stare after him, hating the way he walks, hating how his back muscles move so effortlessly, hating that he magnetizes me to him. I'm shaking. All of me is shaking. My hands. My legs. My heart.

He turns back. "As long as you're here, you are mine. I don't have use for you besides what you were hired to do. So stop trying to make friends, stop trying to lose your pathetic virginity, and stop trying to be somebody you're not."

My mouth pops open. "What do you expect me to say to that?"

"You're the maid, remember? You're not supposed to say anything. You're supposed to clean up our shit and keep your pretty mouth shut."

And then he turns back around and strolls away, all as if he didn't just tear me to shreds.

I don't belong here. I never did. I'm only "his" because his daddy said so. And now he's using it as a way to build a wall between me and everybody else. I should've known better. I should've stayed quiet. Kept my head down. But I played with fire. Of course, I got burned.

Time rolls by and before I know it, it's August. I'm lonely, but I'm used to being lonely. It's a familiar emotion that I know how to handle. I can even find comfort in loneliness sometimes. But people being outright rude to me? Treating me like I'm nothing--or worse than nothing? That's something else entirely.

And that's exactly what has happened with the twins and their friends.

Ethan and Cooper hate me, and Cooper's never-ending parade of women is proof enough of that. Mr. and Mrs. King haven't been here since Independence Day so at least I haven't had to deal with them. And at least I like Camilla. She's the one person that actually treats me with decency and her food is delicious. Camilla is my favorite thing about the job, even if I only get to see her for brief moments throughout the day.

When I arrived at the end of May, I really thought I would love it here. While the island is stunning with a wealthy well-cared-for appeal and gorgeous beaches to spend my evenings, the truth is that I hate Nantucket. I'm counting the days until I can leave.

I want to be the main character in my own life, and on this island, I'm not even a supporting cast member. I'm an extra. I've become the out-of-focus figure blending into the background, easy to replace and easier to forget. I don't expect the whole world to revolve around me, but shouldn't my own world at least center me a little bit?

"Missed a spot," Ethan says, striding past me as I clean his bathroom.

He sure has the main character thing down. Rich. Hot. Confident. Adored. *Douchebag.*

I can't believe I ever thought we could be friends.

"What spot?" I snap.

I'm currently kneeling on the bright white tiles of his bathroom floor, scrubbing them like my life depends on it. Really, I'm timing myself to make my least favorite task go a little faster. If I make a game out of it, I'll forget how hard it is to clean the floors of this monstrous house. There's no carpet to be found, it's all glossy dark wood that I've learned the hard way costs five hundred dollars a square foot, or it's white crisp modern tiles. I don't bother looking for the alleged spot he's saying I missed, because there are many. And no, I haven't missed cleaning them, I simply haven't gotten to them yet.

"Just do your job."

I sit back on my haunches and glare up at him. "It's really

too bad you're such a dick because if you were a nice person, you'd be a force to be reckoned with."

"I'm already a force to be reckoned with," he shoots back.

Sand clings to Ethan's heels and he kicks a clump off. It splatters right where I've been scrubbing a troublesome spot, as if "doing my job" means cleaning up his messes in real-time.

Okay, maybe it does, but still . . . "Do you mind?"

I'm not supposed to challenge them directly but I gave up on that my first week here. Too bad talking back doesn't help. I'm still at my wit's end with Ethan. He's a petulant spoiled man-child who needs to learn manners, and his horny man-child twin isn't any better.

"I do mind," his voice is like gravel. "You're in my bathroom and I need to take a shower."

"Wow, is this how you treat all the women you find in here?" The words come out before I can stop them. Truth is, I haven't seen a single woman sleep over with Ethan all summer.

"Wouldn't you like to know?" he laughs and I want to scream.

This family has more money than God and they act as if they can walk on water, too. It's infuriating, but what can I do? Conrad was right. Paying ten grand for the damaged hardwoods took out a huge chunk of my change. It's not like he's paying me mega bucks here, not when he's providing my room and board. The few thousand I have left will be enough to get me to Boston in time to move into my scholarship-covered dorm, replace my crappy flip phone, and hold me over long enough to get a college job. I had wanted to buy a nice laptop but I'll have to keep saving.

You're almost done, I repeat to myself for what feels like the gazillionth time, *by the end of the month you'll be in Boston.*

At least Cooper has left me alone ever since our failed hook up. But Ethan? Not a chance. He treats me like I'm constantly in his way, as if I want to bother him when I'm pretty sure it's the opposite.

"Listen, Ethan," I try again, gathering all the patience I have left, which is about the size of a grain of salt at this point. "I'll be done here in ten minutes and then the bathroom is all yours."

I gaze up at him, waiting for him to leave like a normal human being. I don't expect an apology, but leaving me to my work would be enough. It's what any decent person would do in our situation. He doesn't respond. Not for a long time. And not for the first time, I want to curse him for being so pleasing to look at, for having the chiseled body of a professional athlete, the troubled blue eyes of a sea-weary sailor, and the heart-shaped mouth of a downright sinner.

The fucker.

"You look good on your knees." He steps closer, his eyes lingering on my mouth for too long. My insides squirm. "But I'm not interested, so leave or don't leave, but I'm taking a shower."

He says this so casually, so cruelly, that I'm stunned, caught up on his insinuation that I'm on my knees to do anything other than clean.

Then true to his word, he begins to peel his swim trunks from his tanned, chiseled body. Right in front of me.

SIXTEEN

My cheeks burn as I quickly avert my eyes and scurry from the bathroom, a glimpse of crisp tan lines on toned muscle seared into my mind. I could tell myself how much I hated what I saw but the truth is I wish I would've seen more of him. It only makes my hatred for the man grow stronger. My one saving grace is that he never looked back at me to witness the hot shame that brandishes my cheeks.

Shame he put there on purpose.

Shame he's put there more than once.

But why should I be ashamed? He's the confusing one, the player of games, the inappropriate asshole. The bully.

The one who hurt me.

His shower blasts on and I want to turn back and demand he clean his own bathroom. I want to tell him he's the biggest jerk I've ever met and that he needs to learn how to respect others, especially women. He's not exempt from human decency just because his family is wealthier than God. People don't choose who they're born to, and he could just as easily be in my position if fate had taken a different turn.

I don't say any of those things, though. A girl doesn't spend her life in foster care and not learn that power dynamics never really change. It's like I said, I've been the background character my entire life. I can handle disappointment.

I don't like it and I don't have to like it.

But that doesn't change it.

It's why I'm determined to rewrite my future as soon as I get to college, but right now, I know when to keep my mouth shut and my head down. I need to get through the rest of the summer. Collect what money I can now that I've sent Conrad the check he required of me.

Then move on to bigger and better things.

Soon...

Soon things will be different.

I'm not going to blow it. I'm going to work hard, study harder, and make something of myself.

Despite the left-out feelings I've had to swallow all summer long, I've resolved not to party or get into any trouble once I get to Boston. Four years of undergrad pursuing a tech degree and I'll never have to be poor or dependent on other people again. I don't mind that it'll be hard, that tech isn't glamorous, or that more people switch out of that major compared to others. The obstacles don't matter because earning that degree will give me more choices than anything else I could reasonably do with four years of a free college education.

I hate blood, so a medical career is out, and I hate public speaking, so law would be a nightmare. With that in mind, I asked my high school guidance counselor what college degree would lead to the highest-paying career. She took one look at my straight A's in math and encouraged a degree in computer technology.

Just thinking about what's to come makes me smile. This

job is almost over and my mind is one hundred percent zeroed in on August 25th, the day I'll be moving into my college dorm.

Two months down and one to go.

I move on to the next dirty floor on my list, which happens to be Cooper's en-suite bathroom. Cooper is probably still at the beach, but even if he's not, he'll ignore me if I interrupt him. He hasn't talked to me in weeks, it's like I've completely disappeared from his radar and no longer exist. The fact that he had my breast in his mouth and his hands pulling off my panties just steps away from this bathroom? Erased.

But when I kneel down to clean his tiles, it's not Cooper I'm angry with anymore. Cooper is weak, doing whatever his brother tells him to do. No, it's Ethan's smug face that I imagine I'm scrubbing into oblivion.

"Arden, could you come in here please?" Mrs. King calls out from the home office and I almost jump at the sound of her voice.

She's been mostly absent this summer but right after I finished with Cooper's bathroom yesterday, she showed up out of the blue, declaring she would be here for the weekend. I've been on my toes ever since, certain she'll find fault in my work.

I set down my cleaning caddy and wipe my hands on my shorts, then stride into the office with a smile on my face. "How can I help you, Mrs. King?" I ask, admiring her understated linen pantsuit.

Her style exudes wealth and is utterly untouchable to someone like me. Her blonde hair is styled in beachy waves and her makeup is done to dewy perfection. I hardly wear makeup, hating the way it feels and looks on my face, but maybe that's because where she shops for makeup and where I shop aren't even in the same zip code.

She's stacking papers on her desk in tidy rows as I stand there fidgeting. Waiting. "Conrad has decided he needs the twins to start work in the Manhattan office as soon as possible. As such, we've decided to end their summer holiday earlier than expected." She acts as if her words don't have massive significance, as if moving from one house to another weeks earlier than scheduled is no big deal.

"Oh, okay." My voice wobbles as my heart rate climbs.

"We're leaving tonight. I'll expect you to clean up after we go and promptly move out by tomorrow at day's end." Her words sound far away. Like this is happening to someone else. Not to me. "The last ferry to Boston is at six and I've already booked you a ticket. It's waiting at will call. Use your security code to lock up behind you."

I'm sinking. Down. Down. Down. Dread floods my body, pulling me under. This can't be happening. I won't have anywhere to go. I blink rapidly, holding back threatening tears. "I'm not supposed to move into my college dorm for another three weeks."

She waves her hand like that's nothing. "You're a bright girl, I'm sure you'll figure it out."

Is she serious? I don't have anyone. I've moved around so often that I stopped trying to form attachments with people. I have no family and no real friends, especially not the kind you can call up out of the blue for a couch to crash on. *Especially not in Boston.* "Can I stay here until August 25th?" I try, hoping I don't sound like I'm begging.

But I'm begging. I'm absolutely begging.

She narrows her eyes shrewdly. They crinkle slightly at the corners, revealing a bit of her age through an otherwise perfectly smooth exterior. "We have been paying you, haven't we?"

I nod once.

But with the repair bill it's not like I've been able to save much. I haven't been irresponsible. I've only bought a few little things all summer--a small silver bracelet with a seashell as a keepsake, toiletries, sunscreen, and a few more books.

All that is to say, I have some money but not enough for a three-week stay in a hotel in Boston.

No. This can't be happening.

The room and board were the main reason I took this job, despite the actual paycheck being low for the amount of hours worked. I bought into the idea of a summer in the sand, but I can see now that was a huge mistake.

"I don't have much money saved up," I try again, my voice growing raspy. "I had to pay for the repairs on the hardwood, remember? It was ten grand." Her face is unreadable, but if I had to guess, I wouldn't count on her being sympathetic to my plight, not when I was the one who damaged the floor in the first place. "There's not a lot left. I need the money for the remaining weeks in my contract or I need to stay here."

She's too quiet.

How could people with staggering wealth be so cheap and so cruel? Because she knows--*she knows*--I'm in trouble now. Maybe his mother is where Ethan gets his mean streak from. Conrad is one thing, but Malory? She's evil if she thinks this is okay behavior.

"But we paid you?" She asks again sharply, as if I didn't answer her question the first time.

"Yes," I admit.

"Well then, fair is fair. There's nothing more to discuss here." She hands me a list of closing instructions and then shoos me from the office.

I fold the list into a square, slipping it into my pocket and beelining to the nearest bathroom. I need to lock myself inside before anyone can witness me dissolving into tears, before the anxiety gets its fangs into me and I'm overcome with helplessness. If Ethan or Cooper see that happen, I'll die. I don't have a lot to float myself for three weeks in Boston, but what little I have will have to be enough. What other choice is there?

Hands catch the door and push me back into the little hallway washroom before I can lock myself inside. Dread knots my stomach. It's Ethan and he's not alone, Cooper slips in after him. This is the first time the three of us have been in such close proximity since Ethan hauled Cooper off my nearly-naked body. Now we're locked in this tiny space and the walls are closing in.

Seventeen

"What do you want?" I demand. My voice cracks and I'm unable to hold back the tears.

Mortified that they're seeing me cry, I stare down at my shoes. I can't feel my legs but my feet are prickling as if ants are crawling in my shoes. It's a new symptom of my panic, or maybe it was always there but I never noticed until now. I wiggle my toes in my socks, trying to squash the ants and force myself to stay calm.

Ethan catches my chin between rough hands and tilts my face up at him. He's so much taller than me that I nearly strain my neck. Cooper leans against the door nonchalantly, like this is a normal Tuesday, like I mean absolutely nothing to him and my ensuing panic attack is a mere inconvenience. How he can turn his feelings on and off so nonchalantly is a mystery to me, a sick and twisted mystery. I can't believe I almost slept with him.

Ethan is close, too close, his eyes two narrowed daggers. "What did Malory say to you?"

I open and close my mouth and frustration paints his gaze.

Cooper sighs languidly. "We haven't got all day, Ardie." My

chest burns at the nickname that he knows I hate. It's a low fucking blow because he hasn't used it in so long. Maybe he didn't get rid of Bree after all. Maybe they meet up to laugh about me and call me Ardie.

"Malory said that you're going back to Manhattan tonight," I croak out. "Why does it matter what she said to me? Go ask her yourself if you have questions."

"What else did she say?" Ethan presses, grip tightening. Not hard enough to bruise but hard enough that I'm stuck here. I try to shove him back but he barely moves an inch from my space. "Think real hard, Arden. Did she say *why* we're leaving early?"

I'm not sure which I hate more, that horrid nickname on Coop's lips, or my real name on Ethan's.

"Get your hands off me," I growl, trying to shove Ethan away but it's no use. He's too strong and my limbs feel weaker by the second.

"Better do as the lady asks." Cooper sounds bored, but he's watching me with surprising interest. It's the first real interest he's shown me since that night in his bedroom. His words must matter to his brother because Ethan releases me.

I press myself against the wall. I want them to leave, but they're clearly not going to let me get past without finishing this bizarre interrogation, and what does it matter? It's not like Mrs. King told me anything private. "She said I had to clean up, lock up, and leave by tomorrow to catch the 6 p.m. ferry for Boston."

"And that's it? She didn't mention anything about our father?" Ethan raises an expectant eyebrow.

"She said he needed you in the office." I shrug.

"And you're to go back to Boston?" He sounds skeptical. Why the fuck does he sound skeptical? It's not like I'm lying.

"Yup. I told her I have nowhere to stay until the 25th but she said I've been paid and I'm smart enough to figure it out."

I don't know what I expect when I confess my predicament to these brothers, but it's not bitter laughter. It rolls out of them like a dark cloud.

"She doesn't know anything," Cooper addressed his brother. Then he gives me a long look, locking eyes with mine. I can't read his expression. I can't even guess. He's completely closed off to me. "Shame. Well, maybe I'll see you in another life . . . I have to pack." Then he opens the door and disappears into the hallway, locking me back in the lion's den with Ethan.

That was the most fucked up goodbye I've ever received.

Now that it's just the two of us, the space feels even smaller than it did before. Impossibly small. How can that be? I suddenly miss Cooper's presence. He was a balm to whatever this festering wound is between me and Ethan. Because as much as I dislike Cooper for how he's treated me this summer, I *hate* Ethan.

"Malory doesn't give a shit about you," Ethan states. "Did you really expect her to care about where you go after this?"

I don't have anything to say to that. He's right. But also, it's called human decency and doesn't Malory have any?

"Besides, we all know you were hired to do more than just clean." His cruel eyes travel up and down my body. "But you failed at that, didn't you?"

Excuse me? He's the one who ripped Cooper's naked body off me. He's also the one who rejected me the few times I thought something might happen between us.

I shouldn't be surprised. It's who Ethan is: cruel.

It's not just his eyes that are cruel. It's his entire personality. The man doesn't just create wounds; he salts them, too.

"I'll have you know, Malory made it explicitly clear that I

wasn't to get involved with either of you, so actually, I didn't fail."

"Nobody gives a fuck what she told you. She has no power here. None."

Wow. Just wow. The way he speaks about his mother is alarming.

Fuming, I curl my hands into tight fists and stand taller. I just need to get through this, get him to leave me alone, and then I can dissolve into panic. But right now? Right now I refuse to spend another second pressed into the wall, shrinking in on myself, giving into the pain, giving in to *him*.

"I have nothing to hide from you. I was hired as your live-in housekeeper from May 25th until August 25th. I worked my ass off all summer so you and Cooper didn't have to lift a finger, and now I'm out of a job three weeks early through no fault of my own." I say it all so fast that I'm gasping for breath by the end, my chest rising and falling in heavy pants.

"Fine, keep playing the victim card." He takes a wayward piece of my hair between two fingers and twirls it. "But if you were smart, you'd realize the easy way out of this little predicament you're in."

As if finding a place to live for three weeks is a little predicament.

"I'm smart enough to know that half the people who go to Harvard only get in because their daddy buys them a place," I snap, enjoying the well-placed dig. He's been wearing his alma mater's insignia on a sweatshirt on and off all summer like some kind of status symbol.

"Is that right?" He smiles. Actually smiles. Has the sky fallen?

"You guys just graduated from Harvard's business school and boy do you want everyone to know it, but as far as I can tell, you're both complete fucking idiots."

"Fucking idiots, or idiots you wanted to fuck all summer? Well, I guess you and I could arrange something. Maybe I can help you out with your little housing crisis if you come upstairs."

Rage. Absolute, pure, unadulterated, *rage*. I slap him across the face. "Go fuck yourself."

His hand covers the blooming handprint on his cheek and he pouts his full lips. "You're jealous. I should've guessed that's why you agreed to work for us in the first place, trying to get a taste of our pie. No matter. I don't need your cunt. But hey, have a nice life." He winks and his sarcasm is so thick it sends me over the edge.

I slow clap, ignoring the hot prickle in my hand, the stark sounds out of place in the washroom. He looks at me like I've lost my marbles. Maybe I have. "Once again, Ethan King. A true gentleman." I'm fighting back for the first time since I met him, letting my true personality come out to play. And guess what? I have claws. He glares and those devil lips turn indifferent.

"I like it when you stand up for yourself, Ardie. You should do it more often. But let me give you some advice. In this fucked up world of ours, it's always better to stand up for yourself with actions. I've found words to be pretty damn worthless."

What the hell is he even saying right now?

I let out a breath, raising my hands in surrender. There's nothing left to do here. "Like I said before, if you want to know what your mom said to me, go ask her yourself."

He steps away and yanks open the door, backing out into the hallway. "That woman is not my mother," he hisses.

I'm rocked by his words, realizing the assumption I made about Malory was all wrong. She's their stepmother? I'm about to say something about that when he slams the door in my face. Our interactions started with a door slam so I guess it's only fitting that they end with one too. Good riddance. I hope to God I never have to lay eyes on Ethan King ever again.

By the time I finish Malory's list of instructions the next day, I'm running late for the ferry. It's extra hot, even for August, and my clothes are soaked through with sweat from the hours of manual labor mixed with the humidity that engulfs the island. There's no time to shower, so I can forget about making myself comfortable before heading back to the mainland. I still don't know what I'll do when I get into Boston.

Ignoring the fear in my gut, I turn off the house's water according to the instructions, then curse the Kings one last time as I grab my luggage, wheeling it out the front door and locking up with my security code. I didn't even get time to say goodbye to the island, not that I'll be missed.

But at least it's done--I'm moving on. Never again will I allow myself to get into a situation where I'm at the mercy of people who don't care about me.

I somehow manage to walk a mile to the bus stop and make it to the dock before the ferry has left. I run up to the counter and tell the attendant that my ticket is waiting for me at will call.

The woman clicks around on her computer and then shakes her head. "I don't see your name."

I frown. "Try Malory King. Or Conrad King." Worry tightens my throat and my words come out in a jumbled mess. "They're my employers. Malory said she bought me a ticket and left it at will call."

The woman's eyebrows rise but she tells me to hold on and walks back to the counter behind her, fingering through a folder of what I assume must be printed will call tickets. Maybe I'm not listed in the computer by mistake. She'll find my ticket and bring it back to me with an apologetic smile.

She returns without a smile. "I'm sorry, but there's nothing here under any of those names."

My heart drops and I step aside to let the next person in line go while I fumble with my phone, calling Malory. She doesn't answer. I try again. Nothing. So I shoot her a quick text but that's all I can do. There's no time to deal with this. I have to board and get the hell out of Nantucket.

I get back in line.

"How much?" I ask the attendant who is eyeing me like I'm about to make her job difficult. I'm not, I'll pay whatever I have to pay and ask the Kings to reimburse me. If they don't, then so be it.

"Fifty-nine, ninety-nine," she says, "but we're sold out tonight. You'll have to come back tomorrow."

I stare at her, then look back at the ferry, then to her again. "How can it be sold out? It's huge."

She shrugs. "Lots of people come and go every day. We sell out all the time."

"Are you sold out for tomorrow?"

She checks her computer. "Not yet. There are three ferries tomorrow, 9 in the morning, 1 in the afternoon, and 6 pm. That's assuming you still want to go to Boston? If you want to go to New York City or Hyannis, we have trips tomorrow as well."

Just the thought of going to another city without a plan makes me squirm. At least if I go to Boston, I'm where I'll need to be for dorm move-in day. "My boss is supposed to pay for my ticket. If I come back tomorrow and she still hasn't paid for it, do you think there will be availability for me to buy my own ticket?"

"The 1 o'clock ferry rarely sells out and we've still got plenty of availability for tomorrow. It's the first and last ferries of the day that usually sell out." She peers around me at the line of impatient people queued up and I have no choice but to tell her thanks and leave.

It'll be fine. It'll all work out . . .

I stand at the bus stop for twenty minutes, watching the ferry drift out to sea with a pit of serpents thrashing around in my belly. There's nothing I can do about this right now, but at least I'll have one more night where I don't have to pay for other lodging.

By the time I'm wheeling my luggage back to the beach house, anger has its punishing grip on me.

This is not okay.

Malory *knows* I don't have a lot of money. And quite frankly, she also knows that I came here from a foster care situation, that I don't have people back home to help me, and that I'm fucking screwed. All that and she still lied to me about the ferry ticket? Why would she do something unnecessarily cruel like that? It doesn't make any sense.

Eighteen

I stand on the driveway of the King's estate, glaring up at it like it's a monster I've come to slay.

I really, really don't want to be here.

Maybe I should find a way to contact Conrad and bypass his wife altogether, but he's the asshole who screwed me over on the repair bills to begin with. Would he really help? Doubtful. Look who he's married to and look who he fathered. Hell, look at everything I've been through this summer. These people are billionaires and they couldn't even treat me with human decency, so what makes me think they're going to help me now?

Conrad said himself they weren't in the business of charity.

My code probably stopped working the second I was supposed to be on that ferry and there are security cameras monitoring the front door and garage. Carrying my suitcase in my arms, I traipse across the side yard to my basement window. There aren't cameras on this side of the house, which is just my luck because the last thing I need is a police escort out of here.

My bedroom window is unlocked because I left it unlocked this morning. At the time I'd thought I was being paranoid but something told me to make sure I had a place to sleep tonight. Thank God I listened to my intuition.

I slide open the window and climb down into the bedroom, then head to the utility room to turn the water back on. I'll try Malory again a little while after I've had a chance to shower and decompress. Returning to the bedroom sanctuary I spent nine awful weeks in, I peel off my sweaty clothing and slip into the shower. The water heater has cooled considerably in the last few hours, but I find the cold water refreshing after my terrible day. I finish up and change into pajamas, then I go upstairs to get something to eat.

The thought strikes me that I'm about to steal food.

It's accompanied by a cruel memory of being hungry as a child.

Sneaking in windows and stealing food isn't what I want for myself but I don't see any other options. Sometimes you have to break a few rules before life breaks you first.

When I was nine, one of my foster sisters taught me how to pick locks. The parents in that particular home kept all the food locked up and didn't feed the two of us as much as they fed their biological kids. Rose would sneak to the pantry and carefully pick the locks, bringing back fruit snacks and granola bars —things the family didn't keep close track of. Eventually I got brave enough to go with her and we managed to steal food nightly for an entire summer until we were caught. We were sent to different homes the next day and I never saw Rose again.

Wherever she is now, I hope she has plenty to eat.

Stomach growling, I pad into the massive kitchen pantry. Camilla removed all the perishables but there's still a hoard of nonperishables lining the shelves, everything neatly organized, and everything organic. There are bags of rice and beans, cans of fruit and vegetables, all kinds of soups, and even a few different varieties of canned meat.

I highly doubt they're going to eat these foods. Most of it will probably expire and get thrown away, only to be replaced with more.

I grab some peaches and bean chili and get to work.

Twenty minutes later, my stomach is satiated and the dishes are cleaned up. I know this house top to bottom, but I never got a chance to enjoy it. The sunset is fading and I don't want to turn on any lights in case the neighbors know it's supposed to be empty. They're not close by, several acres of lawns, gardens, guest houses, and garages separate the homes out here, but they don't have fences.

No, fences would block the views.

Besides, the neighborhood entrance is on a gated street. I could easily get my bike in and out, but cars are stopped by an attendant. An attendant who didn't seem bothered when I strolled up with my suitcase from the bus stop. He's used to my comings and goings.

One of the few things I loved doing this summer was sitting under the gazebo and gazing over the cliff's edge at the coastline and the semi-private beach below. But I can't do that now, because if I can see people, they can see me too. One measly light could land me in a world of trouble. The last thing I need is any more trouble with the Kings.

I'll take care of the ferry ticket myself if I have to.

That night I dream of Boston.

I walk aimlessly through the city, wandering from hotel to hotel only to be turned away at each one. Someone points me to a homeless shelter, but I don't arrive in time to be let in. I end up finding a place to rest in a nearby park, hiding out between scratchy bushes. Just as I start to relax, a group of faceless men appear, ripping my suitcase from my hands. And then one of them grabs me too, so tight round the middle my ribs bruise. He picks me up, hauling me away. I struggle against him and cry out--but nobody stops to help. People are everywhere but they all act as if I'm not even there.

Invisible. I'm always invisible.

I wake with a gasp, my skin sticky and my inhales punishing bursts that bruise my lungs. My hands are shaking, my mind so firmly planted in the realness of that nightmare that it takes a few minutes to calm myself down. It wasn't real. It was a dream. Nothing more.

But I can't shake it. And the next day, I'm too spooked to go to the ferry.

So I stay inside the Kings' house, even when Malory texts asking if I took care of it and I respond with a single word.

Yes.

It's a bald-faced lie, I know that, and my brain tells me I'm taking too big of a risk but my gut says it's better to stay. I'm safe here. I'm alone. Nobody can hurt me. And besides, I can always try for the ferry again tomorrow instead. I just need to gather some courage first, to make myself believe that my fears about being homeless in Boston aren't going to come true.

But I don't go to the ferry the next day either.

And nobody comes for me.

And before long, I've been living in this house for a week, eating bits of their food storage to keep myself fed, reading the last of my books to keep myself occupied, watching their television on low volume, and avoiding thoughts about what I'm really doing--staying here until dorm move-in day.

It's the truth. I'm a liar and I'm staying in this house against their will.

My justification? What the Kings don't know won't hurt them, but going to Boston early could hurt me. I'd rather risk taking advantage of a billionaire family with multiple houses than risk my own life on the streets of a big city. Besides, I was contracted to be here until the 25th. That's in writing, signed on the dotted line.

Is it taking advantage if they're the ones who took advantage of me first? I never should've let Conrad intimidate me into paying those bills before I could really afford to. But I did those things, and now it's time to deal with the consequences.

They hurt me first, right?

I'm only returning the favor, and it's only out of self-preservation. If there's anything I have learned this summer, it's that I have to be the one to take care of myself, to put myself first, because nobody else will.

But it's not the only thing I learned this summer and I'd be smart to remember just how ruthless the Kings can be.

Ten days before school starts, I wake to the sound of male voices. Panic nearly bolts me to my bed. Cursing, I hurry to the window and peek through the curtains. The house has a walkout basement and sloping yard but my bedroom is facing the side yard. That means the window has a small window well blocking most of the view. I crane my neck, searching for whoever's talking but come up dry. The grounds crew are here weekly to take care of the grass and plants, so it could be them, but they were here a few days ago, and besides, they're usually accompanied by the buzz of lawn mowers. I don't hear any lawn mowers.

Could it be the pool guy? He comes weekly too, but he's quick, in and out, and he's always alone.

I take a deep breath and go back to the bed, lying down and staring up at the ceiling. I tell myself to calm down, that nobody knows I'm in here, and slow my breathing back to a normal cadence.

Bang! Bang! Bang!

I squeal and jump back up, sprinting out to the hallway and toward the source of the noise. Keeping to the modern design of the house, the windows are tinted, so it's unlikely anyone will be able to see me in here unless their face is pressed against the glass, but I keep my head down just in case. I peek into the downstairs family room, ignoring the plush leather couches, huge television, and pool table. It's blessedly empty, but two men are standing just outside the rows of glass doors and windows.

Modern or not, the house still has outdoor shutters, and they're covering the windows with them now.

The banging resumes. I watch, transfixed, as they go from one window to the next, darkening the basement. When they get to the glass door that opens to the pool, they haul a piece of plywood from a nearby pile and nail that over the glass. For a brief moment, I imagine them nailing me into the house, but I know that won't happen. The upstairs doors aren't glass, neither is the side door without the camera. I could always make a run for it if needed since they're just covering the ocean-facing glass doors.

I go back to my bedroom and grab my things, bringing everything into the bathroom with me. I lock the door, turn off the light, and crawl into the empty bathtub with a pillow and blanket. It takes hours, but eventually the hammering stops. The world grows eerily quiet, and once I'm sure they're gone, I leave to explore the house.

All the glass has been covered. I can still see through the cracks in the shutters, but the house is cast in shadows. Suddenly, it doesn't feel like August anymore.

Two things come to mind. Either this is typical and they

board up the house every year when they leave to protect it from the elements, or a hurricane is headed toward Nantucket.

Massachusetts *rarely* gets hurricanes.

It's the beginning of hurricane season but big storms don't typically make it this far North. Still, it can happen from time to time. Even a tropical storm can damage any house perched on the Atlantic. I haven't looked at the news or a weather report in ages, haven't even been outside. I've been holed up in here like a little hermit crab, assuming I was safe.

I race to the television and find the remote, flipping through the channels until I get to the local weather station. I cringe at the screen: a satellite image of a swirling hurricane headed straight for Nantucket. The bright blue skies outside are going to give way to a level four storm in less than two days' time.

Suddenly Boston doesn't seem so bad.

Boston is only supposed to get hit with the edge of the storm, it won't be enough to cause much flooding, and it'll be so much safer there than here. This house will lose power and I don't know how long I can stay safe in here, not to mention the piers might get damaged by the storm, preventing ferries from taking people off island for a while. Ten days away from moving into my dorm felt like eternity when I woke up this morning but now it feels like just the right amount of time to spend in Boston before school starts.

Three miserable hours later and I'm back in the house, on the verge of tears and attempting to stay calm. *Poorly.* I took the bus down to the docks only to find out that the ferry was sold out for the entire day.

The attendant registered the look of sheer panic on my face and managed to wrangle me up a ticket on their last boat out *tomorrow*. After that, they're not returning until the storm has passed and the damage is cleaned up--a storm that is expected to ravage the island that very same night.

The island is under complete evacuation orders, even if only those houses down by the water will flood. The Kings' house is much higher above sea-level, but I'm not willing to risk staying here and getting stuck or hurt. The wealthy people can fly off the island but the rest of us have to go by boat. Only the bravest of islanders will hunker down and wait out the storm inside their homes and businesses.

The bravest or the poorest. I'm not sure which.

I'm not used to this way of living. Maybe other people don't see this as a big deal, but the ocean scares the shit out of me, even at low tide. Flashes of what it was like to be sinking under the waves have haunted me since I almost drowned. If that seems bad, what will it look like in the middle of a Category 4 hurricane?

Nineteen

Sleep is a sparse thing all night. I wake several times to thoughts of everything that could go wrong. What if there's nowhere for me to stay in Boston? What if the ferry gets canceled? What if the storm hits earlier than expected and it's while I'm on the ferry? We could get lost at sea.

Sunlight takes ages to arrive, and when it finally does, the Nantucket blue skies I've grown to expect have been replaced with rolling gray storm clouds. It's a terrifying premonition of what's coming tonight. It's going to be choppy as hell out on the water and I'm already dreading getting seasick on the ferry, but I have no other choice.

I force all worries from my mind and get ready. I'm leaving the house as soon as I can, I'd rather wait in the ferry terminal than stay another second in this prison. Since my bedroom window is now boarded up, I have to sneak out the side door for the final time. It might sound an alarm, but I'll be quick and stay away from cameras. And once I'm in the clear, I'm never coming back.

Forget bucket list, Nantucket is officially on my never-again list.

I finish rinsing the last of the conditioner from my hair, and step from the shower, toweling off. The humid air is doubled from the shower and I reach over to draw a giant smiley face on the bathroom mirror as my parting gift, hoping Mrs. King finds it before a cleaning crew does next spring.

I hurry into the bedroom, humming to myself, at last feeling like things are going to work out . . . and nearly drop my towel. My world, my plans, my fears come crashing down around me.

Sitting on the bed, glaring at me with those cold blue eyes, is none other than Ethan King.

"I thought that was you," he says evenly, tone unreadable.

My heart is beating a million miles a minute and my mind scrambles for what to do. I could confess, I could yell at him to get out, or I could play dumb. It's a split second decision, but pretending this is exactly where I'm meant to be is the only chance I've got.

"Yes, it's me," I say nonchalantly. "In my bedroom. What a surprise."

He stares at me, unmoving.

"What do you want?" I try again.

And again, I get nothing.

"If you don't mind, I have to get dressed. I have a ferry to catch." I nod to the suitcase on the bed next to him, but he doesn't follow my gaze. He keeps that unnerving steel-blue gaze on me. Can he hear my heart hammering in my chest? Can he tell that my voice sounds strained? Or see the deception behind my eyes?

It's as if we're waiting for someone to make the first move. But I'm all out of moves.

"Be my guest," he says at last. Then he stands and leaves, closing the door behind him with a soft thud.

Mercy...

Have we ever had such a calm interaction? It was almost normal. I release all air from my lungs and double over, letting the weight of his presence hold me down.

He's really here.

My hands tremble as I hurry to lock the door, then get to dressing myself as quickly as possible. There's no time for hair or makeup or anything beyond the absolute essentials. Nothing else matters. *Ethan is here.* In this house. His house. With me. And he knows I'm not supposed to be here. I'm essentially a squatter. Or is it a trespasser? Which one is worse in the eyes of the law? Will my contract mean anything if the police show up? Will they lock me up in a jail cell and make me wait out the hurricane there?

Either way, one phone call and he'll be able to confirm that I'm not where I'm supposed to be. One phone call and he could have the authorities here. One phone call, and my future could be ruined.

I throw on my travel outfit and an oversized hoodie, comb my tangled mess of hair much faster than the curls appreciate, and brush my teeth in record time. What I should do is go upstairs to explain myself and beg for forgiveness, but what I do instead is sneak upstairs and beeline for the side door.

When I open it, it squeaks and I wince.

Inwardly, I know this is a bad idea. It's not as if I can hide my identity, that the Kings couldn't find me, couldn't make me pay for what I've done. But outwardly, my hands are shaking and I'd do just about anything to get out of this situation. I hoist the bag out in front of me, step through the door, and quietly close it behind me. Time seems to move in slow motion and I'm even slower. My actions are delayed compared to how I'm playing my next moves out in my mind.

Run. You have to run, Arden.

If I'm lucky a bus will be at the stop when I get there, otherwise I'll have to go the whole way on foot. I can't take the bike because I have my suitcase, and also because it's not mine. I don't want to get into any more trouble than I'm already in right now. It's at least five miles to the ferry but it's better to go on foot than to stay here. What a stupid, terrible plan, but it's all I have, and it's a hell of a lot better than facing Ethan.

I'd sprint across the lawn if I could, but the suitcase makes quick movement impossible, so I take a slow and quiet approach instead. Gazing back at the Kings' mansion one last time as I near the road, I take in the modern grandness of it for the last time. Those two descriptive words shouldn't go together, but they perfectly describe it. The tan and white house would look normal if it weren't so massive, if it didn't have two long wings across three stories and a matching guest house and separate garage, if it wasn't set on a grassy outstretched lawn, fields on either side instead of close neighbors. If it didn't overlook the sparkling Atlantic.

In another life, I'd have loved to live somewhere like this, but in this life, I'm shoving this summer so far down into my memory bank that it becomes insignificant.

I hurry away, daring to feel relieved and complete instead of insignificant and afraid. The latter were the two emotions that have shadowed me since I was stranded here.

I'm done. I'm finally done.

Famous last words.

A pair of arms circle my waist and heave me clear off the sidewalk. I scream, dropping the suitcase handle. Ethan's husky voice is low in my ear, sending warning signals through my body. "Didn't want to say goodbye?"

"Put me down!" I wriggle in a pathetic attempt to break free, which only presses me closer against his hard body. He doesn't respond, just turns us around and marches us back towards the house. I try to wedge my elbows into his ribcage, jamming it against him as best I can.

"Your elbows are pointer than they look," he says with a wince.

"Yeah, well, you're just as much of an asshole as you look." It's a lame retort but he chuckles anyway. Low and wolfish, it rumbles his whole body.

"You have no idea," he agrees.

"Pretty sure I have an idea." And that's when I bite down on his arm as hard as I can. He's quick to rip it free, slapping a hand over my mouth before I can do it again.

"If you wanted to bite me, all you had to do was ask." There's a sexual undertone to his words that send a shiver through my center. I hate him, but that doesn't mean I'm not affected by him. From day one, I've never been more physically attracted to someone as I am to Ethan. His brother is a very close second, but Ethan? Ethan was lust at first sight.

And I hate him even more for it.

He leaves my suitcase on the sidewalk and hauls me in through the front door, right into the living room, tossing me onto the luxury sofa like a sack of potatoes.

I suck on my bottom lip and eye the door, freedom is only steps away but a very big Ethan-shaped obstacle is preventing that from happening.

"Someone could steal my bag," I argue.

"Nobody around here wants your bag."

That's the sad truth.

He leans against the wall and stares down at me. "I wouldn't try to run away again if I were you." His calm tone is startling compared to the angry growl from moments ago. And how can he suddenly appear relaxed, as if he doesn't have a care in the world, as if we're not in the middle of a confrontation? Because I'm not staying here, and I'm not listening to him. I stand up from the couch and take a step toward the door.

"It's a funny thing, Arden." His eyes narrow on me as if he knows my deepest darkest secrets. "This house was supposed to be empty."

"And it will be," I argue. "There's a hurricane coming *tonight*. I won't be here when it hits and you shouldn't either."

"Aw, are you worried about me?" His eyes swirl with a storm of their own. "You're the one here illegally," he states dryly.

I swallow hard, scrambling for a different angle to play because I have no idea of the laws for something like this. "You hate Malory," I state matter-of-factly, using her first name because that's how he spoke about her before. "And I hate her too. She's the reason I needed to stay here. Don't give her the satisfaction of turning me in."

"So hating my step monster gives you the right to stay on my property?"

I shake my head slowly. "My contract stated I had room and board here until the twenty-fifth of August. She cut it short even though I had nowhere to go. She knew I'd be homeless." I narrow my eyes. "And you did too."

There's no way he already forgotten about caging me in the tiny washroom to grill me with his asinine questions. I still can't believe I let him see me cry that day, and my cheeks flame at the memory.

"How about we make a deal?" He pushes off the wall and strides forward, standing only inches from me, he leans down close. We're eye to eye now, but we're not equals. I'm still on the couch, still sitting here where I don't belong.

I peer up at him, surprised by his offer of making a deal.

Even though he's so much taller than me, I'm unmoving, unflinching, and refusing to show weakness. In fact, I smirk. "What kind of deal?"

"You stay here with me and wait out the hurricane."

My eyes bug at that. "No, I can't--"

"And I won't call the cops on you," he finishes.

"Or I could just leave now," I challenge, standing up and pushing him back a fraction. We're chest to chest. Well, it's more like we're chest to stomach, but I hold my ground. "It would be your word against mine."

He scoffs, his fingers catching a strand of my red hair. He rolls it between his thumb and then drops it. "Oh yes, the word of a teenage homeless girl against the heir to King Media, in his own home. Whoever will the police believe?"

He's being intentionally cruel--but he has a point.

"Why do you want me to stay here with you?"

His eyes soften but the hard lines of his jaw do not. "I'd like the company."

I find that hard to believe. "Okay, and why are you even on Nantucket to begin with?"

Ethan hardly seems like the type to purposely seek out this kind of an experience. If he wanted a thrill, there are far better ways to get it than hunkering down during a hurricane. Especially not with me. He hates me, has treated me like crap from day one.

"I had to get away."

"So you decided to get away by going to the house that's supposed to be evacuated? Do you have a death wish or something?"

"No more questions," he says firmly, that emotionless mask returning. "Yes or no? Hurricane or cops?"

I doubt either will be pleasant but I can't get in trouble with the law. I don't know what the punishment is for squatting, but the Kings have money and lawyers and power, and I have nothing and nobody. If they came down on me for this, I might lose my scholarship. I might even end up incarcerated. Ethan is making it seem like there's a choice in this, but I don't see one.

"There are no good options, but at least one gets me to school by the twenty-fifth," I bite out, angry to be in this position. He's also making a choice here. He could let me go and be a decent human if he wanted. He obviously doesn't. And now he's telling me I can't even ask questions. "I'll wait out the hurricane with you, but I can't be late for the first day of college, so if the ferry gets delayed, you have to get me off this island another way."

He has resources. He can charter a private plane or helicopter if needed. I refuse to be late for my first day of college, not even for an act of God.

His eyes trail me up and down, that scrutinizing gaze searing into my flesh, then he reaches out his hand. It's so out of character for him, so surprising, I almost don't know who I'm looking at. "Is that a yes?" he questions.

I place a confident hand in his. His is dry and cool--and punishing as we shake. "Why do I feel like I'm shaking the devil's hand right now?"

"Because we both know I'm no angel."

Twenty

He's all business after that, taking inventory of the house and cataloging the pantry. Although I've been eating the food, I've barely made a dent. There's more than enough for us to get through the storm and then some, assuming he's okay with canned goods and not the luxuries he's accustomed to.

"Is there a problem?" I ask, hand on my hips. "I'm sure Camilla is busy, probably already evacuated, so don't you dare call her and put this on her. The woman has enough to deal with and doesn't need to be worrying about you being here."

"*Us* being here," he turns on me, fingers trailing over the cans as he exits the pantry and closes the door. "And no, I'm not going to bother Camilla. What do I need her for?" His eyes sparkle with mischief. "I have you."

"If you think I know how to cook, you're delusional."

He barks out a laugh. "I figured, but it's fine. We have enough food, but we should still go to the grocery store anyway and get what we can."

"It'll probably be picked over if it's not already closed." But then again, the idea of getting out of this house sounds amazing. "But fine, let's go check it out."

He leads me out to the garage where his Range Rover is waiting. "Does this stay here year-round?"

He nods. "It's my Nantucket vehicle."

"Oh, as opposed to your other ones?"

He looks at me side-long. I'm not going to hold back, not one bit, and he knows it. "I have four and I won't apologize for being rich."

I snort. "Your father is the one who's rich."

He slides into the driver's seat and I take the passengers. "I'm also rich," he says. "Besides the business we're set to inherit, my brother and I are worth over a billion each."

My stomach doesn't just drop—it fucking plummets. "What? How?"

He shakes his head and backs out of the garage. "Not that it's any of your business, but our trust funds were well-invested and we inherited them the second we signed our contracts and started working at King."

I wonder what kind of strings are attached to a contract like that. Do they have to keep working for their dad indefinitely? Is there someone who's overseeing the trust funds, making decisions for them? Or when he says they inherited them, does he mean they have complete control now?

But I keep my mouth shut because I don't even know what questions to ask, and also because it's not my business.

Still--the fact that these men are worth over a billion dollars seems unfathomable to me. A billion is one thousand million. I can't even wrap my mind around that kind of wealth.

The things you could do with it. Fun things. Good things. Impactful things.

Not harassing a homeless girl who just needs to get herself to college.

"Is your wealth public knowledge?" I ask, swallowing hard.

His grip flexes on the steering wheel. "Not exactly and I'd prefer to keep it that way. I don't want to have to hire a security detail."

It wouldn't be the worst idea.

But I don't say that, because all I can think is why me? Why tell me this?

"Why am I here?" I ask instead.

He thinks on it for a long moment before he answers. "Because you need help and I'm showing mercy on you."

That surprises me. "By making me try to live through a hurricane?"

"Don't be dramatic, we'll be fine. And what did I say about questions?"

No more questions? Fat chance of that happening. Now that I'm starting to relax and he's speaking to me with something other than animosity for once, the questions come at me like gunfire, and I want to ask them all.

I'm right, there's not a lot left at the grocery store, but at least we get there an hour before it closes, and we still manage to pick up a few pounds of chicken, a basket of produce, a bunch of junk food, and two cases of water.

Everyone is supposed to be evacuating, but there's obviously a lot who are staying on the island from the state of the store. I understand why people wouldn't want to leave. They might have nowhere safe to go. They might not have the money or the resources to leave. Or they just may be stubborn and want to stay with their homes and business.

But Ethan?

Ethan traveled here on purpose. He left Manhattan, a place

that would've just had a crappy storm, and came all the way up to an island set to be ravished.

More than that, he came into my bedroom and waited for me to come out of the shower so he could confront me.

Did he know I was here all along?

The answer is both obvious and terrifying.

I study him as we check out, trying not to be affected by the way he smiles openly at the cashier and the way he chats to the man about the upcoming storm as if we're all going into battle together.

We load everything into the back of the car and he opens my door for me. What? That action alone is bizarre behavior coming from him. I can't take it anymore. I have to know.

"Did you know I was here?" I blurt out.

I expect him to come back with his nonsense line about not asking questions, but turns on me with a wolfish grin.

"Who do you think canceled your ferry ticket?"

The fucker!

I don't want to believe it.

But his grin drops and he looks at me with the kind of intensity that is clearly not a joke. I imagined a lot of scenarios of what could've happened to my ferry ticket but not once did I think Ethan canceled it.

"Why?" I breathe.

"Why do you think?" He says it like I should already know the answer.

"I don't know what to think except you're the reason I got stuck here!"

He turns away, puts the car into drive, and maneuvers us so casually from the parking lot that it's as if we're not even having this conversation.

"No," he finally replies. "You could've bought your own ticket or found a way to get a hold of Malory, but you didn't.

Instead you chose to stay in the house, just like I assumed you would."

My throat is dry as the sand outside our window, a beach off to our left as we drive back toward the house. "Why would you want me to stay at the house?"

I swear, if he keeps avoiding the question, I'm going to strangle him.

"Because you didn't have anywhere else to go."

I don't know what to do with that—don't know what to think. "So you did it out of, what? The kindness of your heart?"

He shrugs. "I'm not the monster you think I am."

Well, he had me fooled.

But I still don't trust it—or him. When things are too good to be true, they usually are. "So this whole time, you knew I was here?"

"I know a local who works for the ferry company. I paid him to contact me when you purchased a ticket. You never did. The only reason why I came here was because you were going to unknowingly ride out a hurricane."

Like I said, too good to be true.

"Then why are we staying for the hurricane?" I raise a brow. "Shouldn't we just leave?" Because it sounds like he came to rescue me, not make me stay here.

His grin pops again. "I decided it would be more fun this way."

And there it is.

"Fun?" Now I really want to punch him. His sense of "fun" is sadistic. "Who would purposely do something like this and call it fun?"

"Okay, maybe not fun, but . . . we will feel," he pauses for a second, considering. The line of his jaw tenses as he swallows, "alive."

The last time I tried to feel alive I almost drowned.

"And you're making me go through it with you?" I practically screech.

He nods and continues driving as if any of this were a normal conversation. He's certifiable. This is not normal, this is not okay, this is not *fun*, and this is not what it means to be alive.

"People die in big storms like this. Do you understand that? It's not a joke. It's not a game or an extreme sport. And it's definitely not something for your sick entertainment." My voice is rising now. I want to get off this island, to get away from him.

I want out.

My vision blurs and my breath starts to come out in short little bursts. I know what's about to happen. If I don't get control of myself soon, I'm going to have a full-blown panic attack. My mind can't simply will this away. If it comes for me, I have to let it take me until it leaves. There's no other way I've found to get out of a panic attack except to go through it. God, I'd give *anything* to have another way out.

"Hey." He grabs my hand. "Are you okay?"

I'm breathing too fast now. The black pin pricks are starting to bloom into ink blots. "I'm . . . going to have . . . a panic . . . attack," I manage between gasps.

Ethan pulls the car over to the side of the road, practically flying out of his door and over to mine. He rips it open, undoes my seatbelt, and lifts me into his arms. There's no beach next to us anymore, just jagged rocks and endless ocean. He sits me on the side of the road, joining me and pulling me into his lap. My back to his front. His heartbeat steady to my erratic thrum.

"Look out there, baby."

I don't want to. I shake my head. The ocean scares me, he knows that, and he thinks this is how to handle a panic attack?

His mouth presses against my ear. "We're not going to die.

This is your chance to face your fears. That house is a fortress and it's too high for the waves to get us. You'll see."

I shake my head. Tears are spilling now. I just want to get off this island. He has no right to force me to face my fears. None of this is okay.

I think I may have said some of those thoughts out loud, I'm not sure, but his face is drained of color and he's looking at me like he's seeing me for the first time.

"You really don't want to do this?"

"Please don't make me." Each word comes between gasping breaths of the salty air.

It's nearly the afternoon now, the sky is even darker than it was hours ago, and the storm is fast approaching. But I've already missed the last ferry out of here. There's no getting off the island today, not unless he charters a plane or a boat.

He must be reading my thoughts because he pulls out his phone and begins arguing with someone on the other end. My mind trails off, following skipping stones to other thoughts as I wait for the panic attack to drift away.

I don't want to hear his conversation. I know what's happening.

It's too late.

Sure, he got a flight out here this morning from Manhattan, but now there's nobody else to take him back. Not even billionaires can pay pilots to put their lives at risk. Nobody is willing to come out here to get us. The hurricane is too close.

It's coming tonight.

He waits until my breathing has slowed to tell me what I already know. "We're staying."

Twenty-One

We return to the house and I'm emotionally numb as we put away the groceries. Ethan doesn't say another word, but he keeps watching me like I'm breakable. He's never looked at me like this before and I don't like it. I don't want to be breakable. I want to be strong. Breakable people don't make it very far in this world.

Either way, I hope he feels like shit for what he's putting me through. I hope he regrets it.

At least the panic has left my body and the aching numbness that follows is starting to fade, too. I'm returning to my normal self. The best way to keep this version of me is to stay busy. If I'm not busy, I'll think. And if I think too much, I'll drop back into the anxiety again.

"Now what?" I turn on him.

"Now we wait."

I shake my head. "Nope. Give me something to do."

He nods slowly. "Okay, should we cook dinner?"

It's early for dinner. Not once this summer did he and

Cooper eat before six and it's only four. Still, cooking sounds good. "Okay. What's the plan?"

"We have options. What do you feel like eating?" He's staring at me, but I don't try to figure out what he's thinking. I already know from experience that he's a closed book.

"Is the power going to go out on us? Maybe we should eat some of the perishables now and save the other stuff for when we're stuck on this island."

"We're not going to be stuck on this island."

"I love how confident you are about that," I snap.

"We won't lose power either," he insists. "We have a top-of-the-line backup generator connected to the house."

A swell of relief rises within me. "You should've led with that."

"I figured you knew."

"Why would I have known that?"

He glances around the kitchen as if to say *"look at this place, what did you expect"* but he keeps his smart mouth shut.

We end up making spaghetti because it's easy. It's strange sitting down for a meal with him. All summer I ate the same meals they did, but I never sat at the dining table. I would eat at the kitchen counter or take my food outside to the patio table or even further to the gazebo. The dining table wasn't my place. It still isn't my place. I can tell, deep down in my gut, that this isn't where I belong and I shouldn't be here.

The food tastes better than I expected, but I have a hard time enjoying it.

We finish up and Ethan gets started on the dishes unprompted. "What is this?" I question skeptically and he turns to me from where he's rinsing plates and loading them into the dishwasher.

"What's what?"

"This whole act?" I demand. "The Ethan King I know would never stoop so low as to do the dishes."

"So you think doing the dishes makes someone low?" He raises a brow. "Do you think so low of yourself then?"

I roll my eyes. "You know what I mean. Your family has staff for this kind of thing."

He nods and his dark hair glistens under the warm kitchen lights. "We do, but we don't have any staff here right now."

I take a step back. "I'm not your staff? I thought I was here to clean up after you while you enjoy a Category 4 hurricane like some kind of sadist."

He wipes his hand on a dishtowel and saunters toward me. "You're no longer in our employ, Arden."

"But the deal . . ."

"Is that you ride out this hurricane with me and that's all." He runs a wet finger over my cheek and it sets me on fire. Opposites in every way. His water to my fire. Or is it the other way around? Doesn't matter, my body wants him, has wanted him from the very first second I laid eyes on him.

No.

No. No. No.

Not happening.

I swallow hard and then he steps back, breaking the spell.

He turns back to the dishes. "Go get your stuff. You're not sleeping downstairs."

I balk. "What?"

"Just in case there is flooding up here, which I don't think is going to happen as we're well above the flood zone, but just in case. We should be careful."

We should be careful? Are those the words of a man who intentionally flies to an island about to be ravaged by a Category 4 hurricane? Apparently so . . . Ethan King is a walking contradiction. And a walking asshole. And a sex god. And about a zillion other things I can't name right now because all I can think is how he demanded I don't sleep downstairs.

"And where will I sleep?"

The curious part of me wants him to say his bed and the rest of me wants him to say anything else. I've become so mixed up since coming to this island and he's the biggest reason why. He makes me crazy. He makes me want things I shouldn't want. He makes me—

"Wherever you want to sleep," his response interrupts my wayward thoughts and my cheeks burn, "as long as it's in one of the upstairs bedrooms."

One of the bedrooms. Doesn't have to be his.

Why did my mind even go there?

Oh, I know why. I shouldn't even have to ask.

I hurry downstairs to get my things before I say or do something that I'll regret. Because I want this man and I know, *I know*, that I'll regret acting on those wants.

Remember why you hate him.

Remember how he's treated you.

Don't forget that you're nothing to him.

This is all just a game.

Don't lose.

We get my stuff moved upstairs and Ethan insists on carrying my suitcase. My cheeks are still burning because of that stupid assumption about Ethan's bed. This place is huge; of course I'd have my own room. He gets me set up in a guest room that's a few doors down from his own bedroom and leaves me alone so I can freshen up.

After I'm done, I shuffle through the house looking for him. I shouldn't feel so awkward, I know this house inside and out, but I can't help it. There's something different between Ethan and I now that the truth is out in the open.

He knew I was here.

He was the one who canceled my ferry ticket, apparently because he wanted me to stay back at the house rather than going to Boston without a plan. It's what he meant when he had me cornered in that little bathroom and told me there was an obvious answer to my problem.

And then he flew out here because he thought I was going to ride out the hurricane and wanted to make sure I didn't do that alone.

Actually, he could've made sure I got off the island but instead he got me to stay in the house with him.

He wants me here.

And he wants to be here *with* me.

I can't trust him, I know that, but this whole situation has me twisting into knots.

Why is he suddenly acting like he wants to be around me when all summer he treated me like a pariah? Is it different now that Cooper is gone? Now that his friends have left? That his father isn't involved? I want to demand answers but what if I don't like what I hear? Or worse, what if I do?

I'm starting to rethink everything about the man.

I find him outside, walking the perimeter of the house. The sun is setting but the clouds are so heavy that there's nothing pretty about it. It's ominous, sending a shiver of fear through me at what's to come. "What are you doing out here? It's going to start raining soon."

"I'm just checking on things. Making sure the contractors got all the glass boarded over like they were supposed to."

He shakes the boards covering the back patio glass and it doesn't move a centimeter. That would satisfy me, but he's got an annoyed scowl on his face.

"Looks like they did a good job," I point out.

"They forgot to bring the patio furniture inside." He nods

to the lounge chairs lined up alongside the pool. "Any one of these could blow into the house or who knows."

"Well, come on then." I roll my eyes and together we begin moving everything into the nearby pool house for safekeeping.

By the time we're done, I'm sweating like a pig and needing a shower. The sun is long gone and the wind is already picking up. It wraps around our limbs like tightropes. Enough pull and it will carry us away.

We need to get inside, but a strange sense of calm takes over me.

I don't want to go inside yet.

I want to see what's coming. Want to feel it. Face it.

I don't let myself overthink, I just act, my feet carrying me down the pathway toward the cliff's edge. I know the way by heart, even in the dark. Ethan chases after me with a cellphone light anyway, his voice calling something that gets lost in the wind.

"Put that away," I demand when he's close enough to hear me. I cover the light with my palm and squeeze until my hand glows. "We don't need that."

He pulls it away and points at me, practically blinding me in the process. "What the hell are you doing? We have to get back to the house."

"And we will."

I turn away and march onward, pushing against the wind like it's a game I'm determined to win. I can't hear Ethan's response, but he turns off the light and chases after me.

The gazebo has built-in benches so there's nothing out here to take back to the house, and that's good because I'm too tired to lift another thing. My legs are jelly and my arms are burning but none of that matters right now.

I just want to see the ocean. Want to hear it. To experience this.

I get it now, what Ethan said about wanting to feel alive. I want the same thing. I want it so fucking bad I will face down the storm for the chance.

The Atlantic is roaring like an angry goddess. Even from all the way up here I can hear the waves slamming against the shore. Despite the heavy cloud cover and the darkness of night, my eyes have adjusted enough to take in the sheer size of them. They're twice as big as any of the waves I've seen all summer. Some more than twice. Three times. At least.

My stomach drops.

"Feeling alive is overrated," I mumble, but my voice is lost in the wind.

"What?" Ethan yells.

"You're sure we're safe up here?" I ask, loud this time.

Ethan rests his hands on my shoulders and leans against my back. His chest is a hard warm wall protecting me from the wind as he speaks against my ear. "From the hurricane, we are."

His words are inviting and terrifying all at once.

I turn around in his arms to face him. I shouldn't encourage him, shouldn't want this, shouldn't even say anything. But I do. "What's the danger?"

He runs his hands down my shoulders, down my arms, down to my waist, his large hands circling the small of my back and then lower. I'm sure he's going to cup my ass but he doesn't. I'm in pajama shorts and a hoodie, and his fingers play at the leg hole of my shorts. One finger slides under the fabric, stroking my thigh, and my breath catches in my lungs.

"Not all danger is bad."

But this kind most definitely is. It's not easy, but I step away. One large step back until it's the railing that's touching me instead of his hands. The empty space between us seems to expand into infinity.

"I'm not going to have sex with you," I blurt out.

I expect him to act cool, or to insult me, or to do or say just about anything besides what comes out of his sinful mouth.

"Get prepared, Arden."

"For the hurricane?

"For me . . ." He steps forward, towering over me like Poseidon himself, equally as powerful as that ocean. His voice is low and languid and certain. "I want you, Arden. And when you're ready to admit that you want me back, you're going to willingly come to my bed, and then I'm going to fuck you so hard that you forget your own name."

Twenty-Two

I gape at him. "You don't know what you're talking about," I lie. So many lies. He knows exactly what he's talking about—I do want him.

But I know better.

A want isn't a need. And while I may want him, I also need to protect myself from this man. This player of games. This god who thinks he can rule over my body.

"We'll see," he challenges. And then he turns away and begins the walk back to the house. "Get your tight ass inside," he calls back to me. "We're not coming back out here until it's over."

I follow, all the while wondering if he's talking about the sex or the storm.

The rain hits us before we make it back inside, the clouds opening up like a curtain to let the downpour fall. I've never experienced rain like this before. It's relentless, buckets of water instead of distinguishable water drops. And it's icy cold.

It mixes with the warm August air in a violent clash.

Conversation with Ethan long forgotten, my body goes into

full-on flight mode. My muscles ache and I feel like I'm running through quicksand as I sprint for the side door that's not boarded up. I fly past Ethan and he chases after me, calling my name and saying something else but I can't hear him. All I can do is run.

Some people fight and others flight.

Me? I'm a flight risk.

Except this time, I don't fly, I fall.

Fall right into the mud and grass, right onto my knees, onto my palms, and onto whatever the hell is left of my pride. The pain is almost enough to knock me out of my panic.

And then Ethan, the man who seems to be everywhere, is here too, and he's lifting me up and carrying me into the house. I don't fight him off but only because I can't—I'm a ball of panic, curled up against his chest like a kitten in need of saving.

I hate that I need saving. But I do. I can't breathe. I can't think.

The panic attacks are getting worse.

He's saying something about being sorry, something about not realizing I would have such a hard time with this. That he didn't know I had panic attacks.

That he's sorry.

He's sorry.

So sorry.

Crack! The lighting wakes me up with a jolt, the room flashing bright and then going dark again. Even through the slants in the shutters, the lightning strikes are bright enough to wake me, but they're not the most alarming part of this moment. What's alarming is that I didn't even realize I had fallen asleep. I sit up, squinting at my surroundings.

I'm not in the guest room.

I'm in Ethan's bed.

And he's staring at me from across the room, sitting at his computer desk, something playing on the screen, a pair of headphones resting around his neck. "You okay?"

"Were you watching me sleep?" I deflect his question with one of my own. Am I okay? That's debatable. But also, do I look okay? I'm not okay. I'm anything but okay.

"Not really," he says, "but after your panic attack I wasn't going to leave you alone."

Who is this man and what has he done with the Ethan I knew all summer?

I reach over to the bedside lamp and turn it on. At least he was right about not losing power, I don't know what I'd do if that was gone too. I take a deep breath and the events from earlier start to filter back to me, piling on the trauma. After carrying me inside, after waiting for me to steady my breathing, he helped me get cleaned up and changed into fresh pajamas, and then he laid me in his bed where I promptly fell asleep.

"What time is it?" I croak.

"One in the morning. You've been asleep for a few hours." He moves to the edge of the bed and I curl my feet in on myself. I can't be too close to him. I don't know what I'll do. The man isn't wearing a shirt and he's got gray sweatpants slung low on his narrow hips. I already knew about his incredible swimmer's body but right now I can't help but stare at it. That's only to distract myself. Distraction is good right now.

Boom! Another crack of lightning. Another deep rumble of thunder. It sends me scurrying into a tight ball. "I'm not afraid of thunderstorms," I'm quick to point out, "but this isn't a regular thunderstorm."

And I'm right. Because the wind has picked up considerably. It's as loud as a freight train and only getting louder by the second.

Ethan stands and I don't know what he's going to do. Go back to watching his computer? Check the window? Leave the room? But instead he tugs the blanket up and crawls into the bed with me. I'm frozen, I can't move with him so close, but he doesn't seem to mind. "Here, put these on." He removes the headphones from around his neck and places them over my ears.

Right away I can hear what's coming from the computer. I don't know what it is but it's much appreciated.

It's the distraction I need.

He shows me how to turn up the sound on the side of the headphones and then I rearrange myself so it's just my face peeking out of the blankets to watch the computer monitor. He tucks me against his shirtless body and I let him hold me. Only for tonight. Only because of these unusual circumstances. No way would I normally go for this.

Liar...

My body relaxes and we watch together, him not being able to hear a thing because of the raging hurricane and me focusing on the voices and music of the story playing out on the screen.

I've seen this film before. It's the version of *Romeo + Juliet* from the 1990s starring Leonardo DiCaprio and Claire Danes. It's about the last thing I expected Ethan King to be watching to keep him occupied during a hurricane, but I don't let myself think about that too much. Soon the tragic tale of young lovers takes me away, my body fully relaxes, and the tiredness from the day sweeps over me again.

My eyes grow heavy and I begin to drift.

At some point the headphones must fall off because I wake to the screeching sound of hurricane winds. Ethan is still holding me and his eyes are open, staring at the ceiling.

"Go back to sleep, Juliet," he whispers.

It's like we're in the middle of some cease-fire. It sounds like a war is raging outside but he's in here calling me Juliet. What do I do with that?

"I don't think I can," I confess, removing the headphones from around my neck. "It's so loud out there."

He nods. "The eye came and went while you were sleeping. We're in the middle of the second wall of the storm right now. A lot of times that's even worse than the first."

I sit up. "Is the house okay?"

"I'm sure it is." If he's so sure then why did he make me sleep upstairs?

I peel off the blankets. "Let's go check."

"We're not going out there until morning."

"Not outside, dummy. But we should at least go see if there's any flooding in the basement."

He assures me there won't be, that his family chose this high elevation property to build on exactly for this purpose, but I don't care. I want to check for myself. It makes me feel like I'm taking action, like I have some control over a situation that I actually have very little control over at all.

Of course, he's right. We go downstairs where there's no flooding.

The house is fine.

"Since sleep is off the table, do you want to play?" He nods toward the pool table.

This thing has been here all summer and I've never once touched it.

With the lights still on it almost feels like we're two normal people in this house, not two idiots waiting out a hurricane when they should've evacuated. "I don't know how to play."

He smirks and those blue eyes flash in playful challenge,

making my stomach dip. "I'll teach you, but I can't promise to let you win."

"Good. I like to win on my own merits."

"I'm sure you do, Juliet."

There it is again. I almost ask about the name and demand he not call me that, but instead I keep my mouth shut and try not to smile.

Not much later I find out that pool is easy to learn but not easy to win. I fail miserably.

"Let me show you a better technique." He saddles up behind me to wrap his arms around my waist and grab hold of the pool stick over my hands. He shifts my hands into the correct position, long fingers lingering over mine for far longer than necessary. I know what this is, I know this is flirting, but I let him do it anyway.

Again, distractions. That's all this is.

"Lean forward," he instructs. I do, taking a risk and pressing my backside against his groin. Maybe this will be my way of winning. Get him all hot and bothered and leave him wanting more. More that I do *not* intend on giving.

He hisses softly then leans his body against mine, his face coming to rest against my cheek. I can feel the scratch of the jawline where facial hair is beginning to grow in, can smell the scent of expensive cologne and warm sleepy skin, can hear the softness of his labored husky breathing. His words keep flashing through my mind. *I'm going to fuck you so hard you forget your own name.*

"Like this." And then he's hitting the white ball and it's slamming into the others, creating a ricochet of pool balls that sends two of my striped ones into pockets.

He returns to standing and I spin in his arms to face him. The cue stick is long forgotten, my hands sliding up his torso, fingers splayed across his still-bare chest. I know he didn't put on a shirt because he wanted to entice me with his ridiculous body, but I don't even care. Because he's affected by me, too, if the skin pebbling under my fingers is any indication. Feeling brave, I gaze up into his eyes. They're molten. Determined.

He leans forward.

So do I.

Crash! We spring apart.

"What the hell was that?" I gasp.

That sound wasn't thunder. It twas too loud for thunder, too close.

He takes my hand and we hurry upstairs, going from room to room until we find the source of the noise. "Fuck," he growls, stepping into the large primary bedroom. Glass is splintered across the wood floors, the storm blowing inside where a massive tree branch has knocked through the entire side of the house.

Forget the shutters, forget the boarded up glass, this is a *huge* branch. The house didn't stand a chance.

The wind is howling something crazy, blowing water, leaves, and bits of glass right at us.

"Come on!" He tugs me from the room and slams the door, then pulls me into the center of the house and the kitchen pantry where there's no windows nearby.

He never expected that to happen, but I did. I did because this is a Category 4 fucking hurricane! Just because we're not in the flood zone doesn't mean we're not in the danger zone. We never should've stayed here. What if the winds tear the house down around us?

Twenty-Three

"Don't panic." He kneels in front of me, hands on my hips and face tilted up. "It's all going to be fine. Just wait here—

"No! Don't go back out there!"

"I'm just going to grab us some blankets and pillows. I'll be fast."

"And we'll stay in here the rest of the night?" I beg, my voice coming out like a child's.

I don't know if I've ever been so scared. Even though I want to be logical, to insist that we're fine, that the odds of more trees breaking through the house are low, that this place is practically a fortress . . . I can't. I'm a bundle of nerves again. I'm walking a tightrope and I've lost my balance, about to plunge to my death.

He gets up and hands me one of the chocolate bars that we bought at the supermarket earlier today as if that's going to help. I'd laugh if I wasn't so freaked out. "Eat this. Think about how it tastes. Let it melt on your tongue. Focus on the chocolate and I'll be back before you finish."

And then before I can protest any more, he's gone and I'm

shoving gourmet chocolate into my mouth and trying not to cry.

He's right though, he's back before I can finish the bar and I hand the rest to him. "I don't want any more."

He plops it into his mouth and chews while he gets to making us a bed, right here on the pantry floor. The lights are on. I don't want to turn them off. I don't know how either of us are going to sleep but right now I don't care about sleep. We can sleep when the storm is gone and this is all over.

Or when we're dead.

We've got two blankets below us for padding and one on top, and he takes my hand and squeezes once before letting go. "I brought my phone, laptop, and headphones," he says. "Do you want to try watching another movie?"

I swallow hard and shake my head, the exhaustion hitting now that the adrenaline has worn off. "I'll be fine. Let's just talk."

I get brave enough to turn off the light but it's so dark that I freeze. He takes my hand and helps me into the makeshift bed. "Okay, what do you want to talk about?"

This is my chance. I don't think he'll leave me alone in here, no matter what I say that could possibly piss him off or make him defensive. And I have so many questions. I borrow against his chest, wrap my arm over his body, and summon my courage.

"Why did you stop me and Cooper from having sex?" I start. "And don't say it's because you claimed me first when you and I both know you treated me like crap all summer. There's something more to it."

He's quiet. Too quiet.

"Just tell me," I press. "I deserve to know."

Nothing.

"Ethan!" I elbow him in the ribcage and he growls.

"Cooper knew better than to get you in that position and he did it anyway."

"But I wanted him to."

He growls again. "No, you didn't. You were both doing it to get back at me."

That shuts me up, the words torn right from my mouth. Is he right? Was I jumping at the chance to hook up with Cooper because I really wanted Ethan and couldn't have him? The truth is mortifying. Because he's right, and I didn't even realize it.

"And why would Cooper want to get back at you?"

"A lot of reasons, but mostly it's because we're competitive and sometimes we can't help ourselves," he says. "Next question."

"Okay, but you have to answer it fully this time," I demand, to which he doesn't agree, but I ask the question anyway. "Why do you keep saying I'm yours?"

"Let's just say you're my type, and everybody who knows me, knows that."

Not what I was expecting. I'm his type? If I'm his type, then why has he pushed me away? Why has he been so mean to me?

"I didn't want you to be my type, Arden, especially with you being so young, but that doesn't change the fact that you are," he continues. "And I'm not going to pretend anymore."

He doesn't elaborate or answer any more questions, and before long the storm begins to quiet and we both fall asleep.

I dream that he kisses my forehead, my check, my nose, his soft mouth hovering over my lips.

Gently. Sweetly.

When I wake the next morning, I wake up alone. My hips are sore from sleeping on the wood floor and my neck is stiff, so I'm slow to crawl from the haven of warm blankets.

Did I only dream of kisses last night or were they real? My mind could be playing tricks on me but I swear at least one of those . . . I shake my head. No. I can't let my imagination take me to the places I won't be able to return from.

The storm has passed, but it's left a mess in its wake. The yard is littered with tree branches and I can only imagine how bad it is down in the flood zones. I hope everyone down there evacuated.

Exploring the outside of the house first, the only damage appears to be the branch that crashed through the primary bedroom. Besides that, the house is relatively unscathed. A few shingles will need to be replaced, but we're lucky.

I'm certain not everyone was as lucky.

I head back inside, looking for Ethan. His bedroom door is open and I slip inside. The shower is going and the bathroom door is open.

I shouldn't look.

Leave, give him privacy.

But does he want privacy? Because these doors have locks and he not only left them unlocked but also open.

Before I can talk myself out of it, I peek around the doorframe.

The glass shower is at the end of the bathroom, faintly steamed up but not enough to hide his lithe body from view. He's standing under the spray, his naked backside to me. I never really got the appeal when girls would say a guy's butt is cute, but I get it now. His ass is perfectly sculpted just like the rest of him and my fingers flex, wanting to know what his skin feels like under that water.

The man is stunning, those muscles gently flexing as he

washes himself, streams of white soap suds running down his tanned skin to pool at the drain. I feel like I just walked on the set of a movie or something because Ethan is movie-star gorgeous. I should leave, but I can't move. I stand there in a daze, watching as he finishes rinsing himself.

And then he turns and I lose all sense of thought. He's in profile as he palms his erection with one hand and presses the other hand to the glass. Slowly, he begins to pump. His eyes are closed, his mouth is open, letting the water in and around him. His hand is large, covering most of his cock, but not everything. It's too big.

He pumps harder and groans, and then he says my name.

Oh. My. God.

I gasp and he whips his head toward me. Our eyes lock.

This is the part where I run away.

But I don't run away. It's as if I couldn't move away if I tried. Something primal comes over me, like I'm channeling someone else, someone brazen who isn't afraid to watch him pleasure himself. To lock eyes with him as he does it.

His stare is fixed on me as he continues to clutch himself, his muscles rippling with each movement. He doesn't say a word and neither do I. We're locked in a staring contest, a game of chicken. Who will spook first?

He continues, faster and harder, his mouth opening and closing, jaw popping, those moody eyes still heavy on me. And I stand there, watching him take his pleasure like it pleases me too. I can't help it. The pressure builds and builds until finally, I can't hold his gaze any longer. I have to look down, to watch exactly what he's doing to himself, to see *all* of him.

He's so big, so hard, so thick and long. Maybe all men look like this, I've only seen Coop's and his was equally impressive, but I have to swallow my nerves at the sight of Ethan's cock. A shiver of intimidated anticipation sweeps right down into my panties. Suddenly, all I want is to go in there with him, to take his cock in my hands and finish what he's started.

But I don't . . .

I don't because I should hate him. Because I can't give him the satisfaction. But mostly, it's because if I go in there, I'll end up naked too. And I'm not sure that I'm ready for that. So I wait until he rears his head back, a primal groan releasing as he explodes.

Fuck.

Foolishly, I thought this would gross me out but it's the opposite. Witnessing Ethan come undone in this way is the most erotic thing I've ever seen. It's also a rude awakening to what I just allowed to happen between us and of how weak I've become. I'm throbbing for more, my desire for him unmistakable.

I turn and sprint from the room, but not before catching his low chuckle and my name on his wicked lips once again.

The flight response practically drop-kicks me in the head. I lock myself inside in my room and lean against the door, my body pissed that I'm in here instead of with Ethan. What could he do to me? I can only imagine the pleasures he could offer.

After fanning myself for a long minute, I take my sweet time showering and getting ready. When I finally have the courage to leave the room, it's only because my stomach is demanding food. And also because I can smell the meal Ethan's cooking downstairs all the way up here. Leave it to bacon to get me out of my hiding place. The unique savory smell has a way of getting to the best of us.

I slip into the kitchen to find him standing over the stove. I'm waiting for him to tease me or tempt me. Whatever it's going to be, I'm already embarrassed. I'm not like the girls he's used to and nothing like the women Cooper paraded around the house all summer. And I don't mean that they're somehow bad and I'm somehow good. I mean that they're cool and sexy, meanwhile I'm inexperienced, introverted, and prefer to keep my love life between my imagination and the books I read.

"How did you sleep?" he asks as if the shower scene never even happened.

I exhale. This is an olive branch and I immediately take it. "Like shit, but that was to be expected. How did you sleep?"

"I slept great." He turns and begins dishing up scrambled eggs, breakfast potatoes, bacon, shredded cheese, and diced avocado into two bowls. If stomachs could cry, mine would out of happiness. This meal looks amazing and smells even better.

"You slept great?" I snort and roll my eyes. "On the pantry floor in the middle of a hurricane, knowing your home has a hole in the side of it and water's blowing in?"

"That's right." He grins and it's so genuine and bright, so not the Ethan I know but the one I wanted him to be on that first day back in May. "Because I was with you."

I nearly melt right then and there.

I want to roll my eyes again, to deflect this moment, but I don't. I just let him have this, let us have this, taking my bowl and squirting ketchup on top. He splashes a generous amount of salsa on his and we go sit at the kitchen table together.

The awkwardness starts to creep back in. Are we really not going to talk about it? He pleasured himself right in front of me and I watched like some kind of pervert. It reminds me of when I first met Cooper and he called me a voyeur. I didn't think I was but maybe Cooper's right about me, at least when it comes to Ethan.

"Did you see anything interesting this morning?" He questions teasingly, but his eyes are hot and I nearly choke. So I guess I'm not off the hook.

"Nope," I say. "Nothing interesting or impressive." He barks out a laugh and my tension melts. I point to the window.

"Well, except for maybe the damage from that storm. Have you gone out to look at it yet?"

That sobers him right up and he nods. "It'll be fine."

It might be, but I'm not sure if I will be, because the fact remains that something changed between us last night and this morning. I can't take it back, and deep down I know I'd be lying to myself if I said I want to.

Twenty-Four

We case the perimeter again but the house seems to be in good shape except for the glaringly obvious tree that has destroyed the primary bedroom.

"What do you want to do about this?" I ask, a frown taking over my face. "Poor tree."

He looks at me sidelong. "Poor tree?"

"Yeah, poor tree." I feel worse for the tree than I do for the owners of this house. This is nothing they can't fix with money. The cost will be like a drop in the bucket for them. But the tree? The tree is a goner.

"Come on, let's get this *poor tree* out of here." He stalks over to the massive limb and begins to heft it, but it's not going anywhere.

I can't help it, I laugh. "You really thought you could just pick that up and move it like some kind of Hercules?"

He drops it in a crash of leaves and turns on me, hands on his hips. "You're right."

And then he struts off in the direction of the garage. He's dressed in plain shorts and a white t-shirt, and I can't help but notice the way his body moves under the clothing. Now that I've seen him naked, I'm not sure I'll ever be able to picture him any other way.

"Did Ethan King just admit that I'm right and he's wrong?" I call out after him, hoping for a distraction. Flirting seems like a good way to go.

"I'm not as stubborn as you seem to think I am."

"Really? Because if the Wicked Witch of the West were to show up and demand my shoes I think I'd be less surprised than I am by the events of the last twenty-four hours, including you just admitting that you're wrong."

He turns on me then and I stop. We're in a standoff, staring at each other like outlaws. My cheeks flame again. His mouth turns up into a slow smile. "The Wizard of Oz starts with a tornado, not a hurricane. Nice analogy though."

I give a little curtsy. "I aim to please."

"That you do," he says slowly, then he whips back around and goes for the garage door.

Like a lovesick puppy dog, I follow.

Considering this isn't a normal garage, I'm not surprised that there's an area in the back with loads of expensive-looking tools. Tools that have probably never been touched. I know for a fact that the lawn care people bring their own stuff with them. But I guess there's a first time for everything, because Ethan pulls out a chainsaw. He opens the cap and sniffs.

"It's got gas."

I snort. "Of course it does. Everything in this place is well-stocked."

He raises his eyebrows. "You saw that for yourself this morning, didn't you?"

Oh my god, he's joking about his well-endowed cock, isn't he?

My cheeks flame but we both laugh, then we put on

gardening gloves and go back to the yard. On the first rip of the cord, the chainsaw roars to life.

"Wait," I call out and he turns on me, brows drawn together.

I remove the sunglasses from my face and step forward, putting them over his eyes. "You need protective eyewear," I yell, but I don't think he can hear me. I can't really even hear myself, the chainsaw is too loud.

I step back and watch him work. He's the picture of masculinity and I have to admit it's sexy as hell. As bits of the tree get broken up, I carefully pick them up to move them out of the way. Before long the sun is back out and it would be like the storm didn't happen if there wasn't such a mess to clean up. The work is hard and we're both covered in sweat. The bright sun hurts my eyes but I don't complain. Sun is my friend after the events of last night.

Ethan finally finishes with the chainsaw, returns the sunglasses, and helps me move the rest of the debris into a pile. "You're burning up." His mouth forms a tightly pinched frown and I shrug.

"I'll be fine."

"Let's take a break."

We head back inside and I immediately go for a cold rinse off. The water soothes my sunburns and I sigh into the stream, letting it fill my mouth and flow down my body. I've caught the burns early enough that I should be fine by tomorrow as long as I take better care with my skin the rest of the day. Maybe I shouldn't have worked outside all morning but it was the most satisfying work I've done all summer.

After a good slather of after-sun lotion and a second layer of sunscreen, I find Ethan in the kitchen making sandwiches. I'm getting used to seeing him here, cooking for me. It's nice. "You look good in the kitchen," I blurt out and he grins boyishly, his eyes catching in the light. They're stunning. He's stunning.

And I'm in big trouble.

"After lunch, let's go see if we can help the first responders."

He considers my request. "That might not be safe. I don't want to put you into any danger."

I sigh and pick up the finished sandwich, taking two big bites and swallowing before I continue. "True, but you already put me into danger the second you asked me to stay through a Category 4 hurricane. We're here. The least we can do is help those in need."

He doesn't have anything to say to that because he knows I'm right. He just watches me, his jaw tense and sandwich untouched.

"I mean it."

After a long pause, he finally nods. "Alright, but on one condition."

"And what's that?"

He steps around the kitchen counter and towers above me. My insides swirl with anticipation. He runs the back of his index finger down the side of my face, then down to my neck, gently pressing against the sunburn. I might spontaneously combust. "You sunscreen this pretty skin of yours."

I nod once. "Already done."

Leaning down, he hovers just between the crook of my neck and shoulder. I swear he's going to kiss me. Time stretches endlessly and that sinful mouth drifts to my ear, whispering against the shell. "Good girl."

Two short words that do more to me than I ever thought possible.

After stacking everything we might need into the back of the SUV, we climb inside.

"The cell phone towers must be down," Ethan explains. "I don't know when they'll be back up, so I can't call ahead to see what's going on. I don't know what we're getting ourselves into."

I didn't know the towers were down because I haven't used my phone in weeks. There's not much you can do with a phone that only texts and calls when you have nobody to text or call. The plastic brick has been sitting plugged in and untouched in my bedroom. I'll admit that his news has me reconsidering our plan. For just a second my selfish side wants to hide in the house but that wouldn't be right. "We need to help."

He nods and pulls out of the drive.

As a whole, Nantucket is wealthy all over and we're staying in one of the most elite areas on the island, but even wealth can't always protect against mother nature. That becomes evident about a quarter mile from the house. The road is a mess. There's nothing to do but clear the debris and press on. It seems like every fifty feet there's another fallen tree we've got to move. It takes hours to make it over the main hill where we can see down into the worst flood zone. My heart sinks. Even from this vantage point, it doesn't look good.

I thought the roads were bad, but this is ten times worse.

The flood waters have mostly retreated, leaving behind thick mud and debris in their wake. I don't know how safe it is to go down there. Maybe Ethan was right, maybe we should've stayed back, but there might be people stranded in that mess who need our help.

"We've got a few hours left before sunset," Ethan says. "Where to first?"

It's overwhelming. I don't even know where to start.

We drive the Range Rover as close as we can get before it's obvious our chainsaw isn't going to be enough and climb out.

Luckily, that's when the Coast Guard pulls up next to us. One of the guys flags for us to get out and we meet him in between the vehicles.

"Can we help with anything?" I ask.

The three men exchanged weary glances and one addresses us. "Normally we'd tell you to go back home. You shouldn't be on the island at all."

"Well, we're here to help," Ethan cuts in. "What can we do that won't get in your way?"

"Okay, you can stick around, but only because we're going to need the help." The guy relents, hand raking down his jaw in worry. "The damage is worse than we anticipated. Some of the structures in the flood zones got completely wiped off the map."

My heart drops.

I try to imagine it and can't. It's too sad. I really hope nobody tried to stick it out in those places, because if they did, they probably didn't survive the night. I remember how scared I was and know that my fear must've paled in comparison to what others faced only a few miles from where we were. Many locals stayed on the island, and I think of Camilla.

What if she lives in the flood zone?

"Where does Camilla live?" I turn on Ethan.

He pales. "I don't know."

My stomach hardens and I really think I'm going to be sick. We need to check on her but if we don't know where she lives and we don't have information on her, there's nothing we can do right now. We'll have to check on her as soon as cell phones work and we can get her address. I want to kick myself for not thinking of her yesterday.

“What can we do?” I turn on the leader, my voice wavering. “Give us a job and we’ll do it.”

“Just come with us,” he instructs, and we follow him and his crew.

We’re on foot, so there’s only so far we can go, but other rescue workers are here, some in boats down in the still-flooded areas. A couple of helicopters circle above.

The remaining daylight fades to darkness as we go from house to house, checking to see if anyone’s home and could need our help. Luckily most of the houses are empty.

But not all.

Twenty-Five

We come across an elderly couple, their home a muddy mess with a dark line along the walls about four feet high. It's a sick reminder of where the flood waters rose and receded. I fight to hold back the tears. They're sitting in a foot of mud on their couch, shaking from shock and cold. Who would leave these elderly people here alone? Why didn't anyone get them out?

The soldiers jump into action, assessing their vitals and then getting them out of the house. These people are too weak to walk far and the roads aren't drivable, so we wait with them until a rescue helicopter arrives.

They take the woman first, strapping her into a chair-like contraption so they can fly her over to the hospital, before coming back for the man. She cries as she goes and her husband cries too. I can't help it, so do I. It's terrible. Nobody should have to go through this. Ethan takes my hand and squeezes, dragging me away from the group.

"Do you want to go?" he asks.

I wipe away the tears and shake my head. "There's more people that need our help."

Rather than wait for the helicopter to come back for the elderly man, Ethan and I head to the next house, marking it as clear for the coast guard. And then the next. And the next. We only come across a few more people in distress, but thankfully no bodies or anybody as heartbreaking as the elderly couple.

It's close to midnight when we're told to go home, that more troops are being deployed and they won't need us to come back in the morning. We thank them for letting us help and start the trek back to Ethan's SUV. It's pitch black out here but luckily Ethan's phone has battery left for the flashlight. What if there are more people stuck in the homes that haven't been checked yet? What if they don't have flashlights? I start crying again. It's not fair. All these homes. All these people. And we weren't even in the worst hit area.

Did people die in this?

"There's nothing else we can do," Ethan says solemnly, taking my hand and squeezing. "But you did good work today. We did what we could."

He's right, but it doesn't make it any better.

We make it back to the SUV and Ethan checks his phone again.

"I've got service," he says relieved, and immediately calls his dad to let him know he's alright and to give the status on the house. I can hear Conrad's booming voice through the other line and hold my breath as I listen. As far as I know, Ethan didn't tell his dad I'm here.

There are a couple of security cameras outside of the house, none inside because the twins demanded privacy, and Conrad tells Ethan that the cameras went down during the storm. They're still not up. Ethan has to be the one to break the news about the damage but Conrad doesn't sound the least bit worried. I fight to roll my eyes—damaged floors in a hallway is the end of the world but an exterior wall caving into the primary bedroom is apparently no big deal.

"How's Camilla? Did she evacuate?" Ethan asks.

The line goes silent and I know exactly what that means. None of the Kings checked up on her before the storm. What a bunch of selfish assholes.

"Are you fucking kidding me?" I grumble, sinking down into my seat.

Ethan shushes me, giving me a dark look and holding his finger over the mic on his phone. "He doesn't know you're with me," he mouths.

Well, I guess that confirms that.

"Give me her address and phone number," Ethan insists to his father. "You must have it somewhere."

"I'll text it to you shortly," Conrad replies. "Stay safe, son. We'll see you when the island is clear."

They hang up and Ethan pauses for a second, a contemplative line between his eyebrows. What is he thinking? But he shakes it off and puts the car into gear.

We drive back to the house which is much easier with the path we cleared on the way down. Ten minutes later and we're sitting in the driveway with Camilla's address. Ethan looks it up on Google Maps before we even head into the house.

"She's nowhere near the flood zone. She's probably fine."

I release the biggest sigh of relief. "See if you can call her."

"Already on it." But she doesn't pick up and I'm right back to square one.

We can't go to her place because it's not close, and it's too dark for the chainsaw. Ethan calls his father back and demands Conrad find a way to check on her and call us back as soon as we know she's okay. I'm sitting next to him in the passenger seat, practically boiling over. These people suck. Out of sight, out of mind, right? Camilla is nothing to them when she's not in their kitchen.

"Just find her," Ethan finishes, hanging up.

"And how long has she been working for your family?" I ask, my tone accusatory but I don't even care. Camilla had told me the exact number, which I forgot, but I know it's been since the twins were boys.

Ethan tenses. "I know I'm an asshole, okay?"

"Good. Glad you know. Now what are you going to do about it?"

He's quiet as he pulls into the garage. I wonder if he's thinking my same thoughts. It's not like Nantucket has slums, anyone who lives here has to have a certain level of wealth, but there's still a big difference between the homes in his neighborhood and some of the homes we visited today. Some of these people have generational homes and businesses. They're not millionaires, let alone billionaires.

When it comes to hurricanes, a lot of people stay back during an evacuation for stupid reasons. People like Ethan. But then there are people who stay back for good reasons, people like that elderly couple who simply didn't have the resources they needed to get away. And people like Ethan? They can just hire someone else to prepare their homes, flying on and off the island whenever they want.

I hate it.

I hate that wealth is so lopsided.

That some people have all the luck, all the connections, everything they could possibly ever need. And then there's other people, people who have to rely on the good will of others. Good will that often doesn't come.

People like me.

I stomp into the house, not even bothering to slam the car door behind me.

Ethan is quick to follow, hot on my heels. "What is your problem?" he demands.

I swing around to face him, poking my finger into his chest. "The fact that you even have to ask that question says everything I need to know."

"And what is it that you think you know?"

My words come hard and fast, biting and cruel. And I don't care. "That you, and your dad and stepmother, and your brother, and your friends, you're all bad people."

"Everyone is a bad person on some level. That's not why you're mad."

I scoff. "There are good people out there, Ethan. You just wouldn't know one if you saw one."

"We all have good parts and bad parts. That's not what this conversation is about."

I step back and he follows, caging me in against the entryway wall. "Enlighten me then."

"You're mad because you're scared."

Well, he's got me there. I'm always scared. "So what? I just went through a terrifying event in the last twenty-four hours. Frankly, I think it's weird that you're not more frightened yourself."

He shakes his head slowly. "That's not the kind of scared I'm talking about."

I swallow the words I was teeing up to throw in his face.

His hands are on either side of me now. There's nowhere for me to go.

"You're scared because you're jealous, because you're alone, but most of all, you're scared because you want me."

How dare he.

How dare he be so conceited, so ridiculous . . . so right.

This would be the part where I throw myself into his arms, where I give in to his seductions. But I'm not that girl. I refuse to be that girl. So instead, I duck under his arm and walk away. I need sleep. And then tomorrow, God willing, I'm getting the hell off this island.

My mind is racing when I finally slip into the guest room blankets, my body so exhausted it feels like I'm being swallowed by the mattress. I should sleep like a baby, but I don't sleep much better than I did during the damn hurricane. It's too quiet, especially compared to last night. It feels like I'm the only one in the house again, but I know that's not true, and then it's like I'm living with a ghost.

Not just living with one, being haunted by one.

The next morning, I wake with the sunrise and walk down to the beach. I'm not getting in the water, but I'd like to say goodbye to the ocean and sand before I head out.

It's the same ocean that greets me, but it's not the same beach.

The storm has changed it, eroding a few areas of the cliff face. The sand is covered in tumbles of seaweed brought in by the waves. With a deep breath, the morning air fills my lungs and I head down the stairs. I'm already imagining the feel of the grainy sand between my toes when I hear Ethan's voice calling out to me.

I ignore him, hurrying down the wooden stairs even faster.

He chases after me. "These stairs could be compromised!"

I freeze, my reply catching in my throat because he's right and I can't believe I didn't think of that. I assess the stairs beneath my feet, shifting my weight side to side to see if I notice a difference. I don't. And the wood is looking only slightly more worn than it was before, even though it's still damp. Of everything on this estate, these stairs are the only things that don't match the upscale high-end elegance of the rest of the house. It's like they were built decades before the house was and I'm a little surprised the Kings haven't replaced them yet. It's only a matter of time before they give out. What's the deal with them? And the old gazebo too? There's got to be a story there as to why they haven't been torn out by now.

I keep going.

"Do you have a death wish?" He sounds angry now. Good.

"You would know about death wishes, wouldn't you?" I yell back, continuing down the stairs without looking up at him. I hear him start to follow, so he must not be all too concerned about these stairs either.

"What's that supposed to mean?"

I scoff. "You're the one who wanted to ride out the hurricane like a lunatic."

Honestly, except for a questionable one towards the bottom, these stairs are in pretty good shape, which is pretty damn amazing considering the beating they must have taken. I reach the beach without any trouble. Unless you consider Ethan King to be trouble, which I do, because he's quick to catch up, grabbing me by the waist and hauling me around to face him.

Twenty-Six

"What's going on with you?" His eyebrows are drawn together, long lashes casting dark shadows over stormy eyes. I can't let it get to me or read into the flutters in my heart.

"I'm saying goodbye to the beach."

"Why? We're not leaving yet."

As hard as it is, I force myself to drag away from his arms. I shouldn't want him to hold me. "I'm leaving. I'm finding a way off this island and you're going to help me. That was the deal we made, remember?"

His eyes flick at the sky, as if searching for strength to deal with my theatrics, and I wonder what thoughts are tumbling through his mind. He's a closed book. Unreadable. "We have a small airport here." His gaze snaps back to me. "I already called and talked to them. The runway was damaged in the storm. They said it'll be a week before it's functional again."

My mouth goes dry. I already know the pier got ravaged. I doubt the ferry will be here any sooner. "What about a helicopter?"

He shakes his head. "They're not willing to come out and get us yet either but that might be an option in a few more days."

"I have to be at school by the twenty-fifth." My voice wobbles and I hate it. I don't want to cry in front of this man again. Not ever.

He nods. "And I have to get back to work. Don't worry, you'll be in Boston and I'll be in Manhattan by the twenty-fifth."

"You promise?" I hate asking him to promise anything. He's never given me the impression that he cares about keeping them.

"Of course." But his voice is thin.

It's the best I'm going to get but I hate that I don't trust it to work out. Or trust him. There's something he's hiding. I can feel it in my bones. I stare at him, searching for cracks, for signs, anything. But he's so fucking unreadable.

Frustrated, I head down toward the water. I'm not getting in but there's a bunch of sea life washed up on the sand, mingled with ropey seaweed and piles of shells. There are even sea stars. I don't think I've ever seen one in person before.

Ethan catches up, his stride matching my own. "We can throw those back." He points to the sea-stars. "They might still be alive."

We get to work, picking up the stars and tossing them back in the water. The beach is littered with several species of them and my heart hurts just thinking of them being ripped up from the ocean floor and left here to dry out in the sun. We should've gotten to them earlier.

This stretch of beach is at least a mile wide, and we spend over an hour barely making a dent in it. At least I remembered to put on sunscreen this morning, but the exhaustion is already starting to get to me and the day has barely begun. And we're here for how many more days? At least a week, he said, but maybe less if he can charter a helicopter.

I need hydration. I need a hat. And most of all, I need to get the hell off Nantucket. Wanting a bit of cool relief, I step into the water, letting it lap at my ankles. I close my eyes and allow a much-needed sense of calm to flow into my nerves. I hate how panicked I can get. I know everyone feels these types of emotions, that anxiety is part of the human experience, but mine can overtake me to the point of exhaustion or illness, sometimes crushing my lungs or making my entire body buzz. If it's really bad, I'll even get itchy and develop hives. There will be a medical center at college that I can go to for help and I'm planning to do that first thing because I can't take this much longer.

"Are you okay?" Ethan's voice is far off.

I vaguely register notes of concern in his voice. Concern and guilt.

Good. He should feel guilty. He had the chance to get me out of here and he didn't. And now look where we are? We're stuck in the middle of a disaster. At least we were able to help some people yesterday. That makes this bearable. He places his hand on my elbow and I flinch slightly, but he doesn't remove it. "Look at me."

I pop my eyes open and turn to him. Yup, I was right. Guilt is written all over his face. Finally, I can read what he's feeling. It's no longer a passing shadow, it looks like a permanent feature.

"I'm sorry," he whispers. "I didn't realize you'd have such a hard time with this."

It's too late for sorry but I don't say that. I don't say anything. His thumb begins to twirl circles on the skin above my elbow and a rush of pleasure floods me. I shouldn't like his touch so much. He shouldn't be able to calm me. My entire body shouldn't relax.

"Sorry." My voice goes hoarse. "As you know, I have problems with anxiety."

Slowly, he wraps me into a hug, holding me against his hard chest. My ear is pressed to the cotton of his t-shirt, his heart thumping beneath the fabric. The fresh scent of the laundry detergent I used on his clothing all summer envelops us. Even more calm floods me, this time enough to drown out the rising panic. Ethan is a lot of things, but he's not going to let me down in this. If he says I'll be back in time for school to start, then I will be. I have to trust that, because the alternative is more unbearable anxiety.

White-hot pain zaps my right ankle. It sears around my foot. Razors dig through the skin. I scream and stumble back, but the pain only increases.

Ethan's eyes are huge but I can't think about that, all I can think about is the pain. I shake out my foot, water flying in every direction.

A jellyfish floats against the surf.

"Fuck," Ethan hisses, picking me up and carrying me away from the water.

I can't think. All I can do is scream. The pain is terrible. Angry welts wrap around my foot and ankle where the tentacles got me. They bounce up and down in my vision and Ethan runs with me in his arms up the beach, up the old stairs, and finally into the house. Each second lasts a lifetime and the pain is an eternity.

"We need to soak it in vinegar," he says and I shake my head, only wanting the coldest water possible.

"But it burns," I cry against his chest.

"I know, baby. Just hang on." He sits me down on the kitchen counter next to the sink and brushes the unruly hair from my face and mouth and wipes away the tears. "Trust me, you don't want fresh water to heal this, you want vinegar, and then cortisone cream. We're going to have to do it twice a day until you're healed."

He says words, smart words that probably make sense, but I don't care right now. I can't stop crying. He disinfects the sink and puts my foot in it. He doesn't touch the faucet. The idea of vinegar on these wounds instead of icy water sends me into a downward spiral. I beg for cold water but he won't listen. I reach for the tap but he pushes my hand away. And then he holds me to his chest and shushes me. It's not helping, I've never felt pain this bad. Is it supposed to be this bad or is there something wrong with me?

I must have said that last bit out loud because he answers in a nurturing tone. "It really does hurt. I've been stung twice and it's terrible, but you might be having an allergic reaction. We'll know soon enough."

That sends my spiral deeper. What happens if I'm allergic? Will I die?

My mind is racing, imagining everything that could go wrong, but he's back to shushing me, assuring me that I'll be fine either way, that he'll get me to the hospital if he has to.

"A hospital that's on the other side of an island covered in hurricane debris?"

Unlikely.

"If I have to, yes. You're going to be okay." But I can hear the slight tremble in his voice, can see the way his hands are starting to shake. He's not sure what's going to happen either. He's just as scared as I am.

He grabs the vinegar and begins to pour it over my foot and ankle. It's terrible at first, igniting the burns. I hold arms around his waist, gripping onto him for dear life.

"Just breathe," he whispers.

But I can't. I hold my breath. He tells me to count to seven and then to release for seven, to breathe in and out slowly, and reluctantly I give it a try. After a few rounds of his method, my breathing slows and my mind focuses. The pain is dissipating. It's still there, but it's like I'm disassociating from it, like it's not so much a part of me as it was a minute ago. And I'm breathing normally again.

We stay that way for a while, long enough for the vinegar to begin to dry, and then he carefully pulls my leg from the sink. I wince at the movement, but the worst of the pain is gone.

"So I'm not going to die?" I ask with a hiccuping laugh.

"Looks like you're going to survive. You don't seem to be allergic and thank God that jellyfish wasn't a box."

"A box?"

"Yeah, the box jellyfish show up here sometimes, especially after bad storms. They're some of the most poisonous to humans." He rakes a hand through his dark hair and frowns. "We shouldn't have gone in the water. We already knew a bunch of stuff had washed up. I'm so sorry, Arden."

"It's not your fault."

"But it is. I knew better." He pauses for a long second and then tells me to stay there while he finds the cortisone cream. "As tempting as it may be, don't put cold water on that. It'll only make it worse, baby."

I lay back on the counter, my feet dangling over the edge, and stare up at the light fixtures, right into the bulb, letting it blind me. It's barely a distraction, but it's enough to keep me from running my foot under cold water. But he must know what he's doing because already the pain is less than it was.

He returns and gently rubs the cream into the wounds. I stay laying back on the countertop, tears pooling into my ears. Then he lifts me up again and carries me upstairs to his bedroom. Lying me down in the center of his king bed, he tucks me into the blankets but leaves my foot exposed to the air. He pours me a glass of water and gets me three ibuprofen, and best of all, an ice pack wrapped in a dish towel.

"You can ice it but don't get it wet."

I agree and he wraps it up with the ice pack, the pain instantly being numbed by the chill. I moan in relief and he smiles softly, though I can still see the grim sense of regret in his eyes. He blames himself and is not going to forgive himself for this one, even if I don't blame him for it. It was an accident. A stupid one that could've been avoided, but an accident all the same.

There's a television mounted to his wall and he turns it on, finding a movie for us to watch. I find myself sinking into the bed. And into him. He's laying right next to me, his body pressed to my uninjured side. I try to get lost in the movie but it's hard, not only because of the pain, but because of his proximity. Because of the kindness he's showing me, the tenderness I haven't seen in him before. Because of how good his body feels being next to mine. And because of the bathroom door that's hanging open and the shower I can see beyond—the memories that won't let me go. The things I've seen. The things I wouldn't mind seeing again, even though I know better.

When I woke up this morning, I was determined to get off this island, but right now, laying in this bed that smells like Ethan, I have to admit the truth. Minus the jellyfish sting, there's nowhere else I'd rather be. And that's more terrifying than anything else that's happened today.

Twenty-Seven

The rest of the day is spent watching movies and getting treated like he's the doctor and I'm his patient. It's strange to let anyone take care of me, let alone Ethan. After my near-drowning incident, he left me alone once I got the all-clear. Today has been entirely different with him at my side nonstop and I don't know how to feel about it.

And he called me baby again. Twice.

When Conrad demanded I pay for the repairs on the Brazilian rosewood, I did it without saying a word to the twins. I assumed they would have sided with their dad considering all evidence pointed to them hating me. But now I'm starting to think Ethan might've had my back. I decide never to tell him. It's over and paid for, so there's no need to admit my failings.

We finish up another movie and he clears the dishes from the dinner he prepared. He's no Camilla, but the tacos weren't half bad and my belly is full and happy. Best of all, my foot is feeling a lot better. It still hurts, especially to walk on it, but the pain has gone down drastically thanks to his care.

"Have you ever thought about going into medicine?"

We're laying on his bed and he's staring up at the ceiling as if it's got the answers to life. His face falters and he looks at me sidelong. "How did you know that?"

"You have a healer's touch." I search his eyes, drawn in by the brilliant blue rings around his iris. I suddenly have the urge to kiss him but I push it down like I always do, swallowing hard.

"The healer's touch, you say?" He smirks. "That's nice."

Saying it sounds a little silly, but I'm being honest. I can easily picture him in an office boardroom, taking control and leading the way to increased profits, but I can also picture him in a hospital setting. I see him healing people, helping them feel better, or at least come to terms with the hardships they're facing.

"When I was a kid, I wanted to be a doctor," he says nonchalantly. His tone reminds me of how someone might talk about believing in Santa Claus as a child, knowing better as an adult that the magic wasn't real. My own experiences with Santa are mostly fraught with confusion and disappointment, but like always, I push them from my mind.

"So why don't you go for it?" I ask. He has everything at his fingertips. I'm sure he could go to a top tier medical school and build a successful career.

"Conrad." He answers like it's obvious.

"Your dad doesn't want you to go into medicine?"

His mouth slips into a self-deprecating smile. "Cooper and I have been raised to take over the family company."

"Both of you? Couldn't you go into medicine and he can do it?"

He looks at me for a long moment. "Have you met Cooper?"

I snort. "I think he's probably more capable than you're giving him credit for."

"That's true," he sighs. "But it doesn't matter because that's not the plan our father has for us. He doesn't want anyone else taking over his company but his own flesh and blood and he's got the board in line with his way of thinking. There's no other choice for us."

"So is that what you're doing now? Taking over for him?"

"Not yet. We're going to work for him until retires in a few years. At that point he'll step down to become chairman of the board, so he'll still have a lot of power. I'll become King Media's next CEO and Cooper will be the CFO. Our pay and workload is structured to be equal, but I'll handle operations and he'll take on financials."

"And what happens if you reject this plan?"

His voice hardens. "Then we lose our inheritance."

I blink at him. "I thought you already got access to your money?"

"We did but we signed our lives away to do it. If we leave King Media, we lose everything and have to start from scratch."

"And you'd never do that, would you?" It seems obvious that he's stuck but it's not like behind golden bars is a horrible place to be. There are worse things in life.

"I don't know," he admits, "but I've thought about it."

To say I'm shocked is an understatement. "I understand why you might want to and I do believe you are capable of success with or without your father's company . . ." My voice trails off. I don't want to say the wrong thing, but this conversation has me unsettled.

"But?" he prods.

"But you have it really good, better than I think you realize."

He's quiet for a moment before muttering, "money isn't everything."

"That's easy to say when you have so much of it that you don't even have to think about it," I argue, heat building.

"You'd feel differently if you were in my shoes. I'd kill to have what you have." My cheeks flush at the admission. But it's true. Well, maybe not *kill*, but I'd definitely trade just about anything for that kind of security. I've never known peace and money might be able to buy it. "I'm not just talking about money. I'm talking about security. You're going to have what you need for the rest of your life. You're in a position that ninety-nine percent of people will never be in no matter how hard they work."

"You probably think I'm ungrateful for complaining."

I don't know what comes over me, maybe I'm challenging another version of myself, the brave one that knows how to touch a man, but I roll closer to him and run my hand along the smooth planes of his jawline. He tenses but I don't stop. The little hairs where his afternoon shadow is growing rub like sandpaper under my fingertips. My bold move sends shivers through my entire body, but I make myself do it anyway. Because I want to feel him. But also because I want him to understand my thoughts. He'll never be able to empathize with them, but he could at least try to understand my perspective.

"I don't think you're ungrateful complaining about your situation." Maybe spoiled and short-sighted, but I don't say those things. "And I do think you'd make a fantastic doctor. But I also think you'll be a kick-ass CEO when the time comes. Could you find it in yourself to enjoy it? Maybe you could create projects that are fulfilling or maybe you could give back to those less fortunate. There's got to be something you can do and I know you're brilliant enough to figure it out. You just have a way about you that others don't have."

I've said too much. His ego is inflating before my eyes.

"And what way is that?" His eyes flare and he inches closer, our breath mingling. We're facing each other now. Lips only a few inches apart.

“A way of getting what you want.” My voice is husky. Needy. A mirror of what I’m feeling inside.

“What is it that I want right now?” The question is a dare, a challenge. One I’m still scared to meet, but that I can’t possibly back away either.

“To feel good,” I breathe, every emotion I’m feeling today pooling right into the apex between my thighs. Anticipation buzzes through me and we haven’t even kissed. At least not in a way that counts. If we don’t kiss, I might cry.

“Like this?”

I expect him to kiss me, but he doesn’t, *he touches me*. His eyes are holding mine, gazes locked together, as he slides his hand between the waistband of my shorts, fingers slipping under my panties. His fingers are pure temptation as he teases them into my heat, gently pinching my sensitive clit. My gasp is instant. The sensation he’s already building in me is intense and addictive. I need more.

I whimper my approval, and he scoots in closer, rubbing the tender flesh. “Does this make you feel good?” I nod into his shoulder, angling my face away from his. Using his free hand, he cups my jaw and tilts it back to look at him. “Keep your eyes on mine, Juliet. I want to see you when you come.”

It’s perhaps the most vulnerable thing I’ve ever experienced, but I do it anyway, keeping our eyes locked as he strokes me. “You’re so wet,” he murmurs his approval. “Do you always get this wet?”

Truthfully, no. “Only for you,” I whisper.

His eyes flare, mouth quirking at the corner. He’s being bold, maybe I should be bold too.

“What do you want?” I ask huskily, because whatever it is, I’m prepared to give it.

He smiles like the devil. “To bury myself in your cunt and make it cry for me.”

Oh. My.

I didn't expect dirty talk, but I must like it because it has my entire body lighting up. The electricity skitters through my entire body. Control slipping, I buck my hips to arch my sex against his fingers, creating more tension.

"You want more?" he chuckles and I nod vigorously. "You want my cock?"

I nod again. I do. God help me, but I do.

He slides his fingers down further, slipping one inside me, and then two. My legs fall open. "You're so tight," he growls, moving his fingers more intently.

"It feels so good," I moan, my voice coming out entirely different than it ever has before, breathy and wanting. I'm so close to release—it's the feeling of being empty and then filled and I want it desperately.

But then he stops, hand frozen mid stroke, his index finger now pressing against my inner wall in a way that almost hurts. Almost. But it also feels incredible and I clench around his fingers, my eyes beginning to water.

"Don't stop." I angle my face up to kiss him, dying to know what his mouth tastes like, but he shifts away from me before I can make contact. I would feel rejected, but I can't feel much of anything right now besides desperate mounting pleasure.

"I want you to beg," he demands, almost cruelly. "Beg me to make you come, little Juliet."

"Please, Ethan. I'll do whatever you want. I'm begging you. Please."

I close my legs around his hand and lean into him, my thoughts dimming at the added tightness it creates. My hands are everywhere. They're on his body. They're on my body. They're pressing against his hand, trying to urge him to finish me. And then they're under his shirt, splayed against his hot skin, sliding under his shorts between us.

I can't see his cock under the blanket but I can feel it, so large and hard, so velvety and ready. I want this. I want more than his fingers inside me. Feeling brave, I grab hold of him and pump. He's been quiet this entire time but not anymore. His groan is raspy. Needy.

It's like pressing an on button because he begins his expert movements again, his palm rubbing against my clit and his two fingers teasing inside me in slow strokes. "I love your innocence, baby."

"I don't want to be innocent anymore," I confess.

His eyes spark. "Of course not. You want to be bad, don't you?"

Oh fuck. Yes. I definitely like this dirty talk. "Yes please."

And then he's kissing my shoulder, lips brushing sinfully over my neck, tongue hot across the curves of the cleavage peeking over my shirt. He leaves shivering trails of pleasure with those kisses, trails that I want to take into oblivion.

"Don't stop," I say. And then I say other things but I can't even follow my own train of thought, let alone what's coming out of my mouth. I'm too wrapped up in the sensation of Ethan.

The pain in my foot is an afterthought compared to everything else I'm feeling. All that matters is him and me and the need that's building between us as we touch each other. I still want to kiss him but we don't even need to. This isn't a love act, there's not even kissing on the lips. It's a sex act, purely carnal, what some would call a sin, but if this is a sin then I'm running straight into hell with Ethan as my guide. Nothing will stop me from this. I don't care. It's all I want. It's everything I need.

I continue to slide my palm up and down on his cock, loving the way it jolts under my touch. He's even larger now than he was when I first started this and I can't imagine what it will feel like to have him inside me, how it will all fit, but I'm desperate to try.

"You're good at that," he hisses, encouraging me.

Is he being honest or is he trying to make me feel better about my inexperience? I want to prove myself to him. Trembling, I slip my other hand down to cup his sack, wondering if he'll like that too. He throws his head back and I smile. This is fun. He's got me surrendering to him but I've got him doing the same thing. Maybe I am good at this.

He changes his movements, working my pussy harder, and swings his other hand up to my breast, fingers prodding under the bra. He rolls my nipple under this thumb and suddenly my oncoming orgasm builds in a new way, a bigger way. It's so much—too much. I start to pull away.

"Fuck no," he growls. "I want you to know what I can do to you."

"I can't—"

"You can. Let yourself."

"I don't know how."

"Yes you fucking do." He kisses my jaw and rasps into my ear. "But I'll help you get there. Promise. What have I been trying to tell you, baby? You're mine."

Twenty-Eight

Those possessive words coupled with his depraved movements send me over the edge. The orgasm rips through me and I scream his name. Seconds later he's coming in my hand and arching into me too, his face softening into a peaceful expression that I've never seen him wear. The pleasure ebbing through me is out of this world. I've never felt anything like this before. The orgasm takes a full minute to release and let me drift back down to earth.

"So *that* was an orgasm?" I breath out the words roughly, almost laughing. "I thought I'd given myself orgasms, but nothing has ever come close to that." Then I do laugh. "Pun intended."

He chuckles and rolls away, slipping his pants back up before I can get an eyeful. He pads to the bathroom and turns on the faucet for a second, so I assume he's cleaning himself up. Then he's back with a warm towel. He hands it to me and all of a sudden, I'm burning up with shyness. This is new for me. Maybe it's normal for the guy to bring something for the girl to clean herself up with, and it certainly is thoughtful, but I wasn't expecting it. We didn't even have sex and already I feel so shy about this, the boldness I had minutes earlier long forgotten. What's it going to be like if we do the real deal?

Please, let us do the real deal.

Now that I've gotten a taste of Ethan, I think I'll die if I don't get more.

A yawn escapes me and I fight it off. I need sleep but I don't want it.

I expect Ethan to get back in bed with me but he leaves the bedroom instead and doesn't come back until hours later, until long after I've cleaned him from my hands, myself from my thighs, until I've thought a zillion spiraling thoughts and eventually fallen asleep . . . still in his bed.

I'm not ready to leave.

I only know he's back because I wake when he slides in next to me, surrounded by darkness and cool AC. I freeze, keeping my eyes closed and my breathing slow. I want him to think I'm asleep because as much as I want to pick up where we left off, I'm not ready to face what we did, especially after he left me for hours by myself.

My back is to him and he softly presses a hand to my spine. "I'm sorry," he whispers, and it's so unlike him that I don't even know how to feel, let alone what to do. We stay like that for a long time, and I wonder if he knows that I'm pretending to sleep. It makes me question what else I could be pretending . . . that he actually cares for me? That he's secretly a good guy? And that this is going to end in a fairy tale? All of the above.

By the next morning my jellyfish sting is feeling good enough that I can walk on my foot again. Ethan is nowhere to be found and I can't sit around in that bed for another day, especially not by myself. It was different when he was watching movies with me, but after the events of last night, I don't think that's going to happen again. Because there's something going on here besides fooling around. He's avoiding me.

He said it himself. *He's sorry.*

Sorry that we ever did anything? It sounded like it.

So I get myself showered and dressed, and I head down to the kitchen to make breakfast.

"What are you doing up?"

I whip around to find Ethan coming in from a run, shirtless and sweat glistening on his body like it's a second skin. Have I ever been jealous of sweat? Only when it comes to Ethan. He tugs his headphones out and glares at me through thick lashes. "You need to stay off your feet."

"I'm feeling much better." I shrug, then turn back to the toaster to retrieve my toast and get to buttering it. And honestly, I am feeling a lot better. The pain isn't totally gone, but it's about eighty percent better already.

"Let me see." He marches around the kitchen island and I stick out my injured bare foot as proof. I'm wearing a little cotton dress today and I may or may not have chosen to forgo any underwear. I smile boldly when the fabric rises high on my thigh.

"It looks a lot better," he agrees. "But you should still be careful with it for the next few days. It could take a while to heal. Sometimes weeks."

I tut. "It won't take weeks." Then I return to preparing my breakfast and Ethan comes to stand behind me. Close. Too close. Who am I kidding? There's no such thing as too close when it comes to this man.

"You smell good," he murmurs into the back of my neck, then picks up my hair and places a kiss on the top of my spine. My body reacts instantly and I try to twist around, but he's got me pinned to the countertop. I can feel his erection growing against my ass and I part my legs ever so slightly. I can't even help it. I'm like an animal in heat for him.

I may smell good, but he smells like he's just been running for an hour. I don't even care though. I just want him to keep touching me, to pick up where we left things last night.

He must feel the same, because he slides his hand down under my dress. "You're obviously not wearing a bra. Are you wearing any panties?"

"Find out for yourself." I'm brave with him standing behind me where I can't actually see him.

"Oh, you do want to be bad, don't you," he growls, finding that I am, in fact, not wearing any underwear.

His hand skirts close to my pussy and I arch into him, ready for this. But then he does the most teasing move imaginable. He removes his hand and grabs a slice of my toast instead, steps back, and walks away eating it.

What the hell?

"That was mine," I argue.

He looks back with a smirk, his eyes lingering on me. "*Everything* in his house is mine, Arden. Everything."

Is he toying with me? If this is a game then I'm playing right into his hands. I'm like putty between his fingers but I can't help it. I need to do better. Two can play at this game. So I take my remaining toast and head out to the back patio where he's stretching. He's already scarfed down his piece in all of three bites.

He gives me a sideways glance as I sit in the nearest chair, letting the fabric of my dress rest way too high on my thighs. I take my time eating, licking my lips between bites and murmuring about how good it tastes. It's stupid, nobody likes toast this much, but Ethan catches the bait anyway. He's staring at my mouth and then my legs and back again, like he doesn't quite know where to look.

"What are you doing?" He steps closer, eyes narrowing.

"Enjoying my breakfast." I lick an invisible crumb off my fingers and moan. "What are you doing?"

"Enjoying you enjoy your breakfast." He smirks, and then he drops to his knees in front of me and presses his hands against my inner thighs. "Maybe I didn't get enough to eat."

Oh good lord. Did he just say what I think he just said?

I'm frozen, my plate in one hand and the last edge of the toast in the other as I stare at him. His eyes are locked on mine as he spreads my legs, as if challenging me to tell him to stop. Despite the nerves rioting in my belly, despite my reddening cheeks, despite the fact that he's probably used to perfectly waxed girls and I only shave down there, I don't stop him. I can't.

His eyes flicker to my exposed skin, feral desire bared in his gaze. Grabbing hold of my thighs, he yanks me to the edge of the chair and I yelp. I'm practically falling off but he doesn't let that happen. He hooks my legs over his shoulders.

Over. His. Shoulders.

"I bet you taste as sweet as you look," he murmurs, and then he's closing the space between his mouth and my most intimate flesh.

The first kiss sends a jolt of surprise through my entire body. Disbelief at the instant pleasure. I never knew something could feel this good. I squirm but he's not letting me go, working my legs further apart. His morning stubble scratches my thighs and his mouth flattens against my clit. We both groan. Then ever so slowly, so deliciously, he glides his tongue up and over the swollen flesh and presses back down. My entire world flips.

"Oh my God," I hiss and he chuckles into my heat.

"This isn't God, Juliet." His face is buried between my thighs and his speech creates a delicious vibration. "Unless I'm your deity now."

Maybe I'm going to hell for thinking it but right now, he most definitely is.

I buck up into his mouth and his tongue gets to work, possessing me, guiding me higher and closer. The sky is an endless baby blue above us, but I swear I see stars as I arch back, trying to breathe, trying to let myself have this. Part of me wants to fight it off again like last night, almost like I don't think I deserve to feel this good. But I do. I must. I have to.

His lips stay kissing me, tongue stroking, and his hands squeeze my ass. One long finger slides into my core, connecting with an inner wall of nerves. It's like a trigger is being pulled inside of my body, shock waves ride through me and I cry out.

I've lost control.

I'm alive with pleasure, with need, with the pain that I don't feel worthy of having something so good but I'm letting myself take it anyway.

The orgasm rockets through me and he doesn't stop, wedging his mouth against me even harder as he holds me to him. The orgasm is longer and bigger than last night's, releasing until I'm practically begging him to stop because I can't take this much pleasure at once. It's too good. "It's too much." My voice is raspy. Desperate. Begging.

But thank God he doesn't stop. He doesn't stop until every last tremble has released from my aching body, until I have to physically push him off, my feet coming down on his shoulders and sending him back onto his haunches. His face is glistening in the morning light with my wetness and he smirks up at me, licking his lips and looking pretty damn proud of himself.

His dick is tented in his shorts and I realize he never

touched it. This was all about me and I don't get it. "Why didn't you touch yourself?" I blurt out.

"Why did you try to stop the orgasm again?" He challenges back.

I sit up and fix my dress, which almost seems fruitless at this point. "I don't know," I mumble. "It was too much."

His smile drops. "You didn't like it?"

I chew the inside of my mouth for a second, trying to figure out how to say this without sounding weird. "I'm not used to feeling good like this."

"I gathered that last night," he stands and brushes himself off. "But you should get used to it."

"Oh?" I'm still breathless.

"Yes," he says with full confidence, "because I plan to ruin you for all other men."

And with that, he takes my plate and strolls into the house, as if that were a typical morning and not one with his mouth doing unspeakable things to me. What he doesn't realize? It's too late. He's already ruined me. Wrecked me. Downright locked me up and threw away the key. Because no other man will ever be him.

Ruin me.

Wreck me.

Fucking own me, Ethan.

But please don't break me.

Twenty-Nine

I want him to kiss me for real. The thought consumes me the rest of the day. The man ravaged my pussy and I still don't know what his mouth tastes like. What does that say about us?

It's killing me that he hasn't done it, and I decide that I'm not going to have sex with him until he does. Am I really going to let my first time be with someone who won't even make out with me? No way. But I also decide that I'm going to have to put on my big girl panties and make the first move. Maybe if I kiss him first, he'll kiss me back. Or maybe I'm going to have to confront him if he doesn't and ultimately walk away.

That's the last thing I want to do.

He's awakened my body. I can't help it, I need to lose my virginity and I need to lose it to him. Today. Because we have limited time together, five days until the airport opens and I have to get to Boston, and I'm not leaving this island with my virginity intact.

He left for the day to go check on Camilla, insisting that I stay back and rest my injury. I wanted to tag along but figured my hobbling around might slow everything down. There's not a lot I can do if I need to stay off my feet for most of the day. So I do my own thing, reading and watching movies. It's not like all the other days I spent alone in this house. It was so much worse knowing that I could be spending time with him, could be touching him . . .

Selfish, I know.

Finally, I hear the car coming up the drive just as I'm finishing making our dinner.

He spends the meal telling me about what he got up to with Camilla, mainly helping her and her husband clear their yard and driveway. He seems satisfied with the work he accomplished.

I can't say the same for myself. I'm needy for something more to happen between us. Five days left is about to turn into four. "I'm going to clean up and then go outside to watch the sunset. Please come?" I ask, setting my plan into motion.

"Whatever you want."

His eyes linger on me as we put away the dishes and head out to the gazebo. The sunsets are to the west and the backyard here faces east, so while we can watch the sunrise over the water here, we have to watch it set over the house and the island. But that doesn't mean that the water isn't a beautiful mirror to the brilliant sky. In fact, sometimes I think the clouds are prettier over here, that looking directly into the sunset can make you ignore the other beauty to be found.

"It's hard to believe that just days ago this was all in the middle of a hurricane," I sigh. "Storms have a way of surprising you, I guess."

"So do people." His tone is a confession and my stomach swoops.

His hands are on the edge of the gazebo's wooden railing, gripping on tight, and I'm not sure if he means that as a good thing or a bad thing. Maybe both. I study his side-profile for a long minute, taking in his mussed dark hair and the sharp cuts of his face, the warmth of his tanned skin and the fan of his eyelashes. What's going on inside that head? Sometimes the man feels like an impenetrable fortress.

"Tell me about Sybil," I blurt out. His ex-girlfriend is probably the worst thing I could ask about but I'm dying to know their history. It's not my business, but I'm also suspecting it's the reason why Ethan hasn't kissed me yet. If I can help him get past whatever lingers there, the two of us can move on together.

He freezes and then turns to me. "There's not much to tell. She's my ex. We were together and then we broke up."

Cooper said they grew up together, dated for years, and got engaged. She sounds like more than an ordinary ex to me. "Are you over her?"

He studies my face, his gaze unreadable. "I've thought about her a lot this summer."

That stings and I look away. He's just using me. That's why his father hired me in the first place.

He steps close, taking my chin and turning it up to face him. "You didn't let me finish."

"So finish."

"I've been thinking about her in the past tense. And now I'm thinking about someone else. Someone I haven't been able to get out of my thoughts."

That depressing pang in my chest transforms into bright hope. Maybe stupid, foolish, immature, idiotic hope. But hope all the same.

"Me?" I question.

He smirks. "Yes, you."

Our gazes are locked, but when his eyes flicker to my mouth, I have to ask. "Then why haven't you kissed me yet?

And don't you dare mention the pecks in the pantry while I was sleeping because those don't count."

He swallows hard. "I don't kiss until it means something."

"So this means nothing?"

"No, it means a lot. It's why I'm being so cautious."

I shake my head. "I don't want your caution."

His smile quirks and he's so beautiful in this moment that I want to learn how to paint just so I can paint him exactly as he is right now. I'm seeing him stripped away from everything else, seeing who he is and who he could be to me.

"Arden, do you want me to kiss you?"

I nod.

Can't he tell that I've wanted to kiss him since the moment I met him? Even despite his asshole-behavior, despite his cruel words, despite his ex-girlfriend, despite the flirtation with his brother, with his friend . . . despite all of that, he's the one that my heart wants.

And now is the perfect moment to do it.

But he doesn't.

He just stays like this, looking at me, hand on my chin, suspended in time.

"What's the big deal with kissing?" I ask.

"Kissing is more intimate than sex."

"That can't be true."

"For me, it is."

"Bullshit. I've seen you kiss girls since I've been here." That first night he was making out with someone on the beach, and again on the Fourth of July.

He softens. "There's a difference between a random make out and a kiss with someone you care about."

"And you care about me?" Because several times throughout the summer, I'd say that's been quite debatable.

This time, he's the one to nod.

"Which is why you don't want to kiss me? Because it's too vulnerable?"

"I said it was vulnerable. I never said I didn't want to do it." Now he's staring at my lips. "I've been wanting to kiss you since the Fourth of July."

I have to roll my eyes. "Is that why you made out with that woman?"

"Wasn't worth it. I should've kissed you instead. The second Perry asked you out, I knew nobody else could touch you but me."

Still holding onto my chin with one hand, his other reaches up to drag a thumb across my lower lip, pressing against the tender flesh. My mouth pops open in surprise and he slides it in erratically. "There's a lot of things I've been wanting to do to this mouth since that night, actually."

I swirl my tongue around his thumb in approval. "Fuck," he groans, and then all too fast, his thumb is gone and we're crashing together, our lips claiming, bruising, wanting, agreeing.

There is nothing tender or sweet about this kiss. It's pure passion. His lips work against mine in a push and pull, as if we're fighting for dominance. But he's winning. Of course, he's winning. Because I want him so badly that I can hardly think. I'm all emotions and nerve endings and *this kiss*.

I open my mouth to him and he darts his tongue inside, our kiss going from zero to one hundred. He grabs my ass and I jump up, wrapping my legs around him. I'm still wearing nothing under my dress. We're separated by measly strips of fabric. His hard pushes against my soft, the perfect combination. Maybe he'll want to do it right here. I can't imagine saying no, not even being out in the open like this. I just want this. I want to take anything he'll give me.

I grind against his erection and he hisses his approval. But he's not going to strip me here, apparently, because he begins walking us up the path. We're making out and he's carrying me but that doesn't seem to get in the way of him taking us back to the house.

Good. I don't want to stop kissing him.

The house is still boarded up except for the side and front doors, and the side is closest. We're in the little hallway that connects to the kitchen and dining room. I don't think we'll make it much further than this.

My hands are everywhere. Under his shirt. On his backside. In his hair.

But my mouth is still firmly on his, enjoying every single caress of those lips and sweep of that tongue, knowing that this is his way of being vulnerable, that kissing isn't something he takes lightly, and that he wants this just as much as I do.

But I have power here too.

And when my fingers slip past his abs and down into his shorts, that power is made evident by the hard erection waiting for me. I grab it and stroke, and he answers by breaking our kiss to catch a breath. His face burns with desire, all because of me.

"Take off your shirt," I demand.

"You like being in control?" He chuckles, stepping back.

He doesn't take off his shirt.

"Maybe I do." I haven't had a lot of control in my life, so I'm not all that surprised that I want to control this.

"Well, so do I," he says. "And tonight, I'm in charge."

His blue eyes are molten with lust, and I know that if I wanted to, if I really wanted to boss him around, I could. It leaves me feeling confident enough to agree to his terms. I want to surrender to him as much as he wants to dominate me.

"Okay." I nod once. "Show me how to make you feel good, Ethan."

He licks his lips and runs his eyes up and down my body. "Take off your dress."

I'm completely naked underneath. He knows that. And he also knows how much I want this. That I agreed to his demands.

So I slip my hands down to the hem of the dress and slowly pull it over my head, tossing it away. Standing naked before him is terrifying and I immediately cover myself with my hands.

"Are you embarrassed?" He sounds angry. "Because if you're shy, that's understandable, but if you're embarrassed, we can't have that."

I shrug. "Maybe. I don't know."

That's a lie. I do know. I'm not being self-deprecating because I know what I look like. Yes, I'm a pretty girl, but I'm not a natural born model and I haven't had plastic surgery. The women he's used to are the kind who fit into one of the categories, if not both. They're worldly and seductive and experienced. I'm just me.

"Don't be," he says sharply. "You're perfect."

My mouth opens with a pop. Nobody has called me perfect before.

"Don't you try to deny it. You're a fucking goddess. You're my Juliet. Don't put yourself down in front of me ever again."

I just blink at him.

"Now let me see you."

I drop my hands to my sides and stick out my chest just a little bit, trying to work with what I've got. I have no shame.

"So fucking beautiful," he says. I expect him to jump on me, or at least touch me, but he does neither. "Go upstairs to my bedroom."

"By myself?"

"Obviously not. I'm going to follow and stare at your naked

ass the whole way." And then he slips a hand down his pants and begins to pleasure himself. "Go," he demands.

I turn and he slaps my ass. *What the fuck!?* I yelp and practically run up the stairs. I can feel my behind bouncing and try not to think too hard about it, Ethan chasing after me with a satisfied laugh. When I make it into his room, he closes the door and stalks me like a wild animal, tossing me onto the bed and crawling up between my thighs. His eyes are everywhere, roaming over my naked flesh like he can't get enough.

"It's my turn to see you," I protest, reaching for his shorts.

He pushes my hand away. "So impatient. Who's in charge here again?"

I bite my lip. "You are."

"Good girl." He's straddling me, his erection threatening to spring from his shorts as he presses it against my bare sex. His mouth is on mine again but only for a moment. He kisses my mouth, my cheek, suckling down my neck, lips sweeping further until he's kissing my nipple. He sucks it into his mouth and teases it with his teeth, swirling his tongue around the tip. It's a painful kind of pleasure, sending a direct line of want straight to my core that I can't satisfy on my own. I buck into him and he chuckles like he's got all the time in the world.

He takes time with each breast and then travels lower, kissing my stomach and then nudging my thighs wider as he angles further south. But I don't want him to kiss me there again. As amazing as it felt, I want more than his tongue this time. I want to reach climax with my legs wrapped around his waist and his cock buried deep.

He must sense it because he tells me to stop being impatient.

"But I can't wait," I argue.

"You can and you will. Women can have multiple orgasms. You know that, right?"

I mean, technically I know that *some* women can, but I can't imagine how that's going to be possible for me. The one he gave me this morning was so big I could hardly move afterward, let alone be touched. I can't imagine doing that again and then having him penetrate me right after.

"I'm in charge, aren't I?"

I nod, my head sinking into the pillow.

"You're wet but I want you soaking for what I'm going to do to you."

My eyes widen, the possibilities catapulting through my mind.

"You ready?"

I nod again and he sinks his mouth to my clit, quick to ravage my sensitive flesh with expert skill. I come even faster than I did this morning, the orgasm taking me to completion within seconds. I cry out, fisting the sheets and bucking against his generous mouth. And when I come back down, I'm panting.

He stands, looking me over with heated eyes. I feel liquefied. My legs are splayed wide and my entire body is bared to him as the pleasure settles over my bones. It's a sweet caress that I could stay in forever. But then he does what I've been waiting for—he starts to remove his clothes—and I'm no longer so relaxed.

His cock springs from his shorts, hard and long. I'm both terrified and excited by his size, and he takes in my reaction with a grin not even the devil himself could rival.

"Don't worry. I'll make sure you feel good, baby."

As nervous as I am, I don't doubt him for a single second. If I'm his Juliet, he's my Romeo, and we're destined to do this. I just hope we're not destined for all the bad things that come next in that tragedy.

THIRTY

He crawls towards me and the anticipation is almost too much. His lips find mine again as he settles his cock against my entrance. He's still grinning like an idiot, like he's won the prize, but really, I think I'm the one who's won because *oh my hell* is he gorgeous and generous. I'm going to hurt at first, but I believe him. He will make sure it's good for me.

"Now," I whisper, husky.

"Almost."

He reaches to his nightstand and retrieves a condom, rips it open and quickly rolls it on. I almost forgot about protection, probably would've had sex without it because I'm so into this moment. It's a good thing he's being responsible because I'm not being responsible at all. I'm the opposite. I'm reckless. Lost. Needy.

And I'm also fearless. "Please," I beg. "Make love to me, Ethan."

His eyes search mine and he runs a finger between us that

makes me groan. "I don't make love, little Juliet. Not like what you're thinking."

I don't even care that his response was a shitty one, I just want to do this. My legs widen and I press against him. He removes his hand and now it's his dick that's sliding up and down, teasing my clit. I find I don't mind the condom at all, it still feels amazing. Everything he does feels it could make me come if he just kept doing it.

"I'll go slow at first," he whispers. "I won't want to keep it gentle, but I will for you. I'll do whatever you need, just talk to me, okay?"

"Okay," I breathe. My heart rate is starting to pick up. I hate that I'm nervous.

"Are you sure this is what you want?"

Is he kidding me? As nervous as I am, I don't care if it hurts, I just care that it happens. I can't go back to the girl I was before this moment. "Yes." I hitch my hips up again, feeling him ready for me.

He kisses me once, long and hard and slow, and then he slides his cock in, inch by wicked lovely inch. It's too tight and it burns, but I can't think about that now. All I can think about is getting closer to him.

I buck against him and something within me snaps, his hardness passing through an inner wall. The pain is instant and I yelp, but he cusses low and guttural, his eyes fluttering like he can't contain himself. And then begins to move within me. Tears burn at the edges of my vision.

It hurts.

I didn't realize it would hurt this much.

He kisses my tears away and continues to rock within me. He's being gentle but I can tell it's hard for him to hold back.

"You okay, Arden?"

I nod, squeezing tightly around him in surrender and he

closes his eyes, lost in the feel of us. I can't say I blame him. My control is slipping too. It's not hurting so much anymore despite the growing intensity. I've never been filled like this, so wholly claimed, so willing to give and receive.

My body naturally flexes around his cock and I lift my legs up to wrap around his lower back. He shifts us lower on the bed until there's no pillow under my head anymore and I tilt my ass up even more to bring him in deeper. The angle is a whole new level of torture but in the best way, the pain lost to the pleasure of him wedged so deep.

"Fuck," he's saying over and over again. "I'm not going to last as long as I thought."

Something about that makes me feel better, like I'm far more in control than he wants to give me credit for, and I buck up against him even harder.

He freezes, holding himself completely still, his muscles flexed. "You're so perfect," he says, staring down at me like I'm the goddess he called me earlier. "Do you have any idea what you're doing to me? Fuck, I've never lost control this fast before."

So there's the truth of it. He says he's in control, but he's not. At least not now that he's inside me. I'm in control now.

I smile, enjoying his words but enjoying his body even more. I can feel his pelvic bone pressing into mine and it's almost as intimate as the sex itself. I take pleasure in the way our bodies are covered in sweat and pressing together, his sun-kissed tan contrasting with my creamy paleness. Everything about this moment is more than I ever dreamed it could be. The pain is gone. It's been replaced with needy desire, with him and us and every tiny delicious movement we make. Each thrust elicits another breathy moan. Each kiss another gasp.

"You doing okay, baby? Does it hurt?"

"Not anymore."

Smirking, he hitches my leg over his shoulder and pushes in even deeper. "How about this?"

"It feels so good," I gasp and we're groaning together, moving together, pumping into each other with so much recklessness that even though it's cliche, I can truly no longer tell where he ends and I begin. Our connection has become bone deep.

And then he's moving faster, harder, slamming into me, the sounds of our pleasure sinfully erotic. I can't hold it in, I'm crying for him to keep going, repeating his name over like a mantra. The most exquisite release is building up within me, threatening to crumble all my defenses, to transform me into a new woman.

His mouth opens to mine, our tongues lazy as our bodies grow more frantic. And then it becomes too much. And it becomes everything. The pleasure spreads over my entire body, radiating from my core. The orgasm takes me away. And he's still rocking into me through the entire process, greedy for more.

And then he goes still and his face takes on a new form. Open. Disbelieving. And completely satisfied. Forget kissing. This is Ethan at his most vulnerable. His eyes flare and his mouth pops open.

He's beautiful.

And all too quickly the rush is over, but the pleasure lingers over us like our tender kisses. I don't want to lose him, and when he pulls away, I feel empty inside in more ways than one. But my heart doesn't, my heart feels full.

He says he doesn't make love, that he just has sex, and that may be true for him, but I realize something in that moment—it's not true for me. Because what I just did? That was all heart. That was making love. That was more than just bodies coming together for sex. It was souls exchanging energy, one binding itself to the other. I'm his now. I'm his and I can't even pretend otherwise.

He's right. We spend the next twenty-four hours repeating what we did. Again in the bed, on the deck, against the wall, the floor, and twice in the shower. I can't get enough of him, and I don't even care that I'm stretched sore and can barely walk. This is the best sex of my life.

It's also the only sex I've had, but I can't imagine how anything could possibly top it.

Yup, I'm most definitely ruined for any other man.

I keep expecting things to get weird between us, waiting for awkward silences or for Ethan to walk away again or say something that taints this bliss bubble, but it never happens. We grow comfortable together when we're not having sex, and even more hot together when we do, getting to know each other's bodies in new ways with each experience.

But our time here is running out. Our bubble is going to pop and we both know it, even if neither of us is willing to acknowledge it. Real life is coming and we can't keep this going. I'm moving to Boston, starting my adult life and focusing on my education, and he's going back to Manhattan to pick up where he left off. Our worlds will once again have nothing to do with each other.

But I want more, fantasizing about what it would be like to actually date him, to be his girlfriend, to fall in love . . .

It's foolish thinking.

Naive musings.

Most girls probably feel this way about their first sexual partner. It's normal.

So I don't dare ask him about what comes after we leave

Nantucket, nor do I give it much thought. I already know I'm going to end up hurt. My heart is already on the line. It will be better to pretend I don't care about him emotionally, to just enjoy the sex while I can and move on with my life when I have to.

"I want to try something," I say, crawling down the bed and hooking my fingers in his boxers. I can't believe what I'm about to ask and I can already feel the embarrassment washing through me.

His eyes flash to mine. "And what is that?"

I chew my lip while rubbing at his newly exposed skin. My cheeks are already burning at the question I'm about to ask. "Can I give you a blow job?"

I've never done it before, and definitely never thought I'd want to, but right now it's the only thing on my mind. He's gone down on me on more than one occasion. Now it's my turn to reciprocate.

"Did you just ask me if you can give me a blow job?" He laughs, sitting up on his elbows, abs flexing in the most perfect way. "What kind of a question is that?"

My cheeks redden and I lean back, dropping my hands. "Umm, I don't know, I just wanted to try it, but I wanted your consent first."

His eyebrow raises and he laughs again. "Let it be known, you will always have my consent to suck me off."

I choke on my giggle. "I'm being serious."

He stares at me, his voice going hoarse in that way that it only does when he's turned on. Already I can see his cock growing under his boxers. "Alright then, but I'm going to teach you how to do it right."

He likes this dynamic and I have to admit I do as well. If I'm going to learn these things, I'm glad it's with someone I'm so attracted to. I wish there was love between us too, but that's scary and having sex for the first time has been scary enough.

God, he's so pretty. He's gazing at me with those lovely ocean eyes and his dark hair is a tousled mess from all the sex. His skin is flawless and his muscles go on for days. Everything about his body could be plucked straight from my wildest fantasies. But his wicked mouth? The sexy things that come out of it? The way he commands me during sex while also making me feel like I'm a goddess in my own right? It's the hottest thing about him.

"Yes, sir," I say and he grins.

"Get on your knees." He points to the edge of the bed and I do as he wishes. He stands in between me and the bed, already hard. I'm in my bra and underwear and nothing else, and his eyes roam over my body as he palms his thick shaft. "On second thought, take off your bra."

"And my underwear?" I bat my eyelashes, already slipping off the bra, my breasts feeling heavier than they used to. I haven't gained weight this summer but sex has a way of making them ache. I'm more aware of them than I've ever been.

"You can keep those on for now." He runs his tongue along his teeth, roping me in with his gaze. "Now cup my balls with one hand, my dick with the other, and suck me into your mouth, using your tongue more than your teeth."

He's talking me through this and honestly, I'm grateful. The details make me blush but also cause liquid heat to pool in my underwear, my body already aching for more. But this isn't about my release—it's about his. His eyes go from clear to hazy when I take hold of him and it urges me on. I pump his cock once and then slip the dark swollen tip into my mouth, swirling my tongue around the head. I run my other hand along his sack and he releases a slow hiss.

"That's it." He fists my hair and urges my mouth down to take him deeper. I taste his warm flesh and the slick precum, finding I don't mind it. I actually love how in control I'm becoming. I've literally got the man by the balls and I'm giving him exactly what he wants, coaxing pleasure from him in a way I haven't done yet.

"Suck," he demands on a rasp, and I do, taking him even deeper into my mouth. He's so large but I hollow out my cheeks and relax my tongue, letting it dance softly against the underside of his cock. And then I squeeze a little tighter with my other hand.

"Fuck!" He growls, and begins thrusting his hips.

Tears sting my eyes and he's moving faster, fucking my mouth.

"Touch yourself," he demands, so I drop a hand to my underwear and slide it inside, pressing the spot that sends my toes curling. It's not like I've never touched myself before, but doing it right now feels so much better than any time before. Ethan has fast become my sexual awakening and I arch my back and take him deeper, opening my throat for him.

"Fuck," he's cussing again. "Arden."

He's losing control and my gag reflex is resisting. I'm trying not to choke, but I refuse to pull away either. I don't want to stop him. Whatever he wants, I've surrendered to it.

"I don't need to teach you a damn thing," he says through a wry grin. "You're a natural."

I mean . . . turns out giving head is not that hard, but okay, I'll take the compliment. I smile, a little laugh coming up my throat, and he fists my scalp harder.

He's normally a quiet man.

But not during sex, and give the man a blow job and he becomes a talker, telling me how good I am, how good it feels, how much he likes it, likes me.

"I'm going to come soon," he hisses, and a little pang of fear urges me to pull back but I don't. He's going to come down my throat and I'm going to let him, even though the thought of it isn't as sexy as I imagined it would be when I first got down on my knees. He says I'm a natural, but I'm really not. This is all so new for me.

I suck harder, swirl my tongue, and relax even more. I have to prove to myself that I can do this. I want to do this. And at the same time, I'm pumping my fingers against myself and coaxing out my own orgasm. It makes the whole experience so much easier and just as I'm about to explode, he's pulling his cock from my mouth and releasing himself on my chest.

His eyes are glassy and his expression is almost stunned as he stares at my exposed breasts. They're heavy and my nipples are hard, everything covered in his seed.

Is this hot or gross? I'm not sure yet.

"Fucking mine," he whispers to himself, his voice like gravel.

Oh yeah, it's hot.

He picks me up, tossing me onto the bed, and tearing my scrap of panties from my jelly-like legs in one delft move. He wastes no time hitching my legs over his shoulders and sinking his mouth into my slick flesh. I arch into him, calling his name as my release washes over me in frenzied waves.

He's right. I am his.

I'm his and as terrifying as that is, I've never been happier.

Thirty-One

That morning he wakes me before sunrise with a long slow kiss. My body is instantly ready for him but then I open my eyes. He's standing over me and is fully dressed, not at all where I need him. I reach my arms around his neck to tug him into bed, but he doesn't budge. "Wake up, Juliet. I want to show you something. You need to get dressed."

"But it's still dark out," I whine.

"Trust me."

I'm tired but he grins like a little kid which perks me awake. Rolling from bed, I quickly get dressed and find him outside in the driveway, standing next to his Range Rover with two coffees in hand. I take a sip of mine and grin. It's an iced caramel latte.

"You made mine exactly how I made it for myself all summer. I didn't realize you were paying attention." Hell, most of the time he wasn't even awake that early.

He shrugs like it's no big deal, then opens the passenger door for me to slide in and goes around to the driver's side.

"Do you want to pick the music?" he asks, pulling out of the driveway.

"No music," I murmur. "Just coffee." I've lost a lot of sleep thanks to all the sex, not that I'm complaining.

Twenty minutes later and we're leaving the main roads for an offshoot. "Hopefully this road has been cleared but I brought the chainsaw just in case," he remarks, peering through the waning darkness.

We're in the middle of the island, nowhere near the beaches or the commercial areas, and I'll admit I'm intrigued. The narrow road goes from paved to dirt and turns bumpy. Tall trees are lining both sides and what was a residential area gives way to a thick forest. By the time we pull into a small parking area, the sun has turned the sky deep blue and will be cresting the horizon any minute. We climb out of the Range Rover and Ethan is quick to retrieve a large duffle from the back.

"Inflatable paddle board," he says and gets to work laying and pumping it up, the hunk of plastic going from limp to fully-inflated in a matter of minutes. His arms flex with each thrust of the pump, his desire to beat the rising sun offering a generous view.

The paddle board is as long as the vehicle and about three feet wide, but paddle boarding is not something I've ever tried before. I'm usually up for adventure but when it comes to water, that's not the case.

"That will hold both of us?" I ask, eyeing the board skeptically.

"This has a five-hundred-pound max capacity. We'll be fine."

Still . . . I eye the lake wearily.

"We're not getting in the water," he assures me, catching on to my fears. "We're just going to float on top. Promise, I won't let you fall in."

He lifts the paddle board easily and drops it into the water's edge, then reaches out for me to get on first. "You can stand or sit, it's stable either way."

Considering I haven't fully woken up enough yet to even think about standing on that thing, I opt to sit criss-crossed in the front and he sits on the back, his legs straddling the board. He presses the paddle into the shore, pushing us off.

He's right, I don't get wet.

The lake is smooth as glass and there's nobody else out here except for the birds singing their wakeup songs and a smattering of ducks floating in the distance. The cool air is refreshing and the sunrise drapes the world in soft shades of pink.

"I had no idea this was here," I sigh and close my eyes, breathing it in.

"There are a few ponds on the island," Ethan replies, "but this one is my favorite."

"I can see why."

The pond is closer to a lake in size, large enough for our paddle board to laze around it but too small to allow motor boats.

"There are usually people here. I've never seen it empty before."

I'm sure that's because of the hurricane, and I know it's selfish, but I'm glad it's just us this morning. We're no longer in the bubble of the Kings' estate but we still get to enjoy our own little world together.

There's a splash twenty feet away where a crane appears, outstretched wings flattening as it settles on the water. It's probably searching for its breakfast. We watch quietly as the world wakes up and the sun rises in the sky, turning the pink to orange and yellow until finally the sunrise finishes and the day begins.

We continue to float for a good hour, talking about anything and everything. Eventually our backs have had enough of sitting on the board and Ethan paddles us to shore. He helps me off by willingly getting his own shoes wet so that mine don't. It's the kind of gesture I'm not used to, someone sacrificing their comfort for mine. The second we're both standing on solid ground, I sling my arms around his shoulders and rise up to claim his lips.

He tastes faintly of coffee and I press myself into him, desperate to capture this moment. He didn't have to bring me here. We could've stayed at the house all day and I would've been fine with that. We could've watched the sunrise from the beach. But he got up early to bring me to one of his favorite spots and that means something. I don't know what it means, but in my gut, I believe it's significant. This thing between us is more than physical. We're becoming friends, which is almost unbelievable, but it's the truth.

I want him to be my friend.

And I want him to be more than my friend.

He breaks the kiss, leaning his forehead against mine. "Are you hungry?"

"Starving." It's true, my stomach started knocking a good hour ago, but I didn't want to answer and break the spell we were under.

"I packed us breakfast." He takes my hand, intertwining our fingers, and leads me back to the car. He parked so the back is facing the lake and he pops the hatch, creating space for us. "It's nothing fancy."

Inside is a blanket that he lays over the edge and we climb inside, my feet dangling and his firmly planted on the ground. He unzips a cooler bag and pulls out two burritos wrapped in tinfoil. I can already smell the melted cheese.

"You woke up early and made us breakfast burritos?" I can hardly believe it. This is not the Ethan that he presented to me all summer. That Ethan wouldn't be caught dead doing something sweet for me. This Ethan? This Ethan shrugs like it's no big deal.

"They're my favorite breakfast and they're easy to make. I also cut up that cantaloupe we picked up from the store and grabbed us some water bottles too."

I go for the water first and then he hands me the warm burrito and I unwrap it in disbelief. This is the kind of thing a boyfriend would do for his girlfriend, not the kind of thing someone does for a hookup. Does Ethan actually like me for more than my body? Is there something deeper going on here than sex?

I almost ask him about it. Almost. But I don't want to break the spell. That, and I don't have the courage to be disappointed. Because what if he laughs at me? What if this is nothing? What if he just wanted to come to the pond and would've brought anyone along and I just happened to be the one available?

We eat in silence, and I keep stealing glances at him. His eyes are fixed on the lake, watching the cranes that have joined the ducks. His face is relaxed. He's so calm, so at peace. This isn't an Ethan I'm familiar with, but I'll admit I like it. Maybe this is the real Ethan, the guy he is underneath all the expectations of his father. Remove the demanding wealthy lifestyle with the demanding strings attached and he's a normal guy.

I snort to myself. Ethan is anything but a normal guy.

"What's so funny?" He raises an eyebrow.

I feel myself blushing and shake my head. "Nothing."

"Tell me," he presses. Of course he does, he's still Ethan.

"I was just thinking about you being a normal guy doing normal guy stuff."

"And that's funny to you?"

I give him a pointed look. "Ethan, you are a lot of things and normal isn't one of them. That's not a bad thing, by the way."

"I could say the same about you."

My cheeks flush. He takes my trash and throws it back into the cooler bag, then stands and comes in front of me, resting between my legs. I expect him to kiss me, to turn this moment sexual because that's what has become standard between us, but he doesn't. He just wraps me in a hug and I find myself leaning into him, my arms tight around his broad back, my thighs resting on either side of his hips. He smells like soap and lake water and his signature spicy cologne. A ripple of comfort stirs something deep within me. Longing. Hope. And fear. He holds me for a long moment, so long that the sound of my rising heartbeat must be louder than the birds.

Then he kisses the top of my head. "Come on, let's get back."

We go home and spend the rest of the day hanging out and talking until eventually I can't take it anymore. Emotionally I'm sated, mentally I'm afraid of what this will lead to, but physically I'm yearning for him again. He's awoken a new side of me these last few days. I don't just want him, I need him.

We finish dinner and while we're cleaning up, he asks what movie I want to watch tonight, saying we should use the theater room for once. I've never used it, and I should want to, but I don't.

I shake my head, take his hand, and lead him up to his bedroom. He doesn't say another word, just closes the door and lays me down, kissing me tenderly, our mouths and bodies and maybe even our souls opening to each other. The first time we had sex I felt that bone-deep connection with him, but this time I feel a soul-deep connection.

This time, it's not just two people having sex, it's two people making love.

I didn't think it could be possible, but it's better than every other time before. It's true intimacy. And it's terrifying. And wonderful. And it makes me fall asleep with a smile on my face for possibly the first time in my life.

Thirty-Two

"I can get us off the island this afternoon," he declares the next morning. He says it evenly and without emotion. We're laying in his bed and I roll over to scrutinize his profile, trying to ignore my sudden shock of disappointment. It's August 23rd, which makes it two days earlier than needed.

"You'll take me to Boston?" I say evenly.

He nods. "The airport has been cleared for flights. I've chartered one. I'll drop you off in Boston before returning to Manhattan."

It's silly to want more than a drop off in Boston . . . but I do. I roll onto my back and stare at the ceiling, same as he's currently doing. "That sounds good," I lie.

I'll be a couple days early for the dorm move in but a few nights in Boston won't be so bad. I'll figure something out.

"I already booked you a hotel across from campus for tonight and tomorrow night and a car to take you there from the airport."

My chest clenches and I roll over to face him. He's still looking up, still in profile, and I rub my hand across his abdomen, my fingers splaying out on his sleepy-warm skin. "Thank you," I say softly, wondering what it all means, because he took the time to make sure I have what I need, even if it is two days earlier than I'd expected.

Don't read too much into it.

It probably doesn't mean anything other than he's keeping his word. He agreed to get me to school if I stayed through the hurricane with him, and now he's holding up his end of the bargain. Simple as that. It has nothing to do with any actual romantic feelings. I may be his, but he's not mine.

He's not mine . . .

But what if he could be?

"You know," I say slowly, summoning all my courage to ask what I need to ask right now. "We could stay here for a few more nights. We don't have to leave yet."

He sighs and sits up, my hand slipping from his chest. His bare back flexes with tense unspoken emotion and dread sinks in my chest. He stands and heads into the bathroom. "Sorry but I've got to get back," is all he says, before he locks himself inside.

The subsequent hiss of the shower turning on makes me feel about two inches tall. He's taking it without me. It's the first shower he's taken alone since we started hooking up.

Is he done with me?

I fist the sheets, angry with myself for caring so much. I knew what this was. He told me he doesn't make love. Hell, the man didn't even want to kiss me at first. I knew . . . but I still let myself believe it could be something more.

They don't call it being a hopeless romantic for nothing.

Maybe it's my age? Eighteen feels so old but I know it's not. When I came here, I thought I had seen enough of people's character to understand them but I've clearly not seen enough of people like Ethan King. I never should've opened my heart.

Does sex always do that? Does it make you feel things you

don't want to feel? If I have sex with people in college, will I fall for them too, or is Ethan special?

I can't help but think he's special. He's different. I wanted him from the very first moment I saw him swimming laps in the pool. The wanting grew with every interaction we had, even though I told myself it wasn't true, lied to myself about hating him. But there's a fine line between love and hate, and with Ethan that line became invisible.

Tears stain the edges of my vision. Stupid, stupid tears. I should go to my guest room to get myself packed and ready. I should wash the tears away. But I don't.

Something else comes over me. Something angry.

I go to his drawers instead, rifling through his things as quickly as I can, ignoring the instant guilt at invading his privacy. He may not be able to give me what I want—he'll never love me—but maybe he can give me what I need.

Answers.

He doesn't have a lot of personal items here and it's quickly apparent that I might not find anything. This is only his summer bedroom, not where he really lives. Just like I'm only his hurricane girl. There are so many things about Ethan that I don't know. He could have a new girlfriend back in the city. He could just be using me. Facts are, I don't even know where he lives. Probably in some expensive New York City apartment somewhere, the kind of bachelor pad that is as masculine and cold as he is. I bet it has a penthouse view of everyone else below him. And I bet he brings women back there so he can fuck them instead of making love to them.

I rub at my tear-stained cheeks and dig through the bottom drawer of his nightstand, past the box of condoms, the random charger cables, until something familiar brushes against my fingers. A photograph. It's tucked into the back corner of the drawer, almost like he doesn't want anyone to know it's there.

Guilt nearly stops me. Guilt and shame.

Guilt because I know better than to snoop like this. It's an invasion, it's immature, and I shouldn't do it. And shame because I shouldn't care so much about someone who doesn't feel the same way about me.

But I can't possibly let go of my curiosity now, not now that I have this hidden photograph at my fingertips. I pull it out, almost expecting something ordinary like a photo of his friends or maybe him and his brother, maybe even his real mother that I don't know anything about because he won't talk about her.

But no . . .

The couple in the photograph is stunning. A younger Ethan with his lips pressed to the cheek of a beautiful girl. She's beaming at the camera. It's not the way they're dressed that is most startling, it's not that her body is amazing, or that their embrace is clearly one of love.

It's the way she looks.

She's got long wavy red hair.

Big green eyes.

Pale skin with a smattering of freckles across her nose.

She looks so much like me.

And it's the names *Sybil + Ethan* written in a feminine cursive scrawl across the bottom.

This is a photograph that Sybil gave to Ethan, one that he kept even though they broke up. One that he kept in his nightstand and brought with him on his summer vacation. He clearly hasn't forgotten her. He's not over her.

It all makes total and horrifying sense. *This* is why Conrad King hired me, why Malory warned me to stay away from the brothers, why Camilla said Ethan would especially be trouble if I pushed his buttons, and why those girls on the Fourth of July were talking about me and Sybil as if we had something to do with each other. "I don't see it" one had said and the other had argued that it was obvious.

And it is obvious.

I look so much like Ethan's ex that I could be mistaken for her little sister. Except for the height and the eye color, she's practically my doppelgänger. And he used me for it.

The shower turns off. I throw the photograph to the back of the nightstand as if the thing burned me, close the drawer, and dart from the bedroom.

It's not until I'm in my own room with the door locked and my own shower running that I allow myself to cry. I lean against the tiled wall and let the sobs rock through me.

He took my virginity.

He claimed me as his own.

But it was never me that he wanted, it was his ex. She was the one who broke his heart, the one who got away, the one that his father wanted to help make him feel better about. And what better way than to provide a second-best lookalike for him to fuck. He probably just wanted me to get her out of his system. When he was inside me, did he imagine he was inside her? When we kissed, was it her lips he tasted?

Because I can't deny the truth—*she's* his Juliet.

My stomach roils and I vomit what little I have in my hollow stomach right there into the shower drain.

It's disgusting but it's nothing to how disgusting I feel inside right now.

And livid.

And stupid.

And . . . and . . . and . . .

There's nothing I can do about it.

It's over. By this afternoon I'll be in Boston and I never have to see Ethan King ever again. This is partly my fault. I knew he wasn't emotionally available and yet I spread my legs for him anyway. How can someone that makes my body feel so damn good also make my heart feel this painfully broken?

Picking myself off the tile floor, I finish my shower and get ready for Boston, taking my sweet-ass time in the process.

Because I don't want to see him.

Ethan doesn't have to know that I know the truth now.

I don't want to fight. I don't want to confront him. And I don't want to give him the satisfaction of seeing me cry. As far as he's concerned, I'm just as unaffected by him as he is by me. This entire experience was transactional—nothing to do with the heart. And I'm ready to move on with my life.

Good riddance to the entire King family.

I head downstairs for lunch feeling like a new woman. I make one sandwich for myself and nothing for him. Not sorry. He can make his own damn sandwich.

He waltzes in from outside and eyes me curiously as I finish up my meal. I don't say a word. I just take my plate over to the sink and wash it.

"Are you okay? You're acting weird."

I turn on him with a fake megawatt smile. "I'm great, just a little nervous for my new life in Boston."

And that's not a lie.

"Is that all?" His eyes narrow.

"When do we leave for the airport?"

He's silent for a long moment. "A car is picking us up in an hour."

So that's it. We're almost done here.

I nod. "Can't wait."

He steps in, pressing me against the countertop. "An hour is enough time for sex."

His words make my skin crawl. This is exactly who he really is and I can't forget it. I want to push him off but instead I consider his proposal for a second. Do I want the last time I have sex with him to be last night when I thought I was falling in love? Or do I want it to be today when I know his true character? I'd like nothing more than to erase any stupid notions of love, so today it is. This way it ends on my terms.

I press my hips against his and slide my hands up his shirt. He leans in for a kiss but I move my lips to his neck instead. I'm not going to kiss his lips ever again. I don't care if he doesn't like it or if he thinks it's weird. More than likely, he won't even notice.

And I'm right. We fuck like animals, taking what we want right there on the kitchen countertop, no kissing necessary, and no love needed either.

Just how he likes it.

Thirty-Three

We take the chartered jet to Boston first and the whole time Ethan leans back in the leather seat like he's as comfortable up in the air as anywhere. I've never been on an airplane before so the experience terrifies me, but I won't let him see my fear. I've shut myself off to revealing anything right now. Anything at all.

Besides the pilots, it's just the two of us. His eyes are heavy and assessing. Maybe he just wants to induct me into the mile high club but I'm not interested. I'm done.

I already said goodbye to his body.

Soon I'll say goodbye to the rest of him.

So I look out the window instead, anticipating the life I'm about to start. A life that is no longer at the mercy of other people. A life where I can find my own family instead of having to hope someone will want me for theirs. A life where I get to choose what I spend my time on and who to spend it with. It's a short flight to Boston so it all starts soon.

When we land, he asks if I want him to drop me off at the hotel.

We're standing on the tarmac of the private part of the airport, the humidity wrapped around us like a wet blanket. Boston is already a lot hotter than Nantucket, a stark reminder that that chapter of my life has closed.

I study him for a long moment, imagining saying yes and seeing what happens from there. But I know better now. It was a hard lesson to learn but boy did he teach me.

"You need to get back to Manhattan," I remark.

He nods, his hands tucked into his pockets, his face hitched toward the cloudless sky. And then he pulls something from his pocket and hands it to me.

It's a business card.

His name, phone number, and email address are engraved underneath the King company logo and his job title.

It takes everything in me not to throw the business card in his face.

"Call me," he says, eyes hard on mine. "Or text. Email. Just . . . don't be a stranger."

I slip the card into my jean pocket and glare at him. "I thought this was goodbye?"

His lips thin. "For now."

I step back. "Not forever? You got what you wanted didn't you?"

The awkwardness is almost as thick as the humidity. "And what do you think I wanted?"

There are a lot of things I should say right now, but the one that I blurt out is perhaps the worst one of all. "To fuck your ex-girlfriend's lookalike and get her out of your system."

He freezes. "What are you talking about?"

"Don't try to deny it, Ethan. I saw the photo of Sybil hidden in your nightstand."

"You went through my stuff?" He says, incredulous.

When he says it like that, it sounds worse than it is. I think any woman in my situation probably would've snooped just a little. But that's not the point, the point is he led me to believe that he wanted me for me. And that was a bold-faced lie. "I did and it was wrong but I'm sure glad I did it anyway. You know all about wrong, don't you Ethan?"

"You're not Sybil."

I laugh. "You don't even know me," I argue. "Name one thing about me that has absolutely nothing to do with the fact that I clearly look like I could be mistaken for Sybil."

He doesn't say a word, proving my point.

I throw my hands up. "Whatever, I don't care, you were good in bed, but now it's over and we never have to see each other again."

"Is that what you want?" His voice is boiling over with anger. "I'll admit that when I first met you I hated you because of how you looked and who you reminded me of, but mostly I hated you because my father was meddling in my private life."

"Oh, is that all? Poor fucking baby."

"And," he goes on, stepping in close, "I hated you because I was attracted to you and so was my brother. You're too young for us, and yeah, you do look like my ex. And how sick was that? I wasn't with Sybil anymore, we were done, but I couldn't stop thinking about you and it was confusing. And it pissed me the hell off that Coop liked you too."

Again. Poor baby.

I roll my eyes and grab the handle of my suitcase, prepared to walk away from this, from him, forever.

"But that changed." His voice drops. "I like you for you. I never would've slept with you otherwise. Why do you think I took so long to come around to it?"

"Oh," I scoff. "So is that why you didn't want to kiss me at first? Is that why you won't call what we did making love? Or maybe it's why you chartered for us to get off the island two days before we actually needed to leave?" His face shutters down, all emotion hidden behind the same mask I've seen all summer. "You don't actually have feelings for *me*, you have feelings for Sybil. If you didn't, you wouldn't still keep her picture in your nightstand." My voice cracks on her name and my heart splits in two.

I hate this.

I hate this so much.

I just want to run and hide and be anywhere but here. But I also want to throw myself into his arms, to kiss him, to forgive him, to let him use me because he can't have her.

But I owe it to myself to be strong.

"It's okay," I add. "Really. I'm not in love with you. You're not in love with me. It was just sex. It was good, but now it's over."

He winces and steps back. Quiet for too long, the moment stretching like a ticking bomb. "Maybe you're right," he says coolly. "Maybe I never wanted you. Maybe I wanted her and couldn't admit it to myself."

His words are brutal, and so I do the only thing I can. I lie. I lie because I'm hurting, because I have to get back at him, because I want the last word. "And I never wanted you. I wanted Cooper. So I guess we both got second best."

His face flames and I can't bear to look at him for another second. That was uncalled for, but so is everything he did to me. I'm so heartbroken, so angry, that I can't stand to be in his presence.

"Goodbye, Ethan." I turn on my heels and strut away, heading into the private airport terminal.

"Goodbye, Juliet," he says to my back.

I almost flip around to tell him not to call me that but I don't. Let me call me whatever he wants, it doesn't matter. It's not real. I'm *not* his Juliet and he sure as fuck isn't my Romeo.

Inside the terminal there's a man with a sign that has my name on it, and maybe it makes me spineless, but I go to that man and let him take me to the hotel that Ethan paid for. I don't feel bad using the hired car or checking into the fancy hotel. Ethan owes me, because not only did he take my virginity, he took my heart.

He took it because I was stupidly willing to give it. And then he didn't just break it, he decimated it.

As soon as I reach my room, I eat the most expensive room service dinner I can manage and crawl into the fluffy bed, attempting to sleep. But I can't. Because I'm so angry. Because I can't stop crying. Because I can't believe what a fool I've been.

I had access to Ethan's bedroom for months. Why didn't I snoop earlier? I could've found the picture of Sybil and learned the truth before I gave myself over to him. I never would've gone to bed with Ethan if I'd known that the real reason I was there was because I bear a striking resemblance to the ex-girlfriend that he's been pining over.

No wonder he always seemed so emotionally shut off from me. He still had emotions, but he had them for someone else. I was nothing but a confusing stand-in.

I think back to the tragedy of Romeo and Juliet, realizing that I was never his Juliet. I was Rosaline. Romeo had thought he was in love with Juliet's cousin Rosaline, but that love was nothing compared to the love he had for Juliet. He was willing to do anything for Juliet and in the end that's what got them both killed.

It's best that I remove Ethan from my life entirely.

Too bad I can't seem to get him out of my head. I keep seeing the photograph of them together over and over again, keep picturing her handwriting across the bottom.

Cooper had said Ethan and Sybil grew up together, that

they had dated for years, that they were briefly engaged before the breakup. I should've known he wasn't done with her.

By the next morning I'm feeling good enough to go explore my new campus. I wander around aimlessly at first, but by the time I get to the library, the excitement finally reaches in and takes hold of my broken heart. It doesn't put it back together yet, but the prospect of my future is enough to hold the pieces together.

The University of Massachusetts is a good school and I'm going to make the most of it here. I can already picture myself studying in this library. It's the tallest building on campus and the inside is renovated to be comfortable for students to spend hours studying. I find the computer lab floor and it has so many machines lined up that I'm certain I'll never struggle to find an open seat. Tomorrow after I move into my dorm, I can get my student ID card and I'm coming right back here first thing.

I've been cut off from the world. It's been months without internet or even any real spending money. It's going to be amazing. I'm going to be able to focus on school and really make something of myself here.

After my campus tour, I plop down in a shady piece of grass and people watch for hours. There aren't a lot of students here yet, but come tomorrow this place is going to be packed with my new life and the people who might fill it.

Finally feeling better about everything, I head back to the hotel. I vaguely note the police cars out front and the two cops waiting in the lobby on my way inside. But when the desk clerk points at me, I startle, my entire body prickling with urgency. The police turn to me and I drop my head down. The tile is black and polished and cold. I wish it would swallow me up.

It's nothing that the police are here. Surely, it's nothing.

"Are you Arden Davis?" one of the officers asks.

I'm glued to the spot as I look up at the tall man, noting the holster with the gun and baton on the way up. "Yes." My voice shakes. I hate that I sound guilty. But what could I possibly have to feel guilty about?

"We'd like you to come with us," the second officer commands. This isn't an ask. There isn't a "please".

"Why?" My voice is wavering. I don't want to go anywhere with them.

"We have some questions for you. We can ask them here or at the station."

People are staring at me now. The hotel clerk has his nose lifted in clear annoyance, like how dare this be happening in the middle of his pristine lobby. He gives me a hard look, as if challenging me not to comply with the police so he can escort me from the premises himself.

"I don't understand," I mumble, but I do as I'm told and follow the police out the revolving glass doors and back into the hot August afternoon.

The second we're out of the lobby, the police drop any semblance of politeness.

"Arden Davis—you are under arrest for trespassing," he's saying more words after that, talking about my rights, about lawyers, and about what's next.

I'm sinking. Down. Down. My eyes are full of tears. This can't be happening. This can't be real. How is this real?

"Please make this easy on yourself," the second cop says in a pitying tone. "We don't have to cuff you. You're not going to jail. If convicted, it's a misdemeanor, not the end of the world. But we need you to get into the back of the car and come with us to the station."

I'm numb as I climb in. It's even hotter in here as the car has been sitting in the sun. The seats are hard plastic. They stick to my thighs. The cops climb into the car and talk about lunch as they drive me away from the hotel. How can they discuss food when my life is falling apart?

Did Ethan do this? He must have. He was the only one who knew I was squatting at the beach house. Either he called the cops himself or he told his father and Conrad took care of it. Either way, Ethan's the one to blame.

But so am I.

Because I did stay back in that house even though I knew I wasn't welcome. But Ethan made a deal with me, he was going to cover me. I held up my end and stayed through the hurricane. He got what he wanted, got *everything* he wanted. This can't be happening.

The business card.

I slide my hands into my shorts, frantically looking for his card, but it's not there.

Because I threw it away.

I never intended to speak with him again.

I need his help, but how much help is he really going to be if he was the one who made this happen? Maybe he's angry that I rejected him, that I called him out on his shit, that he can't treat me like a toy to be discarded. And like a spoiled brat, he's using his power and influence to get revenge.

The cop may be right that a misdemeanor won't send me to prison, but I could get into serious trouble. First Ethan King screwed me, and then he screwed me over. It's not just my heart that he decimated, but my entire fucking future.

Thirty-Four

I need a lawyer. A phone call to someone who can help me. But I don't have anything or anyone. I'm all on my own in this and have no idea what to do. That fact becomes increasingly obvious when I'm brought into the police station, marched into an interrogation room, and peppered with incriminating questions.

"So let me confirm." The police officer writes everything down while I sit across from him, trying not to cry or panic. "Malory King asked you to leave the house three weeks before you actually vacated the property?"

I nod and then I shake my head. "Did you write down the part about my ferry ticket being canceled? Or that Ethan King came and told me I could stay?"

The cop swallows a grimace and a quick nod. "I'll be right back. Make yourself comfortable." He leaves and I'm sitting in the integration room with my glass of water and wondering if his comment about comfort is some kind of sick joke. Just when I feel like I can't take another second alone with my thoughts, he returns, sitting across from me with a pitying expression. "I've spoken with the Kings, told them your side of the story, but they've decided to continue with the charges."

I should reply, should demand *something*, but the words die on my tongue.

"You are free to go but you will need to come to the court on . . ." The officer is talking about my rights and what to do next but I'm not hearing a thing. Everything is buzzing. Everything is too bright.

This can't be happening.

"If I'm convicted, will I go to jail?" I blurt out, fears of being locked up swirling through my mind.

The cop goes quiet for a moment and I make myself focus on what he says next.

"I'm not your lawyer so this isn't legal advice, but since this is your first offense that is unlikely. This is a misdemeanor charge. You need to treat it seriously, but it also doesn't have to ruin your life. If you do get booked, it probably won't be for longer than thirty days, but that all depends on the judge."

I nod because I don't know what else to say. It seems like he wants to add something more, but, with a long sigh, he stands and I follow him to the front of the police station.

"Take my advice and go hire yourself a good lawyer." He pats me on the back.

"I don't have money for a lawyer," I mumble.

He nods like he figured as much. "Kids like you rarely do."

"So what do I do?"

"You hope the court appointed attorney is decent or that the judge takes pity on you. Preferably both." He doesn't say this with a lot of confidence.

"Thanks." What I don't add is that the university will also have to take pity on me. Once they find out about this, there's a good chance I'm going to lose my scholarship. When I got in, I made sure to read the fine print. A criminal misdemeanor means I'm not eligible for scholarships anymore.

I step out the door and start down the sidewalk. A minute later he catches up. He looks both directions and then right into my eyes. His are older, wiser, like they've seen things nobody should have to see. "Take my advice and don't trust people like Conrad King. I see it in my line of work all the time. People like that don't care about people like you." He takes a step back. "Do you need a ride somewhere?"

"No, I'm good."

He nods and then he's gone.

I appreciate that he took the extra time to warn me, but I already know all too well that the King family can't be trusted. I should've taken Camilla's warning from day one and I certainly never should've stayed back at that house by myself.

It doesn't take long to walk back to the hotel because it's less than a mile from the station. I just need to get my stuff and get out of here. Too bad the very same front desk clerk from earlier motions me forward with his index finger like he's motioning a toddler to come forward for a stern talking-to.

He's going to throw me out of his hotel. I just know it. But at this point I don't even care. Tomorrow is finally move-in day. I'll sleep on the street tonight if I must. I'm just so over this whole thing. I'm tired of being scared. I'm tired of losing. I just have to take it day by day and hope I don't end up worse off than I already am.

"Ms. Davis, how are you? Well, I hope." he asks in a professional and kind tone. It throws me off—these are the last words I expected out of his mouth after today's display.

"I've been better." I draw the words out, not sure where this conversation is going.

He nods as if he gets it, as if people get arrested at his hotel every day and it's a necessary inconvenience. "There are some people here to see you."

My stomach drops. "Who?"

"If you'll please follow me." He leads me through the lobby and into the hotel's five-star restaurant. This is a white tablecloth, live classical music, waitstaff-in-tuxedos kind of place. The scent of fine cuisine wafts through the space and my stomach clenches both from not only being hungry but being completely underdressed.

He leads me to a table with a man and a woman I've never seen before. I quickly peg them for mid-fifties. They're both fair-skinned. The woman has gray-streaked auburn hair and the man has gray-streaked black. They both have an air of wealth about them that screams old money. I almost wouldn't recognize it if I hadn't just spent a summer surrounded by these kinds of people in Nantucket.

"I don't understand," I squeak out to the front desk attendant, but he ignores me and pulls out a chair.

"This is Arden Davis," he tells the couple. "Arden, please have a seat."

"I'm sorry, who are you?" I ask the couple.

The man smiles. "Sit down and we'll explain everything."

I hesitate.

"Don't worry," the woman adds, her voice kind and her green eyes watery. "We just want to buy you a meal and talk for a few minutes."

As if on cue, my stomach twists on itself and a server walks by with a plate of prime rib that looks so good I could cry.

I slide into the seat and the front desk clerk is replaced with a waiter. I have a zillion questions, but I don't get a chance to ask them because they're ordering and asking me what I'd like to eat. Finally we're alone again and they're looking at me like I have answers for them. How could I possibly have answers when I'm the one with so many questions?

"So, who are you?" I start.

The woman smiles again but this time she looks like she's about to burst into tears. My anxiety surges. She takes her companion's hand and he nods. "Arden, we didn't even know you existed until a few weeks ago."

I scoot back in my chair, prepared to flee. "What is this about?"

"I'm sorry, we're scaring you, I don't even know where to start—" She originally gave me the impression that she's not the type to mumble her words or confuse her thoughts but she's doing both.

Her husband intercepts. "Arden, we're Gregory and Amelia Laurence."

"Okay—" He declares it like it's supposed to mean something to me.

"We're your aunt and uncle."

My—what?

What do I say to something like that? I've been alone since I can remember. My mother was an addict who died when I was a toddler. My father is an unknown. I don't have memories before foster care. And now this couple shows up claiming they're my long-lost relatives? It's everything I used to dream of but now that it's actually happening, I don't believe it. I can't. Things like this don't happen to me. They happened to cute babies. The Little Princess. Anastasia. Little Orphan Annie.

Not to me.

"You must have me confused with someone else."

Gregory shakes his head. "I assure you we do not." And then he slides a crisp piece of paper across the table. "Take a look at the DNA results."

"Please don't be mad," Amelia adds quickly. "We had to be sure before we approached you."

My stomach sours. DNA results means they somehow had my DNA sample taken when I was unaware. My vision narrows and I want to run but I force myself to study the paper anyway. There are charts I don't understand, statistics I don't know a thing about, but the results are clear. I am a match for Amelia Laurence. We're related.

I look up at her and it feels like I'm looking at her for the first time. She's gazing back at me with the exact same expression. She's studying, assessing. And she's amazed. Does she realize we have the same color of auburn hair? That our skin tones are nearly the same, too? Does she see that our noses are similar, that long Grecian slope. Or that even though her eyes are green and mine are brown, the shapes are both more almond than they are round?

All at once it hits me. Not the similarities. Not the resemblance. But the fact that she knew my mother.

"My mother was your sister?"

She nods. "She was my baby sister. We lost touch with her when she became an addict. After a failed intervention, she wanted nothing to do with our family for several years. I'm sure you already know the ending to her story." She brushes a tear from her cheek and sits up a little taller. "But I swear we never knew you existed."

I sit with her words for a second. She sounds sincere but I find it hard to believe that she really didn't know about me. "The state contacts all next of kin before placing a child in the foster care system. You're telling me that nobody ever contacted you about me?"

She shakes her head adamantly.

"No, they never did," Gregory corroborates her claims. "If they had, you'd have been raised alongside your cousins." He sounds so logical. "Why would we seek you out now if we didn't want you back then?"

I guess he's right. There's no reason to connect with me now if they truly wanted nothing to do with me. Wait ... "Did you just say cousins?"

"That's right. You have three cousins, two boys and a girl."

Amelia pulls out her phone and slides it over to show me a picture. "Sybil is twenty-four and working for the foundation. Chandler is twenty. He has special needs and lives with us. And Hayes is fifteen and in high school."

It's her.

Sybil. The same woman who Ethan was engaged to, the one that looks like me, the one that he never got over so he used me instead. They're on a beach somewhere, dressed for dinner, she's got a wide grin on her face and her arm slung around a lanky teenager who looks like a young Gregory Laurence. Sybil's the spitting image of her mother. Between them is another young man with Down's Syndrome. He also takes after the mother's side of the family.

I flash my eyes at my aunt and wonder if she's who I'll look like when I get older. I can hardly believe it, she's so sophisticated and glamorous. And then I wonder what my own mother looked like. I don't have any pictures.

"Do you have a photo of my mom?" My voice shakes as I slide the phone back to Amelia.

She nods and pulls one up. It's a photograph of a photograph, the two of them are standing in front of a Christmas tree in matching pajamas. Amelia is the taller and older of the two, probably in her late teens. And my mother is standing next to her, a twinkle of mischief in her expression. Just like her sister, just like her niece, and just like me, she's got wavy red hair, pale skin, and a smattering of freckles across her face. She's also got my same brown eyes and the little dimple in my chin. There's no doubt this woman is my mother.

"She looks so happy," I mutter, wondering where it all went wrong.

"Josie had a compulsive personality," Amelia sighs. "She was wild and free. Nobody could tell her what to do. But she was also funny and had a heart of gold. I miss her every day."

Josie? I knew her name was Josephine Davis but that's all. I try to pair the Josephine in my head with the Josie this woman is describing. Sad thing is, I miss her too and I never even knew her.

"I know we've missed out on a lot of time together." Amelia reaches over and takes the phone, replacing it with her hand before I can pull away. She squeezes it tight and our eyes lock. "But I'd love to get to know you, to bring you into the family." Her voice hiccups and I feel like I'm floating. Or maybe I'm just light-headed. I may have forgotten to breathe sometime in the last ten minutes. "We're your blood, Arden. We have a lot of lost time to make up for, but if you'll let us, we'd like to start right now."

Gregory smiles at his wife and then at me and I can't help but wonder if this is really happening. I feel like I'm out of body, watching it happen to someone else. But I'm not. I'm really here. And this is really my life.

These people don't know me and I don't know them. What kind of business do they run? I don't know. Where do they live? I don't know that either. Are they good people? Again, it's a mystery. The only thing I can really gauge about them is that they have a lot of money and the one thing I've learned about wealthy people this summer is that they can't be trusted.

I need to remember what that police officer said. I need to stay vigilant. To be careful.

But dessert comes and we get to talking. One hour turns

into two, then three. There is so much to catch up on. And with each new topic of conversation, my fears begin to fade into the background. This is all I've ever wanted and now it's right in front of me. It's complicated. And messy. And confusing.

But it's mine.

I would be a fool to walk away, so I don't.

Part Two
Two Years Later (Almost)

"These violent delights have violent ends, And in their triumph die, like fire and powder, Which as they kiss consume."

William Shakespeare's Romeo and Juliet

Thirty-Five

Most people start their vacations with so much excitement bubbling over that they can hardly contain themselves. Not me. I'm starting mine with an all-consuming dread. It has drained every ounce of my energy and the vacation hasn't even started.

"I swore I would never return to Nantucket," I groan the second we step onto the tarmac. Sybil just laughs and lifts her hands into the air while spinning as if to proclaim, *how could you give up all of this?*

"Think of it this way." She grins openly, her vibrant green eyes sparkling in that way only people with happy childhoods seem to possess. "You're returning under completely different circumstances. It's going to be a marvelous adventure this time around."

Different circumstances is an understatement. And a marvelous adventure? With Sybil in charge of this trip, that's probably true by most people's standards. But I'm just worried that her idea of adventure and mine won't line up. The last thing I want to do is disappoint her.

"At least it's only for two weeks," I try to say brightly, but it comes out more like a dim flicker. What I don't add is that at least I won't be cleaning up after anybody but myself this time. Not that I'm above that or housekeeping is something I look down upon because I don't. But after my experience with the Kings, I'm sufficiently traumatized.

Never again.

Her mouth pinches. "I know your internship starts soon and I have to get back for work, but can we please not talk about that? While we're here, we're in vacation mode, and you're all mine."

Considering we hang out all the time and she treats every free moment like a mini-vacation anyway, I find her proclamation silly, but I love her enough to go along with whatever she wants. "Okay, deal."

She squeals, radiating so much joy that I can't help but soak it in like a sponge. That's the thing about Sybil, she spreads positivity wherever she goes. She's like a light that can't be turned off. It comes naturally to her, and I know part of that is because she's lived such a blessed life, but I also think it's who she is at her core. If we'd traded places in life, I'd still be a glass half-empty kind of gal and she'd still be a half-full.

But I'm working on it. If anyone can rub some good energy off on me, it's Sybil Laurence.

"I can't wait for you to see the new house." She launches into her explanations, going on and on about why they sold the Hamptons house and built this brand-new place on the Nantucket Sound. I only half-listen because I've heard it before and luxury real estate isn't my thing. Besides, she already knows I'd be happy to travel anywhere that wasn't Nantucket.

Too many memories.

But the Laurences sold their Hamptons place the summer before they found me and bought the lot for this house that same year. They broke ground the summer I was here and took almost two years to build this place to their exact specifications. I still can't believe my shitty luck that out of all the locations they had to choose from, Nantucket was the one they picked. I suspect it has something to do with one-upping the Kings, though I haven't dared ask.

Sybil isn't fazed by my worry. I used to steer clear of people like her, even went so far as to tell myself they were annoying, but deep down I was jealous. I didn't understand why my life was cast in gray shadows while people like Sybil lived under golden hues. Those thoughts used to grind me down, but nothing about Sybil Laurence is a grind and I've learned to let those negative emotions go when it comes to my cousin. The truth is, she's not fake. She's not ungrateful. She's not clueless. She's fucking wonderful.

I've known her for almost two years and to this day I still find it hard imagining her dating someone as crabby as Ethan King. I bet it did him good to be with her, that she brought out all his best traits. Now that I know Sybil, it's obvious why he was so messed up after she ended their engagement, why he grasped at whatever he could to fill the void she left, even if that ended up being me for a short time.

She tugs me to the waiting car and we slip inside while the driver loads our luggage. Twenty minutes later and we're winding up a cobbled driveway to a pristine navy-blue Cape Cod style house overlooking the beach. It's two large stories tall and twice as wide, surrounded by a lush green lawn, full trees, and flowering hydrangea bushes. It's bright and cheery while still being sophisticated, the kind of house that could be clipped out of a luxury magazine spread and pasted on a dream board.

"Wow," is the only word that comes out of my mouth.

"I know, right? I insisted on the Cape Cod style, especially the cedar-shake shingles with the white shutters. It's just so *appropriate* for the location."

She'd told me that she'd had the biggest hand in designing alongside her mother, and to hear the pride in her voice makes me equally proud of them both.

"You obviously know what you're doing. In another life you would've made a great home designer."

"Don't I know it," she tuts playfully.

She tilts her head, her tumble of auburn curls falling down her back as she takes it all in. The light filters through the car windows to reflect off her hair, making her glow in a hazy pink aura. She reminds me of a Cupid's angel, and not just because her birthday is Valentine's Day, but also because she possesses a soft effortless style in every shade of feminine. I know everyone says we look so alike that we could be twins, but that doesn't mean we are twins. There are so many glaring differences between us it's almost laughable.

"What's your favorite thing about it?" she asks and I dart my gaze back to the house, really taking it in this time.

The answer to her question comes easy. "It's not ostentatious."

This is the house of the understated billionaire, and to be quite honest, it's not what I expected. In Manhattan the Laurence family owns a ten thousand square foot penthouse *and* Sybil's trendy loft, and those aren't even their main residences. That's an hour from the city, a gargantuan mansion modeled straight out of the French Renaissance era. Beyond those three, they own property all over the globe, but just like so many other one-percenters, a summer home on the East Coast is a staple.

"I couldn't agree more," she says happily. "It's exactly what I was going for. Thank God Daddy let me design this one. He was going to buy a modern disaster and don't get me wrong, I love a good modern home, but this is *Nantucket*."

She's right. Nantucket has an old money feel about it and I agree that the best houses are designed to look like they were built at the turn of the twentieth century even if they are brand-new. And this place has every detail of Nantucket curb appeal covered, even right down to the cobbled driveway lined with blue hydrangea bushes bursting with the flowers. I can already smell them now, their earthly floral scent wafting through the car's AC system.

But what I love most about this house is that in no way, shape, or form, does it resemble the Kings' Nantucket home. Not only is this place located on the opposite side of the island, we're facing the Nantucket Sound instead of the Atlantic, but this house has established trees and a flat beach walk-out. The homes themselves are much closer together over here and they're not nearly as big either. This entire neighborhood has a different energy, one that feels cozy and welcoming and full of life compared to the breezy open bluffs of the King's neighborhood.

"Don't worry." She grips my knee, her voice dropping. "We're not going to run into anyone we don't want to."

She knows what I'm thinking. Of course she knows. Maybe she's thinking the same thing too. Maybe she's just as nervous as I am, but she's better at hiding it.

"If you really wanted to avoid the King family for the rest of your life, you should've built somewhere else," I point out.

She shakes her head and sits up straighter. "It'll be fine. Even if you do see them, they can't hurt you anymore."

"Just seeing them would hurt me," I confess, and she narrows her eyes.

"Those assholes planned to leave you homeless and they would've sent you to prison if they could've, but guess what?

They couldn't. The court sided with you. Don't let them dictate your life for another second. Why do you think we built this house here? They don't own this island and my family loves Nantucket, too. We used to spend a lot of time on this island back when we were all friends. So guess what?"

"Uh—they can kiss our asses?"

She laughs heartily. "That's right. If we want to be here, then we have every right."

The woman exudes confidence. She lives and breathes coolness and self-assuredness. Sure, I get where she's coming from, but she doesn't know my full story. She doesn't know everything I've been through, doesn't know the thoughts that keep me up at night, the life I've lived, all the shit I've been through, and she certainly doesn't know that I slept with her ex-fiancé. And I plan to keep it that way.

Because what if my darkness dims her light?

Thirty-Six

It's been almost two years since I laid eyes on the King brothers.

I keep telling myself that since Ethan and Cooper are working for their father now, they don't have time to spend another summer here. For all I know they're not even going to set foot on Nantucket at all this year. Hell, the family could've sold that house by now.

But it doesn't matter because I can't get them out of my head. I need to. I need to live as if they never existed and erase them from my mind. Especially Ethan. And especially now that I'm here. Because the truth is, I still think about Ethan every damn day. I hate it. I hate him. And I hate his permanent residence in my mind—but how is this my fault?

He was my first love. I'm just supposed to forget my first time having sex or opening myself up to someone like that? How do you emotionally detach yourself from the first time you fell in love? My first love was also the first time my heart was completely decimated by someone I trusted to take care of it. Ethan took more than just my virginity. He took those experiences from me. He owns them now. They're as much his as they are mine and I can't undo that.

And so yes, the man is always on my mind now, a constant reminder of the foolish girl that I once was, even if nobody else knows the truth but us.

I should tell Sybil. She's proven herself loyal. She would understand because she's been there with Ethan too. And maybe she could even help me through the pain, but I've been too much of a chicken to confess.

At first it was because I was terrified that the Laurences would find out about my trespassing charges and would want nothing to do with me, but when the lawsuit eventually came to light, my new family rallied around me. They were angry on my behalf, becoming warriors of justice, insisting I'd been mistreated. The Kings were the ones to break their contract, not me. The Laurences put their army of lawyers on the problem and made it go away.

But something about this particular confession, that Ethan and I were more than employer and employee—it feels different. Terrifying. Taboo. The end of things.

Because not only did Sybil grow up with Ethan, she was engaged to the man. She wore his ring. Planned their future. They *loved* each other.

These families used to be so interwoven. They vacationed together, helped raise each other's kids, and even owned multiple businesses together before they cut ties. I still don't know the full story behind the break, but I don't have to know everything to understand that it was most likely Conrad King's fault. I experienced firsthand what that man is capable of.

And tearing these families apart? It changed everyone irrevocably.

So how can I bring this up without causing more pain? I don't think that's possible. And what matters to me now is the new family that I've been welcomed into. This is a family that loves me and that I love back. My time with them has been a dream come true and I'm still afraid I'm going to wake up and return to my old life.

That can't happen. What's past is past, and Ethan King is far in the past.

"Earth to Arden." Sybil's standing at the car door waiting for me to get out, a concerned crease between her eyes. "Are you okay in there?"

I blink my troubled thoughts away and force a smile. "Sorry, just thinking about school stuff." The white lie leaves me with a pit of guilt in my stomach.

"You know you don't have to study computer technology *and* business, right?" she says and I slide from the car.

We've had this conversation so many times it's almost as if we've rehearsed it. "I'm studying business for your dad and tech for me. It's fine."

"My dad doesn't really care if you're some business whiz, he'll still give you a job."

"But I want to earn it."

She doesn't say anything more. After I moved to New York City and added on the business classes at my uncle's encouragement, we talked about why a bunch of times. I transferred from the University of Massachusetts to Columbia University before my sophomore year, right after the trespassing charges blew up in my face. I'd kept my secret as long as I could, but eventually my court date was set and the university found out what was going on. I was facing losing my scholarship, but even worse, the possibility of jail time loomed large because I was being charged with not only trespassing, but with theft. I had eaten their food and used their water and electricity without permission.

That was when I got desperate enough to call my aunt and

uncle for help. They swooped in and cleared things up within days, and then they got me enrolled at Columbia the following fall, insisted on paying my tuition, and even invited me to move in with Sybil. They claimed she was feeling lonely living in her swanky upper east side loft all by herself but I'm still not so sure. The woman has countless friends and even more social events. Her calendar is like an episode of Gossip Girl. But in the end, I agreed because they wanted it and I wanted them.

So here I am, getting myself even more entangled with them by vacationing with them for two weeks before starting my summer internship at Laurence International. Sybil and I got here a day later than everyone else because she had an event last night and I agreed to travel with her.

Now we'll be one big happy family in their new beach house.

In just a short time I already owe them so much. They act like they don't see it that way, like they're the ones who owe me. They keep saying how terrible they feel about my upbringing, as if I should blame them for not stepping up when I was orphaned. How could I blame them? They didn't know I existed. If anyone's to blame, it's a broken and underfunded system. That and parents who couldn't take care of me.

"Let me show you your bedroom." Sybil sweeps us into the house and leads me upstairs to a cozy bedroom with dormer windows overlooking the beach. The wood floors are covered in a lush cream wool rug, and the bed is large with a patchwork quilt of peaceful blue hues spread over it. Centered in the room is a glass French door and Sybil grins as she swings it open to reveal an adorable porch balcony with a hanging hammock chair. I immediately picture myself curling up in it, reading the afternoon away.

"This is amazing." I don't have words beyond that. It's like she took my personality and turned it into a bedroom.

"Isn't it perfect?" she beams. "My room is next door and Hayes and Chandler are across the hall. Mom and Dad's master suite is on the main floor. The guest suite is connected to the pool house and has two more bedrooms so maybe next year we'll invite some more people along. This year it's just our family."

Just our family. And I'm a part of that.

Which is exactly why I haven't confessed the truth about Ethan and exactly why I love Sybil so much. She's the sister I never had. The friend I always needed. And I couldn't be more grateful to have her in my life.

She points to the stretch of beach below. The only thing separating it from the house is a crystalline pool, an emerald rectangle of grass, and a line of tall reeds swaying in the breeze. "Now come on, let's go swimming."

I hope she doesn't mean in the ocean.

Thirty-Seven

I imagine my therapist's voice in my head. Dr. Cori would tell me it's healthy to face this fear, but there's no way I'm getting in the ocean again. I'll stick to the pool and be grateful I've come as far as I have. I've been taking swimming lessons for the last two months, ever since I found out about this vacation. I'm still terrible, deep water still makes me panic and freeze up, but at least I can tread water in a pool without sinking to the bottom like a stone. Swimming in the ocean on the other hand? Out of the question.

So as soon as I found out that Sybil absolutely meant to swim in the ocean, I set myself up on the sand with my beach towel and one of the books I bought for this exact situation. She can have the Nantucket Sound. Even if it is far less threatening than the Atlantic side, even if little kids have no problem bouncing around in it, I'm staying right here. Besides, I rarely have time to read fiction anymore now that I'm double-majoring at Columbia. I've been looking forward to getting lost in a fantasy world again and this time I've chosen a dragon rider book that went viral on social media, the unassuming gold cover hiding the action-packed and spicy content inside.

But I barely have time to read a page before a shadow stands over me. I smile up at my Aunt Amelia, admiring the way she's tucked her hair under a wide straw sunhat. It's sophisticated and effortless. I make a mental note to try and replicate it later. Her white swimsuit and gauzy cover-up make her skin look extra tanned. Even at the beach, the woman is pure class. I still find it a bit odd whenever I look at my aunt and cousins for too long and see our similarities. I never had that experience of looking into someone's face and seeing myself there until I met them.

I'm a lot scrawnier than they are, but otherwise we're spitting images and I fit right in with everyone except for Uncle Gregory and his mini-me, Hayes. Those men are all tall and dark and naturally tanned. It's like Gregory and Amelia made cookie-cutter children on purpose.

"She's always been a fish," Amelia nods out to where Sybil is wading in the surf, her outstretched hands v-ing over her head as she dives under a wave. "She gets it from her father. Certainly not from me, I hate the open water."

"And I must get that hatred from you," I reply, dropping the book. "All I can think about are the sharks and jellyfish that could be lurking out there." The jellyfish sting I endured two summers ago may no longer be seared into my flesh, but the memory will forever be seared into my mind. I shiver just thinking about it.

And then I shiver thinking about the days that followed that sting.

The days and the long passionate nights.

"It's a valid concern," she gazes at me sidelong, but I can't make out her expression behind the Tom Ford sunglasses perched on her slim nose.

"I'm not scared of sharks." Chandler bounds up next to his mother and smiles down at me. "Hi, Arden. Do you want to swim with me? We can play sharks and minnows?"

My cousin is two years older but his mental ability is around a ten-year-old's. Despite that, emotionally and socially he's more mature than most people I know. The guy quickly became my favorite person after we met and I'm pretty sure everyone in the family has dubbed him their favorite too. Probably because he's funny as hell. One time he replied to the group chat that he couldn't go to his dad's birthday party because he would be busy that night with his girlfriend. He doesn't have a girlfriend. He was talking about a sexy anime character from the video game he was playing. Another time, he wore a t-shirt that said "Homie with the Extra Chromie" to Easter brunch with extended family, insisting he couldn't dress up in a suit and tie because he needed to represent his people.

"Can I play sharks and minnows with you in the pool later?" I grin up at him. "I don't like the ocean."

"That's weird." He shrugs and takes off toward where Sybil is floating in the surf, dunking her under before she realizes he's there. They both come up laughing.

Amelia watches them with a peaceful lift at the corner of her mouth before directing her hired help toward us. The young man is carrying an umbrella hooked on one arm and several beach chairs over the other. I would fall on my face trying to carry all that but his muscles are popping under his crew neck. Unlike at the Kings' massive estate, the Laurence's Nantucket house is much closer to the beach. There's no bluff here, not a million stairs to descend, so it's a reasonable request to bring chairs and an umbrella right down to the water's edge.

Also not unreasonable to picture a hurricane decimating this place but when I brought that up to Sybil earlier, I was assured that's what flood insurance is for. Must be some pricy insurance, but what do I know? Besides, Sybil had insisted that they only get hurricanes this far north once in a century and the last one was a fluke. I had to bite my tongue on that one, wanting to point out that rising sea temperatures could change things for Nantucket, not to mention the very real hurricane that destroyed parts of this island not even two summers ago could very much become a recurring problem.

Amelia sets up a chair for me to join her, so I do, shaking the sand from my towel and brushing it off my pale legs. Hopefully by the time I leave this vacation I'll have some tanned legs instead of pasty or sunburned. The young man asks if we'd like anything else and Amelia sends him back for drinks. We watch him walk away, and I stare at his backside a little too long. Sorry, but it's hard not to, the guy is a handsome devil. Where was *he* two years ago? It would've been a lot easier had I gotten involved with someone like that instead of Cooper and Ethan.

"Speaking of water, how are the swimming lessons going?" Amelia asks.

My aunt was the one who got me into therapy. She insisted on it from day one, and it was my new therapist in Manhattan who encouraged the swimming lessons when I confessed my fears about the ocean and the upcoming Nantucket trip to the new beach house. I keep most of what goes on in my therapy sessions to myself, but swimming lessons was something I discussed with Amelia.

Amelia swears by therapy. She says the entire family has been in it for years, claiming it's saved her marriage and her kids. I've learned to appreciate it too, but I also suspect her insistence on paying for regular appointments has a lot to do with her guilt over my past more than anything else. I wish she would stop blaming herself. She's been the mother I never got to have, and I love her for that. But it doesn't matter how many times I express my feelings, she still acts like she owes me an unending debt.

"Lessons are going good but I'm still not getting in the ocean." I hook a thumb back toward the house. "Good thing you have a beautiful pool."

She deadpans, "And a beautiful pool boy."

A laugh bursts from my belly. I'm not sure if she's joking or serious. My face prickles and I wonder how much I don't know about my aunt and uncle's relationship. Probably a lot. And probably a lot I don't ever need to know. Are they monogamous? Is she just joking? Who knows, not my business.

"Don't worry," she explains with a smirk. "I can look but I can't touch, but that doesn't mean you can't have a little fun while you're here. You're young and single. You should find someone for a little vacation romance."

My face heats. "That's not really why I'm here--"

She leans back in her chair, face up and eyes unreadable behind her sunglasses. "You know what they say right? Youth is wasted on the young."

I raise an eyebrow. "Is it now?"

"Of course, that's the point. You're too young to realize how good it is to be young."

So I should sleep around? I don't know what to say.

She waves me off. "It's okay, Arden. I won't meddle in your love life, though I can't promise the same for your uncle."

My hackles rise and I sit up taller, pressing my bare feet deeper into the warm sand. "What is that supposed to mean?"

"Oh, you'll find out tomorrow night, but this is me warning you. And remember, just because Gregory wants you to do something doesn't mean you actually have to do it."

My eyebrows rise in question but the attractive helper returns with drinks and a dimpled smile, and she drops the topic in favor of mojitos.

Thirty-Eight

While I was in Boston, I was able to keep to myself. And then I came to Manhattan and I had the excuse of double majoring to keep busy. But right now? Right now I have no excuse but to go to the Nantucket Yacht Club summer kick-off party with my family. It will be my first big social event since meeting them. I knew this day would come, but I still feel woefully unprepared.

My hands sweat and I tug at the elegant champagne slip dress Sybil helped me pick out back in the city. It hugs my curves in an unfamiliar pull, accentuating the areas I usually keep covered under loose-fitting clothing.

"Look in the mirror and tell me you aren't fucking gorgeous," she insists.

"You're the best hype woman." I laugh nervously and let her drag me in front of her full-length mirror. She's right, the dress transforms me into a girl who belongs. I have to admit I like what I see, mostly because I look so grown up and like one of her crew. Sometimes I don't feel like I belong with her, like we're just pretending, what with her upbringing being so different from mine and the fact that she's six years older. She firmly knows who she is and I've just barely figured myself out.

"It's true. This dress makes you look more like a Laurence, see how it accentuates the warm undertones in your hair and brightens your skin so you're not washed out?"

I try to see what she's talking about, but it's lost on me. I only know that the dress is a good one. I shake my head. "I have no idea what you mean. I know I look good, but I couldn't tell you why. I don't have the same eye that you do."

My brain always worked in numbers and now it works in code too. I'm far too left-brained for the creativity it takes to put the right color fabric with the right skin tone, but ask me the difference between javascript and html and I'll have no problem explaining it.

"Trust me, you look incredible and you're going to do great tonight."

I do trust her but I don't know how great I'm going to do. I'm not cut out for this world. I'm better suited behind a computer than out working a crowd. Clearly, if I don't even know what dress looks good enough to make me look more like a Laurence. What makes me think I can handle tonight without embarrassing myself?

A half hour later and we're stepping from my uncle's restored classic Ford Bronco that Amelia says is his newest toy. He had it painted the exact same blue as the house and bought it especially for Nantucket, saying that we needed something that can go "off-road" on the beach. Aunt Amelia had rolled her eyes behind his back and winked at us when he'd said that as we all climbed inside. It's just the two of them and the two of us tonight. Hayes and Chandler stayed back to play video games and eat pizza.

I would've liked to stay back for video games and pizza but instead I was stuck in the back of the Branco, but at least it's not the ostentatious Bugatti Uncle Gregory typically drives back home. I like the Bronco better. It feels more normal even though I'm sure the restoration cost as much as some people's houses.

"Why didn't you warn me?" I gasp at the sheer size of the party.

"We didn't think you'd come," Sybil whispers, tucking my hand into her arm and tugging me along. Don't they know me better than that by now? I would've come because they asked me to come, plain and simple.

"It's fine. I knew this was going to happen eventually."

"Dad wants to show us off to his friends and their eligible sons," she warns. "But don't worry, he's not going to actually make you date anyone."

So that's what Aunt Amelia meant yesterday.

"Great," I reply sarcastically. It's not that I never wanted to be introduced to their social circles or that I think I'm too good for anyone, it's that I'm still terrible in social situations. My medication has helped with a lot of things, and therapy even more, but nothing can stop my social anxiety. Not yet, anyway.

I just don't want to disappoint anyone.

I'm not like the Sybils and Hayes of this world who were bred for socializing. I'm not like the Chandlers who gets a pass when he doesn't fit into places, and not because he lacks anything, but because the world is lacking the right accommodations.

I'm just me. I'm just Arden. The girl who doesn't know the appropriate things to say or how to draw the right kind of attention. People may consider me a Laurence now but deep down I'll always be a Davis. I never knew the man that gave me my last name, why he wasn't on the birth certificate, or why my mother chose Arden, but sometimes I think their genes must run strong in me.

Still—I'd like to belong. I'd like to be better. More confident. And nobody can give that to me. I have to fight for it myself.

"I'll do my best to try," I say to Sybil and she smiles like she believes in me.

She's so pretty. So perfect. Maybe if I try to emulate her, I'll do okay.

She's wearing a strappy black gown that fits her body like a glove and walks like she's as comfortable here at this party as she would be at home. Her jewels sparkle alongside the demure smile on her perfectly made-up face. Her hair is slicked back to one side, curls cascading over her slender shoulder.

She was meant for this, the kind of person expected to arrive fashionably late.

I wasn't meant for this, but I'll fake it.

There's the yacht club building with a sprawling lawn next to it, and beyond that are rows and rows of docks with boats of varying sizes in the slips. A massive white party tent has been set up with warm twinkle lights strung across the top, tables on one side and a dance floor on the other. The waitstaff are probably melting in their suits as they circle with trays of beautiful hors d'oeuvres and flutes of bubbly champagne, but you wouldn't know it from the pleasant expressions on their faces.

I was hungry before we left the house but now my stomach is wound tight and I'm not sure I can eat. At least Sybil didn't make me wear the high heels she originally chose for this outfit. What a disaster that would've been.

"Just smile and look pretty. I'll handle the rest." Uncle Greg slips his arm through mine and leads me away from Sybil and into the thickest part of the crowd.

I stomp down my annoyance at his comment. All I have to do is look pretty and be quiet and I'll be accepted by these people? That's messed up. Did he mean it like he agrees or was he trying to make me feel better about everything? My uncle Gregory doesn't normally say things that are so blatantly misogynistic, so I give him a pass and go along with his request. It's not long before everyone we speak to knows I'm his niece who's going to college at Columbia and that I'll be interning for him this summer. It's intimidating but at least they're all unrecognizable— that is until I catch sight of a familiar face.

"Perry Hargrove, how are you, son? Have you met my niece Arden yet?" Gregory booms, patting Perry's broad shoulder.

I smile up into Perry's dark and handsome face, noting the same dimples that caught my eye two years ago. There's a different air about him tonight than there was before, a more confident one, as if he's had recent victories.

"We've met before, actually," Perry replies warmly, his approving gaze sweeping over me. "As I recall, she turned me down for a date."

My smile falls. Just like the spidering-smoke shadows left behind when fireworks burn out, that Fourth of July night is imprinted on my memory. I had said yes to the date with Perry but Ethan got involved and nothing ever came of Perry's brief flirtation. I assumed the guy forgot all about me. And let's not forget how I ended up holding Ethan's hand that night while simultaneously cuddling with Cooper. The whole night had been a lesson in confusion.

"I never turned you down." I can't help challenging him. "I agreed to the date, but you never followed through."

Perry's eyes flash with something unreadable, something a lot like amusement and a little like irritation. "Then please forgive me. We'll have to rectify that missed opportunity."

Uncle Gregory pats me on the back. "She's single. She'd love to go out with you."

I blink up at him. *Excuse me? Don't I get a say in this?*

"Great. I'll call you." Perry says it like he actually means it and then he slips back into the crowd. I'm left standing here wondering what the hell just happened. Perry doesn't even have my phone number, not that it will stop him now that he's got Uncle Gregory's blessing. Hopefully he wasn't being serious because I'm not looking to date anyone right now.

Especially not someone with ties to Ethan King.

My uncle chuckles and leans in close. "Perry Hargrove is an excellent choice. His family has deep roots in oil and gas, but he's gone out on his own and is doing very well for himself. He works in television production of all things."

Television immediately makes me think of the Kings' media company, but neither of us say a word about the Kings. We never do. It's like an unspoken rule between us, a rule I caught onto real quick. Fine by me. I'd rather forget I ever knew that horrible family.

As fate would have it, it's at that exact moment that they arrive.

THIRTY-NINE

My uncle spots them the same moment that I do. A wave of anxiety passes through me. I quickly look down, heat flooding my system all the way down to my toes.

"What are they doing here?" His voice is hard. "Conrad hates boats. Always said yachts were a bad investment when really he was covering up his pathetic fear of drowning."

Drowning is also my fear so I guess that makes me pathetic, too.

My uncle is not actually talking to me, he's just venting out loud to himself, not that I would know how to properly reply. It's hard to imagine Conrad King fearing anything, let alone having the same fear I have. But the truth is, I know very little about Conrad King aside from what he did to me.

Aunt Amelia appears next to us, whispering to her husband in a hushed tone. She turns to me, her face ashen. "We'll be right back, Arden. Please continue to enjoy yourself."

I nod even though I wasn't enjoying myself.

The pair of them traipses over to where Conrad and a

woman who is definitely not Malory King stand hand in hand, Conrad's sons not far behind them.

A stronger woman would find somewhere else to rest her eyes, but my weakness gets the better of me, because mine land firmly on Ethan.

I can't look away.

Because it's Ethan—*he's* my weakness, pulling me right back into his gravitational field. It's been twenty-one months since I've seen him. Twenty-one months of hating him and missing him, of wishing I'd never met him while also reminiscing of the day we did. Two years ago, on a May day much like this one, I saw him for the first time and everything changed.

I hate him for the hold he has on me, for the way my entire body turns toward him without even thinking about it. That even after two years, being near him makes my heart squeeze as if he's responsible for the blood pumping through my veins. But most of all, I hate him for taking my heart and breaking it into a million little pieces.

He turns, our eyes meet, and the world fades.

It's as if we're the only two people here. His mouth slackens and he's staring at me like he's staring at a ghost and all I can hope is that I've haunted him as much as he's haunted me. Please, God. Please let me be not some insignificant hook-up from his past but someone who actually takes up space in his mind.

Our gazes stay locked as if in a stand-off. It's like we're counting down from ten. Who is going to pull the trigger first? I don't move and he doesn't either. It's just the two of us and our shared history between us. It's like an invisible force, like ghost hands twisting around our necks, threatening us. *Do not move. Don't even breathe.*

I won't be the first to look away, but I don't want him to be the first to do so either.

Like always, he disappoints me, breaking our eye contact and turning toward his father and whoever this new woman is. Amelia and Gregory are right there, right in their faces. The confrontation appears to escalate. Bodies tense and voices become clipped. I can't hear what anyone is saying, but I can imagine it's something like *what are you doing here? You weren't invited,* followed by something else like *actually I was invited because I bought a gazillion dollar boat that's much bigger than yours.*

Ethan speaks, his eyes pinned on my uncle, and Cooper shakes his head in frustration.

I can't do this.

I. Can't. Be. Here.

I don't know where Sybil is, I don't know where the bathroom is, I don't have anyone to talk to, there's nobody to save me from this moment. Like a coward, I flee the scene, heading in the opposite direction of the party, which happens to be the docks.

Twenty minutes later and I'm walking up and down the maze of them, my body finally starting to relax after fighting off a panic attack. I'm on anti-anxiety medication now, something my psychiatrist says I may need to take for the rest of my life. I only take a low dose each morning because I don't tolerate the side effects well, so it's not enough medication to stop the panic attacks completely. But it helps, and with the tools I've learned in therapy, I can usually stop an attack if I catch it early.

The doctor says I have generalized anxiety disorder. I live with it and have every day since I can remember. I don't know if I was born with it or if I developed it, but my psychiatrist and therapist have helped me come to accept this as a part of myself. Some people have poor vision, some people struggle with autoimmune diseases, with chronic pain, or other invisible illnesses. Me? I have a tense snake coiled in my chest, ready to strike at a moment's notice. So I've become a snake charmer, learning the art of keeping that snake from lashing out and sending my nervous system into fight or flight.

This is one of those snake-charming moments.

There are so many docks here, each with a dozen slips filled with rigs bigger than the last. I know I shouldn't be wandering among them. It's not like I have a boat, and this area is not why my family brought me to their party, but I can't let myself think about that too much. Being here is better than going back there, and it's far better than seeing the Kings again.

I stop, close my eyes, and take in long steadying breaths because I know what has to come next. I can't run away forever. I'm going to have to go back before my family comes looking for me. I'm still close enough to the party that I can hear occasional wisps of orchestra music floating through the breeze like champagne bubbles. It's not like I'm lost. I'll be able to make my way back there in a few minutes, even if I'm not quite ready.

I run my sweaty palms over my dress and wish for the umptheenth time that I had brought my phone tonight. I don't carry it everywhere at the suggestion of my doctor because smart phones are proven to increase anxiety and that's very true for me. Sometimes I consider going back to a basic flip phone. Isn't it funny how the things you want so badly sometimes become the things you hate the most?

That's proven true with people too.

So I don't have a phone and now my fingers are itching for the distraction I can hold in my hands. Not to mention, I need to contact Sybil. If I could text her, she could let me know when it's time to head back. I wouldn't have to return to the party at all. The Kings and Laurences are all back there trying to exact revenge on something I still have yet to understand.

I just hope they're not talking about me.

"I've been looking for you."

It's him . . .

Relief. Unease. Concern. Familiarity.

All the emotions crash through me at once and I'm not sure if it's the rough timbre of his voice that is making me feel these things or if I'm picking up on his emotions too.

Ethan. His voice is exactly as I remember it. I know that voice like the back of my hand. It's the voice that haunts my dreams, that refuses to let me go, that I've been simultaneously dreading and secretly wishing to hear again since he last said goodbye.

Goodbye, Juliet.

Of course I don't have to turn around to know it's him. I don't have to move. Don't even have to breathe. It's him and he moves closer.

"We should talk," he rasps, and it all comes rushing back.

The pain. The betrayal. The love gone wrong.

No. He doesn't deserve to talk to me. I release my held breath, keeping my vocals steady. "I have nothing to say to you."

"That's a lie and we both know it." He chuckles, low and torturous. I'm reminded of the old Ethan, of things better left to the past, of the desperate girl I used to be that would've done anything for his attention.

I whip around, my shoulders back and my chin high. "So you're calling me the liar?"

His eyes are hooded in shadow. The sun has set and there's not as much light out here, but I can still see the stormy blues I used to get lost in. My heart lurches and I shift back. He inches forward. A game of push and pull. How far will he follow? How much dare I retreat?

"You're lying about this," he says. "You're bursting with things you want to say to me." I shake my head and he tuts. "You want to yell at me, to tell me what an asshole I've been. You want—"

"Stop," my voice cracks, giving me away. "I have nothing to say. What's done is done."

"And what was done?" His eyes travel up and down my face, lingering over my lips before jumping back to my gaze. "Are you one of them now? Are you a Laurence?"

Are we enemies?

"They're good to me." It's my only defense but it's enough.

"The family you always wanted." He says it blankly, like it means nothing to him either way, but how can that be true? The woman he once loved is a Laurence girl. Whatever he thinks of them now, Sybil cannot be erased.

"That's right." I stand up a little taller even though he towers over me. I have to crane my neck up. "They're wonderful people."

"Gregory isn't." He says it like it's a fact, like I already know and would obviously agree with him. Well, I don't.

"Gregory is great," I snide. "You don't know him like I know him."

And okay, I don't know his history all that well, but I do know his heart. He took me in and treated me like his own since day one. A bad man wouldn't do that and I don't care what Ethan has to say on the matter.

Ethan laughs at that though, laughs like it's all a big joke. "Gregory is a liar, a cheater, and an all-around piece of shit."

I slap him. Hard.

Right across the face.

And then I gasp, stumbling back. My hand is red, fingers stinging. I don't know what just came over me except that Ethan deserved it. I should've slapped him ten times over the course of our summer together.

He cups his face, expression emboldened like he's finally seeing the new me. Good, he should get used to it. I've changed and I'm not going back.

"You really don't know," he sighs. The tone is not what I expected. There's no anger there, only regret.

"Stop." There's nothing more to know, I already have enough information.

But he doesn't stop. Not even a little bit. He stalks in close and I shift back until my spine is flat up against a dock post. He's cornered me. We're only an inch apart. Less than that. He's the predator. I'm the prey. But remember, I have a snake coiled inside me.

And snakes have fangs.

Forty

"Your uncle had an affair with my mother." His words are brutalizing. Startling. Like a knife held to a neck. There's no going back after that statement.

"W–what?"

"And when she died, he didn't let their secret die with her. Instead, the bastard flaunted like it was some kind of badge of honor, like he had a fucking right to mourn her deeper than her own husband and children."

Sinking. I'm sinking into the deck, down into the water, to the ocean floor. Either that or it's coming up to swallow me whole.

I don't want to believe what I'm hearing but his words click puzzle pieces into place, confirming little things I've picked up on. The therapy that the family is in, how Amelia said they've been doing it for years, that it saved their marriage. The random comments about mistakes made in the past. The way Amelia got teary and Gregory got defensive the few times the Kings have been brought into conversation. The fact that I sensed there was something they weren't telling me.

I thought the families had split up over business disagreements and that the breakup between Sybil and Ethan was part of that. I never knew it was something more.

Something this devastating.

But it's not my business. It's in the past, my aunt obviously forgave my uncle, Sybil broke up with Ethan, and everyone has moved on. I should too.

"That has nothing to do with me," I manage.

I can tell Ethan wants to say more, that he wants to go off about what terrible people the Laurences are, but he doesn't. He stays quiet, eyes searching mine. It's like he's trying to convey a hidden message, like he expects me to understand, to side with him, to say and do the right thing. But I can't. I never could.

The moment stretches between us like a live-wire dragging me into his gaze and sparking something deep within me. All of a sudden it's like I'm right back to where I was two summers ago, right back to wanting him, maybe even loving him. Ethan is electric and I have to get away fast. I've removed myself from him before and I can do it again.

I will do it again.

"Goodbye Ethan," I say, and then I duck under his arm and walk away.

With each step I take I should be feeling lighter, more free. Empowered.

But I don't feel anything but heartache.

And I'm filled with the kind of questions that require an answer, the kind that I suspect will take hold of me and refuse to let go even long after I find out the truth.

I'm almost back to the party when I spot Sybil and Cooper up ahead on the docks. "It's none of your fucking business," she is saying. She sounds rushed and heated—not like herself. I know that voice, but I don't know that tone. I've never heard my cousin talk this way to anyone.

I approach cautiously, my hackles on full alert. Cooper is as handsome as he ever was, but his hair is shorter and his jaw is cut in a sharper line than it used to be. He's grown into his face even more somehow, becoming devastating in the process. His scathing glare is directed at Sybil. I don't recognize this level of anger on him. This isn't the guy I used to know but maybe this is the man he's become.

A pang of sadness overwhelms me as I watch him. Where's the fun-loving, easy-going, devil-may-care playboy from two summers ago? This Cooper is intense. He's dark. He's … like Ethan.

Defensiveness for my cousin takes over, the mama-bear in me coming out with claws and teeth, and I stride right up to the pair.

"Are you okay?" I direct my question at Sybil but they both answer with a quick, "We're fine."

"You don't look fine." I fold my arms over my chest and shift to stand between them. Cooper tears his gaze from Sybil. They rake over me with no inhibitions. His intense perusal of me makes me squirm.

What happened to Cooper?

"This is a new look," he says coolly.

"What's that supposed to mean?"

"Just that you're different. I didn't say it was bad. Maybe it's a good thing."

I'm not sure if he's referring to my outfit or my attitude or just being with Sybil, maybe it's all three. Or maybe he thinks it's funny that I'm getting between two people who are taller than me. Does he find it amusing or am I sticking my nose where it doesn't belong?

Sybil grabs my hand from behind and squeezes. "I was looking for you. We're leaving."

She marches us back to the party, hellbent on getting as far away from Cooper King as possible. I peer back at him, trying to understand what just happened. His hands are stuffed into his suit pockets and his dark eyes are jumping from me to my cousin and back again. He seems to be debating something, and when our gazes lock he makes up his mind. He catches up to us and Sybil practically growls her frustration.

"I should've realized you were related to the Laurences the first time I saw you, Arden," he says apologetically. "I can't believe I chalked it up to coincidence. You two look even more alike in person."

"Like I said," Sybil shoots back at him. "It's none of your business."

He ignores her, still intent on talking to me. "You should've called me. At least when you met her and learned the truth about everything, you could have picked up the phone. We don't have to hate each other just because our parents were idiots."

"Are you kidding? Am I forgetting the part where you gave me your number? Oh, that's right, you didn't. You pulled that frosty cold-shoulder bullshit on me for weeks before you left. Even if I could have called you, I wouldn't have."

Sybil whips around on him, dropping my hand and practically punching his chest. He's an iron wall but she's a bulldozer. "And actually, *you* should have called *me*. The second Arden walked into your house and you saw the resemblance you should have called me. But you didn't, did you? I had to find out from my parents *months* after you guys met her."

"So I guess we're even," he growls.

She shakes her head. "We're not even. We're not *anything*."

Cooper instantly returns to the guy I don't recognize.

This fight seems to be about me, about a lack of communication and trust. But it's deeper than that and I can't deal with it. I don't want in on the drama.

"Let's go." I tug Sybil back to my side and we walk out of the party together.

This time Cooper doesn't follow.

My aunt and uncle are already waiting in the Bronco as we climb in, the air conditioning on full blast despite the day's heat fading. Maybe Amelia's hot flashes are acting up but more likely they're overheated from being upset. I feel like we arrived seconds after they finished a screaming match; the energy is too tense. Everyone is silent as we drive. I don't know what to say, but maybe for once, none of them know what to say either.

I learned things tonight that I wish I'd never have known, but now the truth is out there and I can't take it back. I try to study my uncle's profile as he drives us home, but I can't look at him for too long without imagining him cheating on my aunt. The fact that the family is still together is nothing short of a miracle. I'm sure marriage can be hard and sometimes cheating happens and spouses can forgive and make it work, but I personally can't imagine forgiving infidelity. Especially not at that level.

This wasn't a random hookup.

This wasn't a drunken mistake.

This was a full-fledged affair with one of their best friends. I would never be able to let someone back in after a betrayal so deep and public. How much therapy have they gone through and is my aunt really okay with everything? She obviously hasn't healed if tonight is any indication, but then again, I can't judge. I have no idea what healing from that would even look like. Ethan and I were never together for real, never married, no cheating—and I still have miles to go before I'm healed from what happened.

Poor Amelia.

I can't help but see their marriage through a whole new lens. Maybe they only appear to be perfect. The outside could be an illusion when on the inside they're barely hanging on. They could be on the brink of divorce for all I know. So what would happen if they found out the truth about me and Ethan? Would it tip the scales too far in the wrong direction?

And that's when the question hits me, the thought that cuts the deepest, that takes my world and sends it spiraling completely off its axis. *Did Ethan know who I was the whole time?*

Because not only did I look like his ex, but I was related to his ex. I was orphaned, working for them, essentially homeless, but I was cousins with the one that got away.

All this time I thought he wanted me because of my resemblance to Sybil but what if he wanted me as some sick game to get back at her?

And to get back at Gregory too.

Which would explain why Conrad wanted me to hook up with him in the first place and why Cooper wasn't allowed to. Because Coop never dated or was engaged to a Laurence. My stomach goes hollow at these thoughts and suddenly I'm carsick and shifting my weight over so the AC is blasting on my face. I close my eyes and try to relax.

If this is all true, then it's only a matter of time before the Kings tell everyone about what Ethan and I did. Because if they want to take down the already crumbling Laurence family once and for all, exposing my affair with Ethan could be exactly how they accomplish it.

Clank! Clank! I wake with a start, eyes popping open. I sit upright and peer through the darkness. Adrenaline ping-pongs through me as my inner alarms blare. I attempt to clear my mind, to wade through a fog of unsettled dreams.

Then I hear it again. It's a light tapping on the glass door to my balcony. I should scream but I don't. I should run away but I stand, my nightshirt dropping to my thighs, and pad to that door. With a slow breath, I slide the curtains aside.

The man standing there is a broken one.

Not a conniving one. Not one set on revenge or on destroying a family.

The expression on his face is of utter devastation.

Maybe it's because I'm still half-asleep but before I can think what it means or talk myself out of it, I unlock the door and slide it open, stepping outside. "Ethan? What are you doing here?" I whisper.

He's quiet for a moment. "Can we talk?"

"We already talked."

A moment passes between us. There's so much left to say and we both know it, but I can't be around him without spilling my guts.

It's been two days since the yacht club party.

Two days and I haven't been able to get him out of my mind. He's part of me now, under my skin and in my blood. Seeing him again made me realize how much I missed him and how angry I've been that he hurt me. The truth is that I fell in love with him. I didn't even have a choice. And even now I still feel that love underneath all the hurt. I still feel forever connected to the man who calls me Juliet even though he shouldn't.

It wouldn't hurt if it wasn't love.

And how is that fair? I don't want to feel this way, so

burdened by heartbreak every fucking second. I don't want the memories. I didn't ask for this.

"Please." His voice catches and suddenly he's not the cold-hearted man I got that last day together in August. He's someone else, someone who tended to me through panic attacks and jellyfish stings, someone who wanted me. Maybe I should take pity on us both and let him say what he has to say. It's dangerous, I'm already teetering on the edge, but sometimes a girl needs a little danger to feel alive. Ethan taught me that.

Forty-One

I nod and peer around the darkened landscape. It's late and quiet, the only sound is the rolling of the ocean waves and my own pounding heart. At least Sybil's bedroom light next door is out. I'm sure she's fast asleep. That woman has the opposite of insomnia. As soon as her head hits the pillow, she's in dreamland. Always so comfortable with her world, always so safe. It's another confirmation that even though we look alike, we couldn't be more different.

"Wait." I pin Ethan with a glare, a sudden thought coming to me. "How did you know this was my bedroom?"

He exhales a slow breath, his voice wooden when he answers. "I followed you home after the party, walked along the beach and watched the house for you. You came out here."

He's right. I did come out to the balcony. The second we got home, everyone hid away to their different corners of the house, and I ended up out here with my reading light and my fantasy book, not that I got much reading done. My mind was a mess then and my mind is a mess now.

"Isn't that kind of creepy?" I raise a brow.

"I wasn't done looking at you."

Definitely creepy if it was anybody else. With Ethan it's not exactly a compliment as much as it's a revelation. *He wasn't done looking at me.*

There's one question I have to know the answer to before I send him away, one question that would make sense of so many torments. "Did you know I was a Laurence before I did?"

He stares at me like whatever he's about to say next holds the weight of the world. It tips the scales and I already know the answer. My heart sinks.

"Say it," I whisper my demand, voice laced with the pain of betrayal.

"I suspected," he admits. "But I didn't know until the day I flew you to Boston."

The day I found the photograph of Sybil.

"You wanted nothing to do with me because I was a Laurence or because you realized I didn't only look like Sybil but was actually related to her?"

His expression fills with regret and he takes my hands. I should pull away, but I let him. "I wanted *everything* to do with you, but you being a Laurence made it impossible."

I squeeze those hands. "For who?" My voice is shaking. Maybe my hands are too. Maybe all of me is. "I didn't even know about them and you certainly weren't the one to tell me."

"And I should have. I realize that now."

I start to pull away, already imagining going back into my room and leaving him out here to stew in his own self-loathing. As far as I'm concerned, he should feel terrible about not telling me the truth. He should feel like an asshole about all of it, especially the part where I ended up with legal trouble despite following through with our agreement. But those things don't hurt nearly as much as what he did with me. Taking my virginity because he wasn't over someone else is unforgivable.

And dumping me in Boston when I confronted him with the truth is not something I can get over. But worst of all was allowing me to fall in love with him.

"Please, Arden." He's practically begging. If I asked him to get on his knees and grovel right now, I think he would. "Let me explain everything."

Against my better judgment, I decide to let him.

"We can't have this conversation out here." I shouldn't be doing this, but I need answers. "Come on then." I ignore the alarm bells in my head and let him into my room.

It's dark and cool and quiet in here tonight, and as I slide the glass door shut, he lingers closer than a shadow. His presence is too big, his energy too magnetic. I can't be in the dark alone with this man. I don't know how to make good decisions around him or how to be the grown-up woman I've become instead of the insecure girl I was two years ago.

I slip away from him and flip on the bedside lamp. The light makes this moment more real somehow, illuminating the truth of being together. This isn't a memory or a dream or a fantasy, this is really him. I catch his eyes sweeping over my bare legs before they spring up to my face. Is he remembering what my legs looked like wrapped around his body? I hate myself for remembering the very same thing, but the memories simply won't let me go.

"Explain yourself." My voice is a low demanding whisper, but I sound strong and confident despite unraveling inside. Am I taking steps backwards toward the old me instead of forward to the new one? I can't let that happen.

I've had sex with three other men since my time with Ethan but none of them came close to making me feel the way that he did. The first was during a college party my first semester, a one-night stand just so that I could say Ethan wasn't the last man to touch me. It was rushed and terrible. The other two were mediocre boyfriends, the romances fizzling out within a few months. Sometimes I worry that I'll be looking for what Ethan gave my body for the rest of my life, that I'll never be able to find someone who can make me feel the way he did.

And yet here he is, looking like a tortured Romeo here to woo his Juliet. We even have the balcony to prove it. The warring families. But that story ended in tragedy. And while technically ours did too, we're both still alive. We don't have to go back there or test our luck. But first, I need answers. Answers might not give me peace, but at least I'll be able to finally move on.

"You look good, Juliet," he says, as if reading my mind and I suck in a breath.

"Don't you dare call me that."

He holds up his hands. "Arden. Sorry."

And then he's quiet, like he knows I have to process not being his Juliet afterall. It takes a full minute for me to calm myself. "Go on."

He nods once and stays standing there in the middle of the room as he quietly explains himself. "It's true that I wasn't over Sybil when I first met you." My heart twists at the confession. Hearing it confirmed makes it all so much more real. "But there's so much more to the story. I wish I could change some of the things that happened that summer. I fucking hate myself for the way I treated you."

"Can you get to the part where you explain why you didn't tell me who *I* was?" I'm back to angry, but part of me knows that's only because I don't want to face all the other emotions bubbling under the surface. Anger is easy. Anger is safe.

Rejected? Hurt? Passionate? Hopeful?

Not going there.

"I suspected the family connection. You look so much like Sybil. But your background didn't make sense to be a Laurence.

Plus, you're built so much smaller than the rest of them. I thought it was a coincidence and let it go." He steps closer again. "My father was the one to confirm it but he didn't tell me until that last morning. You were asleep when he called to let me know that not only did he know you were at the house with me, but that you were related to the Laurences." He swallows hard and I track the bob of his Adam's apple in his throat. "All summer he had been encouraging me to hook up with you. He said he felt bad about what had happened with Sybil so when your application and photo came through the system, and Malory showed him the resemblance, he insisted we hire you." He shakes his head. "I didn't trust a word he said. I still don't trust his reasons, to be honest."

My gut clenches, my suspicions confirmed. Whatever Conrad's true intentions were, the fact remains that I wasn't really qualified for the job I was hired to do. I was there to fill an entirely different role.

Stupid me. I played that role exactly as Conrad wanted.

"He was the one who thought I needed to sleep with you to get her out of my system. I promise, that was never my plan." He says this last bit so adamantly that I let myself believe him. God knows I shouldn't, but I do anyway. "That last morning together, he called to demand I take you to him," he finishes. "That's when I knew he had nefarious plans for you."

I blink rapidly, trying to make sense of this. "But why would he want me to go to him?"

"Could be for a multitude of reasons but I'm sure it was to use you against his enemy. I still don't know what his plan was and I don't care. He's ruthless when it comes to Gregory Laurence. He'd do anything to hurt your uncle for what he did to our family. I'm serious, Arden. *Anything.*"

"Your mother was part of that too, though." I point out. "It takes two to have an affair."

He grimaces and I sense he's fighting anger because his eyes are hard. "I know," he admits. "And Conrad has accountability too. He may have been physically loyal to my mother as far as I know, but emotionally he was a shitty husband, not that he'll ever admit it. Why do you think he's already on his third wife?" So that's who that woman at the party tonight was, the new wife. I wonder what happened to Malory, but then again, I don't really care. She was just as awful as the rest of them. "Anyway, I couldn't take you to him and let him turn you into some pawn for his revenge game, so I took you to Boston as promised."

"But you still didn't tell me the truth."

"And I should have, but I was embarrassed when you said it was Cooper you wanted all along. My pride got in the way."

"I was lying," I confess, ashamed of myself. "I'm sorry. I was hurt and wanted to hurt you back. Didn't you realize that was a lie?"

"I did. I knew it then and I know it now, but you have to understand that although Cooper and I have always been best friends, we've also always been in direct competition. Maybe it's a twin brother thing or maybe it's a King family thing, but it's just how our relationship works. When you said that you wanted him and I was your second choice, it was easier to believe you." He reaches up and rakes a hand through his hair, letting it fall back down in a dark tumble. "I mean, he did get you naked."

My cheeks heat. "That was a mistake. I never should've done that."

"I know. He knew it too. Why do you think he gave you up so quickly? I told him he couldn't take your virginity unless he was willing to actually date you and be exclusive for the rest of the summer. You can imagine how that went over."

Coop never wanted to be my boyfriend and that should

hurt but it doesn't. Cooper wasn't the one I wanted. He wasn't then and he isn't now. Same as he didn't want me for more than a one-time hook-up and maybe to prove something to his brother.

Again, Ethan steps closer. I'm still frozen, standing by the lamp with the warm light basking the bedroom in a gentle glow. I'm still unable to move away whenever Ethan is near. He's still my gravity. He'll always be my gravity . . .

"I realized something bigger that day though," he continues. "You always wanted a family and this was your chance. Being with me would've taken that away from you. It's no secret that the Laurences and the Kings hate each other. You couldn't have dated me while also getting to know your new family. Here you were about to embark on this new life at college, the whole world at your fingertips, and now you were going to be a Laurence too. I couldn't take that away from you, so I took you to Boston instead and then I called Gregory myself."

Of all the things he could have said, I never expected it would be that. "You called my uncle?"

"Turns out Amelia and Greg had already found out about Sybil's doppelganger working for the King family. Word got out. They obtained genetic confirmation without your consent."

"I already know about that," I mumble.

I still don't know exactly how they did it, but money can move mountains. I never asked for the specifics. My guess is they hired one of the twins' friends or Cooper's girls to secure it when they were visiting the house. It wouldn't have been hard to steal a hair sample out of my bathroom. Whoever did it, I'm honestly grateful. They changed my life for the better.

"Thing was, they couldn't find you after the results came in. They didn't know you were still hiding out at the Nantucket house. I was the one to let them know what hotel you were going to be in. I demanded they get to you right away."

And they did . . . "The very next day I met them and my whole life changed, but that wasn't before I got picked up by the cops for trespassing on your property."

He's displayed practically every emotion since we've been talking, but the anger simmering under the surface finally boils over. No anger, complete *loathing*. It pours out of his voice, fills his eyes, corrupts his entire demeanor. "My father pressed charges against you when I didn't bring you to him like he'd asked. It was a way to punish us both. He didn't tell me it was happening. Cooper and I didn't know about it right away or I swear to God we would've intervened, Arden. But the charges were dropped, weren't they?"

"Months later, only after I got my uncle involved."

He shakes his head, his breath leaving in an emphatic scoff. "That's *not* what happened."

Forty-Two

My uncle saved me, that's a fact. The man has done so much for me but that was the one thing he did to really solidify my trust in him. He truly loves me like his own. I believe that with my whole heart and it's why I agreed to transfer colleges and live with Sybil, why I added a business degree to my studies and plan to join Laurence International. And you know what? Thank God Ethan let me go when he did. He was right, I needed to be free of the Kings. I needed a real family. As much as it sucks that he hurt me, he gave me so much more than a broken heart that day.

"I knew nothing of the charges at first," he explains. "I only learned what was going on when the lawyers tried to set up a mediation meeting with me and Cooper. *We're* the reason your case was dropped, not Gregory's lawyers, although I'm not surprised he took credit."

I shake my head. "You must be mistaken."

"I'm not. The Nantucket house was put in mine and Cooper's trust when we started working for our father. We own it. We're the ones who get to say what happens there, which means we're also the ones who get to say if we're pressing charges. Conrad was trying to do it behind our backs as a fuck you to Gregory, but Coop and I dropped the charges the second we found out about them."

I stand frozen, a million thoughts bombarding me at once.

A million feelings too.

There are moments in life that shape you as a person. The moment I realized that Ethan had betrayed me, that he had told his father and gotten me charged with trespassing, I had changed into someone different. Someone harder. I wouldn't say I stopped believing in love, but I definitely stopped believing I could trust men like Ethan. But that was all a lie. So will this moment reshape me again? Because Ethan wasn't the one who pressed charges; he was the one who dropped them. And he wasn't trying to hurt me by dropping me off in Boston; he was trying to help me. He was giving me a family.

It's all too much.

"And what about Sybil?" I squeak out.

"What about her?"

He takes another step closer and so do I. This time it's both of us moving toward the other. Somehow during this conversation, we went from standing on opposite sides of the room to being a foot apart. The space between us pulses with energy, with memories, with confessions, with hurt, and maybe . . . maybe even with love.

Was it love? It was for me but I can't speak for him.

"Did I help you get over her?" My voice quivers knowing the answer could hurt me. He said himself that he wasn't over her at the beginning of that summer.

For the first time tonight, he smiles. "Yes. And faster than I wanted to admit. It wasn't months of being around you that finally made me stop thinking of her, Arden. It was days. It was minutes. Seconds. I wanted you from the moment I laid eyes on you. Do you remember? You were on the beach, it was night, and I was making out with someone else like a fucking idiot. I saw you and something inside of me knew you were mine."

"Actually, I saw you in the pool earlier that day," I confess. "That was the first time for me. The beach was the second."

His eyes heat with hope and lust and maybe, maybe even love. "Such a fucking shame I didn't see you then too because I'd die for one more memory of you."

My heart skips over a beat. I can hardly believe what he's saying, but why lie about something like this? What does he stand to gain from coming here? Nothing, except for getting through to me. Maybe that gravity thing works both ways. Maybe he's drawn to me just as much as I am to him. I might be the one that steadies him right back.

"After things ended with Sybil, I thought I could get over you like I got over her, that time would erase you or that I would meet somebody new who would change everything, but it never happened." Closer. Closer. Closer we move together. "And then I saw you and for a second I thought it was her. I was angry and confused. But then I looked again and I saw you for you. You weren't Sybil. You were you. A girl who stood like she was unsure of herself, who didn't know anyone on that beach. Your hair was windswept and as beautiful as that bonfire. You had this deep longing in your eyes and this raw honest innocence about you, too. You weren't like the people I knew." He clears his throat. "I wanted you."

"And you got me and then you left me in Boston."

"I know. Fuck Gregory but the rest of the Laurences are decent people. I left you there because I wanted you to be happy."

"And I am happy," I breathe. But I'm also missing something. He gave me something and then he took it away and I don't know how to get it back without him.

"God, I missed you. I thought of you constantly. For two years you've been on my mind. I almost came to you when I found out about the lawsuit but by then you were established with the Laurences and I didn't want to mess that up."

"But you're here now," I point out.

"Because when I saw you the other night, I knew I'd made a mistake. I never should've let you go. I'm so fucking sorry for everything, especially letting you walk away."

I almost want to tell him it's okay, but I can't.

"I'm going to be selfish now, baby. I want you back."

It's like all my broken pieces have a chance to come back together.

This confession is everything a girl wants to hear. I've missed him too. I've longed to rewind time and fix things between us, to take back my harsh words, to make him see that we were good together, to make him love me more than he loved Sybil. I was angry and hurt but I never stopped wanting him.

"And now I'm here because I needed to make sure you knew what really happened." He swallows hard and then every so lightly, he cups my chin between his fingers and angles my face up toward his. My breathing turns erratic, every nerve sizzling under his touch. "I'm sorry, Arden. I hurt you and I messed up. I don't expect you to forgive me, and I don't expect you to still have feelings for me, but I couldn't go another minute without telling you the truth."

In the movies, this is the part where the couple kisses and makes up. In books it's where the internal dialogue of the character is interrupted by an explosive kiss, by confessions, maybe a few rounds of amazing sex, and then everything works out. The third act break up is over. They get to live happily ever after. The end.

That's not our story.

Ethan does lean down to kiss me, but I don't let him.

I shut it all off.

Push him back.

Turn away.

"Thank you for telling me the truth but I've moved on and you should too." He was right about one thing, I'm a Laurence now.

As much as I want him, *I can't lose them*.

"Does it make it easier to belong to them if you hate me?"

"Yes." *No. God, I don't know.*

"It's okay. I understand."

I don't know what I expect, more groveling? Him falling to his knees? But I get none of that, instead I get exactly what I asked for because *he understands*. The energy in the room shifts, the shadows recede, the glass door opens and shuts, and just as quickly as he appeared, Ethan King is gone.

If Sybil and Chandler are the big sister and brother I always dreamed of, then Hayes holds the title of goofy kid brother. The kid is hysterical and brilliantly gifted, and he's also a giant pain in the ass. Of course, I love him for it.

"Can you please stop that?" Sybil all but screeches for the fourth time in an hour.

We're laying out by the pool and Hayes keeps intentionally splashing us while simultaneously feigning innocence. He's seventeen and going into his senior year of high school, so you would think he's mature enough to know better, but no. Around Sybil especially, he's a little shit.

"Are you talking to me, *sister*?" He pops up on the side of the pool deck, arms propped on the edge. "Sorry, I couldn't hear you, there's water in my ears." He grins devilishly and shakes his head like he's clearing his ears.

I can't help but snort.

"Yes, I'm talking to you," Sybil snaps, dropping her phone a fraction to glare at him.

The woman is addicted to her iPhone, but part of that is because she's just as dialed in on social media as she is dialed in socially with Manhattan's elite. She was bred to be a socialite and plays the part exceptionally well, posting beautifully curated content that garners a lot of attention for Laurence International's charitable foundation. "You know what you're doing, *brother*. Grow up. You're not a child anymore so stop acting like one."

"You're right." Hayes lifts himself from the pool and strides right for his sister. "I always appreciate your constructive criticism. Thank you."

He leans over into an awkward side hug, dripping pool water all down the front of her designer sundress. She screeches and shoves him away, and he just laughs and tells us he's going to see if Chandler wants to come swim before sauntering back into the house. Even though he's nine years younger than Sybil and she's taller than most women, he's got at least fifty pounds of muscle on her and several inches. The kid shot up like a rocket shortly after I met him, partly because he spends an ungodly amount of time in the gym. He's almost eighteen and I can imagine he'll be a force as he grows into a man.

"I swear, it's a miracle I haven't killed him yet," she growls. "If he wasn't so important to Chandler, I probably would."

I just grin at her because I think it's funny and also because she has no idea how good she's got it. I'd love to have a real sibling, not just cousins that I've only known for a few years. The three of them have a special bond and no matter how much they bring me into the fold, it'll never be the same. We don't share the same memories or upbringing.

But that's okay. Because this is still better than anything I could've hoped for.

This is what I wanted.

What I choose.

It's exactly why I'm here with them instead of with Ethan right now.

They are my people now.

My family.

She turns on me, her sunhat and oversized sunglasses hiding most of her expression. "So, are you finally going to tell me what happened with Ethan?"

Forty-Three

My lips part and my stomach twists. "What do you mean?"

"I mean, what happened at the party? I saw him break away from the others to go look for you. I can only imagine why."

A million thoughts swirl through my brain. "Are you going to tell me what that conversation was between you and Cooper?" I deflect.

"It was nothing." Her reply is so careful that I know she's bullshitting me.

"Didn't look like nothing." I sink further into my lounger, hoping that if my face is red right now, it just looks like I got too much sun.

I'm avoiding her questions. I tell myself it's because I hate keeping secrets, but I have good reason to keep them. Sure, a better person would tell her everything. I know she deserves the truth, even if my past with Ethan is going to stay there. But at the end of the day, she was engaged to Ethan. She knew his body the way I did, his heart too. Maybe even more so because they had years of history. And she also knows the pain he leaves in his wake.

I don't want to be the one to drudge all that up again.

"If you must know, I was telling him to keep his family away from ours," she says, pulling her sunhat further down on her forehead. "So what about you and Ethan? What did he want?"

"He told me about the affair." I let out a little wince.

Her shoulders tense but her voice softens. "Fuck, why can't they just let it go?"

"He thought I deserved to know the truth." And honestly, I agree. It's not my business but it's also my family, and if everyone else already knows about what happened, it's helpful for me to know too. At least this way I won't accidentally put my foot in my mouth and say the wrong thing.

"I guess so . . ."

"It's all over though, right? Your dad hasn't done anything else?"

"It's over, but I kinda doubt things will ever go back to the way they were before. Too much has changed. Sometimes I feel like I was Dorothy on the yellow brick road and believed my dad was this all-powerful wizard who had all the magic. But once I saw behind the curtain and knew who he really was, that it was all a bunch of smoke and mirrors and he was a flawed man like the rest of them, I couldn't go back to believing in him the way I used to."

"Shit," I mutter. "That's sad. I'm sorry."

She shrugs. "I think Mom feels the same way. Why do you think she's so into therapy? Ever since that whole thing came out it's been her life's mission to keep this family together. At least she's been successful at it."

"I don't know what to say."

"What is there to say? It sucks. Dad made a huge mistake,

Mom forgave him, and eventually Hayes and I did too. Chandler . . . nobody told Chandler."

I guess I can understand that. I had preconceived notions about Down syndrome when I met Chandler, but the truth was I didn't really ever get to spend a significant amount of time with someone who had it until I was introduced to my sweet cousin. He's the same as other people in a lot of ways, but in others, he's undeniably different. There are limitations to what he can process. He lives a full life in his own way. The family keeping this information from him probably isn't because he can't take it but because they don't want him to have to.

"I'm glad things worked out," I say softly.

She nods. "Well, you know my father. He's not a shitty person, he just did a shitty thing. He's actually got a really good heart. Anyway, it's all over now."

But I can't help but wonder if that's true.

Of course it's over with Victoria King because she passed away, but what if there are other women? And what if she'd never died, would he still be fooling around with her in secret? And if that was the case, would Sybil and Ethan be married by now? Or maybe something else would've happened. Maybe Victoria and Gregory would've left their spouses to be together. If things had happened differently, there's a good chance that I never would've found my family. I wouldn't even be here right now.

I ask the question I've been dying to ask, the one that makes me feel like I'm walking on the sharp edge of a blade. "Do you ever regret what their affair did to your engagement?"

"No." Her answer is immediate.

I sit up, turning to face her and swinging my legs over the edge of my lounge chair. Her answer feels like the most important one of this entire conversation. "Why not?"

She sits up too, facing me. Our knees rub together but

neither of us shifts away. The scent of her spicy-sweet perfume mixed with the sunscreen we applied earlier wafts between us. "Ethan and I would've ended up like our parents."

My eyebrows pop up. "Cheating on each other?"

She nods. "We didn't love each other enough to make it through the long haul. Sure, we cared deeply, but there was always something missing with us. By the end we only got engaged because that's what was expected of us."

I wonder if Ethan feels the same way and I doubt it. The man I met was completely hung up on Sybil. He never acted like their relationship was a lie. Maybe her father's affair hit her harder than she lets on. Maybe she really did think they were going to make it but discovering her father wasn't faithful shook her foundation. Could she be looking back on that relationship with a jaded attitude instead of seeing the love they shared?

"I'm sorry." I take her hand and squeeze. She squeezes back and offers a smile.

"It was hard to break up with Ethan at the time, but it was for the best for a multitude of reasons. We're both better off."

"You really think so?"

"Hell yeah. I love being single. Playing the field isn't just for guys, you know."

Something within me relaxes, like a tight tangle of knots finally slipping loose. This is the perfect opportunity to tell her about my history with Ethan. She'll understand that I didn't know her at the time. She won't be angry with me and if anything she'll be upset on my behalf. Maybe it will bring us closer together. We can even bitch about Ethan together.

"Stay away from the Kings," she warns. "Take it from me, they're bad news."

"Well I agree with you there--" This is it. Tell her.

She fans her neck and sits forward. "I'm too hot. I'm heading in."

Before I can gain the courage to stop her, Chandler and Hayes are back, racing each other to the pool, and Sybil's up and drifting into the house like she doesn't have a care in the world.

Wouldn't that be nice?

My tennis shoes slap against the hard sand where the surf has left an extra layer of density. I keep having to dodge the water whenever a larger wave rushes up the bank, but overall, running on the beach isn't too bad. I'm sure I could move onto the loose stuff and make it ten times harder. No thanks.

I still run almost every morning. It's my favorite exercise—I love starting my day out with an endorphin-fueled sense of accomplishment. Plus, running is accessible and cheap, and while I wouldn't call it easy, it's not too intense either. I went with Sybil to one of her cycling classes shortly after I moved in and that was much more difficult. When she tried to drag me to a Pilates reformer class the next week, claiming that it would make my butt rounder, I'd told her I would start going with her when she started running in the early mornings with me. She laughed and dropped the issue.

After almost a week on the island I've let myself get lazy, skipping all my morning runs. So this morning I'm running on the beach to punish my laziness, and I can already feel the inactivity biting at my sides and chasing my heels as a warning not to get too complacent. How fair is it that good conditioning can take months to build up but can disappear as quickly as the sand flinging behind my shoes?

"Hey!" someone calls out, blending into the background

ambiance of my thoughts, but the calling continues. "Hey! Arden!"

I stop and turn around to find Cooper jogging down the beach. I let him catch up even though I don't really want to talk to him. Sybil was right, I need to stay away from these people.

"How are you?" Sweat drips down his bare chest and he's got a tattoo on his arm that wasn't there when I last saw him shirtless. The black ink portrays angel wings with a Roman soldier's helmet in front and a sword going through the whole thing. I'll admit it's an attractive addition to his physique. I wonder what it means but I don't ask.

"You're a runner now?" I ask instead.

The Cooper I knew never went running. He surfed and hit the home gym, but most of his cardio seemed to be spent in bed with his revolving door of women. And he certainly wasn't ever awake this early.

He nods. "Yeah, I started last year." Interesting. I wonder what happened last year to make him change his habits. "You didn't answer my question. How are you?"

"I'm fine. What are you doing here?" The Kings' estate isn't on this side of the island. If he picked up running on the beach, good for him, but shouldn't he stick to his territory?

"Looking for you."

And there it is.

I shouldn't be surprised he came right out with it. Cooper never was one to play games, often saying what he thought exactly when he thought it, even when that meant sticking his foot in his mouth.

"Why?" My eyes narrow.

He shifts his weight from one leg to the other. "Can we talk?"

I peer over my shoulder, as if expecting one of the Laurences to be watching. That's silly because none of them are morning runners and I'm a few miles from the house. Either way, people like to gossip and I know better than to talk to Cooper out in the open.

Yet, I do it anyway.

"Sure." I motion to the direction I was headed and start walking. My eyes stay trained on the darkened sand, waiting for another big wave to dodge.

Cooper walks beside me, our steps in sync for a minute before he begins. "Ethan has changed." He announces this like it's some kind of revelation.

"Okay? And you came all the way over here to tell me that?"

He nods.

"Why?"

"Because you're the one who changed him."

Forty-Four

A longing blooms in my chest but I quickly stomp it out. "What is this really about?"

I stop and turn on him, taking in the lines of his face. He's barely aged, still looks like the same carefree guy I knew, but there's a maturity behind his eyes that was never there before. How much has happened to him in the time since he finished grad school and started working for his father? And how much has happened to Ethan?

"I *am* being honest," he says. "He told me what happened between you guys. I know everything."

This revelation comes with mixed feelings. Half of me feels vindicated, like I wasn't just a footnote in Ethan's life. And the other half is jealous that Ethan had someone to talk to when I had nobody. I went through that shit on all my own.

"And what did he tell you?" Because I'm curious but I'm also suspicious that it's not the full truth. Ethan doesn't strike me as the kind of person to take accountability for his actions, no matter how much I wish he would. *But he came to you, he told you everything. He groveled and you kicked him out*—this thought grabs on tight and won't let go.

"I know about the hurricane and how you ended things."

"Do you mean how I ended things or how he ended things? Because there are two sides to that story."

"Both. And I also know about the lawsuit. My father was an ass but that's not the surprising part. If only you knew the hoops we've had to jump through with him, you'd understand why my brother and I are so fucked up."

We're not walking anymore, we're just standing here face to face as the surf occasionally splashes around our feet. Forget trying to save my tennis shoes. Mine are sinking deeper into the sand, water seeping in, but it's like I've forgotten how to move. All I know how to do is have this conversion with him, to seek healing for festering wounds that won't close.

"So tell me, what is the surprising part? Because I already know that you guys were the ones to drop the charges, not Conrad."

"That my brother, a guy who gets every damn thing he wants, who isn't afraid to go after anything, that has never had trouble with women before, is so fucking hung up on you that he hasn't even been able to look at another woman in two years."

That leaves me speechless.

"And you're not even going to give him a chance."

That doesn't.

I step back, breaking free. "Give him a chance? You can't be serious."

"I'm dead serious."

"But I'm a Laurence now—–"

"I don't give a fuck if you're a Laurence or he's a King. You want him. He wants you."

"I don't want him."

He laughs. "I'm not blind. You've wanted him since the day we met you. And guess what? You guys can be together. It's not that complicated."

But it is that complicated.

"The girl I knew was head over heels for my brother." I open my mouth to argue but he beats me to it. "Don't even try to deny it, we both know it's true. You never took your eyes off him all summer."

I scoff. "How would you know? You were busy burying your dick in women all summer."

His eyebrows shoot up. "And why the fuck do you think I never had sex with *you*?"

I ball my hands into fists, the shame of that experience surfacing. The rejection. Being ignored. Forgotten. "You didn't have sex with me because your brother talked some sense into you and told you that if you did, you'd have to seriously date me and you don't seriously date anyone."

His voice softens. "Look, for one, I'm sorry about that. I never should've treated you like that. I didn't know how to handle things with you back then."

"No kidding."

"But for two, that's only partly true. I knew you wanted Ethan. And I was a competitive little shit about it so I wanted your eyes on me instead. But when he pulled me off you like that? That's when I knew he wanted you back. I wasn't going to get in the way."

Oh... "I never thought of it like that."

He nods and visibly relaxes. "Because he's my brother and I love him, so I wanted him to be happy. And if the Laurences really love you, they'll want you to be happy too."

"But what about Sybil and all the bad blood?"

"Sybil doesn't love Ethan. You love Ethan. That's what

matters. And as for the rest of it, that's between our parents, not us."

Maybe, but what happens if I let Ethan into my heart again and he breaks it twice? I don't know if I can go through that again.

I'm not brave enough to ask this question, but it's like Cooper reads it on my face because he answers it anyway.

"For the last two years, he hasn't dated anyone. I couldn't figure it out but now that he's told me everything that went down with you two, it's clear as fucking crystal. Trust me, my brother has missed you. He's paid his dues. He's not like me, he's not a fuckboy. Ethan is a relationship guy. Monogamy or nothing. But nobody interested him."

I snort. "You're calling yourself a fuckboy?"

"We both know I am." He laughs it off. "And then we saw you at that party and all the pieces clicked into place. I know my brother better than anybody, so I confronted him about it and he finally told me everything that went down. He hasn't moved on because he's still hung up on you."

The worst part of this is that I'm equally hung up on him, but what does it matter? I'm not going backwards. I have a new life now. A better life. Even if I don't have romantic love, I have family love. I have Sybil and Chandler and Hayes and Amelia and Gregory.

"I'm not saying he's your soulmate or that you're going to get married, but I am saying that you both owe it to yourselves to give this thing a real shot." He clicks his tongue. "Trust me. I know what I'm talking about."

That gives me pause and I step back, giving him my most skeptical look. "Since when do you know the first thing about relationships? Have you ever even been in one?"

His face falls and I wince inwardly. It might've been a low blow, but it's the truth.

"Never anything serious or public or *real* and that's exactly why I know what I'm talking about. I date around a lot. I know what's out there."

That's the understatement of the century. He must be able to read what I'm thinking on my face because his cheeks go adorably pink and he shakes his head earnestly. "The kind of spark you guys have isn't something that comes along every day, okay? You're taking it for granted."

"I'm not."

"You are. What if this love you guys have is the best either of you are ever going to find? What if he's your person and you're being too stubborn to forgive him?"

I don't know what to say to that. This all feels too fast while simultaneously feeling like it's been years in the making.

"Just think about it." He rakes a hand through his sun-kissed brown hair and shakes it out, looking like he's exactly where he belongs on this beach.

"You really care about him, don't you?"

"He's my twin brother, of course I do. Yeah, we're competitive as shit and give each other a hard time sometimes, but at the end of the day he's my person and I want him to be happy."

"And you think I'll make him happy?"

"I know so . . ." He worries his lip between his teeth and nods once as if resolving something in his head. "You know those docks you guys were at during the party?" He doesn't wait for me to answer. "You can find him there most days. He goes sailing in the mornings and finishes up by early afternoon. We're here for another week. Longer if there's reason to stay."

"Sailing, huh?"

"It's his new thing, apparently," Cooper chuckles and winks. "Whatever floats your boat. Pun intended."

I playfully punch him in the arm. "You're so weird."

"Our slip is on the very end of dock seven. Go see for yourself."

So I wouldn't even have to go by the Kings' residence if I wanted to see him.

Coop tugs me into a quick hug and then walks away, setting into his easy familiar swagger at first and then picking up pace to run.

Running wasn't his thing, but it looks natural on him now, so maybe he really has changed. And if he's changed, doesn't that mean Ethan has as well?

I certainly know I have.

Maybe that's what happens with time. Maybe we all change, and if we're smart about it, we mature, too. But even so, I can't help but think some things will always stay the same. Like the sun that rises in the east and sets in the west. Like the way I felt when I first laid eyes on Ethan. I never believed in love at first sight but that must've been it because I also never believed I could hurt as much as he hurt me.

Only love can hurt so good.

I pick up my pace too, needing to run until my lungs burn and my mind clears and I don't have to think about what the hell just happened. Unfortunately, I'm not fast enough. I can't outrun the truth in my heart, nor can I outrun my family obligation to stay away from the Kings.

Forty-Five

That night we skip the high-end restaurants and the private chefs the Laurence family are accustomed to and make dinner ourselves. Aunt Amelia loves to cook and has passed down her skills to her children. Me on the other hand? No chance. But still, it's fun to sit around the kitchen and watch the masters at work, helping out with whatever odd jobs are needed.

I'm chopping up cucumbers for the salad when Aunt Amelia turns on me with an appraising gaze. "We can finish up here. Why don't you and Sybil go upstairs and freshen up?"

I frown at my linen shorts and plain t-shirt. Is this not appropriate for dinner? There's still so much about their world that I have to learn, like apparently we should wear nice clothes to dinner in our own houses with our own family. My voice wavers. "What kind of outfit should I wear?"

"Sybil will help you."

"Yes I will!" Sybil drops the dish towel she was just using to wipe off her hands.

"She looks fine," Hayes says nonchalantly. He's standing

over the stove doing something magical with the chicken. At only seventeen, it's pretty impressive. Whenever I try to make chicken it turns out dry and flavorless.

"Thanks for having my back." I shoot him a wink and he nods sagely. He really is growing up.

"I'm not changing," he states. The kid is in tie dye board shorts and a band t-shirt. So okay, maybe not so grown up. "Arden shouldn't have to either. It's dinner at home. Who cares?"

Sybil turns on her mother, the two communicating with their eyes alone. Amelia gives a little nod. "Stay out of it, Hayes," Sybil chirps, her mouth twisting into a sly smirk.

"Stay out of what?" Chandler asks. He's setting the dining table and is meticulous about every item being placed perfectly. He's usually the type to ignore family drama but this conversation has him wide-eyed and curious.

"You'll find out soon enough." Sybil hands the spatula off to Amelia like a baton. "Let's go." She grabs my hand and tugs me upstairs before I have a chance to finish my job, leaving the cucumber half-chopped on the cutting board.

"What aren't you telling me?" I ask the second she drags me into her room. She turns on me with a knowing grin.

"We have dinner guests tonight."

I narrow my eyes. "What dinner guests?"

"The kind that includes a single twenty-six-year-old hottie who just so happens to be interested in you."

I stare at her. "You guys are setting me up? I don't want to be set up."

"Don't worry, you like him."

"I like him?" My frown deepens.

She really has no idea what's been going on in my head lately. No new guy is going to have a chance with me when I'm so hung up on Ethan. Still, it doesn't hurt to humor her. This is what my family wants and it's not like I have to marry the guy, but I can give him a chance.

"Who is he?"

"Perry Hargrove," she announces, then prattles on about how she's known him for years, that he's rich and handsome, and how admirable it is that he went out on his own instead of joining the family business like all their other friends. "He's an executive producer for a hit television show called The Verb. Have you ever heard of it?"

"I'm not much of a TV person," I remind her.

She waves that off. "It's really edgy. Anyway, he splits his time between California and Manhattan. He hasn't dated anyone in a while but he's into you. And you've met him, so you already know he's a good catch."

If he's such a good catch, why doesn't she date him?

But I keep my mouth shut and allow her to dress me. Really, this woman should've been a stylist on top of an interior designer. She's got the eye and the personality for it, but on the other hand she's doing a lot of good with Laurence International's charitable foundation. She styles me in a long beachy dress with a slit up the side to reveal my thigh, gold understated jewelry, and then manages to tame my hair into loose waves. "You really don't need much makeup but let's accentuate those gorgeous eyes."

I snort. "They're boring brown." Nothing like her vibrant green.

"Don't say that. They're a stunning honey and I love them."

Twenty minutes later and we're heading back downstairs, following the low hum of conversation leading to the outdoor dining area. There are voices I don't recognize. They must belong to Perry and his family. And of course, when we slide through the back door and out onto the patio, we're greeted by the ever-so-handsome Perry Hargrove, his sophisticated mother and father, and teenage twin sisters who are busy huddled together over their phones.

Perry looks me up and down, eyes appreciative, and grinning at me like we're the only ones here. It should make my stomach swoop in excitement, not twist in on itself like I'm going to be sick. I know I told myself I'd give him a chance, but now that I'm faced with it, I don't think that's possible.

Besides the brief conversation at the yacht club party, I haven't seen Perry since the Fourth of July two summers ago. Even still, it would be impossible to forget a face like his. He's the classic Hollywood type and could easily be the one in front of the camera instead of behind it if he wanted to be a movie star.

Sybil elbows me gently before strutting forward and throwing her arms around his neck. "It's good to see you again, Perry."

"You too, Sybil. It's been too long." His reply sounds genuine, but his eyes are on me. If I wasn't sure what someone blatantly checking me out looked like before, I sure know what it looks like now. "Arden, it's so great to see you as well." He finishes his hug with Sybil and then wraps me in an even tighter one. I stiffen under the touch. It's not like we're old friends. I've only had two conversations with him.

We settle into our spots around the table and no surprise, I'm placed right next to Perry. The food smells and looks wonderful but I can hardly taste it. It's not Perry himself that bothers me—it's this blatant setup.

First my uncle swoops in and claims to save me from a lawsuit, then he moves me to Manhattan and gives me a place to stay, pays for my college, ensures I have a job at his company, and now he's trying to set me up with his friend's son. Don't get me wrong, I know I've been blessed, but sometimes I feel like I've lost control of my life. The girl I used to be is gone but I still don't know the person I'm supposed to be in her place.

After dinner, the group heads out to the beach to watch the sunset and I soon find myself standing alone with Perry.

"I haven't scared you away, have I?" he asks.

I laugh lightly. "I don't know, you're pretty scary."

"And you're beautiful."

I go tense and look up at him, trying to search out if he's being genuine or just playing a part.

"It's true," he says. "You're even more beautiful now than you were two summers ago."

He's staring down at me with dreamy dark eyes, dimples popping in his smooth African American skin, a bewildered smile bright on his mouth. He's so handsome that it would be easy to get swept away by him. And this is the kind of brazen compliment that I'm not used to receiving, the kind of thing that probably would've worked on me when I was younger and eager for affection. I wanted love so badly back then, but now his words do nothing for me.

"Perry, I don't know what you want from this, but I just want us to be friends."

His mouth twists and he lets out a labored breath. "Wow, I really read this all wrong. I'm sorry."

"There's nothing to apologize for. I'm flattered."

He rocks back on his heels and smiles again. "So you won't let me take you out on that date?"

Why should I? He dropped me the second Ethan got in the way and now that our families have decided that we'd make a great couple, suddenly he's back to being interested? It's not all that romantic. "I don't think friends go on dates, but we could hang out with Sybil if you want."

He shrugs. "If that's what you want. It's okay. I'm not going to beg. We can just be friends." He says it honestly, not an ounce of annoyance or expectation, and I finally relax, my limbs loosening like coiled springs releasing.

"Why don't you take Sybil out?" I suggest. It's obvious to me that they'd make a great couple. They have so much in common and seem to get along really well.

Sybil is a gorgeous woman who has men knocking down her door. I would know, I live with her. She has multiple dates a week and is always off to some event or another. I also know all about her active sex life, but she never stays with anyone for long. Getting into a real relationship would probably do her good and Perry is at a stage in life where he's looking for one.

"Don't think I haven't tried," Perry laughs. "But Sybil's just like you. It's friend-zone only with her."

Hmm . . . that's interesting. Maybe it's because Perry actually is an old friend and she doesn't want to do anything to mess it up? Or maybe there's more to the story? I can't forget how I met Perry in the first place—through the King twins. The ties to her old flame could be a deal-breaker for her like it is to me.

"Guess my parents will have to get over it," he finishes. "A Hargrove-Laurence match isn't in the cards no matter how much they want it."

And how much my aunt and uncle want it.

I smirk. "So you admit your parents set this up? Way to make a girl feel special."

"Oh, I'd still love to date you, but trust me, they'd love it just as much. They're constantly trying to get me to date their friend's daughters."

"You say that like you don't normally do it."

He tilts his head up to the sky, smirking as the breeze catches his hair. "Oh, I don't."

"Why not?"

"Do you want the whole truth?"

"I can handle it."

"A few reasons. I wasn't looking for anything serious until recently and casually dating someone in my parents' social circles would've had them planning my nuptials. That, and most of those girls aren't half as hot as you and Sybil are."

"So you're admitting you're shallow," I tease.

"Oh, absolutely. I'm as shallow as they come. Why do you think I got into television production?"

We laugh and things become easy after that. Before long the others join us, and we head back to the patio where we spend the rest of the evening chatting. The sunset is stunning, the sky going bright crimson before giving way to darkness. The Hargroves eventually leave and my uncle corners me on my way up the stairs as I'm about to turn in for the night.

"What is your impression of Perry?" He folds his thick arms over his chest and studies me in that pensive way of his.

I falter, grasping for the right thing to say. I knew this conversation was coming so at least handling it now means we can get it over with.

"I think he's a nice guy and a nice friend." I don't want to disappoint anybody but I'm also not going to let my uncle dictate who I date.

"He's a great guy and comes from a respectable family," Gregory points out. "And he's got his eye on you. If anyone could catch Perry Hargrove, I think it could be you."

I sigh, leaning against the banister and wishing I could be different. It would be so much easier to give in and let Uncle Gregory choose this life for me, but I just can't. Not when I know what it feels like to be so drawn to someone that they're with you even when they're not. "I'm sorry but I don't think there's any chemistry between us."

Gregory studies me for a long moment, his mouth slowly setting in disappointment. I almost expect him to argue, but he doesn't. He just nods once, as if it's done. "Very well. We'll just have to find you someone more to your liking."

"Please don't."

He chuckles. "Between you and Sybil I've got my work cut out for me, but never you mind, I'll take care of everything."

"I know you mean well, but I'm only twenty. I'm not old enough for all this."

"You're a smart girl," he says. "Thinking about your future means more than school and a career. Who you marry is going to be the most important decision you'll ever make."

The key in that sentence is it'll be a decision that *I* will make, but he doesn't seem to get that, and I don't know how to make him understand.

He leaves with the final word, bounding back down the stairs and striding away, as if all of this is normal, as if I should be thrilled that he wants to play matchmaker to my future. Maybe that's normal in this world of elite one-percenters, but it's not normal to me. The last thing I need is to end up in some kind of arranged marriage situation.

There are a lot of things I would do to please that man, but adjusting my love life to suit him isn't one of them.

Except, that's a lie, because if I truly didn't care what Gregory thought, I would be with Ethan right now.

Forty-Six

"What do you think you're doing?" Sybil marches into my room a few nights later, eyes bugging at the sight of my pajamas.

"Going to bed?" I state the obvious.

She snorts. "Oh no. We're going out."

I run my hands along the cool silk shorts, inwardly groaning at the thought of changing out of them. My legs are freshly shaved and lotioned, and all I wanted to do was lay down between my crisp sheets and read my book. "I'm not twenty-one, remember? You're just going to have to wait another summer before I can go to the bars with you."

"Don't worry, I've got that covered. You need to let loose and I need to show you around the fun side of Nantucket. No more snooty uptight rich people shit."

"I'm not saying you're snooty or uptight, but you do know you're richer than most of the people around here, right?"

"And yet we haven't had any fun," she pouts.

"That's not true. I've had fun."

Since we've been here I've already done more than I did in

the entire summer I spent with the Kings. We've gone to eat at all her favorite spots, shopped at several boutiques, laid out at the beach every day, swam in the pool, watched loads of romcoms on the massive flatscreen, and we even had a picnic lunch at a nearby lake that I had no idea existed. Thank God it wasn't the same lake Ethan took me to—I don't know how I would've reacted had it been.

"Well, *I* haven't had near enough fun. Now get dressed, we're going out."

An hour later we're walking into the very same club that Bree had tricked me into getting turned away at the door. A pit eats at my stomach at the memories of Ethan taking me home. He'd been such a dick about it, but now I look back on those memories a little differently. I'd been so naive that night, riding my bike out here and thinking I could just walk in this place. He may not have been nice about it, but he was protecting me when nobody else cared.

I'm sure I'm going to be stopped and humiliated, but this time the bouncer is a different man and I'm with Sybil. She hands him several crisp one-hundred-dollar bills and the guy lets us in without question, he doesn't even ask to see our IDs at all.

"Wait," I whisper to her. "That was illegal."

She laughs and gives me a wink. "Lifestyles of the rich and the famous, babe. Get used to it."

I don't know if I want to . . .

We head over to the bar and Sybil orders us cocktails. We drink them faster than we should and then she's leading me out toward a group of hot guys who've been eyeing us, one of which just happens to be all too familiar. "Well, lookie who it is. Perry-Fucking-Hargrove," Sybil slightly slurs his name and I could kill her.

"Was this another set up?" I say under my breath but she either doesn't hear me or she pretends not to hear me. Perry is with three other men, all looking great and all with devilish grins plastered on their inebriated faces. Sybil eats it up, handing me off to Perry so she can flirt with the others.

"It's good to see you again." Perry's voice is husky, his eyes lingering on my lips. I shift uncomfortably, and not because I'm wearing heels but because I thought we left things in a good place, that we'd agreed to be friends and nothing more. Now I'm not so sure he was being honest.

"Hello, Perry." My voice is frosty.

He inches closer, the scent of alcohol a cloud around us. "Dance with me."

It's not a request, it's an expectation, and before I can answer he's taking my hand and we're in the throng of people gyrating their bodies to the pulsing club music. His hands are on my body and he's too close. Part of me wants to close my eyes and relax, maybe even pretend he's somebody else. Maybe this isn't a big deal, maybe friends dance with each other like this and he's not angling for more.

My buzz makes everything go fuzzy and I find myself dancing with Perry, letting myself have fun instead of staying pissed off. Dancing with him, even dirty dancing, doesn't have to mean anything. If I was Sybil, it might even mean a couple of hookups and nothing more. It won't mean sex with me, it will just mean dancing, but that's okay.

The song changes, the beat turning sultry, and Perry slides in behind me. His face nears the crook of my neck and his breath sends goosebumps skittering across my skin. He takes hold of my hips and presses me back against his hard chest. My dress is already too short and now it's riding up. He slides his hand down the length of my body, fingers digging into the flesh of my upper thigh. I can feel his erection growing against my backside and he groans into my ear. "What kind of friends do you want to be?"

I step away and he lets me.

"Sorry, too forward?" Everyone dancing around us seems to be closing in, pushing us back together. He reaches out to tug me back against him. "No worries, Arden. I get it. Let's just dance."

But I'm done dancing.

"She doesn't want you to touch her." Someone growls over the music.

"What the fuck would you know about it?" Perry snaps back and I whip around to find Ethan and Cooper standing not two feet away from us.

These guys are all friends. Ethan and Cooper were the ones to introduce me to Perry in the first place. So why do they look like they want to rip each other's heads off?

"Come on Arden, let's get out of here." Perry grabs for my hand, fingers digging into my wrist.

Ethan lunges at him.

It happens so fast I barely have a chance to register the moment Cooper yanks me behind him. Ethan's fist connects with Perry's face and Perry stumbles back, blood spurting from his nose. But he's quick to recover, ramming his shoulder into Ethan's stomach and taking him down.

All hell breaks loose.

The crowd separates for the fight and the men don't hold back. They're yelling obscenities and fighting with ruthless drunken abandon. Sybil is suddenly there, pulling me away from the fight, and then so are Perry's friends. With Cooper's help, they manage to peel the guys off each other. And then the bouncer is there too, and we're all getting our asses kicked out of the club.

We stumble out into the parking lot and only then does the gravity of the situation hit me—these men fought over me.

What idiots. How old are they again? Twenty-six? And here I'd thought they'd matured with age.

"I can take care of myself," I hiss at Ethan and then turn on Perry, "and you should know better. I said just friends and I meant it."

Everyone's staring at me like they're seeing me for the first time, especially Sybil. I reach out for her hand. "Let's go home."

"You guys need to grow up and leave us alone," she yells at Cooper and Ethan, as if taking Perry's side is a given. It irks me.

"That's what I've been telling them," Perry says.

"Oh, shut up, Perry," Sybil adds and I'm not so irked anymore.

Hand in hand, my cousin and I stride away.

"I'm so sorry," Sybil rushes her words. "I didn't realize I was sending you into that mess. Last I heard Perry had a falling out with the twins. I didn't realize it was bad enough for them to fight about it."

Or about me . . . but I don't say as much.

I tell her it's okay and then unable to stop myself, I look back at the group of men. They're not arguing or fighting anymore, they're just watching us. All five of them. Of course it's Ethan's fiery gaze that captures mine. His lip is bloodied, his hair is a mess, and his shirt is ripped. But none of those things compare to the intensity in his eyes.

And the hopelessness.

Hours later, after combing over every detail in my mind, I finally fall asleep, and those hopeless eyes haunt my dreams. Because as much as I wish I didn't, I understand exactly how Ethan feels.

The next morning I'm eating breakfast at the kitchen island when Chandler carries in the most beautiful bouquet of flowers I've ever seen. At least three dozen velvety red roses lay intermixed with sprigs of baby's breath and small fig leaves. They're in a crystal vase and he sets it down right in front of me without saying a word, going to the fridge and retrieving the gallon of orange juice.

"These are pretty," I say, admiring the arrangement. I've always loved flower arrangements even if I've never been on the receiving end of one.

"I don't like roses," he states so matter-of-factly that I snort.

"What's wrong with roses?"

"Too smelly." He makes a face as he pours the OJ all the way up to the rim of his glass, then carefully lifts it to his mouth and drinks, releasing an audible *ahhh* when he's finished with the first large gulp. "Hope you like roses though."

"Why?"

"They're for you."

My heart flutters. For me? I assumed Aunt Amelia had them delivered to brighten up the house. She loves fresh flowers, always has them around. I quickly locate the little white card tucked between roses with my name scrawled across the front and open it. The message is short and penned in neat boxy handwriting.

Sin from my lips? O, trespass sweetly urged. Give me my sin again.

PS: I'm sorry.

As cliche as it is, I swear my heart skips a beat. I know exactly who sent these flowers and penned this note.

Memories of laying in Ethan's bed and watching the Leonardo DiCaprio and Claire Danes film version of Shakespeare's tragedy flit through my mind. He started calling me Juliet after that. This quote is direct from the star-crossed lovers themselves when Juliet said it was a sin to kiss Romeo and he replied with how sweet it was to sin, that he wanted to do it again.

Ethan and I have become those star-crossed lovers with our family obligations keeping us apart—and our pride. He's an idiot for fighting with Perry last night but this apology might just make up for that display of masculine toxicity. It may even make up for a few other mistakes he's made with me.

I take the flowers up to my room, placing them on the dresser, then sit and stare at the card for the better part of an hour, my thumb running over the words again and again.

Forty-Seven

"Did you ever get your driver's license?" I corner Hayes after lunch. My aunt and uncle are gone for the afternoon and Sybil is laying down for a nap after our morning on the beach. As for me? I can't stop thinking about Ethan. He's like the sunburn on my shoulders, persistent and irritating and begging for relief.

"Yeahhh," Hayes draws out his answer but doesn't look at me.

He's sprawled out on the downstairs couch playing video games while Chandler watches with rapt attention. Their vacation has consisted of more Zelda than anything else, so it's no surprise that the animated princess holds their attention far better than I currently am.

"Do you think you could give me a ride?"

Pausing his game, he turns on me with a raised eyebrow. "You don't know how to drive?"

"Hey, don't pause it," Chandler groans.

"Sorry, but I need to talk to Hayes."

Chandler rolls his eyes and reaches out for the controller. "My turn?"

Hayes passes him the remote and Chandler resumes playing, his focus entirely on the television screen.

"I never learned to drive," I admit, plopping down next to Hayes and watching Zelda climb a tower. "It's on my list of things to do. Can you give me a ride or what?"

"Ask Sybil."

No way in hell I'm asking Sybil. "She's sleeping. She's got a migraine."

"What about Mom or Dad?"

"They're on the boat, remember?" And also, they can't know about this either. But they went out deep sea fishing at the butt crack of dawn and tried to get us to go with them. Nobody wanted to get up that early and I certainly didn't want to get on a boat. They are convinced I'm going to change my mind about boats by the end of our trip.

He sighs, gives a look of longing at the remote in Chandler's hands, then back to me. "Where am I taking you?"

I don't like lying to people and I especially don't like lying to Hayes, but I also can't tell him the complete truth. He wouldn't understand. "I just need to go back to the yacht club."

"Why?"

"I left something there," I lie, immediately wishing I hadn't.

His eyebrow quirks. "What did you leave?"

One lie always leads to two and I need to backtrack. "Why are you being so nosy? I thought you liked driving and will make any excuse to drive, or was your mom exaggerating?"

"You're right." He peels himself off the couch, acting like he's doing me some huge favor, but I can already tell he's excited to get behind the wheel.

Five minutes later we're in his dad's prized Bronco and Hayes decides to answer my question seemingly out of the blue.

"I've always been nosy. It's a misconception that girls are nosy and guys aren't. We're just as curious as anyone else." He's back to his peppy-self and the kid I'm used to. "So what did you forget at the yacht club?"

My pride. My heart. Take your pick. "Um--a necklace." My voice comes out all wobbly.

God, I'm such a bad liar and guilt hits me immediately for lying. "The little one with the seashell that you wear all the time?"

My cheeks flame. "I didn't realize you noticed." I bought that necklace two summers ago. It's my one physical souvenir from that summer and I can't seem to let it go. However, I'm not wearing it today. It's currently sitting on my dresser next to the roses.

"Umm—" my voice trails off. I really don't want to lie.

"You can tell me the truth, you know."

I eye him sidelong, wondering if that's actually true. I want to trust him, but he's a seventeen-year-old kid who might accidentally blurt something out at the most inopportune moment. "Since when did you become so perceptive?" I say instead. "Don't worry about me."

We find parking and he climbs out after I do. "It's okay." I assure him. "I'll find a ride back."

He scoffs at that and I realize my mistake. "What the hell is going on with you? You said you needed a ride. You'll be done in five minutes and I'll wait for you right here."

"I'll just Uber back." God, I sound like an idiot right now.

"You're not making any sense. You could've just done that to begin with."

There's a reason why I asked Hayes to help me and it was because I didn't think he would ask questions. Clearly, that was the wrong assumption. I should've called a car; it was stupid not to. My mistake is glaringly obvious now.

"Please, just trust me to get home safe, okay Hayes?"

He stares at me like he's trying to figure me out, but he finally takes a step back and nods. "Okay, if you say so, but call me if you need anything."

This is a level of maturity I haven't seen in a seventeen-year-old boy before. I really expected him to keep pushing the issue. "Thanks, Hayes. I owe you one."

I head off in the direction of the yachts, finding dock number seven that Cooper told me about. I have no idea what Ethan's sailboat looks like or where to find him, or even if he's here today, but I don't have his phone number and there's no way I'm going to his house. I'm just going to have to hope that Cooper was right and I could find him here.

The ocean breeze wraps around my bare legs and the sun beats down cruelly. We're eight days into our two-week trip and this is by far the warmest day we've had. I'm glad for the breeze but it does little to cool me, let alone to settle my nerves. There's no turning back now though, so I head toward the last slip, searching for Ethan.

Maybe this is a stupid idea.

Maybe I shouldn't have trekked out here.

Maybe I should've told Sybil the truth.

Maybe I'm wrong about everything . . .

My hands start to sweat and I think back to this morning, mentally revisiting the moment I took my medication to make sure I didn't forget. But I didn't, I had it with breakfast like I always do. Slowly, I breathe in and then out, counting to keep it steady.

"Arden?" Ethan's voice softens my anxiety.

I turn around and there he is.

He's standing on the deck of a gorgeous white sailboat, the name Juliet scrawled across the side in blue script. My mouth drops open and something shifts in my chest.

"You named your boat Juliet?"

He's quick, striding to the edge of the boat and jumping the few feet down to the dock. His hair is sticking up in places, like it's either windblown or he's been running his fingers through it or both. As he approaches, I catch the light reflecting off his eyes. They're made even bluer out here by the water. Deeper too.

"Yes, I did . . . after you."

"Why?"

"Boats are named after women and you're my favorite one."

Just. Like. That. I realize why I'm really here. I want this man back just as much as he wants me back. I'm putty in his fingers and he hasn't even touched me yet. "Why me?" My voice cracks. I can't believe this is happening.

I thought I would hate him forever, but I don't hate him. Not even a little bit.

"Because you're smart. You challenge me. You're kind and strong. And most of all, because you're so damn easy to love."

I'm unable to speak.

He takes my face into his palms and stares down at me, voice intentional, eyes convincing. "I'm in love with you, Arden. I love you. I have for years but I was too immature and lost to realize it at the time. You don't have to love me back. God knows I don't deserve it."

I told myself I came here to get clarity but that was a lie. I've been clear. I am clear. I'm not ready to confess those words but I want to anyway. Ready or not, I'm tired of denying myself the truth. "I love you, too."

Everything changes. We're standing on the edge of eternity, jumping off the cliff into the unknown together. He smiles and it's time to show him exactly how I feel. No more speaking when words can't express it like actions can. Rising to my tiptoes, my lips crash to his.

Kissing him is like falling, but in the best way. A rush of inertia that offers both relief and intensity.

He groans and takes me into his arms, lifting me up. My legs wrap around his center so naturally and he palms my ass. Need burns through me. It doesn't matter that we're in public or that it's the middle of the afternoon. All that matters is him and us and being together. We're not lost in this moment, but we're not lost in each other—*we're found.*

I feel so close to him but want to be closer. I never quite understood what people meant when they talked about emotional intimacy during sex until that day we spent at the pond and the night that followed. And now I'm about to experience it again because I have to have him.

He sets me down, breaking away, those gorgeous eyes searching mine. "Can I show you my boat?"

I snort. Something about that sentence paired with this moment is hilarious. "I'd love to see your boat."

And more. I'd love to see so much more than his boat.

He eagerly leads me inside. The sailboat is large and pristine, all scrubbed white surfaces and polished whiskey-colored cedar. This vessel isn't a yacht, it's meant to be smaller and move faster. The cabin itself is modest, holding a couch, a single bed, a kitchenette, and a small door that probably leads to a bathroom. I'm particularly interested in the narrow bed.

I turn back to him. "Is this really happening?"

"Only if you want it to."

I nod and then his lips are back on mine, no longer questioning. He loves me and I love him. What else is there? At the back of my mind, I know that's a ridiculous question. There's our families. There's a history of hurt and pain and lies. Those things alone are practically an ocean separating us but I don't care about that right now. All I care about are his mouth and his hands and that he uses both to take my clothes off.

He prods my mouth open with his own, deepening our kiss. I press myself more firmly against him. When I feel his hardness against my softness, my pulse skitters and I'm so overcome with emotion that I could cry. I need this. I need him inside of me, need to feel him taking me, need it in the most desperate way.

Between kisses I peel off my shirt and he tugs his over the top of his head, flinging it into the kitchenette. Watching the way his chest is revealed to me, the tanned skin, the even broader shoulders than I remember, the tapered waist and the flex of his muscles—it makes me want to weep. He's so beautiful. So perfect. And it's not just that he's conventionally attractive, it's that he's proven himself to me. It's that he's mine and I'm his in a way I've never belonged to anybody before.

His voice is ragged. Desperate. A man wholly undone by love. "Come here, Juliet. Let me look at you."

Forty-Eight

He tugs me forward again and with one deft move, unhooks my bra. My breasts are full, my nipples tight, and he takes one into his hand and the other into his warm mouth, grating his tongue around the tip. After giving it sufficient care, he moves to the next one, this time nipping at it with his teeth. I gasp and he chuckles, sucking in more of my breast and reaching his other hand down to my shorts. He slips it right under the hem without hesitating.

"You're soaked," he rasps. He sounds pretty fucking proud of himself. He should be. None of the other men I was with were ever able to get me this wet this quickly. Only Ethan. Only ever him.

It's been too long without him.

He slips his fingers through the slick flesh and rubs at the nub, then pushes in even further inside. "Fuck, that's good."

"So good," I mirror.

If I thought I was putty in this man's hands before then I had no idea what that word really meant because this--this is it. This is what it means to give yourself to someone. He can do whatever he wants with me now, mold me into any shape, and I'll gladly let him.

But I'm not powerless either so I slide my hand into his shorts too and cup his erection, first a light squeeze and then more firm. He groans, eyes fluttering, entire body going still. He's a large man who's filled out even more in the last two years but with a single touch I've taken control.

It's like someone has set a timer because suddenly we're off.

"I need you," I say, stroking with one hand and wrapping my other arm up around his neck. Our eyes lock as I tell him what I need. "Don't hold back."

"Okay, baby. I won't."

"Good, now stop talking and fuck me."

His eyes flash, pure masculinity radiating through his body. He tears down my shorts and underwear in one go, then drops to his knees and thrusts his face into my core. It happens so fast I barely have a chance to see it coming, let alone to gain balance. But I don't need it because he's holding me up with his face and my hands are gripping his shoulders. His tongue is a sinfully delicious thing, sliding up and down my swollen center. His greedy hands knead into my backside.

The orgasm rips through me fast and furious. I scream his name and heaven only knows what else as my legs shake and he savors every last drop of my orgasm.

Then he stands, wiping his face, and slipping from his shorts. His erection is just as big as I remember. The satisfaction of the orgasm he just tore from me is nothing compared to the one I want to ride out on his cock. So I step back to lay down on the bed, trying to pull him down with me, but he shakes his head, tugging me until I'm flush against his naked body. "We'll use the bed for the next one. For this one, I need you to hold on. Just let me get a condom."

"No," I say without thinking, but I've never had sex

without a condom and I'm desperate to feel him inside me bare. I can't stand the thought of anything separating us ever again.

He stares at me. "Are you sure that's safe?"

"Are you clean?" I ask.

"Yes, I promise."

"Thank God, because I'm clean and I'm on the pill," I say.

A wicked grin quirks his lips. "You have no idea what those words just did to me."

He's on me in a second, lifting me like I'm weightless. I know I'm a lot smaller than him but I still don't expect it and I squeal, anticipation building. I wrap my arms around his shoulders and my legs around his torso, holding on for dear life as he slides his cock home.

I gasp, the oxygen leaving my body. He's so thick and pressed to the base, seated and full. I don't think he's ever been this deep before. "Oh my God," I gasp.

"Does it hurt?" He kisses my earlobe as he whispers into my ear.

"No," I'm quick to reply. "I said don't hold back and I meant it."

Standing in the middle of the room, the boat lightly rocking from the waves, his hands on my ass and my legs around him, Ethan begins to pump. We both groan. "So fucking good," I murmur.

"You want more?"

"Please."

So he does, bending slightly and then thrusting up, harder and faster. My breasts bounce against his chest and I throw my head back, my moan growing louder. I don't even care. I've lost all sense of self-preservation at this point. *Make me scream, Ethan. I'll do it.*

He chuckles. "Oh, I plan to."

Wait—did I just say that out loud? My cheeks flame but there's no time for embarrassment.

"You're so perfect," he growls. "I love you so much."

"I. Love. You. Too," I reply between throaty gasps.

I think I say it over and over again, but I can't be sure because I lose myself in the feel of him. He's never fucked me like this before. Never so raw, so rough, and so deep. I'm mad for him. I wouldn't be surprised if I'll be able to feel him inside me for the rest of my life.

I'm getting too close too fast. "Put me down," I beg.

Let's do this on the bed. Against the wall. The floor. Anything. But I can't orgasm with him holding me up like this. It feels too vulnerable, too reliant on him to carry me through it.

"Don't deny yourself, baby," he chokes out. "I said hold on and I meant it." He kisses my lips once. Twice. "Do you trust me?"

"Yes." Damn it, but I do.

"Then let me take this one. All you need to do is hold on."

And so I do. My nails dig into his skin and my thighs tighten around him as the climax roars from deep within. It vibrates through my entire body, pleasure pulsing into every corner of my body and soul, and I can't help but cry.

"I know." His voice is husky and thick. "Let it all out."

He doesn't stop pumping as the orgasm continues. It's overwhelming. I've never felt this good before. Just when I can't think I can't take another moment, he continues to hold me there, continues to slam into me, his bare cock hitting deep inside as my wetness grows between us. Even his pelvis is sliding against my clit in the most perfect way. My legs are jelly and my nipples are hard and the added wetness makes the moment stretch into oblivion.

How long can a woman have an orgasm? It feels like forever

but I know it's probably only a few minutes, maybe even a few seconds. And then he's kissing me, releasing a gasp into my mouth as he spills his seed deep within. It's a beautiful thing, knowing what I'm doing to him, that he's releasing a part of himself inside of me.

He holds himself there until we're both ready to come down from the high, and then he gently sets me down, removing his cock from me, the evidence of our pleasure all over us both. I thought I would find something like this gross but I don't. It just makes me happy knowing that I've surrendered my heart and body to someone I love so deeply.

"That was, without a doubt, the best sex I've ever had," he states.

I smile, savoring the heated look in his eye. I know he'll need more than a few minutes, but if he was ready to go again right now, I would try.

"Mine too." I nod towards the captains-wheel that's perfectly framed outside the window. "Now why don't you take me sailing?"

Suddenly, I'm no longer afraid of boats. I guess Ethan makes me brave.

He chuckles. "Okay Juliet, I'll take you sailing under one condition."

"And what's that?"

"Once we're out on the water and alone, you let me make love to you on that deck."

"Make love, you say?" I tease. "I thought you only had sex."

He shakes his head, his hair tumbling into his eyes. "With you there's definitely a lot of both happening."

I grin, imagining being out there in the ocean on this boat, rolling waves giving us the perfect tempo to move as he covers my body with his. "You've got yourself a deal."

FORTY-NINE

I arrive home that night well after dark. Ethan took me all around the island, showing me how to sail, and then as the sun set, he laid me out on the deck and took me again. Or rather, he gave, because I swear his mouth traveled to every square inch of my body and when we finally came together, this time at a slower pace, the explosion was just as powerful as any before it.

I think I'll always remember the way our eyes stayed locked together while he rocked inside of me, mouth worshiping mine between soft confessions of love and pleading apologies for everything that has happened between us. He'd promised me that one way or another, we were going to be together.

God help me, but I believe him.

I love him and I trust that he loves me back. I know we're going to figure this out one way or another. But for now, I want to keep our relationship a secret from most people, at least until we have a solid plan. But I still want to tell Sybil about us. Not just want to, I need to. She's been nothing but wonderful to me and I owe her the truth.

Ethan doesn't love the idea, but he understands why I can't lie to her. She's become my best friend and she's like a sister to me. That, and she was engaged to Ethan, so she deserves to know what's going on between us.

After a hot shower and a bit of procrastination, I find her on her bedroom patio watching a TV show from her phone. "Where did you run off to?" She frowns up at me. "I've been blowing up your phone."

It's true. I have two missed calls and three texts from her, but I'd sent her a quick text back earlier that I was fine and would fill her in when I got home.

There's no backing out now.

"I met someone."

She jumps out of her seat, strays of red hair flying out of her messy bun. "What? You horny bitch!" she squeals. "Tell me everything right now."

I laugh but inside I'm a nervous wreck. I'm not good at confrontation because I've never been close enough to anyone long enough to learn how to do it right. There's a way to have hard conversations without destroying a relationship and I make a mental note to ask Dr. Cory for tips at our next therapy session. If Sybil was someone I didn't love then this conversation wouldn't be so bad, but I do love her and I want her to keep me around. I already know she's going to judge me for what's about to come out of my mouth. Maybe that's not fair, but I just have this sinking feeling that things are about to change for the worse.

"Let's go inside."

Her eyes round. "Oh, is this serious?"

"You could say that."

Her room is decorated similar to mine but in shades of pale pink and white instead of blue. It makes sense, she's the pink to my blue. We sit criss-crossed on her bed and I play with the hem of my pajama shorts, way too nervous to not be fidgety.

"Out with it, woman! I've known you for almost two years and have never seen you like this. It doesn't matter who it is, you could be in love with the pool boy for all I care. I'm just happy to see you happy."

"Even though it's not Perry Hargrove that I was out with?"

"Are you kidding? Perry can kiss my ass," she snorts. "And my dad can get over it. He doesn't get to set you up, this isn't the olden days. We're sex-positive, modern women."

But does she really believe everything she's saying? Because if she did, then she'd be okay with me dating a King.

"So I met this guy a few years ago but we just recently reconnected. Turns out we've both been holding out for each other." A smile creeps on my face. "And we're in love."

"Who is it?" Her voice is calmer now, more collected. More guarded.

"Just please understand that I never intended for this to happen."

"Who?" Her face is draining of color and it's my fault. She must already suspect what I'm about to confirm.

I swallow hard and force his name from my lips. "It's Ethan." The silence is an endless chasm between us. I expect her to say something, but she doesn't. "Please let me explain."

"Go ahead." Her voice is stony. Cold.

"You know we met two summers ago when I worked for them. At first I hated him, but over time he grew on me." She stiffens and I decide to make this quick. "Anyway, long story short, by the end of that summer, we started sleeping together."

"Was he your first?" Her voice sounds bitter and I nod. "Mine too," she tuts. "Go on. The story doesn't end there. Finish your explanation."

I can do this and she deserves the truth.

"We broke it off because I found a picture of you and thought he was using me to get over you." She doesn't say anything to this so I continue. "And he found out about the connection to you guys, and he knew how much I wanted a family." My voice cracks at that part and I love him so much more for understanding me on a level that other people never have. "He was actually the one to call your father and tell him where to find me."

She tilts her head, studying me for a long moment. "And now you've reunited and want to be together?"

"Yes."

She nods slowly and then lays back on the bed, her tired gaze staring at the ceiling as she continues. "First, let me start by saying I'm not mad at you but I am mad at him. He knows better. Second, this relationship is doomed to fail. Trust me, I've already been through this with him."

"I know, but--"

"But we were *engaged*, Arden," she says tiredly. "We dated for years. And we couldn't make it work because of all the family drama. What makes you think you two will be any better off?"

"I never knew his mom. I wasn't involved in any of that."

She sits back up, seemingly labored by the process. My news is already heavy on her heart, weighing her down. "That's not the point. A King and a Laurence can't be together. You're going to have to make a choice, same as I did. I choose my family. I choose being a Laurence." Her eyes fill with tears and heartbreak laces her tone. "I don't want to lose you."

"You won't."

"But I will, and Ethan will be the one to take you away."

"No."

"You can't be with him. You have to promise you'll end it."

I shake my head. "Please don't do this."

"Listen, Victoria King's death nearly killed my mother. They were best friends. So imagine how she felt when she found out that her best friend had been sleeping with her husband behind her back? She's not here to defend herself, so we'll never know why she did it." She shakes her head regretfully and I wonder how deep the betrayal feels to her too. She probably looked up to Victoria like a second mother.

"Dad's fucking lucky Mom forgave him, but it wasn't without a lot of hard work and a shit ton of tears. If you start dating Ethan, it's going to bring all that drama right back to the surface. Do you really want to do that to my parents? They've taken you in. Mom treats you like her own daughter. Please, Arden, you're one of us now. Don't do this."

She's right and it kills me that she's right. I nod numbly, feeling like my entire world is crashing down and nobody understands. When I asked her about her breakup with Ethan, she didn't seem that devastated by it. Not like I would be to lose him again. "I wish you understood."

"I do. I know how hard this is for you. I understand better than anybody. I loved him and I gave him up. If I can do it, you can do it."

But did she really love him? She said their marriage would've failed, that they would've ended up cheating, and that's not at all how I feel about Ethan, especially after today. I truly believe that if we were given the chance, we could prove to everyone that we're strong enough to not only survive but to thrive. We're good together. I make him softer, open him up, and he makes me stronger, gives me faith in myself. We're not destined to fail because of ourselves but we might be destined to fail because of everybody else.

"It will be okay. You'll get over him." She wraps me into a hug. We're sitting awkwardly on the bed, our crossed knees pressing together, hugging but I don't feel any closer to her. I feel so much further away. Miles away. Light-years. I wanted her approval and in my wildest dreams I'd hoped she would take this issue to my aunt and uncle and plead our case. "Don't worry. You will fall in love with someone else eventually. Someone better."

By someone better she means someone her family approves of, and what a bunch of shit that is considering she just said I could be in love with the pool boy and she wouldn't care. I love my cousin, I do, but she let her family obligations change the trajectory of her life and now she's assuming I'm going to do the same. I'm not her, I am me, and I want to keep this love, even if that means I have to keep it to myself.

FIFTY

I have his number now and I also have Cooper's. I made sure to get them before Ethan dropped me off at the gate yesterday and I walked back up to the house. But I also have five people in this house who want to keep me busy during our final days of vacation.

Ethan thinks it'll be easier to date secretly back in New York. We hate that we have to keep this a secret, it feels like we're ashamed to be together when we're not, but we also understand how much is at stake. If we come out with the truth, people who claim to love us will do everything in their power to rip us apart.

Eventually it will come to that, but until then we can pretend it never will.

And maybe we can figure out a way to be public.

Still, I can't wait until this vacation is over to see him. And he must feel the same because he texts me and we make plans to meet up again. I'm going to sneak away tonight and walk down the beach to a more private area where he'll be waiting. So all day, even as we lay out at the beach and as we eat our meals together, as we chat and enjoy each other's company, I know I'm betraying my family because I can only think of Ethan.

But it's either betray them or betray myself, and my heart is stuck in the middle.

I say goodnight to everyone and head up to my room to get ready to meet Ethan. My heart pounds and my hands shake with anticipation. I have to admit this forbidden lovers thing is exciting. Does that make me a bad person? Maybe, but I don't think so. I'm letting myself have something I really want. It's not my fault my uncle and Ethan's mother had an affair. Ethan and I shouldn't be the ones to pay for that. So as I get ready, taming my hair into soft curls and applying strawberry ChapStick to my lips, I push the guilt aside and focus on what I want, and right now that's to spend time with Ethan.

When it's sufficiently late enough that everyone has gone to bed, I use my security code to quietly leave the house and sneak out to the beach, my heart pounding with each measured step. It's dark out here and maybe not the safest decision, but I don't let that stop me. After a few minutes of speed walking, my vision adjusts and there he is, a tall figure waiting in the dark. There's nobody else out here, we choose a secluded section of beach away from the homes, so when I reach him, I don't even hesitate.

We come together like magnets, our mouths first and then our bodies. He's laid out a blanket on the sand and it takes us no time to lay down on it together. His body weighted over mine releases all the tension I've held inside since we last parted.

"This can't be wrong," I whisper between hot kisses.

"It's not, baby. It's right. It's so fucking right."

Well, if it is wrong then I don't care to be right. It's a cliche sentiment but it applies to us. Maybe this is wrong or maybe it's simply that what's right for the two of us isn't right for other people. We're not bad for putting ourselves first, for giving in to what feels like peace.

He kisses down my neck and onto my collarbone, then licks his way down to where my breasts are tight underneath my shirt. I'm not wearing a bra. He nips at the peaks through the cotton and I arch into his mouth, not caring if he leaves a mark. After a minute he kisses back up to my neck again and the cool left behind where his hot tongue trails across my skin dissolves into gooseflesh. I shiver and shift until my legs are spread. I'm wearing a long nightshirt and nothing else. There were no promises between us that we would make love again tonight, but when his rough hand slides up my thigh and he doesn't find any underwear, he practically growls. "You're fucking killing me, Juliet."

I roll my eyes but I'm definitely pleased with my decision to go naked underneath my nightdress. "You'd better show me exactly how much I'm killing you."

It's only been a day since we were together but it's all I've been thinking about. The images of our lovemaking keep flashing through my mind on an erotic loop, and I just want more. I'm greedy for the man.

He bites my nipples through the cotton and then all at once, he's sitting me up and lifting the shirt over my head, tossing it into the sand. The half-moon is my audience, as is the ocean, the sand, the stars, the tall grass behind us--and him. Most of all him.

I'm pale but under this light I'm practically glowing. Suddenly shy, I cover my breasts with my palms and shift my position so that my stomach looks smaller. I've gained some weight in the last few years and I don't want to disappoint him that I've changed.

"Don't you dare hide your body," he growls. "You're damn beautiful."

I don't know about beautiful but damned might be right.

He lifts my hands away from where I'm covering myself, savoring my naked form, then he nudges my legs apart so he can see me there too--I'm completely bared to him. It might be the most vulnerable I've ever been with him except for the moment I told him I loved him.

He's still completely dressed as he begins kissing my body, but I'm too impatient to wait like I did on our sunset cruise. I sit up and fumble with his shirt. Why did he have to wear something with buttons? "Are you ready for me, baby?" he chuckles low. "So impatient."

I nod eagerly and he rips the shirt apart, buttons flying, then makes quick work of his shorts. As soon as he's naked, I push him back, loving the way his brawny form feels underneath my greedy fingertips. The back of his head is in the sand and not on the blanket but neither of us cares. We don't know how much time we have because what if someone comes out here? This is considered public indecency, not to mention, if one of my family members decides to go on a late-night stroll, we're screwed.

I climb on top, clutching his hips and lowering myself onto his cock until fully mounted. We simultaneously moan and I begin to ride him. I rock and arch, rolling my sensitive clit against him with each movement. His eyelids flutter as he lets me take the lead. This might be the first time he's let me do it and I grin as the need for release grows and grows. It's wonderful and I'm in a rush for it to take over.

Just as I near climax, he lifts up onto his elbows and buries his face into my bouncing breasts. The movement changes our position and slows us down. He bites down on one and a pained pleasure courses through me. My motions become frantic.

"I'm not ready for this to end," he says, lifting me off him carefully. "Slow down, baby."

"I'm going to punch you," I deadpan and he laughs. "Being out here makes me nervous that we'll get caught," I confess. "I don't mind making this one quick."

His mouth quirks. "I got you, baby. Relax."

"I don't know how."

He kisses my cheek and whispers against my ear. "Get on your hands and knees."

He's taking charge again, and that alone relaxes me. I trust him and do as I'm told, my knees sinking into the blanket and hands in the sand. I squeeze it between my fingers as he positions himself behind me.

"You follow instructions so well," he says, his breath tickling my spine. "You're such a good girl."

The praise fills me with happiness as he thrusts back inside. The angle draws a gasp from my lungs and I buck back against him.

"Widen your legs." His hands are on my hips and then tracing down the curves of my ass as I do as he asks. "Good."

From this angle, I can't help but arch my ass up, guiding him in deeper. My breasts hang full and he palms one possessively. He begins to pump and the pressure is by far the deepest I've taken him before. It hollows me out and fills me again with each drive of his cock.

"Sure this is going to slow us down?" I pant.

The new angle is intense and I buck back in equal measure. This isn't going to take long, I'm already so close, and from the sounds he's making, he's on the edge right there with me.

"I changed my mind," he rasps. "We're not slowing down. Fuck that."

Thank God because I don't have control anymore, I've lost

it, handed it right over to this man who knows exactly how to send me over the edge.

The pressure builds, mindless pleasure spreading through me, and he tightens his grip on my hips, fingers splayed across my skin. He kisses along my back and I arch up into him, but it's not as deep and I need the depth. I need to feel all of him, everywhere. So I sink my face down into the sand, my breasts pressed against the blanket, knees wide and digging into the earth. He rears back with a guttural hiss, pounding into me like a man about to come undone.

Sand is all over my face now, in my hair and against the side of my cheek. I'm grabbing onto the beach around me for dear life but the sand slips between my desperate fists. Just when I can't take it anymore, the pressure builds to a crescendo and I fight to muffle a scream. There's nothing quiet about this moment, but at least the crashing waves help to drown out the sounds of our lovemaking. Fuck it, I scream his name anyway.

"Say it again," he commands.

"Ethan!" My voice is a keening sob. I'm ablaze with pure adrenaline. The pleasure rolls through me like the crashing waves in front of us, taking command of my body and soul.

Just as I start to come down from the high, he speeds up until he's cussing and releasing deep inside. I'm a whimpering mess but I truly don't care. This is too good. He is too good.

We are too good.

He pulls me into his arms, cradling me against his chest, and wraps the blanket around us. He kisses my cheek, my mouth, the top of my head. "Just let me hold you," he whispers.

Does he realize what an ask that is? Because he's not just holding my bared body to his, but my bared heart. All of me is here with him, given freely. It's the scariest thing I've ever done. I watch the dark ocean waves as they tumble into the shore, thinking of the night of the hurricane. As terrifying as that was, it doesn't hold a candle to what this moment means for me.

He could break me. He could destroy me.

And if not him, our families hold that power to do it for us.

"You're crying."

I shake my head. I'm not crying. But then I lift my hands to my cheeks and find the salty wetness there. He's right. "I'm just scared," I confess, "because I'm so happy."

"I know exactly what you mean." He holds me tighter. "But I promise you, I'm never going to hurt you again and I'm not letting you go. We'll figure this out. We're a team now, okay?"

I nod against his warm skin, breathing in the spicy masculine scent of him, memorizing the way the stubble on his chin feels against my forehead and the way his arms cradle me like I'm something to be cherished. His words are exactly what I want to hear, but they're also exactly what scare me. Because if we're a team, then that means there's a game at play, and the only games I know are the ones that end with a winner and a loser.

Fifty-One

It's the tenth night of vacation, which means I've still got three full days left. Tomorrow Ethan is supposed to head back to the city, and I can't help but daydream about what could be if he stayed and we got to be together openly. We could go to the beaches and the lakes, wander around the boutiques and pick out cheesy postcards together. He would take me out to dinner and then we'd spend the night in each other's beds. We could date for real. But this isn't that world. That world is a wish. And this one? This one belongs to warring families who will never stop.

At least Cooper is on our side, but I know Sybil never will be. I can't even say I blame her for that. But I also can't let her dictate my choices either, so for right now, I'm going to have to keep secrets, and I hate keeping secrets.

Sybil and I are out at a dive bar tonight, and this time she's invited a man along. Reid is an old friend turned casual hookup who's in town. The three of us are sharing a booth over drinks and I've never felt more of a third wheel than I do right now. Sybil and Reid are all over each other and every touch spears me with jealousy that I can't be public with my man.

Reid breaks away to go grab another round of drinks and Sybil scoots in closer, her green eyes bright. "I think I'm going home with him tonight. Is that okay?"

I sit up taller. "More than okay. You go have fun and I'll get a cab home."

"Are you sure?" She peers over to where Reid is already on his way back with drinks. The guy is already undressing Sybil with his eyes, the sexual chemistry between them thick.

"Of course, I'll see you in the morning," I insist, because she can do what she wants but also because this opens up the perfect opportunity for me to do what *I* want.

She kisses my cheek, jumps up, downs her shot, hands me mine, and then promptly hooks her arm through Reid's to drag him away, whispering in his ear as she goes. He follows her out the door willingly, not once looking back. I can't say I blame him; the man is about to get lucky with a beautiful woman.

I leave my untouched shot on the table and call Ethan. We weren't going to be able to see each other tonight, but it looks like fate is being kind. My aunt and uncle haven't been keeping close tabs on Sybil and I, so as long as Ethan gets me home before Sybil returns, nobody will be the wiser.

Ten minutes later, a familiar black Range Rover rolls up to the side street next to the bar. Cooper jumps out of the passenger seat and holds open the door for me.

"Hi, Cooper," I say, climbing in. "Fancy seeing you here."

"We were on our way out for the night when you interrupted us," he replies with an exaggerated sigh, closing me into the SUV and leaning into the opened window to speak to his brother. "If I'd known you two were going to hook up, I would have driven my own car."

"Sorry," I mutter as Ethan shoots him a glare.

"Don't be," Ethan says to me, then to Cooper he adds, "I think you'll survive."

"Where's Sybil?" Cooper asks, stepping back with a little frown to peer around the quiet street. "Isn't she supposed to be with you?"

"She . . . doesn't know I'm dating Ethan."

His eyebrows furrow and those brown eyes darken. "You didn't tell her?"

"Oh, I did, but she doesn't support it. She insisted I break things off."

Ethan has the maturity to keep his mouth shut during this exchange. Nobody has forgotten about his history with Sybil.

Coop shakes his head, and thankfully, his face softens. "That sucks. So where is she now?"

"She went home with a friend of hers. Some guy named Reid. He seemed pretty cool. Do you know him?"

Cooper scoffs. "Reid Havish? Of course she did . . ." He steps back and pats the side of the vehicle. "Alright, you can leave me here. I will get my own ride home later. I need a stiff drink anyway."

And then he's striding into the bar and Ethan and I are alone. I roll up the window and turn to Ethan with a huge smile.

"Hi," I say.

"Hi." He smiles right back and my stomach swoops low. The man really should smile more often but maybe the fact that they're rare makes them that much more special.

"Where do you want to go?" I ask coyly.

He puts the car into gear. "Let's go to the *Juliet*."

It's a good idea. We can be alone on the docked sailboat and it even has a small bed and bathroom. We don't need much to have a good time, just a little privacy and each other.

An hour later we're cuddled under the sheets, naked and

blissful on the twin bed. It's way too small for two people, especially one as tall as Ethan, but we make it work. The sailboat is docked and bobs slightly on the surf. I press my face into the crook of his neck, kissing the warm salty flesh of his clavicle and loving the way his hair at the nape of his neck has curled from the humidity we created in the small cabin. The thrill of good sex has given way to the exhaustion of the day and my body feels like it's slowly filling up with sand. I want nothing more than to stay the night here and let him hold me until sunrise.

But I can't risk it.

"I think you should take me back before we fall asleep," I whisper between the kisses I press to his neck.

"You could spend the night." His throat vibrates under my lips.

"I can't. You know what happened when I told Sybil about us." I let out a long, frustrated sigh and roll over onto my back, taking his hand and threading it through mine as I consider how to put this in a way that won't hurt his feelings. "We'll figure it out when we get back to the city, but while I'm under the same roof as my aunt and uncle, I don't want something to escalate the situation. Besides, I love the bubble we've created for ourselves. Nantucket is special for us and I don't want anything to ruin that."

He squeezes my hand. "It's okay, baby. I get it." We fall into companionable silence for a long moment before he speaks again. "But I couldn't do it. I told Conrad about us this afternoon."

Worry prickles through me and I drop his hand, sitting upright to stare down at him. In the faint light, I can barely make out his expression. He's being dead-serious, maybe even more than I've ever seen him before.

"And what happened?" I whisper.

"He took it surprisingly well, actually. We still got into an argument because I made him swear not to use us against Gregory. This is our private business. You and me are real, and it's not something for him to angle for his own benefit. He didn't like that but if he values his relationship with me, he'll stay out of my love life." A smile plays at his lips, but his eyes remain hard. "I'll be taking over as CEO soon. The plan is in motion and I've proved myself. He can't control me anymore and that's difficult for him to accept. I called him out on that, as well as some other bullshit. He didn't like that either."

"I don't know what to say. I'm sorry, Ethan."

"I'm not sorry." He pulls the back of my hand to his lips and kisses my knuckles, his soft breath warm and heady. "It's our house so Cooper and I could've told him to leave, but he got mad and left early. Him and his new wife are already back in Manhattan."

I let this sink in. Ethan did something brave for me, stood up for me, and here I am not willing to do the same thing with my family. Not yet, anyway. I will, I know I will. I just have to gather the courage first. I'm not so brave with my love.

"Okay, so what happens next?" I ask carefully.

"Coop and I are staying on the island until you leave. I'm not taking any chances leaving you here without me close by, especially now that Conrad is aware of our relationship. But when we get back to Manhattan, when you're ready, we'll tell our families that they can either accept us, or they can lose their relationship with us."

Lose us? The warm fuzzies floating around my chest turn to ice.

"Don't worry," he adds quickly. "They'll accept us."

But I'm not so sure about that.

That ice sinks deep into my belly but I keep my mouth shut. Ethan sounds so confident and I don't want to upset him. I know I want to be with him, but Sybil made really good points, and Amelia and Gregory are probably going to feel the exact same way. There's a very good chance my family won't accept our relationship and I really will have to choose.

Is Ethan clouded by love? Is that why he's being so positive? I don't know what to say to him that won't come out all pessimistic. Turns out, I don't have to say anything, because Ethan leans up to kiss me, his mouth lazily exploring mine until passion takes hold of us again and my thoughts give way to actions.

The next morning I wake up in my own bed, but the panic is already clawing up my throat and squeezing off my air supply. My skin crawls with itchy heat, stress hives forming.

I sit up and grab my throat, sucking in oxygen. Tears roll from the corners of my eyes, salty tracks leaving reminders on my cheeks that I am still Arden Davis. It doesn't matter that I changed my last name to Laurence, I can't erase the past.

Breath, I tell myself. *Remember what Dr. Cory taught you. You're overwhelmed and you drank too much last night. That's why you're having anxiety. This will pass.*

Just breathe.

My brain wants to cling onto my past, to insist I can't get through this. I'll always be that girl who experienced years of childhood neglect. I'll always have to live with generalized anxiety disorder.

In for one, two, three.

I hold for another three seconds and let the fear pass through me, allowing myself to feel the darkness move though my body without inviting it to stay.

Release for one, two, three, four, five, six.

I continue Dr. Cory's method of breathing until I slowly

come back to myself, my thoughts evening out and my physical reactions softening. After a few minutes, I'm not so sweaty, not so itchy, not overcome with unwanted adrenaline.

Despite everything, I smile.

Every time I can work myself through an anxiety attack and come out feeling alright about it, I get a little bit prouder, my self-confidence growing. I'm learning to have my own back.

With a final deep breath, I peel myself from my bed, go to the bathroom, and splash my face with cold water, then go down to breakfast still in my pajamas.

We've got a whole spread set up for us today, and even Sybil has returned from her night with Reid to enjoy it. We're all together and enjoy a wonderful breakfast, joking and laughing and eating—the picture of a happy family on a Saturday morning. And when we're done, my aunt and uncle each give me a hug. Gregory kisses the top of my head and Amelia tells me I'm a sweet girl. Maybe they noticed the red splotches on my neck and knew I needed a little extra love, or maybe they just wanted to remind me that I belong to them.

I can feel their love like it's a physical thing, something that cannot be easily killed, and I get a sense that it's all going to be alright. When we get back to the city, I will explain everything. They won't like me dating Ethan, but they love me, so they'll understand.

They have to understand.

Fifty-Two

The sunset reminds me of a creamsicle, all dreamy oranges mixed with swathy white clouds. Sitting at the front of my uncle's sailboat, I bask in the sensation of the ocean air whipping past. Uncle Gregory loves his boats. Not only does he have a yacht currently docked somewhere in the Caribbean, but he's got a sporty little speedboat and a luxury sailboat both docked here in Nantucket.

Tonight he finally convinced me to go out on the speedboat.

Hayes and Sybil have way more experience on this thing than I do. As far as the Laurence's are concerned, I've never been on a boat before at all. Ethan's boat is a secret I'm holding close to my chest, even if it does make me feel guilty.

It's my last day on Nantucket and I'm not risking seeing Ethan tonight. I've seen him everyday since we got back together and our affair is starting to eat away at me. I don't know how this is going to play out, but I just know I'll be with him.

We speed out from the docks and float for a while in the Nantucket Sound. Aunt Amelia pulls out a bottle of champagne and we toast to our successful family vacation. "I have to hand it to you." She smiles at her daughter. "You were right about selling the Hamptons house and building out here. It's so much more . . . rustic."

I nearly choke on my expensive champagne. If they consider their upscale Nantucket home rustic, I can only imagine how fancy the Hamptons one was.

"I like it better too," Sybil agrees. "And I love that Nantucket isn't nearly as crowded as the Hamptons."

Hayes grumbles that he liked the Hamptons house because he had friends there and Chandler says that both are fun, but he likes being at home best.

"Cheers to many new memories here." Uncle Gregory raises his flute and we clink them together. It's the kind of surreal moment I never thought would happen for me.

The guilt deepens, wedging itself right there next to the gratitude.

My eyes water and I hate that I'm on the verge of tears. I rarely cry in front of people and I've never cried in front of the Laurences. I'm grateful for my oversized sunglasses because I certainly don't want anyone to see what's going on behind them. After finishing our drinks and catching the last of the sunset, Uncle Gregory tells us to sit down so we can get going and Amelia busies herself with putting away the champagne flutes and bottle.

Sybil scooches in right next to me, swinging her arm over my shoulder. "Are you okay, babe? You seem sad." Can she tell why I'm feeling emotional?

"Yeah, I'm okay," I answer but my voice wobbles, giving me away. I am very much not okay.

"It only hurts now. It will get better," she says softly.

We don't have to go into details, we both know what and who she's talking about. She thinks I've ended things with

Ethan. I never outright told her I would, but I also led her to believe that I agreed with her. How am I going to do this? If push comes to shove, am I prepared to give these people up for him?

It's so unfair. Family is supposed to support one another. If they really loved me then wouldn't they understand? Wouldn't they want me to be happy and to be with the person I love?

"You've got to be kidding me!" Hayes points into the distance, a sour expression taking over his young face in a way I don't recognize. He suddenly looks ten years older. "That's the Kings' new sailboat, isn't it?"

I bristle, panic coursing through me. This can't be happening right now.

But sure enough, only a few hundred yards away, the *Juliet* bobs on the water. Atop it two males are silhouetted against the backdrop of fiery red sky—Ethan and Cooper.

"Let's go," Amelia's voice is hard. She shoves the picnic basket into one of the sleek compartments and finds her seat.

"They don't want us in Nantucket," Gregory scoffs. "As if they own the island. Conrad built that place twenty years ago but he acts like they're a Nantucket generational family and we should be the ones to leave."

Sybil's voice is even as she gives my hand a squeeze. "Mom's right. Let's go. Forget them."

But Gregory won't stop. He's standing up at the steering wheel instead of sitting, his tirade far from over as the rest of us sit here helpless to listen. "They should be the ones to leave. Conrad is a bastard. Look at everything he did coming after Arden the way he did, just to jab at us. He wanted her locked up for his poor treatment of his employee. It's deplorable."

He conveniently leaves his affair out, and since Chandler is here, he knows nobody will say anything. He looks over at me and I can't help but tip my chin down and stare at him over the tops of my sunglasses.

"But they dropped the case," I point out.

He waves that off. "Conrad ran with his tail between his legs when he knew our lawyers were right and he couldn't beat us."

He's lying. That's not what happened and he knows it, but he doesn't know that I know it. My emotions are wreaking havoc on me. Before I can stop myself, I blurt out the truth. "But Conrad doesn't own that house anymore. It was trusted to his sons, and they already had ownership. They're the ones who dropped the case, not Conrad. All your lawyers had to do was bring it to their attention. Conrad would've kept fighting you if he could."

Same as Gregory would've done the same, because it would've been one more pissing contest between them, and neither would've been willing to let it go.

"Wait. Is this true?" Sybil asks.

"How do you know that?" Gregory's eyes narrow on me. "Have you been talking to them?"

Hayes snorts. "She's been doing a lot more than talking."

My body goes cold.

I turn on him, my mouth falling open. What the fuck?

His face instantly pales, and he mouths "sorry" at me before looking away. *You can trust me*, my ass! Hayes told me he was nosy and I should've believed him. It's obvious to me now that he followed me after he dropped me off. What all did he see? I hope no more than us kissing on the dock. I'll never be able to look him in the eye again if I found out he saw more than that.

"What are you talking about?" Amelia questions Hayes before whipping around to face me. "What is he talking about, Arden?"

Beside me, Sybil lets out a long-frustrated groan.

"Have you been seeing one of them?" My uncle's voice is

calm and steady, but the anger behind his eyes is something I've never witnessed before.

It's pure venom.

I swallow hard and take off my sunglasses. We need eye to eye contact for the conversation that's about to happen.

"It's Ethan." Sybil grabs my hand in solidarity. "She dated him two years ago and they hooked up again recently, but she broke it off." Her voice turns icy. "I explained everything to her, Daddy. She knows why she can't be with a King. It's over."

"Is it over?" He asks and they all turn on me expectantly.

This is it. I could lie to them, could go on pretending, but that's not who I want to be. I'm tired of making excuses for myself. I need to be strong enough to be honest. "It's not over," I confess. "I'm in love with Ethan King. We're still together."

Sybil drops my hand.

Fifty-Three

My uncle is a handsome man; some might even say he's a silver fox, but he's ugly as hell when he's bright red with anger. The veins in his forehead look about ready to burst. For the first time since I've met him, I feel afraid of him.

"You may love Ethan, but he doesn't love you. He's using you to get back at us!"

He's yelling at me, lethal and patronizing, but he's wrong.

He's wrong.

"You don't know him like I do."

"And you don't know him like we do!"

Silence. And then the sound of the engine as he turns the key in the ignition and the boat rumbles to life.

"That's it," he yells over the motor. Since it's a small boat that barely fits the five of us, there's no problem hearing him over the roar. "I'm going to settle this once and for all."

He doesn't sit which worries me because this boat doesn't even have a roof. It's made for speed. And he presses the gas with one hand and steers with the other, heading right toward the *Juliet*.

"What are you doing?" Amelia screams at her husband, but Gregory is unmoved.

"What I should've done a long time ago. I'm going to teach that spoiled punk a lesson."

I'm shocked, glued to my seat. I knew they wouldn't react well to my news but I never imagined the reaction would be dangerous.

Amelia is frantic, standing up and trying to get life jackets out of the seat she's been sitting on. We wore them on the way out but took them off and put them away for the champagne toast. We would've put them back on before leaving. She hands the first one to Chandler and Hayes helps him with it, then she tosses them to us.

I manage to get mine on but my hands fumble with the straps, unable to buckle anything. We hit a wave and I bounce too high. A scream rips through me.

"Just hold on tight," Sybil says, her voice shrill in my ear. I can barely hear it over the noise. Forgetting the straps, I grab onto the seat below me.

"Leave Ethan alone!"

Nobody reacts except for Sybil to speak low against my ear. "Ethan was the one who leaked the affair. Dad's still pissed about that."

That's no excuse. This reaction is total bullshit. Back then Ethan was a college kid who had just lost his mother, and now he's to blame? Gregory is the middle-aged adult and he's the one who is accountable for what happened.

"Let's talk about this at home," I yell, but Gregory is too focused and we're gaining speed.

He's angled the boat so we're headed directly toward Ethan

and Cooper. We'll crash. Hayes jumps up and goes for the wheel, trying to intervene, but his father pushes him away. Hayes falls back on the small deck space between us with a thud. We all scream. Hayes crawls onto his hands and knees, blood streaking his forehead. The sight of it is a stark realization to our situation as he slips back into his spot between Amelia and Chandler.

We're truly in danger. None of us are wearing our life-jackets properly except for Chandler, and Gregory doesn't have one on at all. This was just supposed to be a gentle sunset cruise. What the fuck happened? My heart slams against my chest and I grip onto my seat as tightly as possible but it's not nearly enough.

I focus on the sailboat up ahead.

Ethan and Cooper have caught on to what's happening because they're lifting up their sails, movements frantic, but there's no time. We're too fast. Ethan dives for his steering wheel and Cooper stays at the front of the boat doing something with the sails.

"You're going to get somebody killed!" Amelia screams.

"I know how to drive!"

"So slow down," Sybil screeches.

"After I teach the Kings to stay away from my family!"

Do I not know my uncle at all? My cousins and aunt are hanging on for dear life, but none of them appear all that surprised by this behavior. Not even Chandler. It's like everyone knows this dark angry side of my uncle except for me.

We hit a big wave and Gregory's hand accidently jabs down on the gas when we land, increasing the speed. We're sent flying over the surface at a breakneck speed. Everyone is screaming. Everyone is falling.

And then we crash.

I'm whiplashed forward. The booming crack of metal smashing wood assaults my eardrums. I hit the deck first—then

I'm airborne. The ocean comes at me so fast. When I hit the water, the unbuckled lifejacket slips right off my body.

Cold salty water fills my throat and burns my eyes. I sink deep and then I kick out, pushing for the surface and crying out for breath when I reach it. I look around but I can't see the lifejacket, it's lost in the debris from the sailboat getting hit by the speedboat.

I've worked on my swimming, but no lesson could've prepared me for this. The entire left side of my body screams in pain. I hit the deck hard. My ears are ringing. My lungs have water in them. I'm coughing. Coughing. Coughing. The water is too dark and too cold. My eyes burn. It's so salty. So terrifying. So wrong.

I scream but that quickly takes the last of my oxygen, so I kick instead, trying to get a sense of exactly where I am and how to get to safety. Is everyone in the water? Did Ethan and Cooper take a direct hit? I can't see anyone else, so I start screaming for Ethan, screaming for Sybil, screaming for Hayes, and Amelia, and Cooper, and even screaming for Gregory. Where is everybody? Are they okay? Are they alive?

My yells go unanswered and make me so much more tired. I have to stop.

This watery nightmare is made worse by the pain in my side. It's so fierce I can hardly move my limbs. I tell myself to take a deep breath, to kick through the pain and tread water. Don't pass out. Find something to float on. But I'm losing faith. My head is throbbing and my vision is tunneling, a panic attack closing in fast. I can't let the fear take me, because if it does, I'm certain I'll drown.

So I kick, but it hurts.

And I count in my head, but it's too fast.

And I slow my breathing, but I'm still hyperventilating.

It's all too much and I can't control what's happening. I

swim toward the wreckage, pushing through the splintered wood bobbing on the ocean's surface. This is bad. This is really, really fucking bad. My ears are still ringing and I try to yell again, but every time I do I end up swallowing more water and losing energy. I don't hear anyone. I don't see them.

My legs seize up.

The panic chases me and now that my muscles are cramping, it's going to catch me. I'm not going to make it.

Sybil.

She's screaming. I hold onto her sound like a lifeline. Further up ahead I spot my uncle's boat. It's still floating, looking relatively unscathed, and it sounds like she's on there. I just need to get to her, to keep going.

I can do this.

I can do this.

I can't. The waves are too strong.

I can't. The cramps are too intense.

The panic takes hold, as if it's an invisible force wrapping itself through and around my body. The serpent has returned and it pulls me under.

Fifty-Four

Somehow, miraculously, I focus on the surface and make it back up there with my arms alone. My legs are useless to me, the panic still owns them.

And that's when I see Ethan. He's coming for me.

Blood stains his hair and face, but his arms are rotating in frantic arcs as he swims. He yells my name like it's a desperate prayer and pulls me against his body just before my face is about to dip beneath the surface again. "I've got you," he promises. "You're okay."

He's so much faster than I am, able to swim us over to the speedboat in record time. I blink, grateful that this boat took less damage than the Kings' boat, that it's still floating. The *Juliet* is completely decimated and already half under the dark waves. A few more minutes and it will disappear beneath them entirely.

I crane my neck, searching for everybody. There's Chandler and Amelia and Sybil and Hayes.

But I don't see my uncle anywhere, and I don't see Cooper either.

Oh my god . . . oh my God!

With Hayes's help, Ethan hoists me onto the boat and then immediately dives back into the water. The world is darkening by the minute.

We're all bleeding. Hayes still from his forehead, Sybil from her forearm which looks broken, Chandler has a split lip, and Amelia already has a blackening eye and bloodied nose. My left leg is all scuffed up and my hip hurts like a mother fucker. I'm sure it's going to be purple for a week. But none of that matters right now. I can't look away from the water where Ethan disappeared beneath the surface.

"Where are they?" I beg. "Where is Ethan and Cooper? Where's Uncle Gregory?"

Nobody has an answer for me.

Amelia ignores me as she frantically digs through the area underneath the bench, yanking out another lifejacket and tossing it to me. Seems a little late for that but at least we'll all have them on if this boat starts to go down too. She turns to Hayes and begins instructions for contacting authorities to send out a distress signal. Surprisingly, he's the one with the least amount of damage to his body.

I'm shivering and Sybil finds a towel, draping it over me. We sit side by side, staring down into the lapping waves. Her hands are covering her mouth and she's crying.

"Cooper was right there in the water a minute ago," she says between sobs. "He was yelling at us. And then there was blood in the water and he just sank."

My heart rate speeds. It's an image I don't want in my mind. I can only imagine the three of them under that water right now, all drowning and being pulled away by the current. Lost to the sea forever.

"What about your dad?" I whisper.

She shakes her head. "He went in after Cooper about a minute before Ethan did."

Then she stands, hoisting her leg over the side of the boat as she fumbles with her lifejacket to remove it.

"No!" I grab onto her. "Can you swim?"

"I'm good enough."

Amelia is there, helping me to pull Sybil back. "You can't go down there, you are bleeding and you're not a great swimmer." Her voice goes quiet, the undercurrent of fear unmistakable. "Losing blood isn't good for swimming and it's not good for the sharks either."

Did she just say sharks?

"Because there *are* sharks in these waters," she continues. "We're all bleeding. It's not safe."

"I'm going after Dad." Hayes doesn't wait for permission, his life jacket is off in seconds and he dives over the edge.

Sybil starts screaming again.

Bile rises up to my throat, panic setting in all over again. My vision narrows around the edges, too bright in the center and too dark around the sides. I can't focus, can't grab onto a thought long enough to process through it. My emotions are as volatile as this horrible crash.

I stare into the murky water, imagining the sharks circling. Imagining what else they might be doing. I can picture the blood and hear the watery screams that come out as gurgles.

Someone is screaming with Sybil. They're screaming for Ethan and Cooper and Gregory. And it's only after Sybil shakes me, do I realize that the screaming voice is my own.

It doesn't help. They don't resurface.

Until finally, something bubbles and Ethan's head pops back up, followed by Cooper and Hayes.

"I can't find Dad!" Hayes is desperate.

And Cooper? Cooper looks like he's already gone. He's not responsive, his eyes are closed, and his face is way too pale.

"Help me get him up," Ethan yells, and immediately he's at the edge of the boat and the three of us women are yanking Coop into our small deck space.

There's blood everywhere.

"I'm going back to look for Dad," Hayes says and then he's back in the water.

Ethan is already in emergency CPR-mode. Amelia is yelling at him to leave Cooper to us, to go back into the water to help Hayes and Gregory. But Ethan isn't listening to her, she could be invisible for all he cares. He's solely focused on his twin.

Tears stream down my face, mixing with my own blood. Cooper and salt. I can only stare at Ethan and Cooper in shock because I think . . . I think Cooper might be dead.

Not only is he not breathing, but his right leg is completely decimated.

From the wreck? From a shark?

Oh God, I don't know.

There's not much of it left besides some bone and sinew. It's the goriest thing I've ever witnessed. Like something out of a horror film. And he's losing way too much blood. The coppery scent of it overwhelms everything else.

Sybil falls to her knees next to Ethan. She's got a rope in her hand and she's tying it tightly around Coop's upper thigh. That's smart. I've seen that in movies. She's trying to keep him from bleeding out.

She's at least being useful. I think Chandler and I might be in shock.

Ethan practically pounds on Cooper's chest, then swoops down again to blow oxygen into his brother's slack mouth. He does this over and over again until Cooper coughs up water and foam, his entire body seeming to rise and fall with the action.

Coop blinks and gazes down at his leg, and then the obscenities start flying. He's not the only one yelling. Where is Uncle Gregory? Where are the authorities? Is our boat going to sink? It's all too much, and my gaze fixates on Cooper's bloody shredded leg even though I know I should look away if I want to calm down. But I can't. My vision narrows even further. I reach for a breath, but I can't find it, there's nothing there, I may as well be on the bottom of that ocean for all the oxygen I can manage.

That's when arms are thrown around me. It's Chandler. He's crying. I've never seen him cry before. I gaze up into his eyes and force myself to breathe, to focus on him instead of everything else going on around us.

"It's going to be okay." I squeeze his hand and pray to God I'm not lying, even though deep down, I know I am.

Fifty-Five

"Can you tell me your name?" The paramedic asks.

"A-Arden Dav-Davis," I try not to stutter but it's impossible. Now that everything is over, my body is in even more shock. "Actually, I-I changed my name last year," I manage. "It's Arden La-Laurence."

"Okay, Arden, you're injured and experiencing shock. We're going to take you by ambulance to the hospital."

I blink at her. We're back at the boat dock. The police arrived shortly after they got Cooper awake. They rushed him and his brother away immediately on a speed boat and took us back on a second boat. The authorities stayed behind to search for my uncle.

"Where are Cooper and Ethan? Are they already at the hospital?"

"Not locally," she says. "They were taken by helicopter to Boston. Cooper is going to need surgery and will be admitted to the ICU."

"His brother Ethan went with him?"

She nods and I let out a sob. I'm glad he's with Cooper. "Did you assess Ethan for injuries too?"

"Quickly. He looked okay but they'll check him out in Boston to make sure."

Ethan will live but Cooper can't die. There's no way someone so full of life could just be here one second and gone the next.

Except I know that's not true. That's not how life works.

And if Coop dies, Ethan might as well too because it will absolutely destroy him.

Another paramedic joins the woman standing over me and they help me into the back of the waiting ambulance. There is another ambulance here too that Sybil has already been loaded into for her broken arm. I wonder if the break is bad enough that she'll need surgery too. Amelia, Hayes, and Chandler insisted on staying back. Their injuries aren't as bad and they want to stay on the docks for when they find my uncle.

Because he never came out of that water.

"No word on Gregory Laurence yet?" I'm almost scared to ask.

The paramedics exchange quick glances and then shake their heads.

That's it. All the confirmation I need. My uncle is gone.

"We're very sorry. He hasn't been recovered. The search and rescue team are still out there though. They won't stop for a while yet."

But it's dark out. He was underwater. There was so much blood. He was likely injured, maybe even a head injury that nobody saw him sustain.

There's no way he's still alive.

Tears spring from my eyes and silent grief pours down my face. Maybe by some miracle Uncle Gregory survived, but I don't have much hope for that. He jumped in to help Cooper. If he was anything like the rest of us, he wasn't in good shape to save anyone. Maybe he passed out in the water or maybe the sharks got to him. Whatever it was, I'm certain it's too late for him.

After a miserable seventy-two hours, the authorities call off the search and Gregory is declared lost at sea. All evidence points to him being gone so sometime after the funeral there will be a presumptive death hearing. Once a judge rules him dead, his trust will be distributed to the beneficiaries, and we'll all be expected to move on with our lives.

What a horrific way to go. Every time I try to imagine what he went through, how terrifying those final moments must have been, my palms itch and my chest aches. My panic attacks have been full-out since the accident. An accident that started with a rescue mission, turned into a recovery mission, and dissolved into defeat. Nothing more could be done.

The chances that we ever find his body are slim to none. Amelia agrees that it's time to leave the island, plan a funeral, and find a new normal. We all fly home together on the private jet. Nobody talks. Nobody brings up Ethan or Cooper. Nobody even brings up the erratic way Uncle Gregory caused the accident in the first place. We don't even talk about our injuries, not even the cast that Sybil will have to wear for weeks.

I have no idea what was said to the police, but when the officers showed up at the hospital room to get my statement, I told them the truth. They didn't seem the least bit surprised.

By the next weekend, it's time for the funeral I've been dreading. The fanfare over my uncle's death has been startling, to say the least. The accident made international news and there has been no shortage of debate as to whether to feel sorry for billionaires dying in boating accidents. The hashtag #nantucket-boatgate starts trending on social media. Condolences get sent to the family by the hundreds. They come in the form of flowers, cards, phone calls, messages, and meals. Sybil's loft smells like a nursery and paparazzi start circling.

I go to the penthouse that Amelia and Gregory shared to meet everyone before the funeral. There are even more flowers here. Are flowers supposed to make anyone feel better? They only make this more real.

"Are you ready?" Amelia's voice is stoic when she finds the four of us sitting in the foyer, waiting for her.

"Yes." We stand and I brush out my conservative black dress.

"Let's go then."

She turns on her heels and strides away and we all follow her out the door. It might be the first time she doesn't comment on our nice appearances when leaving the penthouse together. And she certainly doesn't meet my eye. None of them do except for Chandler. It's not that I have high expectations of them right now because I don't. It's that I blame myself and I think they do too, which is another barb forever lodged in my heart. Grief is isolating for all of us, but in my case, I deserve to feel every ounce of pain.

The church is packed. People offer condolences but not many people know who I am, so I stand back. We sit in the front row for the service and the funeral goes by in a blur. I'm heartbroken too, but my feelings are more complicated. I was just learning who my uncle really was when he died. I was angry at him and now he's gone before we can repair anything that was said or done. How could he do this? He died because of his temper and Cooper is still in the ICU. Ethan and I have exchanged a few texts but that's all. Everything is a mess.

After the burial and the luncheon, I climb into the town car with Sybil. The driver is supposed to take us back to her loft apartment, but she gives him other directions and we end up in midtown instead. Parked in front of a tall shining high rise, she shifts her body toward mine. Her eyes are red rimmed from crying and her makeup is gone.

"Ethan's penthouse is on the top floor," she says stoically.

A spark of hope lights but I quickly snuff it out. I shouldn't even be thinking about seeing Ethan today. We'll reunite when things are easier.

"Okay . . . why did you bring me here?" I question.

She gives me a haunted look.

"Because it's time you break things off with him." Her voice is hollow but I know there's burning anger underneath. So this confirms it. I blame myself for her father's death and apparently, she does too. "Or you don't break it off, in which case that's your decision to be loyal to the Kings instead of us, and you can stay with Ethan."

She turns away, looking forward, eyes glacial. It's not just the air conditioning that is making it so frosty in here. Sybil has become an ice-queen. "I don't *ever* want to see Ethan or Cooper King again. You must understand that. So please, go make your choice."

Heart shattering, I climb from the car. I expect it to drive away but it doesn't. She plans to wait? She expects me to choose her. At least the paparazzi didn't follow us here. It doesn't feel real when I walk into the building.

The doorman stops me, and I tell him my name and that I'm here to see Ethan. Recognition lights his eyes. "Oh yes, you're already on the list, Miss Laurence. Go on up to the top floor."

I stride into the elevator and press the button. Never did I imagine the moment I would see his place would be after coming straight from a funeral. Never could I have thought in my worst nightmares that it would be under these circumstances.

But here we are—life is fucking cruel.

The door slides open and I'm faced with a small chrome entryway and a single steel door. I ring the doorbell and wait. Maybe he's not here. Maybe I'll have to come back later.

But the door swings open a few seconds later and Ethan stands there.

He looks terrible. He's normally so put together but right now his hair is a mess and his eyes are red, heavy bags that look like bruises under each one.

He pulls me into his arms.

"Thank God you're here," he breathes against my ear. His presence alone sends a sense of calm through my entire body. After a minute in his arms, he brings me inside, closing the door behind us. He drops a kiss to my forehead. "I thought I had lost you. I don't want to live without you."

"I don't want to live without you either." My words come out in a choking sob. He was under that water for so long, I really thought he was gone. I was so close to throwing myself into that water to go after him. I probably would've drowned if I had.

We both almost lost our lives that night. And we can't forget who actually did. And who else was hurt.

"How's Cooper?" I ask and he steps back, his eyes pained.

"Cooper lost the leg."

My heart falls. I knew this was coming but we hadn't discussed it yet. Confirmation doesn't make it any easier. "I'm so sorry."

"Me too. If Gregory wasn't already dead, I swear I'd kill him."

Speaking ill of the dead is taboo but I completely understand his anger. "I don't know what came over him. He found out about us, and he saw you guys out there and he just lost his mind. Everything got out of hand so quickly."

"The only redemption that piece of shit has is that he died trying to save my brother," he grits out. "But he's still responsible for the leg. He crushed it with his fucking boat and changed Cooper's life forever."

"He broke Sybil's arm too. It's in a cast but it will heal. Amelia, Chandler, and Hayes are okay though. They got a little banged up but they're okay. And so am I. Nothing is broken." I suck my lip between my lips and grimace. "But that doesn't change the fact that my uncle is gone."

He pulls me into a hug again and I can feel his heart pounding against his breastbone. He really was terrified he lost me. I know exactly how that feels.

How am I going to break up with him? It seems impossible, but I don't know what else I can do. Shaking, I step out of his embrace and peer up into his troubled eyes. I just have to say it. "Ethan, we can't do this. It's over."

Fifty-Six

I expect his eyes to go cold, for his jaw to set in harsh lines, for him to dismiss me. He does none of that. "No," he states, like it's simple. "We're not breaking up."

I let out a pained laugh. "It's not up to you. This is my decision."

I seem to reach him this time, because his expression falls.

"I just got you back, we've been through a terrible trauma, and I can't lose you again." He drags the palms of his hands up his cheeks. "Fuck!"

I briefly close my eyes because I get exactly how he feels, but it doesn't change what happened. Maybe we could've found a way to make this work before the boating accident, but now it's impossible. The pain between the Kings and the Laurences is too much. I have to choose which way to break my heart. "It's either I get you or I get my family. What am I supposed to do?"

"I'm your family now too. The kind you chose."

And he is family to me because I love him. But I also love Chandler and Amelia and Sybil and Hayes. This is the hardest decision I've ever had to make. I swipe away the tears that splash down my face. I thought I'd cried myself out at the funeral. How wrong I was.

"And what about your family? What about Cooper? Your father? They're not going to want us to be together either after what happened to Coop's leg. It's too much."

"I don't fucking care what they want," he growls.

But that's not true. He loves Cooper. What if Cooper is like Sybil and blames me for what happened? The man lost his leg for Christ's sake. He'll never be able to look me in the eye again. Our relationship will put a rift between the brothers, and I can't do that to Ethan. I don't want to be the reason he ends up estranged from the one person who was born to be his best friend.

"No," he states again, emphatically. He takes my hands between his and tugs me against his chest again. "Kiss me and tell me that we're not meant to be together. You have to mean it. Because Arden, nobody has ever made me feel even close to the way you make me feel."

"You're making this too hard."

He leans down, his lips brushing away the tears from my cheeks with sweet kisses. He's the only person who can make me feel better and I hate that I have to give him up. Doesn't he understand the stakes? But then his mouth is on mine and damn it if I don't kiss him right back. I gasp into him and he takes the opportunity to slide his tongue inside, deepening the kiss. This is a battle and he's determined to prove how much he cares.

But he doesn't have to prove anything. I already know our love is real. That's not the problem.

I should leave, should force him away, but I don't have the strength.

One last time, I decide. It will be our goodbye.

He carries me to his bedroom and lays me down on a soft

gray comforter. I sink into it, my hair fanning around me in a halo. He crawls over me, peeling off my black layers one by one—the heels, the pantyhose, the dress, the black panties and matching bra.

I'm usually vocal during sex but right now I can't speak. If I do, he'll know how greedy I'm being by letting this happen. How broken I've become.

He's quick to remove his clothes and then he's climbing over me, kissing away the last of my tears. There's no foreplay, neither of us can wait. I'm already ready as I wrap my legs around his hips. He slides home with one powerful thrust. He begins to rock and it's immediately apparent that the man has something to prove, and boy does he prove himself to be the best lover I could possibly want. The feel of him so deeply inside of me delivers pleasure through my entire body. We exhale together and then we're kissing again as he languidly slides in and out, a tempo of sinful possession. Our lips never part, not even when I lift my legs to his shoulders so he can slide in deeper, not even when the movements grow frantic. The heat between us is as hot as our kiss.

But the emotion—the emotion is overwhelming. This can't be a goodbye, I don't want to accept it, but deep down I know I already have. And I suspect he has too because he slows down just before we come to take his time with me, like he can't let this moment end. Maybe if we can stretch it out into forever, the rest of the world will be forced to move on and let us be.

We make love until neither of us can hold back, until our orgasms demand to be felt and then together give in. "You're mine and I'm yours," he demands, the climax ripping through us. "Say it."

"I'm yours." My voice is a husky whisper.

He pumps harder and my world is destroyed.

"Again."

"I'm yours. I'm yours."

My vision tunnels and he jerks inside of me, finishing deep and true. I want to keep him there inside of me forever, because he is mine. And I'll always be his.

Always . . .

After it's over, he stays inside of me as long as he can before finally pulling out and falling onto his back, eyes fluttering closed. The man is desperate for sleep and he gives into it immediately.

I watch him for a few minutes, tears burning the entire time.

I need to go. They're waiting for me and I've already taken too long. It's the hardest thing I've ever done, but I manage to slip from the bed, clean myself up, and head downstairs without looking back at Ethan even once.

I force the tears to dry up before I leave the building, but I put on big sunglasses just in case before getting back into the waiting car.

Of course, Sybil waited. She knows me and she knew I would do the same thing she had to do once upon a time.

One day, he'll fall for someone else and he'll be grateful I had the strength to leave.

One day, I'll have peace with this decision too, even if I never love like this again.

As much as I hate it, I've finally made my choice.

The days that follow are some of my hardest. I block Ethan's number and try not to think about him, which is like trying not to breathe. At least Sybil is starting to warm up to me again. She says she wants to get back to work, that she needs to find her new normal sooner rather than later. I don't know how to do the same.

The internship is still waiting for me and just the thought of it leaves me either numb or skirting a panic attack. How am I supposed to move on after all this?

But that's life. It keeps going.

So after an emotional session with my therapist and a productive one with my psychiatrist, I adopt a "can-do" attitude and a higher dose of my anti-anxiety medication.

Laurence International's board votes one of its members in as an interim-CEO until they can agree on someone long-term. I go to work, meeting Mr. Vale along with the other new interns. He doesn't treat me any differently than the others, not like Gregory probably would've, so at least that's good. I never wanted to be singled out. But still, seeing this new leader makes me think of my uncle and sends me down a negative shame spiral.

This is Gregory's livelihood, his place of business, his legacy---not Vale's and not mine. Do I really have a right to be here?

The internship is with the tech department which turns out to be a good fit. I get to wear headphones while I work and have very few group projects. Sybil and I meet for lunch twice that first week and Aunt Amelia even comes in to check on us. She still treats me like her own daughter, and I don't understand how she can be so forgiving. At least she's still got Chandler and Hayes at home. Chandler keeps her busy and Hayes is focused on his SAT prep for the rest of the summer, alongside training for his upcoming varsity football season. The family seems to be accepting their new normal despite everything. Grief hits everybody differently and I'm certainly not the judge.

Before I know it, three weeks pass without Ethan. I count every day in my head like I'm a prisoner tracking time. We only had a week where we were actually together this summer, and only a week the two summers previous. How is it that those two weeks had such an impact on me? They felt like years, but they also felt like no time at all.

The emotional and physical intimacy that we shared was special, and even though I'm only twenty year -old, I don't think I'll ever find something as deep again. People would say I'm too young to know the difference but I'd disagree. I'll always love Ethan and I'll always be grateful that I got to experience his love for me, even if we broke each other in the end.

Maybe we were like Romeo and Juliet after all—marked for a tragedy.

After a particularly good day in the office, the kind that is busy and makes the clock spin faster, I stride out onto the street and head towards the subway entrance. I finally have a smile on my face and I let myself have it. Passing a newspaper stand, an image catches my attention. I turn, staring at the picture with the startling headline, reading it over and over in disbelief.

"*Billionaire Heir Arrested for Manslaughter of Rival Businessman*," the headline reads, followed by three images of Ethan. The first is a corporate headshot of him in a suit and tie, the second is of a younger Ethan standing between his father and Gregory on a fishing trip, and the final shot is of him being taken into police custody.

Fifty-Seven

This is the front page of the New York Times. Oh my God. Word of this must be spreading like wildfire. And I went all day without knowing? *Shit. Shit. Shit.* Why was Ethan arrested? He didn't do anything wrong. He was a victim in the boating accident. My uncle's death wasn't his fault. I want to believe this is paparazzi drivel, but I know it's not.

With shaking hands, I buy a copy of the paper, then read the front page while standing right there on the busy sidewalk. I blink several times and my hands shake in disbelief as I read.

Ethan King, son of self-made billionaire Conrad King of King Media, was arrested Thursday for voluntary manslaughter in connection with the death of billionaire Gregory Laurence of Laurence International. The Massachusetts prosecutor's office in conjunction with the New York City Police Department made the arrest after a weeks-long investigation into the June 4 boating accident that took the life of Mr. Laurence, who was lost at sea and is presumed dead. The prosecution asserts they've gathered sufficient evidence that Mr. King knowingly caused the accident with the intent to harm Mr. Laurence and his family. More on page 8.

No fucking way I can read another word of whatever the hell is on page 8.

I toss the paper in the trash and call Amelia, but she doesn't answer. This has got to be some sick joke. Why would *Ethan* get arrested? The whole thing was caused by my uncle. Ethan and I may have fueled my uncle's rage with my confession, but Gregory was the one driving recklessly. He was the one who crashed into them. He caused his own death. If the prosecutors want to lay blame on someone, lay it on Gregory, but not Ethan.

Instead of taking the train to my building, I go to Aunt Amelia's penthouse in hopes that she's here in Manhattan and not an hour away at the Greenwich, Connecticut house where she and the kids spend most of their time. Or worse, vacationing at one of the other houses and screening my phone calls. I stride into the opulent Upper East Side building overlooking Central Park, the kind with marble floors and million-dollar artwork in the lobby, and ask the security to let her know I'm here.

"You're in luck," he says. "She just got in today."

I'm sent right up and she opens the door for me as if it's the most normal thing in the world for me to be here.

She gives me a hug but I'm stiff and awkward. She's put together, wearing black dress pants and a burgundy blouse that compliments her hair. Her signature perfume encircles us, a spring floral scent that was always so comforting to me because she told me that my mother used to wear the same one when they were teenagers. Now it feels like a betrayal. She releases me from the hug and takes my hand. "Come in then. Let's have some tea."

Fuck tea. "They arrested Ethan."

A flush creeps up her neck. "Yes."

"Why? Ethan didn't do anything wrong."

She releases a bitter sigh and drops my hand. "That's your opinion. The Massachusetts prosecutor's office has a different one. We should let them do their job."

My knees weaken and I would sit down right there on her stupid hand knotted Turkish rug if I didn't think it would make me look weak. "Gregory was the one that crashed into them, he almost killed us, he broke Sybil's arm, and he caused Cooper to lose his leg. It's a tragedy that Greg died, but why should Ethan have to face false charges over it?"

She waves her hands as if I'm being dramatic. "Ethan King will get off. There's not enough evidence and he's got an arsenal of lawyers."

"Okay . . . so what did you say to the police? Did you lie to them?"

"I'm not a bad person." She's defensive and grieving. Grief makes people do crazy things but that's still no excuse. "Listen, Arden, it was either our reputation or it was theirs. You saw the hashtags, the way this blew up online? The media needs to blame someone for the accident and the Kings have gotten away with far worse. Ethan won't end up in prison over this but it's an opportunity for their family to face some real consequences for once."

So this is about reputations. It's about pride. And it's about getting back at her cheating dead best friend by taking down her survivors.

"Are you even listening to yourself? This is wrong. This isn't you."

Her face goes slack and then hard. "You don't have to understand it."

"What would my mother think?" Maybe this is why she ended up estranged from her family and on drugs. Maybe they were conniving and led her down a dark path. What if not telling them about me was her way of protecting me?

Her eyes go sad. "I don't know what she would've thought. She never valued family the way I do. She left."

This is not what I signed up for. We're supposed to take care of each other, but this is not the way to do it. "If being a Laurence means lying and manipulation, then I'd rather go back to being a Davis."

I'd rather leave too.

"Davis? That wasn't even Josie's real last name. She changed it to that just to get away from us. Davis means nothing. Laurence means everything." Her eyes water and I hate myself for hurting her, but she's hurting me too. "Do you know what I've been doing today?" She takes my hand and leads me further into the penthouse.

This building is one of the most iconic in the city and my aunt and uncle have three entire floors to themselves. The real estate alone is worth over a hundred million dollars and that doesn't include all the priceless artwork and furniture housed inside. I was out of my mind if I ever thought I could fit in with these people, blood relation or not.

But the feel of her hand in mine reminds me of just how kind she's been to me. How is this the same person who would let Ethan go down like this? She helped raise him. He saw her as a second mother, she saw him as another son.

And now she's going to help ruin his life?

She leads me into her bedroom where boxes are lined up with Gregory's clothing. "Your uncle wasn't a bad man just because he wasn't perfect. He cheated on me, and he had a terrible temper that got him killed, but we loved each other, we were partners, and now I have to pack his life away in boxes and attempt to move on. We met in college and got married right after graduation. Did you know that? I've been with him for over thirty years. I don't know who I am without him."

And so she wants to make the Kings hurt because she's hurting? "Cooper lost his leg. Isn't that punishment enough?"

She drops my hand to touch one of the boxes, like she's holding vigil over it. "She was my best friend. Have you ever had a female best friend? You become like sisters. I was there with her through so much, through the children and the cancer and everything. And for years she was cheating with my husband."

"It's terrible what she did, but punishing her kids isn't going to make you feel any better."

She turns away. "It's done. Like I said, Ethan will get off. There's not enough evidence. You don't need to worry about him anymore. Sybil said you two broke it off. Is that true?"

"It's true," my voice cracks and my fists ball. "I did it for you guys, not for myself. I love him. He loves me."

She scoffs and begins mindlessly moving boxes around.

"It's true," I force myself to say the words she needs to hear, even if it hurts us both. "Your husband and Victoria King are responsible for what they did to you and Conrad, but the two of you are responsible for the pain you're causing now. Don't you see what you're doing to us? None of this is our fault but you're making your children pay the price. Those two may be gone now, but we're all forced to live with their ghosts."

She drops a box and turns on me, face ashen. "You can leave now."

"Fine. Push me away, just like you did to my mother," I continue. "You loved your little sister, right? You hated when she became estranged? Tried to make it up to her memory by taking me in? Well, have you ever stopped to wonder that maybe you pushed her away just like you're doing to me because she didn't fit in with your perfectly pretty little boxes?" I point to the boxes filling the room. "So put me away too, just like you're doing to Gregory, just like you did to my mother. Keep me at arm's length." The tears are flowing now. I can't help it. "But I love you, I do. And I love Sybil. Chandler and Hayes. And I loved Uncle Greg more than you know. And yes, I also desperately love Ethan. And I wish, I just wish, that you would let me love who I want, that love could be enough."

I've struck a chord and she doesn't have to accept it, but I'm right. I think deep down she knows that. But she doesn't respond, so I turn and leave, ready to move on with my life.

Fifty-Eight

I go to Cooper first. He's been moved to a rehabilitation floor and is open to visitors. He's watching television when I walk into the private room and looks to be in better shape than I expected. Any bruising on his face is gone but I know that under his hospital blanket is an amputated leg.

"Hi, Cooper," I say tentatively.

He looks over, his eyes traveling me up and down, and then he smiles. It's a grim one, but it's a smile, and it fills me with relief. "Hey, Arden. I was wondering when you were coming around. It's good to see you."

"Can I come hang out?"

He points to the end of the bed, the side without a leg. "I've got plenty of room." My chest tightens and he chuckles. "Ah, come on."

I sit down and immediately jump into my apology. I can't go another second without getting this out. "I'm so sorry. I blame myself for what happened to you. I understand if you hate me."

His eyebrows shoot up. "And why is this your fault?"

"Because my uncle found out I was with Ethan and lost his shit. If I had handled things better this never would've happened."

He shakes his head. "I fucking hate that guy and I always will even if he's dead, but he's the one that did this. Not you. I wanted you with my brother, remember? This isn't on you."

An immense weight lifts from my shoulders. I didn't realize how heavy it was until Cooper said his piece. I'm still not sure I can forgive myself for everything though. Cooper takes my hand and squeezes.

"What if the roles were reversed? Would you blame me if I was you and you were me?"

I shake my head. "No. I guess you're right."

"Yeah, I'm right."

We talk about his prognosis and how he'll be ready soon to learn how to walk with his new prosthetic. He seems to be in good spirits, but I know Cooper and underneath all the bravado, he's angry. I can't say I blame him. Here's this young man in the prime of his life, and he loses his leg because someone who he used to see as a role model couldn't let go of rage. I'd be angry too.

"Have you heard from Ethan recently?" I ask, gazing down and running my fingers along the edge of the bed.

He tuts, his expression turning hard. It's like the kind, open guy I was just talking to has been immediately replaced with another much more defensive one. I guess I deserve it.

"Is he okay?" I try again.

"Wouldn't you like to know?" His tone goes cold, this is no longer the man putting on the brave face. This is a man protecting his brother.

"I would like to know." I look up and his jaw is tense. He shakes his head.

"Sorry, Arden, but you lost that right when you broke up with him and blocked his number."

"I did it for my family." Shouldn't they understand that? Ethan wanted me to have the Laurences to begin with.

"Our father has threatened all sorts of shit on my brother over the years and yet Ethan would've never let you go over some shit Conrad wanted. But what did you do? You called it off. And now he's facing a disgusting lawsuit. It's going to ruin his reputation. So I'm sorry if I'm being a dick about this, and we can still be friends, but you don't have a right to talk with me about Ethan anymore."

"I deserve that." My bottom lip trembles and tears blur my vision, but I'm not going to cry here, not in front of Cooper. I messed up but I want to fix it. "Don't you think this rivalry between the Laurences and the Kings needs to end?"

Cooper's entire body tightens. "No. I don't see how it can."

"But—"

"But what? Can you get me back my leg?" There's nothing I can say to that. "And I've seen the court documents, Arden. They're not okay. Amelia, Hayes, and Sybil all testified that Ethan was the one to run into your boat and not the other way around."

I lose my breath. This is news to me. "But—but that's ridiculous. There's so much proof that says otherwise."

"I know and we'll get Ethan off, no judge in their right mind would convict, but the damage to King Media and Ethan's reputation has already been done. People think he's a monster."

"So what am I supposed to do?"

"You've already made your choice, Arden. Now you've got to live with it."

His words echo the exact same sentiment I'd told myself

when I'd walked out on Ethan. "Can't I change my mind? Go back?"

"Go back?" He sighs, gazing down at the space where his leg is supposed to be. "Sorry, but no, you can't go back. Not this time."

"Maybe, but I still believe in forgiveness."

He shrugs and I'm overcome with sadness. Has anyone in these families learned to forgive? Have I? Maybe it's why I pushed Ethan away instead of trying to find a way to make our relationship work. I hadn't truly forgiven him for the hurt he'd caused me. I'd spent years grieving him and the loss of my innocence. Taking him back didn't mean I was over what happened between us. Me being the one to walk out was a form of punishment, but I was punishing myself too.

"I don't think forgiveness is always possible." He shuts down after that, face going hard and eyes distant. There's nothing more I can say, so I stand and give him a side hug, wishing him well before I leave.

I go back to the loft to find Sybil laying in her bed. It's Friday night, normally she'd be going out, but things are different now. I don't want to push her with everything she's going through, but I need to talk to her about Ethan's charges. I stand in her doorway and wait for her to acknowledge me, but she doesn't act like I'm even there.

"I talked to Cooper today."

That makes her drop her phone and look up. "Is he okay?"

"He's starting rehabilitation tomorrow to learn how to walk with a prosthetic leg, so what do you think?"

Her eyes drop to her bedspread, and she picks at an invisible piece of lint. "It's sad. I'm glad he's alive though."

"Are you? Even though your dad died trying to save him?"

Her head pops back up. "My dad died because of his own stupid mistakes."

"And yet you're willing to pin it on Ethan."

She rolls her eyes. "Ethan is a billionaire. Are we supposed to feel bad for him? He won't even be convicted. My guess is this gets dropped within a week."

"But not before the media has a field day with it, right?"

"What is this about, Arden?" She snaps.

"It's about telling the truth. Cooper read the court documents. He says the affidavits are bullshit. And all for what? For revenge?"

"It's what Mom wants." But she sounds just as upset about it as I am. "What was I supposed to do? She never asks anything of us."

I have to bite my tongue from truly saying everything I want. "I love you, Sybil. If I didn't love you, I wouldn't have broken my heart for you. But this is wrong and I'm so disappointed."

I turn and go to my bedroom, locking myself inside. If I had the money, I would move out but I don't have much of anything. Maybe I'll get something from my uncle's will after his presumption of death hearing coming up, but I don't want to count on that. In fact, I'm not sure I'll take a dime even if I'm offered it. I need to come up with an exit strategy that's mine and mine alone.

The summer internship is two months long but hardly pays anything. After that I'm supposed to start back with classes at Columbia, classes paid for by the Laurences. What if I was able to get my old scholarship back? I could leave New York and start over. As far as I know, it never got revoked. My uncle convinced me to transfer colleges, but could I go back to Boston?

I've already lost Ethan. I'm going to lose my family if they don't do the right thing. At least, I don't see myself being close with them anymore. There's nothing else keeping me in Manhattan.

Opening my laptop, I research the grant program for foster kids, and after reading through some hopeful information about my age and status, I shoot out a couple of emails. One to my old case worker and one to my previous college.

And then I do what I've been afraid of for far too long—I type my mother's real name into the search bar. Her maiden name and not the one she changed it to. The name that could've been mine had things been different. Not Laurence. Not Davis.

Astor.

I always thought of her as Josephine Davis, but she was Josephine Astor for most of her life, nicknamed Josie, and only changed it when she became estranged from the family. I don't know why she changed her last name beyond that, like maybe she chose Davis because it belonged to my father, or maybe she picked something random and generic to protect me from him so he couldn't find us. There's no information on who he could be and he's not on my birth certificate. All I do know is that she got pregnant with me while in active addiction. That's probably why I'm so much smaller than my family members even though I look like them. As a toddler I was pulled out of a drug home when she overdosed and died.

I got out of there. She never did.

Pictures of a beautiful young woman flood the computer screen. A woman who was full of life. A woman who used to look just like I do now, young and full of possibility. A woman that my aunt knew as her little sister. She was Josie. Josie Astor.

And I cry.

Did she have anxiety too? Did she ask for help? What led her to the path that ultimately killed her? I don't think I'll ever have all the answers and I decide that's okay. I can live without knowing all the sad details because the point is that I do get to live. And I can live for the young woman on my computer screen whose life was cut short. I will make the healthy choices that she couldn't, carving a path that's all my own. She was my mother, after all. I'd like to believe it's what she would've wanted for her daughter.

Fifty-Nine

It happens fast—six weeks later and I've officially wrapped up my life in Manhattan. I've switched colleges and can use my old scholarship to pay for school. I've finished my internship with Laurence International and packed up my bedroom. My uncle's presumption of death hearing is set for next month, but it doesn't matter. I'm not taking any money even if I get offered something. It's no secret that I'm leaving but there's nothing anyone can do to stop me.

Last month I unblocked Ethan's number and sent him an apology text, but he never replied. I called Cooper shortly after and he told me that Ethan was out on bail but under house arrest and that I shouldn't contact him again. Ethan will be the one to contact me when he's ready—if he's ever ready. I'm starting to think I'll never see him again.

I've pled Ethan's case to Sybil, Amelia, and Hayes on more than one occasion, but they won't budge. I won't budge on my feelings about it either. There's nothing left to do but leave Manhattan and start over.

Again.

I roll my suitcase out into the family room and find Sybil sitting primly on the couch. "So that's it? You're really leaving?" She eyes me up and down, hurt crumpling her pretty face.

"Yes, I really am."

Ethan wanted me to choose him and in a way, I am, but I'm also choosing myself. I don't want to be like them and staying here would slowly chip away at me until I resembled them on the inside and not just the outside. They lead lives of vindictiveness and anger and making decisions based on grudges and social status. I can't do that to myself, so if it means I have to be on my own out in Boston again, then so be it.

"I'm going to miss you." I can tell she means it.

"I'm going to miss you too." I also mean it and wish things could be different.

"Can I at least ride with you to the train station?" She stands and motions to my suitcase, but I shake my head.

"This is something I need to do on my own."

She looks away, gazing out the window to the city skyline. "You're braver than me. I'm ashamed of my actions."

"So do something about it," I try. "Ethan was your love once too. Don't you still care about him? This isn't fair, so go talk to the police or someone in the prosecutor's office and tell them the truth."

"I can't. I promised Mom."

"Keeping a promise for something like this isn't noble. It's actually the opposite."

A tear slips down her face and her chin wobbles. "I know."

I let out a breath and wheel my suitcase over the door. This is it. This is goodbye. But a knock sounds on the door and I open it with a frown.

Amelia and Hayes are standing on the other side.

I've barely seen Hayes all summer but he's looking at me like he's happy to see me and Amelia is her normal self. Maybe they came to say goodbye? That's fine. As angry as I am, I still care about them, but I wish they would've brought Chandler along. He's still my favorite, especially after everything that's happened. He's the best of us. We should all try to be more like Chandler. If we were, maybe we wouldn't be saying goodbye right now.

"I need to show you two something," Amelia announces, sweeping into the apartment and setting a thin piece of printer paper on the coffee table. "Hayes has already read it."

Sybil is closer and grabs it first, her eyes scanning the print. They widen as her hand flies to her mouth. She exchanges a glance with her mother, who nods, and then she hands the paper to me with trembling fingers.

It looks like an email exchange and I scan the email addresses first. This is correspondence between my uncle and a Massachusetts social worker. This time my hands are the ones that tremble as I read the words, immediately understanding the significance they hold.

To Mr. and Mrs. Laurence,

I have been trying to contact you for some time, but my calls are being screened. I'm writing to inform you that your niece, Arden Davis, has been taken into state custody. Unfortunately, Arden's mother has passed away and we don't have information on her father. We're seeking next of kin to take custody of Arden. She's a darling one-year-old in need of a loving family. Please respond immediately so we can discuss the details.

Sincerely,

Stacy Peirce

Child Protection Caseworker

. . .

To Ms. Peirce,

My wife and I have talked it over at length and have decided it's best to leave Arden in your custody. Arden's mother was a drug addict who caused us a lot of pain and we've since moved on with our lives. We have no doubt that Arden will have been born addicted to drugs and will have special needs, which we are not prepared to accommodate. We already have two children, one of which was born with special needs of his own. As much as we hope Arden gets the care she deserves, we need to do what is best for the children already in our home. Please do not contact us again or I will be forced to file a harassment claim against your office.

Best Wishes,

Gregory Laurence

Best wishes? Those words hit me like a punch to the gut.

I've never been the most confident kid. Growing up in the system can take whatever spark you have and stomp it out. When my family found me, that spark started to light again, and even with everything that happened, that spark was still there inside of me. But now? Now that spark is extinguished.

I sink to the floor and hang my head between my knees.

They never wanted me.

The puzzle pieces fall into place and the picture isn't pretty. They would've happily gone on with their lives, never acknowledging my existence at all if I hadn't showed up at the Kings and been recognized. It's only because their rivals found out about me that my aunt and uncle changed their minds.

I can't say I blame them—they had their work cut out for them already but the rejection still stings.

And the lies still feel like someone is twisting a knife into my back.

Amelia sits down in front of me, gently placing her hands on my knees. "Arden, I need you to look at me."

Shame doesn't want me to do that. Shame wants me to run away and never look at Amelia Laurence again. I can't let shame win so I gaze up at her, but not before schooling my features into a mask of indifference.

Her watery green eyes stare into mine, intent and focused. "I swear on my life, I never knew you existed back then. That email my husband wrote all those years ago was full of lies. Had I known about you, I would've taken you in and raised you as my own."

I believe her. Maybe that's naive, but she's more earnest than I've ever seen her.

"Uncle Gregory thought I was a crack baby." My voice is hollow. "He didn't want to raise me. And you know what? I probably *was* born addicted to drugs. I don't know the specifics about my history, but it makes sense doesn't it? I'm not like you guys. I'm too small. And my anxiety—"

"Anxiety runs in the family," she interrupts. "And even if you would've had special needs, I still would've loved you like my own. Actually, I would've loved you even more because you would've needed me even more. Ask Hayes and Sybil, they understand why we all love Chandler the most."

A tear slips down my cheek.

"My sister had issues, but does that mean I didn't love her? Of course not. I loved Josie fiercely. When she ran away for the last time, I spent months looking for her. I even hired a private investigator, but she'd disappeared."

Because she was living in a drug house and changed her name. She didn't want to be found. Maybe she was pregnant by then, maybe not. But she'd raised me there until she'd overdosed and I had to be placed into state custody. Honestly, it's a miracle that I'm alive. I know all this and

I'm grateful to be here, but that doesn't take away the hurt.

"I'm so angry at her that sometimes I hate her," I confess.

Her face drops and she nods. "I know, honey. And it's not your fault. What she did was wrong, but she also wasn't in her right mind. There's no excuse but if you had known the girl I knew, you'd know that she loved you."

"How can a mother do that to her baby?"

Her eyes go distant and she glances back at her kids before returning to me. "We had very abusive parents. They're gone now and I won't get into the details of what we went through, but I'll just say it's a miracle that I didn't end up like she did. I don't blame her for finding solace in drugs, though I wish everyday she would've chosen something different."

"Do you think she had an anxiety disorder, too?"

"Undiagnosed, but yes."

Where would I be now if Aunt Amelia hadn't gotten me into therapy and working with a good psychiatrist that understands the chemicals in my brain? My own disorder has been hard to manage and that's with help.

"Now, as for my husband, he has no excuse for his behavior, and if he was still alive, I'd divorce him."

I let out a scoff. "You don't mean that."

"I do," her voice is stiff. "He's put me through enough. This?" She picks up the piece of paper and squeezes it between her fingers. "This is unforgivable."

"And we'd support you, Mom," Sybil adds and Hayes nods. They look stricken, like they're sick to their stomachs, and guilt is written all over their faces.

"But he's gone and that's his own fault, too. It's not your fault, do you hear me?" Amelia drops the paper and squeezes my hands instead. "Falling in love with a King was not your fault. The accident was not your fault. Your upbringing was not your fault. And your mom's death was not your fault either. You have done nothing wrong."

She's saying everything I need to hear but it's hard to let the words have impact. I've been carrying so many what-ifs on my back that they've been crippling me, but don't know how to put them down.

"And the accident wasn't Ethan's fault either," she admits. "I got access into Greg's emails yesterday and found this exchange last night. First thing this morning, Hayes and I contacted the Massachusetts prosecutors office and recanted our statements. They've already dropped the charges against Ethan."

I sit back with a gasp. This means that Ethan is free, that this whole thing can be put behind him. The media damage can't be entirely undone though. "And what about his reputation?"

"Don't worry about that. I'll think of something to get the media off their backs. Ethan will be back under golden light soon, I promise."

I wish I could go to him. If anything, I just want to give him a hug, but Coop made it pretty clear that Ethan and I are over.

"I'm so sorry for everything. I hope you'll forgive me, that we can be the family we were always meant to be. No more games. No more expectations. You can live your life how you want, love who you want, and do what you need to do. We're not going to stop you."

With shaking legs, Amelia helps me stand and we hug. It might just be the best hug of my life. I know she's not my mother, but for a moment I imagine she is. That doesn't quite feel right, so I imagine her arms wrapping around my mother, that this is what their hugs must have felt like. That makes me burst into tears all over again, but this time it's not so sad. This time there's a silver lining to it all. Because my vow hasn't changed—I'm going to live my life to its fullest.

"Now can you please stay in Manhattan?" Sybil blurts out.

I laugh but I can't answer that until I speak with Ethan face to face. If he wants me here, I'll stay, but if he doesn't, then my heart needs me in Boston.

Sixty

But Ethan isn't at his penthouse, so I call Cooper in the cab ride back to Sybil's place and he tells me Ethan left the city. "He's been through a lot, Arden. He needed a break from Manhattan and the media frenzy this has all caused, not to mention he needed a break from our father."

"Do you think he'll want to see me?"

Cooper's long pause isn't a good sign. "Give him space. He'll come to you when he's ready."

If he's ever ready.

"Can you at least tell me where he is?"

He hesitates. "Nantucket."

A bright ray of hope lights me up. If Ethan's in Nantucket, then he's not afraid to face what happened. Maybe he'll face me soon, too.

"How's the rehabilitation coming along?" I try to change the subject, and I really am interested in how Coop is recovering, but my voice couldn't sound any more distracted. I just want to see Ethan. I feel like I'll die if I don't at least clear the air between us. I don't expect him to take me back but I don't want him to hate me either.

"It's going as well as can be expected. Therapy is a bitch. My prosthetic is even more of a bitch. But my hot nurse is an angel and she's making me feel better if you know what I mean."

I laugh and he chuckles right along with me. I'll always feel terrible for what happened to his leg but I'll also always thank God that he made it out of that water alive.

"Cooper, I'm really glad you're still here, and I'm glad we're friends, but thank God I didn't sleep with you because you are quite the manwhore."

A laugh bursts from him through the line and I smile. "Believe me, that would've been a mistake. I've learned the hard way that women may want to fuck me, but it's Ethan who they want to love."

"Hey, don't say that. You're lovable."

His voice darkens. "I'm not asking for compliments or sympathy, Arden. I know what I can offer and I'm okay with it."

"If you say so." I wonder how many women have given their bodies to Coop but held onto their hearts with Ethan in mind?

Ouch.

Cooper and I hang up shortly after that and the cab stops in front of Sybil's building. I head back inside and go right to my bedroom, throwing the covers over my head and trying not to cry. I'm so fucking sick of tears, I could puke just thinking about crying.

I postponed my train up to Boston for a few days but there's not a lot of time before school starts and I don't want to leave here without that conversation. I can't help but hope that Ethan will forgive me and I'll end up staying in Manhattan after all. I'm not sure what that will look like for schooling, maybe I'll have to take the semester off.

A knock raps on the door and Sybil asks to come inside. I pop my head from my pathetic cocoon of sadness. "Come in." She crawls right into the blankets with me and that's when the words pour out of me, confessions I've been dying to reveal to her for weeks. When I explain my fears about losing Ethan, she hugs me tight.

"Oh honey, I'm so sorry. This is my fault. I used my own experiences with Ethan to try to dictate yours and that was wrong. Do you want me to call him?"

I shake my head. "Maybe I need to let him go."

"Is that what you want to do?"

Just the thought of it hurts. "No."

"Then you have to go to Nantucket."

"What if he doesn't want to see me?"

"He might not, but that doesn't mean he doesn't love you. I bet he'll want to hear you out." She pins me with a confident smirk. "Cooper doesn't know everything."

I'm not so sure.

After the funeral, Ethan begged me to stay together, we made love, and then I left him while he was sleeping and blocked his number. It was a fucked up thing to do and I wish I could go back and handle that moment so much differently. I ended us, and then from his perspective, I stood by while my family raked him across the coals. He might even think I lied to the police too. He might hate me.

"You're going to Nantucket," Sybil presses, jumping out of bed and grabbing my suitcase that is still packed and sitting in the corner of the room. "Look, you're already packed."

I roll my eyes. "My whole life is in that suitcase. I don't need to haul it to Nantucket."

"Then take an overnight bag instead. Or just go and take nothing. This is your grand gesture." Ethan's grand gesture when he named a boat after me, so this would be the least I could do. "I'll book the flight," she continues. "You need answers. You're going."

She's right.

And it just might be the most terrifying thing I'll ever do, but I agree to go.

The first time I came to Nantucket, it was with a cheap ferry ticket and a tattered suitcase holding everything I owned. This time, I fly first class with Sybil's Prada overnight bag slung over my shoulder. It's filled with things that I might not even need. If this conversation doesn't go well, I'm not staying here tonight. I can't face being on this island knowing we're through.

The plane lands smoothly and a car service greets me at the arrival gate. Sybil arranged that too. She says feels terrible and wants to help make things right, but I also think she enjoys arranging other people's lives, same way she enjoys planning the parties and decorating the homes. She's good at making things run smoothly. It'll take a bit of time to fully trust her again, but I still believe she has a good heart.

The driver is a chatty older gentleman. I don't normally like talking to strangers, but this time is different because I need the distraction. He drives me to the Kings' estate, the gate attendant not giving us any trouble, thank God. When we pull up to the driveway, I have to hold my breath. The house looks exactly as I remember it. Seeing it again is like seeing Ethan again too. It's overwhelming and nostalgic, terrifying and hopeful, beautiful and intimidating.

There's no turning back.

I climb from the car and pay the driver to wait out front for twenty minutes. "If I don't come back, you can leave. And if I do come back, I'll need a ride to the airport."

"Works for me," he smiles and whips out his phone. "I've got a level on Candy Crush to beat anyway."

I laugh, feeling a little less guilty for potentially wasting his time.

"You have a number you can call if you need help, little lady?"

"I do, thank you."

"Good luck." He winks and rolls up the tinted window.

I wish luck was enough to get through what I'm about to do. After everything my family has done to Ethan, I'm not even sure if the man loves me anymore.

As I walk up the drive, memories of us return with each step I take.

The first moment I saw Ethan he was swimming and he looked like a god under that water. It was love at first sight for me. Well, maybe not love, but definitely lust. It never mattered to me that he was off-limits. Even when he was an ass to me before he started to change, he still occupied my thoughts. And then he'd tried to teach me how to swim in that pool and the attraction between us was unlike anything I'd experienced in my life. He'd pulled away when he found out I was a virgin, but it wasn't too much later when he'd been one to take that virginity.

No, not take. I'd given it to him freely.

Staying with him through the hurricane had been the craziest thing I'd ever done, but look where it got me—into his arms and into his heart.

I don't know for certain if people are made for each other or if fate is real, but I'd like to believe so because how else can I explain our story? Nobody has ever fought for my heart the way he did.

Taking a deep breath, I square my shoulders and ring the doorbell.

Camilla answers. She looks the exact same, her curly hair up in a huge bun on top of her head and the same yellow apron tied around her waist. Flour is smudged across her left cheek and her brown eyes widen as she takes me in.

"Hi Camilla—" I start but she doesn't give me a chance to finish.

"Arden!" She throws her arms around me, squeezing me into her bosom. "My girl, I never thought I'd see you again, but I should've known you'd be back. You're here for Ethan, no? He's down at the beach."

She speaks a million miles a minute, her Italian accent coming in thicker than usual, and I peel myself away from her embrace with a tentative smile. "Do you think he'll want to see me?" my voice wobbles.

She nods emphatically. "He wouldn't be here moping about if he didn't want to see you."

"What do you mean by that?"

"Nantucket means Arden. He told me that the summer after you left. Why would he come back here if he didn't want to be reminded of you? The boys aren't here as often as they used to be, I'm just part time help now, but they still talk about you. Especially Ethan."

I relax. All hope isn't lost. If he still talks about me, still thinks about me, then maybe he still wants to be with me enough that he can forgive my mistakes. "Thank you."

She waves me off. "I know what love looks like, believe me, I've experienced it myself." She smiles, her eyes glancing away as a far-off expression transforms her face. "I met the love of my life when I was only eighteen too. Frank was on holiday in my village back in Italy and I was his waitress on his first night there. He asked me out and two weeks later I went back home with him. The rest is history."

I smile, picturing a young Camilla falling in love. "That's beautiful."

"Love always is, even when it's messy." She smiles, gaze dreamy and confident. "Anyway, I was just leaving for the day. I'm sure I'll see you later. Now go."

I don't know if she's making herself scarce for our privacy or if she really is finished with her day, but I leave her on the front steps and head around the side of the house towards the beach. I'm not sure what he's doing down there, it could be surfing or swimming or just lounging in the sand like I always used to do.

It's the perfect August day as I round the back of the house, but once I catch sight of the crystalline pool with all its memories, the nerves return.

I hope Camilla is right. Cooper was pretty adamant that Ethan wanted space from me, but I need to hold on to what Camilla said. Ethan wouldn't have come here if he didn't want to be reminded of me. I can relate, because everything about this place reminds me of him.

Striding down the worn path, I eye the familiar wind-worn gazebo up ahead. It's been two years since I last stood in that gazebo looking out at the ocean, two years since Ethan and I ended things the first time. I've grown so much in those two years and still have so much growing left to do.

I want to do all of it with Ethan by my side.

The gazebo still has the best view and I use it to search the beach for him. It's depressingly empty, which might be the first time I've been sad to see the beach empty. Where is he?

My eyes catch on a figure out on the horizon, a surfer catching a wave. Even from this far off distance, even with his wetsuit on, I recognize Ethan's silhouette instantly. His inky hair curls in the wind and his legs flex as he expertly rides the wave toward the shoreline. He finishes beautifully and then paddles back out, arms rotating in that same assured way that first drew me to him. He hasn't seen me yet. I could turn back now and let him go. I wouldn't have to face these nerves. I could take the coward's way out.

But I would regret that for the rest of my life, and I'm done with regret.

Taking a deep breath, I head toward the stairs. They're still wind-worn, still the same old stairs that I remember. They must not have replaced them after the hurricane, just repaired what needed attention.

What's that phrase people say about making assumptions? Assuming makes an ass out of you and me? In this case, assuming makes me fall on my ass, because about six stairs from the bottom, one creaks and loosens before breaking entirely.

Sixty-One

My fall is fast. One second I'm looking down at the sand below and the next I'm landing on it, pain shooting up my backside and spine. It's not so bad that I immediately think I broke something, but it sure as hell knocks the wind right out of my lungs.

I'm on my back facing the cloudy sky with its puffs of white against a vibrant blue. Thank God my vision is normal. I slowly catch my breath, willing myself to sit up.

And then Ethan is here, he's yelling my name and lifting me into his wet arms.

He asks if I'm okay, but I can't speak yet. Cursing, he carries me back up the stairs, stepping over the one I just broke. He's saying something about how they've been meaning to get that one fixed and how sorry he is.

I'm sorry too, but not for a dumb step.

"I'm fine," I finally cough out. "It wasn't that bad."

"Can you feel your legs? Move your toes for me," he demands as we reach the top of the bluff. He gently sets me down on the floor of the gazebo and inspects me while I wiggle my toes.

"I'm fine," I insist. "I'll probably have a bruise but that's all. The sand caught me."

"Thank God." He's kneeling beside me, his head hanging low and water dripping from the ends. "That stair has been a problem for two years. We've just been skipping over it every time we use them. Cooper and I haven't wanted to tear down the old gazebo and stairs because our mom loved them. They were here on the original property when my parents bought it and Conrad promised to keep them for her. After she died, we let them get worse. They should've been fixed or replaced. I'm sorry. So sorry."

He's speaking so fast, and all the while his hands are trailing over my body, trailing down my arms, around my sides, over my legs. He's checking for injuries, searching for something he can fix, but it's my heart that needs his attention right now.

"I'm okay," I say again. Had I landed on rocks, or fallen from higher up, I probably wouldn't be, but it wasn't as bad as it probably looked. "My ego is bruised more than anything. Coming here was supposed to be my grand gesture."

He sits back on his haunches and meets my gaze, holding me steady within the depths of his eyes. They remind me so much of the ocean and maybe that's why I find them so intriguing. The ocean has always been this fearful thing for me but if he asked me to go swimming with him in there right now I would gladly face my fears and do it.

He's so beautiful. Attractive, yes, but it's more than that. It's not just his expressive eyes framed by thick lashes, or his shapely muscles, or his thick wet hair that's half covered in sand. Those are all things I love about him, but it's his heart that I love most. He's become a wonderful man, someone who will do anything for the people he loves. Someone who would've done anything for me until I pushed him away.

Hell, he risked his life to try to save his enemy because he knew I loved that enemy.

"Is that why you're here?" he asks and it's time to face this.

"There's something I need to say to you." I sit up, tucking my feet under me, and cling to whatever courage I can muster. "I was wrong. I got so caught up in trying to please my family that I let them hurt you and I let them hurt me, but worst of all, *I* hurt you."

He's silent, sitting with my words, but he hasn't argued or left me yet, so that gives me hope. Hope is all I can ask for right now.

"And I'm sorry," I continue. "I'm so sorry for everything. I don't expect you to forgive me, but I wanted you to hear it from me that I'm leaving Manhattan. I'm going back to school in Boston."

His eyes flicker with something unreadable, something that I fear is about to be rejection. Or worse. Indifference.

"You wanted to do some grand gesture to . . . win me back?"

My cheeks warm and I nod. "Stupid, I know."

I expect him to tell me off but instead he shakes his head once and then slides his fingers into my hair, gripping my scalp and tugging me toward him. Between one breath and the next, his mouth claims mine. And I get it. Because what are words when actions are so much better?

But I like the words too, especially words like "good girl" and "Juliet" and "Arden" and "fuck that's good" all the other praises he's so great at saying when he's with me. I don't know what that says about me, maybe that I was desperate for love and attention as a child, but I don't care. This is part of who I am. And Ethan? He knows me.

"Of course, I forgive you," he answers between kisses. "I'll always forgive you."

Soon we're laying down in the gazebo, blocked from view and surrounded by the storm-weathered wood that has seen us through arguments and confessions. This place has survived a hurricane. It has stood strong through so many tests. Ethan and I? We may have been damaged along the way, but our relationship is still standing too.

He takes his time with me, stripping us bare between long languid kisses. And then when we're ready, we make love like it's the first time. Careful at first, considerate and slow, until the need is too much and the movements grow frenzied.

Through it all, I'm met with a sense of belonging that I've never experienced so deeply before this moment. I truly trust Ethan with my whole heart, but also with my body, mind, and soul. He means the world to me. I'll do anything to keep him. And I know he feels the same way about me. It's a pure, forgiving, all-consuming love I've never been on the receiving end of before.

We've been through so much together, through pain and pleasure, through grief and glory. What's next? Life will be easy and life will be cruel, but I have confidence that we'll weather every storm together.

As we make love, our connection grows deeper, stronger, better with each confessing stroke. When my body nears completion, he takes my hands between one large palm and holds them above my head.

"Hold on to me, baby," he growls into my mouth. "Never let me go."

I do just that, knowing that I'm not just holding onto his hands, but onto what we are. And I'll gladly hold on to this man forever.

Pinpricks flicker through my vision and I lose all sense of

time and space, my body growing hot with angst. I'm writhing beneath his sinful hips, whimpering and panting until we come together. There's nothing that will ever separate us again.

Once finished, he says exactly what I need to hear. "I love you. Please don't go to Boston."

"I love you too," I sigh, rolling into him and smiling against his warm cheek. He smells of the ocean and spicy cologne and delicious sex. "But I already got everything worked out to leave." Not that I wouldn't change my plans for him because I would. I absolutely would.

"Fine, then I'm coming with you."

I laugh. "Your life is in Manhattan."

And it's true. He's got his career and his brother. He's working toward becoming the CEO of King Media. He has friends and a social life and a reputation to rebuild. He can't just leave Manhattan. There's too much at stake.

"Have you learned nothing?" He brushes his lips against mine before pulling back to gaze into my eyes. "My life is you. Where you go, I go."

I know he's being honest because I understand exactly how that feels.

Where you go, I go.

Epilogue

Later That Year

"My bounty is as boundless as the sea, My love as deep; the more I give to thee, The more I have, for both are infinite."

William Shakespeare's Romeo and Juliet

Sybil claims that there's nowhere better to spend New Year's Eve than in New York City. She's not talking about Times Square with its monstrous crowds waiting for the ball to drop, though that's obviously a popular event. Rather, she is talking about the myriad of upscale parties to choose from, many of which are catered exclusively to the rich and famous. For someone who considers herself a socialite, this is her Super Bowl, and she made me come over to get ready with her for the better part of the day.

Now we're dressed to the nines in shimmery designer gowns and walking into some upscale hotel nightclub, a place exclusively reserved only for Manhattan's elite to ring in the new year.

Right away I can tell this is totally her thing and is most definitely not mine. It takes all of a minute for me to decide I'd rather be at home. Sure, the decorations fit the iconic black and gold theme perfectly and the glamorous people are dressed to blend right in, but the party is loud and crowded and it feels like everyone is staring at us. Probably because they are—ever since my uncle died, it's been a media shitstorm for both the Kings and the Laurences.

I shrink into myself under the scrutiny, but Sybil lets it feed her, standing taller and lifting her chin high. She takes my hand and leads me through throngs of people to the bar. Luckily, one of the men at the bar just so happens to be a very handsome Ethan King who also just so happens to be waiting for me. He's standing next to his brother and they look at the two of us with completely opposite expressions. Ethan's eyes are on me, hot and possessive. Cooper's eyes are on Sybil, cold and annoyed.

"Here's your woman," she sighs dramatically at Ethan, then to me she adds, "Guess I'll be seeing you later then."

Without another word, she flips her hair in Cooper's face. Ethan doesn't seem to care one way or the other, he's focused solely on me. But Cooper? Cooper takes a swig of his drink and mutters something under his breath that sounds an awful lot like "fucking bitch". I would tell him off, but the guy has had it so rough lately. His first prosthetic leg didn't work out and his second hasn't been an easy adjustment whatsoever. He's finally up and walking, but I have to fight to keep my gaze from flicking down to his pant leg. I'm sure most people here that know about Cooper's accident have no shame in staring.

Not that Cooper should be ashamed. He absolutely shouldn't, but that doesn't change the fact that being different can make you a target for gossip and unwanted glances.

As far as I know, this is the first time Sybil and Cooper have been in the same room since May, so I can't expect too much of them. Coop lost his leg, but Sybil lost her *dad*.

Ethan offers to get me a drink, but I decline, so he leads me out to the dance floor where we spend the rest of the night. Every three or four songs someone will come up and ask for introductions but that's about it. We're not the center of attention even though I'm sure there's plenty of gossip circulating about the infamous King and Laurence feud, and the star-crossed lovers who refuse to give each other up.

As fun as it is to be with Ethan, this isn't my thing and the night passes too slow. Eventually the countdown begins and I sigh with relief, counting down with the rest of the crowd and kissing Ethan when we get to the cheers of "Happy New Year" and people start making out.

His lips are bruising and passionate, and I kiss him back with equal measure for at least a minute before we break apart. He presses his forehead to mine. "Happy New Year, baby."

"Happy Ne—" I start to reply, but I'm cut off by a familiar voice yelling not too far away.

"Stay the fuck away from me, Cooper," Sybil yells, and I turn to find her rushing past me, her face red and her eyes two hard slits.

"Oh fuck," Ethan mutters. "Do you want to go after her?"

Well, I'm not going to be a shitty cousin and let her run out of this party by herself. "I'd better," I say, giving him one last peck before taking off after Sybil.

I find her outside of the lobby, hand raised to catch a cab, but it's busy tonight and none of the yellow cabs are available yet. I'm surprised she didn't have a car waiting or a security detail here to get her. Things have been different lately with all the media attention. Sybil is usually on top of these things, but then again, she probably didn't expect to leave the party right at midnight.

"Hey, are you okay?" I ask between pants from running to catch up.

"Oh, I'm great," she snaps. "What a fucking pleasant evening this has been."

Shit. I pretty much ignored her all night. No wonder her tone is stark. She's mad at me. "I'm sorry," I wince. "I shouldn't have ditched you for Ethan."

She sighs and drops her arm, turning to me. The air is cold and her breath puffs out in little clouds. "It's fine, I get it. This isn't your thing and it's totally mine. And actually, I had a great time right up until the end."

"Why? What happened?"

Her face pinks and not because of the cold. That is one thing we definitely have in common. "I kissed the wrong person at midnight."

My eyes bug. "Cooper?"

She lets out a scoff. "In his dreams. Anyway, let's just say Cooper decided to put his nose where it didn't belong, just like he always does."

"How so?"

"Oh!" She spots a vacant cab and holds up her hand again. It stops next to us, and she opens the door. "Come home with me and I'll tell you all about it."

I falter because I really wanted to spend the night with Ethan. It's not that I have to be with him all the time, but it's New Year's Eve and that kiss stirred something in me.

"It's fine." She rolls her eyes, clearly not as pissed as I

thought she was. "Go home with Ethan and we can talk another time."

With that, she slips into the backseat of the cab and closes the door behind her. The cab drives off and I can only guess what happened between her and Cooper. I turn back to the hotel to find Ethan coming out of the sliding doors. He's not alone.

Cooper's arm is slung around Ethan's slightly taller frame and his head is hung low. The guy appears to be more than just a little intoxicated. He's plastered.

"Let's take him home," Ethan says to me as he helps his brother stumble to the sidewalk. "I've got a car already on the way."

"What happened?" I ask.

Cooper groans and the scent of alcohol permeates the January midnight air. "Not so loud, you two love birds," he slurs. "I've got a headache."

Ethan's mouth thins. "I don't know exactly, but I'm sick of the drama."

I nod because I feel the same way. We knew it would be an issue, and honestly, it's a small price to pay to be together, but that still doesn't mean we have to like it. Our families have been mostly civil about our relationship these last four months, though they usually just pretend the other family doesn't exist. We should've known putting alcohol into the mix with Cooper, Sybil, and all their mutual friends, was a recipe for disaster.

"It's okay." I grin up at Ethan, reminding him of our upcoming plans. "Only two more sleeps and then we're on our vacation. Just you and me."

His face softens. "Can't come soon enough."

"Are you ready for this?" Ethan asks and I hesitate. He smiles knowingly. "Yeah, you're ready. You've got this, baby."

He's right, I do. Or I don't, but I'm going to pretend like I do anyway. Before I can talk myself out of it, I take off running into the surf.

The sand flings from my heels and Ethan is quick to catch up. He doesn't take my hand or say another word, but I feel his support. He believes in me and that's great, but what's even better is I believe in myself.

I know I can do this. Fear or not, the ocean isn't going to hurt me today.

The water rushes up as if greeting an old friend, sprays of salty foam gathering around my ankles, then thighs, and then stomach as I hurry into the aquamarine depths. The waters of the Maldives are not nearly as cold as the waters surrounding Nantucket, thank goodness. This water here is welcoming, an invitation to sink down even further into its lovely warmth.

With a deep breath, I dive under a wave, letting it roll over me as I swim further out. Tiny air bubbles tickle my back and legs. I pop back up for air, a smile plastered to my face.

"This is so nice and refreshing."

"You like it okay?" Ethan asks earnestly.

"I love it." I say it because it's true, but also because I know how much this vacation means to him, how he planned it for us as my Christmas gift and made sure to leave after New Year's because he knew I'd want to spend the holidays with my family. We're here for a week, just us.

He swims next to me because he's my safety net out here, but also because we simply want to be near each other. It's been like this from the moment we left Nantucket in August and told our friends and families that we were together, that we were going to be living together, and that there wasn't anything anybody could do to stop us. Not everyone supports the idea of us, but we don't care. We're in love and that's more powerful than anything else.

The water glistens on his bare chest and I swim towards him, splaying my fingers against his pecks. Ethan truly is the perfect specimen, could easily be a male swimsuit model, and my greedy eyes can't help but linger on his body.

"Hey Arden, my eyes are up here," he teases.

He doesn't call me Juliet anymore because I asked him not to. Her story ended in tragedy and his boat ended up on the bottom of the ocean. Romeo and Juliet aren't our future. Our love may be as all-consuming as theirs was, but our story is going to be much, much better.

We're Ethan and Arden, and I like us.

I laugh and playfully punch his arm, and he uses that as an opportunity to sweep me into his. "Can I kiss you now?"

"As if you have to ask." I roll my eyes and lean up to meet him.

His mouth is delicious mixed with the faint taste of salt water and I can already tell we're going to have a hot vacation together. It's just him and me, this warm ocean, and this beautiful new place to explore when we're not relaxing in our private villa. Ethan booked one right on the beach, saying that if I wanted to switch to one of the more popular overwater ones that it could be arranged. I declined, because as much as I'm ready to swim in the ocean, I'm not quite ready to be sleeping right above it.

Maybe someday.

He breaks our kiss and peers into my eyes. "Do you want to keep swimming?"

I nod and he lets me go. I dive under the waves a few more times before laying on my back and letting my body float up and over the gentle waves. After a few minutes, I relax like I never have in water before, any remnants of fear cleansed away.

Swimming in Nantucket again might be a different story, but we'll write that when we get to it next summer. Whatever it is, be it an adventure or a romance, it won't be another tragedy.

I never did move back to Boston, so after this vacation we'll return to Manhattan where I'll pick up where I left off with my studies at Columbia University, focusing solely on my interest in computer science. I dropped the business degree. Ethan will continue to work alongside his brother at King Media and navigate the manipulations of Conrad King. It won't be easy, but at the end of the day, we'll both get to come home together. And maybe someday he'll be brave enough to cut ties with his father entirely, but even if he doesn't, it won't change my love for the man. And my respect.

Because over these last few months, he's really shown me the kind of man he is. Loyal. Smart. Dedicated. Hard-working. And yes, he's even kind. Right after we left Nantucket in August, I moved in with him, and it's turned out to be one of the best decisions I've ever made. It already feels like we've been living comfortably together for years, loving each other for even longer. For infinity. Ethan is my home, the kind of stability I've been craving my whole life.

He's the family I chose.

Also By Nina Walker

Book two of Devious Delights, *Collateral Damage*,

will release December 2024 as

Sybil and Cooper continue the story

. . .

A Letter From Nina

I'm new here so if you liked *Crushed by Love*, please do me a favor and leave a review and tell a friend.

Would you like to read a bonus scene from Ethan's POV? Join my Facebook Reader Group at FB.com/groups/NinaVeronas-ReaderRoom to get it. You can also find me on socials at @Author.nina.verona.

Book Two, *Collateral Damage*, is loosely based on Shakespeare's Julius Caesar and is Cooper and Sybil's story.

Many thanks to my beta readers, arc team, cover designer Natasha Snow, editor Dani Galliaro, and my supportive husband. I couldn't do this without the support!

All The Love,
Nina Verona

Please Note: I'm a happily married woman who choose a pen name due to the sexual nature of this genre. While drama is an author's day job, personal privacy is important to us too. Thank you!

About the Author

Crushed by Love is Nina Verona's debut spicy contemporary romance. Follow her on just about any social media platform to interact and learn the latest news.

In her free time she enjoys books and film and television. Her obsession with stories is probably a good thing given her line of work. She also loves spending time with friends and family, as well as hiking and traveling, starting (but not necessarily finishing) random art projects, cuddling with her cats, and a really good chai tea.

@Author.Nina.Verona.

Printed in Great Britain
by Amazon